Missing

DJ Cowdall

CONTENTS

ACKNOWLEDGMENTS

Thank you to Claudette Cruz for the final edit on this book.

Cover art and design by Perie Wolford

Other Works By DJ Cowdall

Novels

The Dog Under The Bed 1

The Dog Under The Bed 2: Arthur On The Streets

Two Dogs In Africa

Hypnofear

I Was A Teenage Necromancer: Book 1

I Was A Teenage Necromancer: Book 2: Supernature

The Magic Christmas Tree

The Kids of Pirate Island

53%

Short Stories

Inferno

Kites

Sacrifice

A Breath of Magic

Available from all good booksellers

1

COLD MORNINGS

August 1980

Life is tough, and for that there are no exceptions. For most people, life begins with an alarm clock, often before daylight pokes its unwarranted head out above the horizon.

The first thought in Liz's mind was the scream of the alarm beside her bed. It wasn't so loud, but it was unwelcome and sounded all the worse for it. Before she had a mind to throw the thing at the wall, the chill air surrounding them reminded her of just how difficult things could be.

"I guess it's going to be cold getting up again this morning," she said, wiping her eyes as the shrill siren continued to sound.

"I'm awake, you can put it off now," Jack said, sounding as if he had only just gotten into bed minutes earlier.

"Sure, I'll do that for you. Would you like a foot massage too?" Liz asked, leaning over to hit the clock hard with the palm of her hand.

Jack remained in bed, wondering if she might have meant it. He waited, wondering if the air between them might signify something positive for the day ahead. Instead he turned over towards his wife of twenty-seven years, placing a cool arm across her warmth.

"We've got time for a cuddle, haven't we?" Jack asked, opening his eyes for the first time. As he did, he noticed Liz looking at him, her gentle smile offering the kind of morning welcome that in most times had been desired, but not now, now it was different. As light finally seeped into the room, he could see her face, her fine darkish brown wispy hair, the jowls of her cheeks that had fallen seemingly with each day. Her eyes remained the same, that fine deep blue, but in other respects, the ways that mattered to him, she no longer seemed quite who she was.

"I guess no time for that," Jack said, turning abruptly away just as

1

Liz had allowed herself a moment to share their warmth. Common sense told her that he was right, time was always short for something, but still, those quiet moments they had together seemed so rare these days, she couldn't help but wonder where it had all gone.

Ignoring the signals in her mind, Liz turned over, swept back the quilt covers, and placed her feet onto the cold carpet.

"I forgot to tell you," Jack said, now standing up. He had dropped his pajamas onto the floor, standing there naked for all the world to see. He was tall, and still fairly muscular, but his stomach stood out as if he were expectant. Liz often looked at him like that and laughed mentally over it, but it was fine, it was such a minor thing about the only man she had ever really truly loved.

"Well, get some clothes on and tell me what you forgot," Liz said, turning away before she giggled openly. She didn't look back as she dressed, knowing what the day ahead held, so dressed accordingly.

"I'm going on a business trip today, so might be a bit late back tonight," he said, struggling to pull on a pair of black trousers and standing at the same time.

Liz looked at him, half-clothed in a worn blouse, holding it across her front, staring ahead. "And you figured you would only just tell me now?" she said, not wanting to sound as negative as she felt over it.

"Sorry, I just forgot about it. I'll try not to be too late," he replied, rushing to put on his shirt.

"Why the haste?" Liz asked, walking around the bed to assist him.

"Oh, no, it's OK," he said, pulling away as the shirt finally settled across his stomach.

Jack wore a plain smile on his face, looking with the same deep blue eyes as he always did at her. He was never quite the most attractive man, but to her he had been quite perfect, a gentleman and still the only man she had ever wanted. For all of his faults—his many faults, she figured—she still loved him.

"Are you wearing that?" Jack asked, looking at her with a hint of disdain.

Liz looked back at him, feeling the awkward gaze. It was an unusual moment between them, not so isolated that it had never happened before, but still not something she liked. It made her feel uncomfortable, as if she were standing in the presence of a stranger. As positive as she always tried to be, she couldn't help but feel that things weren't quite as good as they should be.

"Well, I was going to clean the house today, things need doing, so I just dressed accordingly."

"Of course," Jack replied, wrapping a too thick tie around his neck.

"Here, let me do that," Liz offered, holding her hands out towards him as if she were a supplicant.

"No, I've done it now, I have to get going," Jack insisted, clearly struggling with his tie but obviously keeping a distance.

Without another word they both walked out of the bedroom. The air between them changed the moment he saw her in the first light of day. For Liz, nothing changed, except how she felt of what existed between them.

Jack walked ahead down the landing towards the bathroom as Liz turned to another door. She rapped her knuckles on the plain white door, leaning into it as if it had an invisible window she could peer through.

"John, get up, you'll be late for school," she shouted, before waiting for a response. It was a typical morning ritual; one she knew very well wouldn't result in a response from her son—it never did—but it was the ritual that had to be observed. It seemed only yesterday when she could open the door and go in to shake her beautiful son, then look into his loving eyes and catch that beautiful smile. How and when things changed, she couldn't remember, but now it was a polite knock on the door, and don't go in, must avoid mutual embarrassment.

"Did you hear me? I'll throw a bucket of water over you," Liz offered playfully. She never wanted him to be late, but still she understood how he felt as a cold draught wound its way around the house.

Jack returned from the bathroom, the toilet flushing as he walked out. He looked back at his wife, offered a half smile and looked away.

Liz looked at him, his light blue shirt covered in water splashes.

"You're supposed to get washed before you get dressed," she said, standing before him, hands on her hips like a schoolmarm.

"Yeah, yeah, I know," Jack sighed, appreciating the sentiment.

"You'll never get a promotion going into work covered in toothpaste stains and water marks," Liz continued. The moment she uttered the words, she regretted it, knowing she had said something that could never be undone. Jack didn't reply. He just looked away, standing as if waiting for her permission to leave. It was the last thing she wanted, forcing more of a wedge into the invisible barrier between them, but the unspoken connection between them had long since disappeared.

"I know," Jack said, walking towards the stairs. Liz turned away, her mind on other things, preparing for the day ahead.

"Come on, John, I won't tell you again," Liz barked, peering towards her son's door, as if she might look at it and he would know.

As she leaned in, the door suddenly opened, as John stood there, still dressed in his pajamas, shoulders slumped, eyes firmly closed as he yawned.

"Will you be going to school like that?" Liz asked. As she spoke, he opened his eyes wearily, blinking heavily, trying to see.

"I figure I'll take a day off today, get some downtime, work through some things and generally catch up with my sleep," John said, before breaking out into another yawn.

"Oh, OK then, that's fine, you go back to bed."

"Really?" John asked, suddenly wide-eyed.

"No, get ready for school, quick," Liz insisted, before walking away. John shook his head as he closed his door. The idea occurred to him that he might close the door, get back into bed, and forget about it, but he knew all too well how she could be, so did as he was told.

Liz turned to the final door on the landing, ready to knock as the door swung open.

"Yes, I'm fine, all ready to go," Patricia said. She was fully dressed smartly in a light white blouse and black leggings. Her makeup, as always, was perfect, having spent since daylight dawned sitting in front of a mirror, preparing.

"Don't be late for college, love," Liz insisted, walking away. She knew full well that her daughter wouldn't be late, that she would be up, but still old habits died hard, and she would continue to be there every morning.

"When was I ever late, Mom?" Patricia asked. Though it was barely eight in the morning, she was chewing gum and ready for anything. From her demeanor, she often appeared aloof, but deep down she was anything but.

John's door swung open dramatically, as he stepped out from his bedroom. He was wearing his school uniform, long gray trousers matching his height, and a white shirt with a baggy gray blazer.

"You're always late, Patricia," John insisted, looking towards the bathroom.

"Funny, you're always looking gray," Patricia replied, snapping on her gum nonchalantly.

"Yeah, well, it's not my fault the school makes us wear gray," John snapped back.

"I didn't mean your uniform," Patricia said once more, quickly heading down the stairs before he could say anything.

As she walked down, she could hear voices from below, at first thinking nothing of it as she drew closer to the downstairs hall door. Just as she was about to push it open and walk in, something alerted her to wait.

"I'm sorry, I didn't mean to sound so funny about that what I said of your shirt. You look fine."

Patricia hesitated, not wanting to get involved in anything personal between her parents. It was difficult, as aware as she was of the changing times between them. It was a concern, but given how long they had been together, she knew it would work out in the end, simply because it always did.

"It's fine, don't worry about it, you were right," Jack said. After the few words, it all went quiet, as if everyone was waiting for an entrance or an invitation.

"What are you waiting for?" a voice asked, abruptly interrupting the moment as John stood over Patricia, hovering over her like a tall building.

"John, you made me jump," Patricia said, realizing she would have to go in to avoid further embarrassment. As she pushed open the door and walked in, she could feel eyes on her, as if they were wondering how long she had been standing outside.

Liz looked at her silently, her expression blank, as if she feared for what might be said.

"So, what's for breakfast?" John asked, completely oblivious to it all. It was just what was needed, a chance to move on quickly.

"Er, nothing. You're going to be late for your bus," Liz said, grinning at her son.

"Mooom," John said, pulling a face at her.

"Relax, I'm joking. I'll get you some cereal."

While the conversation was going on, Jack was standing in the corner of the open dining room. He remained with his arms folded, expressionless, almost lost in a daydream.

"Penny for your thoughts, Dad?" Patricia asked, looking at him.

Jack focused his eyes on her, without otherwise moving. The delay in his response was obvious, as if he were lost in thought.

"No, no, I'm fine," he replied, taking in a deep breath.

Patricia returned an awkward smile. "Yeah, I know you're fine, just wondered what you were thinking," she continued, looking at him inquisitively.

"I said I'm fine, just thinking about the day ahead," Jack insisted, unfolding his arms and smiling.

Whatever it was, he could see nobody was buying it. Liz looked at him, then back to Patricia, wanting above all else to avoid an argument.

"It's OK, it's just Dad has a meeting and something he has to do today, and he's going to be late in, that's all," Liz said, hoping to get through the morning and then get on with a better day.

"One problem," John said, once again offering a welcome interruption.

"What's that?" Liz asked.

"I still don't have any cereal," he replied, looking to all the world completely lost.

"Seriously, get it yourself!" Patricia demanded, throwing her arms out as if she were trying to manage a very young child. John ignored her, looking at his mother.

"Right, I will get you some," Liz said, walking quickly into the kitchen.

"Yeah, I'd best get going, lots to do," Jack said, turning to take hold of his work satchel. Most of his colleagues used briefcases, but he never liked how studious they seemed—an executive appeal, much like suits—so he kept a bag instead.

As he opened the front door to leave, something tapped him on the shoulder. As he turned to look, he saw Liz standing behind him.

"Take care, won't you?" she said, looking up at him, clearly uncertain.

"Yeah, I'll be fine," Jack replied.

"Funny, you've not even brushed your hair," Liz said, laughing quietly.

"You always have to pick at everything, don't you?" he replied. He looked at her, mulling over his thoughts, wondering if he should voice just how he felt, but as much as he felt, he still didn't want to openly hurt her.

"I didn't mean anything, I was just—" Liz began, but before she could finish, he waved at her, smiled briefly, and walked off to meet his lift to work.

She watched him go, feeling a sense of deep unease in her stomach. Things hadn't been too good for so long, she knew as much. As bad as she felt, she was a fighter deep down, and whatever it took, she knew they would work it out.

As she turned to walk back in, she felt a sense of relief as she noticed both Patricia and John sitting at the dining room table, eating and talking. She walked over to them, feeling better.

"So you won't starve after all then?" Liz asked, smiling broadly. John ignored her, too busy enjoying food to think of anything else.

"Yeah, I figured I would save you the trouble, because we know he can't manage it," Patricia said, offering her mother a knowing look. She could see things weren't great, but it wasn't the first time, and wouldn't be the last. Whatever, once the holidays began, everything would blow over.

"Hey," John said, wondering if he could stop eating from his huge bowl of cereal long enough to protest against his sister. As soon as he realized he couldn't, he began nibbling away again.

"Right, I'm off, must get my bus to college," Patricia said, standing up to get her jacket. Liz nodded at her, immediately thinking she wished her daughter could stay with her, to do something with her. As much as she felt the need for company, she knew she couldn't make such demands. Her daughter had her future to work towards, and didn't need such burdens.

Grabbing her bag, Patricia turned to kiss Liz on the cheek then headed for the door.

Liz looked on for a moment, thinking she would need to give her son a push, because of course if she didn't he wouldn't, and nobody would.

"Hold on, I'm coming," John said suddenly, grabbing his own bag and rushing for the door, spoon in hand. His abrupt change had caught Liz by surprise, having expected to talk with him. No chance now.

"Right, bye, Mom," John said, heading out the door and

disappearing without a second thought. Liz envied him of his naivety towards life.

Patricia watched him go, feeling bemused, before turning to her mother. "Are you going to be all right?" she asked, sounding much older than she was.

"Yes, I'll be fine. Your dad and I have been through everything together. We will both be fine. You go on and I will get sorting here."

Patricia smiled before heading out, content that she was right.

Then there was silence, and being alone. The house was finally empty as sun shone in through the large front windows and warm air circulated around. Liz mirrored how Jack had been, folding her arms, wondering if her emotions would get the better of her. They didn't, she wouldn't allow it. She was being foolish. It would be fine. It always was.

2

NO TIME FOR GOODBYE

Jack stood, waiting patiently as he always did. The weather was good, which helped, but he never looked forward to having to do so in winter, soaked to the skin when raining, freezing cold when it was icy or snowing, and then there were the times when his lift never turned up. That would mean going in to work with excuses, falling behind on what he had to do, not to mention the anger and annoyance of those around him.

As he looked around at the local village, his mind was a river of thoughts, back to when they had first moved in, how things always seemed the same, how his life was. He recalled the decision to move to the area, his employers deciding that it would be cheaper to manufacture in the north of England, and how nice it could all be. They were right, it was nice, "nice" being a four-letter word which suggested stagnation, boredom, end of life. It was as if he were stuck in a dead-end job in a dead-end place, surrounded by dead-end people. If that were the case, then why did he stay? He had no answers…

Just as his frustration threatened to boil over, a honking sound interrupted his thoughts. His ride had arrived. Alan Laker pulled up in his bright red Ford Cortina, leaning his head into the windscreen, peering at Jack. He had that same silly grin on his face, the one which suggested he was pleasant, but in reality meant he would stab his own mother in the back if it meant he might get a promotion.

"Well, come on then, we'll be late for work," Alan said, winding his side window down to speak. His hair was a mess, and he had again forgotten his tie, which in their management role was a requirement. Somehow, for all his poor dress and attitude, he still ended up getting promotions and favors.

Jack looked at him, unable to comprehend how he might be better than him. He failed to understand that Alan was likeable and decent, fundamentally a good man, whereas he was simply seen as being aloof, arrogant, and annoying.

"Morning," Jack said, pulling open the car door and stepping in.

"Morning, Jack," Alan said loudly, still grinning.

Annoying as ever, Jack thought.

"Mind you don't," Alan began to say, too late as Jack slammed the door so hard that it rattled. It was as much a part of their daily routine as anything, good and bad.

"Sorry," Jack said without looking at his colleague. He knew what he had done, and often did, but it was too bad.

"Ready for a new day?" Alan asked, sounding far more cheerful than anyone should, especially for someone working as a line manager in a furniture business.

"I guess so," Jack replied, looking out of his window.

"Not feeling so great then?" Alan asked.

"Not really."

"Why, what's up now?" Alan continued, but deep down aware how Jack could be angry at anything. Nothing ever seemed to make him truly satisfied, nothing made him happy.

"I don't know. I moved here, to Elton, this little village, surrounded by people who all seem the same."

"That's a good thing, isn't it?"

"No, because it's the same thing, day in day out, and the only way a lot of these people get on is by climbing over each other, by being horrible with each other and stabbing each other in the back." As Jack spoke, his mind bristled at the thought of what he was saying, and who he was saying it to. If Alan had lived in the same village, he would have understood it.

"Well, anyway," Alan said, pulling away. The engine of his car whined, making Jack chuckle to himself, though he didn't feel so happy that he should laugh, but he couldn't help but associate the whine of the car with the whine of the man.

"At least you have your family," Alan said, trying to begin the day positively.

"Sure, the old ball and chain."

It was enough. There was clearly nothing more to be said. As they drove, neither spoke nor looked at one another as Jack stared out of the window.

"Do me a favor," Jack said suddenly.

"Sure, what is it?"

"Will you drop me off at the local shops here?"

Alan turned briefly to look at his passenger. "What's up, forgot something?" he asked, turning away from their usual destination.

"Yeah," Jack replied, without smiling.

"OK then. We'll have to be quick, though, otherwise we'll be late for work."

Alan drove silently to the shops he knew well. There were a few of the usual ones from around, but it occurred to him to wonder what he might need. Jack had never seemed the type to shop.

As they pulled up outside a newsagents, Alan turned to speak, but before he could say anything, Jack opened the door and stepped out quickly.

"Sorry, mate, I just thought of something. I'm not gonna make it in today. Can you make an excuse for me? I'll see you soon," Jack said.

"Well, I—" Alan began, but before he could finish his sentence, the door slammed, once again so hard it rattled. Even for someone as nice as Alan, such behavior grated.

"Sure, mate, I'll do that, mate, I'll do that for you," Alan mumbled, quickly accelerating in reverse. As he turned the car to move away, he watched the man as he walked off. He sat, waiting and watching, as his work colleague walked off down the path, ignoring the shops, disappearing down a side alley. Just as he thought to go after him to say something, a loud sound behind him broke his concentration. As he looked in the mirror, he saw several cars waiting behind for him to move, so he did, and with it all thoughts of his colleague were gone.

3

SHOCKS AND SURPRISES

Liz stared at the wall, not quite thinking about anything. The haze and fuss of the morning had died down, Jack and the kids had left, and for the moment she could breathe a little, take a moment for herself. A flopping sound from the front door interrupted her moment as a batch of letters dropped rudely onto the doormat. Liz turned to look at it, wondering what she had been doing. Still, it was nice to switch off for a time, forget all the trials and issues of the day ahead.

Bills, bills, and more bills, or so she thought. A brown envelope suggested a tax letter, another white one with fine writing was clearly a bill for electric, one more for her catalogue payments. Of course the catalogue was worth it, to keep the children in clothes, except soon they would no longer be kids, and then what? Besides, she thought, if she didn't have the catalogue, who would buy the clothes? Liz stopped mid-thought, berating herself for being so negative towards her husband. So what if it was true, so what if he never bought anything personal for his family? His money paid the mortgage, as he was so fond of reminding her, and for the car they no longer had, and the holidays which they no longer went on. Discussions of money were always a dead end, leading to discussions about his life, where things were going. Deep down she felt such optimism, but no matter how hard she tried, it seemed he never shared her feelings.

As she walked across the living room, bare feet against the soft carpet, she felt mixed, on one hand happy that she had such a nice home and a loving family, but on the other torn over her relationship with her man. He was far from perfect, but for all his problems he was a fundamentally good man, and most importantly she still loved him. Such negativity had no place in a loving heart, and so she determined no more, she would plan ahead, get to it and make it work.

First there would be the bedrooms, then the washing, then the dusting, then, then there would be something else. There always was. Liz climbed the winding stairs. When she had first seen the house, she had an immediate sense that it was wrong, because who wanted their sole form of winter heating to be under-floor and nothing else? But as time passed, even with all the unfinished work, it was still a beautiful home to her. She stood at the top of the stairs, deciding which room to tackle, before heading to John's, feeling a glib sense of mock shock as she entered the teenager's room.

As she swung the white door open, it was as if she had stepped into a mix of a warzone and a dream, or perhaps a nightmare. Clothes were strewn all over the floor, with plates piled up on a bedside cabinet. A small radio at the end of his bed played music, its tiny speaker vibrating annoyingly. The curtains remained closed, and every drawer and door wide open, clothes and covers hanging out from each, as if they were all trying to escape the maddening mess.

"John, John, John. Where do I begin?" Liz whispered to herself, as a sudden image flashed into her mind of a bonfire with all his rubbish in it. The moment she thought of it she giggled to herself, before feeling foolish that she should be so merry while alone, let alone about something like that. Still, it would save some time. For a few seconds she allowed herself to wonder about it, sorting the whole day's cleaning, all by bonfire!

It had become something of a ritual for her, ours is not to reason why... working on the house, ensuring the family had what they needed, ignoring her own needs. It had been her mother's way to do such things, and it had never occurred to her to do anything differently.

At which point Liz went back to autopilot, ignoring anything private or unsavory, throwing sheets, covers, and clothes to the middle of the floor, and putting away anything that had a home, while clearing and cleaning as she went. As annoying and repetitive as she felt it was to do everything over and over, week in week out, she couldn't help but feel a sense of satisfaction when it was all finished.

Time had no concern for her as she worked, simply allowing her mind to focus on each task at hand. Occasionally she would wonder if anyone really appreciated what she did, but truthfully she knew it mattered that she did it, because she loved them all so much, and it was her way of being a part of what made their family work.

As she picked up the large bundle of washing, she looked around, seeing the stark changes she had brought about. It looked like a home, like a room anyone would want to be in. The sun shone brightly through the window, reminding her how much dust floated around. In no time at all it may well be back as it was, but for now it was fine.

Liz looked at the posters on the walls, a video game character carrying a gun, a music group that she had never heard of, and never wanted to, and a trio of posters of barely clothed females. The latter were reminders that her son was growing up, and like her daughter would soon fly the coop and then it would be just her and Jack. As much as she had looked forward to the idea, she knew in part that it would never happen, they would always be there. A deep-rooted sense of unease threatened to overwhelm her, a nagging voice about the man she loved, her doubts, his doubts. Before she could dwell on it, she flushed them from her mind, once again focusing on nothing but her family and the day ahead.

As she dropped the pile of washing into the basket, a shrill sound screamed from downstairs. It was the telephone. For the umpteenth time she mentally berated herself for only having one telephone, downstairs. At least it was an opportunity for a break, so she dropped everything and headed down. The phone rang, a cacophony, shrill and demanding as she approached it. She wondered who might call at such an unusual hour.

The moment Liz picked up the receiver, a voice blared at her down the line.

"Hello, Elizabeth, is that you?" the voice hollered. Liz figured the telephone didn't need a volume control, her sister did. She could always tell it was her, not just from her Yorkshire accent, but from how loudly she always spoke.

"Hello, Brenda," Liz said, at first speaking so loudly she felt annoyed with herself.

"Hi, how's everything?" Brenda asked. How loud she often was made it difficult to determine what kind of mood she was in. As she had grown older, she had mellowed as a sister, but never quite managed to lower her tone. Whether such behavior was endearing to anyone, Liz was never sure, but she had grown used to it anyway.

"I'm fine."

"How are the kids?"

"They're fine, absolutely great."

"How's Jack?" The moment the question was asked, Liz felt a chill come between them. Her mind lit up as if there was a battle inside of her, where one side screamed how much she loved him, but the other demanded that she stand up for herself, to admit what was wrong.

"Oh, he's good, no problems. John is in school, Patricia is at college. Jack is at work, and he's fine."

"Well, that's good."

"How are you?" Liz asked. She couldn't help herself, feeling it was so much of a dance, getting things out of the way, the same old routine, before they could talk properly.

"I'm good, been busy, doing cakes for the holidays, as usual. We're all fine here.

"So, what are you up to, then?" Brenda asked. Still as loud as ever.

"Just cleaning the house. It seems to be never-ending."

"Yeah, I know. Daft, isn't it? You should come up and see us, it's been a while."

The thought of traveling to Yorkshire wasn't one that filled her with joy. As much as she always loved seeing family, going back to where she was born held little interest for her. She had seen and done everything there, and being such a forward-looking person, she could never countenance the thought of going back.

"I know, it would be nice to see you all. Maybe in the new year I can come up, or you can come here?"

Brenda laughed. "Yeah, come and spend some time with you and the kids, and Jack. Happy Jack."

Liz hesitated. "Why did you say that?"

"Say what?"

"Happy Jack."

Now Brenda hesitated. "Oh no, nothing really. I just haven't seen him in ages, and when I have, he never seemed very happy."

Liz stood, remaining silent, holding the phone to her cheek, trying not to give way to her emotions. She tensed, feeling her cheeks burning as her eyes welled. She would not allow it, wouldn't give in to anything negative. It was fine, all fine.

"Are you there, Liz?" Silence continued.

"I'll have to ring back, sounds like she's gone."

"No, no, I'm still here. Sorry, just had a dry throat. I nearly started coughing."

"Oh, how daft," Brenda said, laughing.

Silence descended upon them both again. Liz struggled internally, knowing she needed to say something, anything, otherwise it would provoke. Too late.

"Are you all right, Liz?" She could never hide her emotions from her sister, or anyone really.

"Yes, yes, I'm fine. We're all OK, and me and Jack are fine too, so don't worry."

"OK, sis. Did I tell you about what happened to Ernie?"

"Oh, no, you didn't. What trouble has he gotten into now?"

At which point all concerns and worries were left behind in an hour of chatter and fun. Liz relaxed, knowing that come what may, she always had her sister to talk to. She knew full well if things were really bad, she would be on a train straight there, sorting everything out, or at least trying to.

*

A rapping sound on the door interrupted the fun, just as the wooden clock standing in the corner chimed to say it was two o' clock. Liz looked up from the door to the clock, stopping what she was saying mid-sentence. It was of such importance that the interruption instantly blanked her mind, no memory of what they were talking about.

"Brenda, look at the time. We've been chatting for so long, and I've got nothing done."

"Oh, me neither. OK, I'll let you go. Call me if you need to." At which they both agreed to talk soon. Just as Liz was about to place the receiver on the hook, the rapping on the door grew louder.

"Hold on, I'm coming," Liz insisted, annoyed by the belligerence.

As she approached the door, a shadow cast at the side of the frame as whoever it was attempted to peer through the frosted glass. Again the person tapped on the door, then on the window, exaggerating their impatience.

As the caller went to knock again, Liz quickly opened the door. "Can you not be a bit more patient?" she demanded, looking at the person furiously. It was a short man, wearing a raincoat. He was smartly dressed, with a deep brown tie, and was clean shaven, looking so serious, and yet he smiled in the most pleasant way.

"Oh, good morning. Please forgive me for being so persistent. I wasn't sure you might have heard me."

The man's demeanor caught Liz off guard. She had expected him to behave differently. As annoyed as she was over the knocking, she felt disarmed by his approach. "Sorry, yes, what was it you wanted again?"

"Well," the man said, pulling a bundle of papers from a leather satchel.

"Sorry, if you're selling something, I'm not interested at this time," Liz said, thinking to herself that there never would be a time, because money was tight.

The man gave her a wry smile. "Let me explain," he said in a quiet voice, looking directly at her. "You see, I am from the bank, and I am calling about your credit card."

"Oh, right, have we won something?"

The man laughed, trying not to, for fear what came next might cause greater offense.

"No. You see, the bill hasn't been paid, and the spending is well over its limit."

"Really?" Liz asked, a frown on her face. "We always pay that on time, and last time I looked a couple of months ago we had plenty left."

The man looked up at her, aware of her genuine confusion. "Well, perhaps we should go inside to discuss it?"

"Well no, because my son will be due in soon, and I don't want to discuss this in front of him. I'll ask my husband Jack to call you to sort it out. OK?"

The man looked around, then down and finally back at her. "I'm so sorry to have to be persistent, but you see, the limit is five thousand pounds, and given his excellent track record, and your having been with us for over twenty years, we allowed the limit to be exceeded."

"Well, that's very kind of you, but I had no idea."

"The balance now is over eight thousand pounds, and we haven't had a payment on the account now for two months."

The words hit her like a bullet. It was a simple matter. Jack's wages weren't amazing, but they managed—just. The amount was like a siren call to her mind, berating her with what it meant. The man looked at her, understanding how she appeared, what it had done to her, but he knew he had a job to do.

"Please forgive me for dropping this on you. Normally we would simply recall the debt and involve other collectors, but you have been with the bank so long, and we wanted to put this behind us if we could."

"Well, I don't think we have that kind of money. Are you sure there hasn't been a mistake, or fraud or something?"

"Oh, no," the man said. As he spoke, he withdrew at the suggestion, placing his papers back in his satchel. "Well, if payments are not brought immediately up to date, then I am sorry to say we will have to commence court action."

Liz just looked at him, wide eyed, unable to speak. She had never been in such a position before. They would often speak about money, but Jack, being the only earner in the family, handled all the payments. Usually all spending would be handled by him. Now, like a stream of worry trickling down her spine, it seemed as if she were losing any control she might have had.

"Right, yes, I'll speak to my husband about it; he will deal with it soon." As soon as Liz finished her sentence, she became aware of her immediate neighbor, standing in her doorway, looking out at nothing. It was a familiar sight, the woman who always had a kind word and a nosey look. Any excuse to have a cup, and a chat, and a gossip, and spread the word, or make it up. A neighbor to be tolerated, Liz thought, but now she could see exactly what she was doing.

"Afternoon, Pam," Liz said loudly, staring at her neighbor. She was a large woman, short hair, often dressed in cream slacks. Liz wondered if she didn't wear so much makeup people might think she was a man, before again berating herself for being so mean.

"Oh, hello, Liz. Just getting some air," Pam replied, smiling broadly. She cupped her hands together as if giving thanks to the Lord. Liz smiled, trying her best not to show her disdain, but she was angry that by tea time the entire neighborhood would know all their business.

"OK, I'll get my husband to call you as soon as he comes in."

The man smiled at her cheerfully. "That would be so good, if he could just catch up with these last payments immediately, then that's fine."

"What is the total to pay now?" Liz asked, regretting it, but needing to know. The last thing she wanted was to worry about it until Jack came home.

"Well, including charges, and interest, and what will shortly be three months' payments, you should be looking to pay three hundred and eighty-six pounds."

Liz felt that same sense of shock again. The eight thousand was like a bullet, but the thought of paying nearly four hundred was like a cannon.

"Well, I think we'll have to call and work it out, but I'm sure it will be sorted by the end of the month."

"Oh, no, we will need that payment now, by close of business tomorrow. Otherwise further action will have to be taken, and then there will be collection charges, and court charges, and the amount will increase substantially."

Liz felt breathless, like she had stood up too quickly and all the air had been taken away. She was at a giddy height, looking down from debt mountain. She felt sick in a way she never had before.

"I'll... I'll sort it," Liz stumbled, trying to speak and close the front door, looking for a way out. The man nodded at her, assured the gravity of the situation had sunk in. He walked away as Liz closed the door, stepping back from it, wanting to fall to the floor and cry.

Just as her emotions were about to explode, whether to scream or cry as loud as she could, the door banged again. Each tap on the hard wood was like a tap on her heart. She lay awkwardly, feeling a mixture of anger that the man should dare to return, but fear for what he might say, or do. She had no choice, but she wouldn't shy away this time.

Standing up quickly, she grabbed at the door, swinging it open wide. "Look, I have told you," she began, only to see her son John standing before her, a look of shock on his face.

"Oh, oh, sorry. What are you doing home?"

"Mom, it's three fifteen, I'm home from school."

John stepped beside her, walked in, and threw his bag to the middle of the floor. He slumped down on the sofa, so hard it slid backwards on the soft carpet.

"John, I've told you before don't crash down like that." He looked at her, a mixture of disinterest in her point, and annoyance that he couldn't simply sit and do nothing, not even think.

"And look at the state of your uniform, a mess as usual. I'm sick of it," Liz said, relieved that she had a softer target to pick on.

John looked down at himself, pulling his school blazer closed, only now becoming aware of how he looked. He remained silent, but the look he gave her was no longer one of dissent, but a fragile one, where he no longer seemed so assured in his argument, but was uncertain who he was talking to. He didn't need words to convey it, just that look, which horrified her.

"John, I'm so sorry," she said. The moment the words came out, she realized it was all she had been saying and feeling, sorry for everything. She wondered if she was saying sorry for things that hadn't happened yet.

"It's fine. Put the TV on," he said, instantly changing the mood, satisfied she was just having a moment. Being so young, his moods were as fickle as hers. In such a respect, he was bulletproof.

"Are you—" Liz began to say, before stopping herself short as she closed the door. She was going to ask if he was hungry, but of course it was a silly thing to ask him. Even when he was asleep he was hungry. John looked at her with a blank look, vaguely aware she had spoken, but more interested in other things than what she had to say.

"TV, Mom," was all he said, before looking back at the blank box in the corner. It was as if he no longer functioned. He had done his bit, been to school as instructed, as expected, and now he was back in the cradle of his mother's arms, ready to be protected with cartoons and chips.

Liz breathed out, as much a sigh of relief for normality as exasperation over her son. Still, she didn't mind too much; for her it was all part of the family, doing for each other. She ignored the bit about her son doing for her—that would come much, much later, she hoped. She grabbed the remote control, which was sitting right next to him, clicked the on button, and dropped it into his lap.

"Unh," John grunted, a thank you of sorts.

"Cheese?" Liz asked.

"Cheese what?"

"Sandwiches."

"What about them?"

"You asked for a sandwich, what do you want?"

"A sandwich, that's what I asked for," John said confidently, wondering about his mother.

"Yes, but." She gave up, figuring it just wasn't worth the effort. If he objected to what they were, he could wear them.

As she walked into the kitchen, she stopped, thinking of something she should have asked before. "John, why didn't you use your door key to come in?"

"Er, I lost it, I think."

"Again?"

"Yeah, sorry."

Arguing about it wouldn't do any good, even if it was the fourth key in three months. It was just something to put up with, something else.

As thoughts dwelt on keys, the sound of a key in the lock became clear. Liz felt her heart leap again as she prepared herself mentally. It would be Jack, he would come in, take his shoes and tie off, and say something. She must hold it together, must not be rude, no need to argue with him, not in front of their son. Liz peered round the frame, looking along the living room, to see the door open.

"Finally, I'm home," a voice called. It was Patricia, arms full of carrier bags, struggling to manage the door and her entrance.

"Oh, it's you," Liz said, unable to stop herself before she said it.

"Oh, thanks, Mom, nice way to be welcomed home."

"Sorry." There it was again, that word. It was like a bell ringing in her head, the same thing over and over, that she had to apologize for silly things she had done, but also things that she was going to do, for what was coming.

"Check this out," Patricia said. As Liz looked at her, she dropped the entire batch of bags, slammed the front door shut, and began rifling through to find something. After a moment's pause and a growing sense of melodrama, Patricia pulled out a long black dress, covered in sequins, held up by a string like threads of differing colors.

"I thought I would wear it for the pub tonight, cause Dan is picking me up," Patricia said, smiling happily. John looked at her, stared for a moment before returning to the television, searching for cartoons.

Liz looked likewise at the dress, then her daughter. "So, you say you're off out tonight?" she asked, a look of concern on her face.

"Yeah, he's coming on his motorbike. Gonna take me out for food and a quick drink." Ordinarily it would be a good thing, nice to see her children going out with others, even if it was on a motorbike.

Tonight felt different, as if she were vulnerable, needing her children around her.

"Well, that will be… well, I thought we might all stay in and watch a movie," Liz said, holding her hands together as if they were too cold. She rubbed them, as if to ward off a sudden onset of ice around her.

"Mom, please, I said the other day we were going out, we can't do that," Patricia said. Liz looked at her wounded, feeling hurt, but somehow still managing to smile with it. She wanted to say it clearly, how she felt, how much she loved and needed them, but as much as she felt it, instinctively she just needed to protect them.

"Well, yes, it's fine, I can do us some tea before you go out."

"No, Mom, I said we're eating out, and drinks."

Liz nodded patiently. "All right, yes, that's fine. I'll do something for John and myself."

Liz struggled to be positive, but for all her emotions deep down she knew she was being foolish. It was a day no different than any other, and come what may, as it always did, things would be fine. Patricia looked down at her bags, without actually opening anything. She quickly glanced up to see her mother, frozen in time, like a puppy waiting for some love.

Without saying another word, Patricia walked over to Liz, opened her arms, and wrapped them around her. She embraced her strongly, pushing her head into her mother's shoulder. It was all a surprise to Liz, an unexpected show of affection. As much of a shock as it was, such a deeply personal display, it was so welcome, so personal, but most of all, so understanding. Her daughter was at an age where she could read emotions, and see how brittle and fragile she was, even if she had no idea why.

She looked at her, the wispy blonde hair which used to be brown, those same fine blue eyes and that easy smile. She was proud of her daughter, a good person deep down. Liz often chuckled to herself how alike they had become, as her daughter wore similar clothes to her, even now wearing simple flat shoes, which she promptly flicked off the moment she was indoors.

"Dan can pick me up, and how about we go the local chippy, get us all a curry and fries, rice, drinks, and we all eat in here, together?" Patricia asked, pulling away from her mother, looking at her with eyes older than her years.

"Yes, that would be really nice," Liz said, her mood much brighter now.

"Yeees," John said boldly, still not bothering to look at them. "I'll have a fish with mine too," he said, as his eyes fixated on a cartoon on television.

"I suppose you want a boiled egg on top of that too," Patricia said, looking at her brother. He had sunk down, as if he were melting, lazing across the arms of the sofa, shoes kicked off, eyes half open as he wallowed sloth-like in pure comfort.

"Nah, fried," John said quietly.

"What about your dad, are you gonna get him something?" Liz asked.

"Yeah, we'll get him his usual box of kippers and fried rice," Patricia replied, looking wryly at her mother.

"Funny, you know he doesn't like kippers."

"No? Well, when he gets in and Dan is here we'll see what he wants." Patricia loved her father, but their relationship was never the strongest. It never helped he and Dan not getting on well, but nobody openly said anything. Nobody wanted to upset anyone else. So things that needed airing remained hidden.

"Mom," John said, interrupting the moment between them.

"Yes, love?"

"What's for tea?" John asked, pulling his socks off and throwing them across the rug.

Patricia laughed. "Oh, John," she said, walking over to him. "Don't ever change," she said, slapping him easily on the arm.

"Mom, Patricia's hitting me," John said, still not looking away from the television.

Liz walked away, ignoring his cries. She quickly prepared a cheese sandwich, then returned, lowering into her son's eye line, otherwise he might never know it was ready.

Briefly he looked at the sandwich, then her. "What's that?"

"Cheese."

"I don't want cheese."

Liz looked at him, mock fury on her face. "I did ask," she said loudly. Again he looked at her, before allowing his attention to slowly refocus on the television.

"So, what do you want?" Liz asked.

"Curry, and fries, and a fish," John replied. Before his mother could express herself, Patricia leaned over, took one of the sandwiches, and thrust it into his face, gently grinding it into his mouth.

"Yuck," John said loudly, suddenly bolting from the sofa, wiping bread and cheese from his mouth.

"Ohhh," Liz said, struggling not to laugh.

Patricia ran away, thinking he would try to repay her, but it was John, and one thing he always hated was running. In the end, as John wiped himself down, Patricia and Liz laughed at each other, enjoying the moment, a shared memory for them all, to remind them that come what may, family could overcome anything.

4

THE WAITING GAME

"So, how's you?" Dan asked. He stepped in through the front doorway, bringing in with him a waft of cool Autumn air. He was wearing a red leather biker jacket and black leather trousers. His boots went right up his legs, with buckles on the side, as if he were a modern day knight, ready to joust with his mechanical beast. He was looking directly at Liz, a polite smile on his face. His short, black curly hair was matted to his head, a clear sign of motorbike helmet hair.

"Oh, I'm fine, thanks for asking," Liz replied. Night had fallen as evening set in and orange lights outside lit up one by one. As they chatted, Patricia walked in, wearing jeans and a blouse, holding a black leather jacket.

"Oh, we not going to the pub tonight, then?" Dan asked, looking at her.

"No. Well, I said to mom that we would stay in here tonight, but maybe go the chippy and get a big order in."

Dan nodded.

One of the characteristics she liked about him was how affable he could be, but mostly how much he could appreciate the importance of family to them. "Sure, sounds good to me," he said.

"What's Dad having?" John asked, stretching.

It was only then Liz noticed he was still in his school uniform. It was the perfect opportunity to avoid the question. "You go and get changed and have a wash," Liz insisted, folding her arms, as if to emphasize she meant it.

"Yeah, smelly, go get washed," Patricia said quickly. Dan smiled at them, unsure of what to do or say.

"Ignore them, Dan, you get used to it after a while," Liz said.

"Fancy a game of darts in the garage later?" John asked, finally managing to stand up.

"Yeah, sure, if you're still awake," Dan replied.

Before anyone could say another word, John ducked down and

headed through to the small hall and up the stairs. It was cold, and he was tired, but the thought of food called to him, blocking anything else from his mind.

After he had gone, Patricia looked at Liz. "Where is Dad? He's never usually this late."

"I don't know, love. I called his work an hour ago, but no answer."

"Maybe he's just stuck in traffic. Pretty bad out there at the moment," Dan said, trying to remain positive. It was past seven o' clock, but he knew they would achieve little from worrying.

"Maybe," Liz said, refusing to make eye contact. She knew if she did, she might not be able to hold a straight face over it. "Just get him a fish and fries, and I'll put it in the oven for him."

"OK, Mom," Patricia said, sliding on her jacket. She leaned over, kissing her mother on the cheek. "It'll be fine," she said, before leading Dan out the front door.

"I'll get some plates and things ready, and try his number again," Liz said, watching them go. The sight of the two, looking so connected, so happy, reminded her of days gone by, when she and Jack were so young. Anything seemed possible. She knew where all the time had gone, raising children, but couldn't understand how the optimism had died.

"Keep safe," Liz said to no one in particular. She knew she was alone, but felt the need to express her sentiment. She turned to go about what she had promised, to get things ready for their return. As she flicked on the kitchen lights, she noticed the cordless phone on the counter. She picked it up, flicking through the address book, clicking on Jack's work number again. Placing it to her ear, she internally waited for the ringing sound, dreading anything else, hoping for a voice. A voice came, lighting up her hopes, only to be dashed as a mechanical voice suggested the caller couldn't be reached.

Liz placed the phone back on the counter, wondering whether to call again, and again. She wanted to keep calling, as if her mind might somehow connect to him, to tell him to answer. Images demanded to flash into her mind of the worst things. Ideas whispered to her, car crash, hurt, hospital. She refused to listen, determined to remain calm. Above all, she was a mother, a protector. She would do that for her children. She could bear any amount of suffering and grief, if it meant protecting the children that made her life worthwhile.

The hall door burst open, making Liz jump, as John rushed in again. "What's on TV, Mom?" he asked, as usual oblivious to what was going on. His mind functioned on a single circuit, one designed to ensure he had fun and was happy. That was fine for Liz. It meant one less thing to worry about. He was like a beacon of hope, where little could affect his positivity and belief that everything could always be worked out, and with patience, everything would always be right. It wasn't a thoughtful choice for him, just that his mind simply worked that way, what was fun, good, enjoyable, and anything else was superfluous.

"I have no idea, love, why not find out?" Liz said, smiling at him, feeling a little better. She was surprised he hadn't commented about Jack not returning.

As John flicked through channels, once again finding his sweet spot on the sofa, Liz picked up the phone again and wandered into a corner of the kitchen. She flicked through the address book on the display, pulled up Jack's work number, and rang. The dial tone clicked before buzzing as it rang.

"Hello, Staines Furniture, can I help you?" a voice called, sounding like a robotic human being.

"Hi, I'm calling about my husband, Jack Cornwell. He hasn't returned home yet, and I'm wondering if you could tell me if he is still there?"

"Oh right, well I'm afraid I'm only night staff. There's no one in at the moment that I could ask. Could you call back in the morning?"

Liz breathed out heavily, annoyed at the suggestion. The lack of empathy from the other end, knowing she was worried for where her husband was, infuriated her.

"I guess I'll have to."

"Sorry I can't help you." On the last syllable of the last word, the phone clicked off, as if the woman she had spoken to couldn't wait to hang up.

"That's so nice of you, thanks," Liz said, slowly placing the phone on the counter. She stood a moment, half thinking of things and half allowing her mind to wander to nothing. An idea entered her head to burst into tears, but then it was replaced by a question as to why she should. Just as she was about to give way, the front door slammed as a blast of cold air came in. Liz pushed herself away from the counter quickly, one last vestige of hope that it would be Jack. Patricia and Dan walked quickly in, carrying thin white carrier bags full of hot, delicious chip shop food.

"That does smell nice," Liz said, smiling again, looking as if she had never felt a bad thing in her life.

"Yeah, can't wait," Dan said as he dropped bags onto the counter in the kitchen.

"Have you not put plates and cutlery out, Mom?" Patricia asked as she followed.

"Oh no, I was miles away," Liz said, quickly turning to help out.

Patricia turned to look at Dan, a knowing glance. He looked back briefly, unsure of what he might say and do.

"No sign of Dad?" Patricia asked as she placed food onto plates.

"No, nothing. Let's just eat food and think about it later," Liz suggested.

"Come on, John, food's out," Dan shouted. The moment he did, John leapt up like a gazelle.

"Wow, you never move that fast if food isn't on the table," Dan offered, laughing a little. John didn't answer, simply sitting, eyes wide at the mountain of food on his plate.

"That's curry, rice, fries and fish on there. If you don't eat it all, next time you don't get a fish," Patricia said playfully. She knew full well John would devour it all in no time, knowing his appetite.

As the four all eventually sat at the table, food was eaten, drinks enjoyed, and a quiet moment shared. Often they would eat separately, and even when together they used trays for their plates, sitting at the sofa or chairs. Table meals were rare, but when they ordered in food, it was a special treat to share.

"Where's Dad?" John blurted out, mouth full of food, struggling to speak.

Patricia stopped mid-bite, and Dan looked down at his plate as if he were praying. Liz did the opposite of both, looking up at her loud son, eyes wide, continuing to enjoy her food. She paused a moment, biding her time as he divided his attention between eating and looking at her.

"Eat that up, because that's all you're getting tonight."

John continued to chew feverishly. Just as Liz looked down again, and quiet descended once more, John looked up brightly. "So when's he back, then?" he asked again.

Patricia dropped her fork to the plate with a clang. "John!"

"We don't know. When we do, I'll tell you," Liz said, glaring at him.

"Right, I only asked."

The food was good, making up for the awkward air around the place. Nobody spoke, focusing on the food, ignoring what was to come.

Nothing more needed to be said. Dan helped Patricia clean plates away, then bade goodbye to her and the others and left. John slunk back to his favorite spot on the sofa as Patricia and Liz sat at the cleared table, silently thinking.

"Have you called him again?" Patricia asked finally.

"Yep, his work, nothing," Liz said, nodding gently.

Patricia looked up at the clock on the dining room wall, noticing it was approaching ten at night. "Maybe we should call the police?"

Liz felt her heart sink, a depressed sensation tugging at the pit of her stomach. Until then she had been clinging to the idea that there was still time, that he might come in at any moment, in a temper, angry at the delay, hungry, hugging, normal. It was like an icicle into her, leaving no room for doubt.

"I don't know, I think they will say he might be delayed. I do think they ask you to wait like a day or something. Otherwise any time someone was late, people would be calling the police."

Patricia nodded, unsure of what to do. She trusted her mother to know best, but as calm as she appeared, inside she was a mess of emotion and confusion. Her relationship with him had not been great for years, as he struggled to come to terms with her growing independence, and she struggled to adapt to her changing life, but they still loved each other.

"You and John go to bed. I'll wait up a bit longer, clean up, and if there is any sign of him, I'll let you know," Liz suggested, doing her best to be positive.

"OK," Patricia said. As if he had bat-like hearing, the moment Patricia agreed, John jumped up, springing off the sofa over to his mom.

"Right, going to bed. Good night," he said, kissing his mother on the cheek. It brought with it a well of emotion for Liz, but she held on, remaining tight-lipped. Patricia followed suit, kissing Liz on the cheek before going up. Liz remained at the table, elbows on it, supporting her depressed face as she leaned over, allowing her mind to wander again. An odd thought occurred to her, how Jack often criticized her for elbows on the table, insisting she show more decorum. He had his odd ways, annoying too often, but after so long together, twenty-seven years of marriage, she would never do without him.

A chill air grew around her, but she ignored it as the under-floor heating turned off. Little really mattered. In all of the years they had been together, they had their fair share of arguments, even refusing to speak for a time, but it always blew over. She knew deep down whatever problems they had would be dealt with, but the difference now was he wasn't home. He had never done such a thing before.

The night crept in as a frost crept across the land outside. Liz felt tired beyond her years, but for now she would just sit a while, and wait.

5

A CALL TO ACTION

A shrill alarm sound rang, interrupting what little sleep Liz had been enjoying. It was that same alarm from that same clock that had woken them for so long, she no longer remember how they even got it. She lay there, hand under her face, feeling sick after a wretched night of worry and a night in a bed alone for the first time in so long, it seemed like an eternity.

The routine, the life, the same old things every morning. The same things happen for so long that you get sick of them, and it becomes a trial to keep going. But when it stops or something changes, it's like your life has been thrown into a tumble dryer and come out different. The thing you came to dislike ends up being the thing that you miss the most, not the people or the events, but the routine, the safety of it, the normality.

The air felt colder, as if any last claim summer might have had on the season was gone. Liz felt different, not just inside, but outside. The skin on her face felt different, cold, but loose, as if she had aged overnight. As she lay on her back, looking up at the ceiling, it felt as if all the air above were pressing down on her, forcing her flat, that all the vitality and life had been pressed out of her. If she stood up now, she would look paper-thin, so blank in presence that she could wander around and nobody would notice her.

All the while she waited, her mind reminded her, nagging her over and over, remember the phone, think about the phone, it will ring, it might ring. Any moment, the call would come and she would have an answer, and all the problems ahead would be known and dealt with. At times as she lay, she wondered if she were hearing a ringing, that she had been called and been so busy thinking about it that she had missed it. It was a kind of madness, where all she could see were her own thoughts and all she could hear was a bell which never really came.

Occasional thoughts pervaded her mind, duties, obligations, the need to move and get on. She had been raised in tough times, father died early, mother raised her and half a dozen brothers and sisters. There was no room for slacking then, there were chores to do, assisting with everything to make life work in the house. Deep down, as much as she struggled emotionally to cope, she still held that instinct, to go on till the last, to never stop trying until she was truly beaten. Life was hard, it hurt sometimes, but you still had to live it.

Finally she jumped up, not so much like a gazelle, more like a weak puppy crawling away from the warmth of its mother for the first time. The skies outside were gray and listless, much like her inside. It would be an empty day whatever happened, because things had changed, for the worse if such were possible. Everything around was so still, it seemed as if all the air had been sucked out, that she stood in a vacuum, where only she existed.

The mirror stood before her, the wretched full-length mirror, which reminded her of how old she was, all of forty-seven years, and looking every bit of it. Her nightdress was the best thing about her morning, white but covered in pretty yellow flowers. She had wanted new pajamas, remembered the row she and Jack had had over it, but of course he needed a new suit for work, and that always came first, so she did without.

Like a mother's tale, where everyone else mattered more than she did, where she would live forever, never asking for anything, not expecting anything, and never getting anything. She was fine with it, because to her all that mattered was her children were well, and safe, and entered each day with a smile on their faces. Even dull, always-unhappy Jack mattered more than she, because it was the duty of a wife and a mother to put others before herself. At least that was how she was raised, her mother insisting the man of the house must be obeyed. Nobody told her what to do when the great man was wrong.

So it began, the walk through the house, and the merry dance began on her new life.

*

"John, if you don't get up right now, I'm going to come in there, grab you by the ankles, and drag you downstairs, head banging on each stair as I go, bump, bump, bump," Liz shouted, surprising herself in the process. She wasn't a loud person, more the wallflower type, smile and hope kind of person.

"Mom, that's the funniest thing I've ever heard you say," a voice offered, making her jump. Liz looked sideways to see Patricia standing beside her, still in her dressing gown, hair all a mess. As surprising as it was seeing her there, she couldn't help but stare at how badly prepared she was.

"Pat, you gave me the fright of my life. Why aren't you ready for college?"

Patricia smiled at her knowingly. Before she could say anything, John's door swung wide open as he stood before them, looking half-asleep and decidedly annoyed.

"Why are you going to drag me down the stairs?"

Again Patricia smiled, forcing herself not to laugh.

"Because you're going to be late for school," Liz insisted, folding her arms to show how serious she was.

"It's Saturday," both answered her in chorus, as if they had rehearsed it. Liz looked at them both, eyes wide, shocked at her own state of mind.

"Goodnight, Mom," John said, closing the door, ready to head back to the land of sleep.

"I'm staying up, now you've made such a racket," Patricia said politely.

Liz shrugged internally, feeling a sudden urge to cry. Of course she wouldn't; that was something she would never burden her children with. Not yet, anyway.

"Right, I'll go do breakfast," Liz finally said, head down, looking as if she were going back to sleep herself.

"I'm not really hungry," Patricia said. The moment she finished her sentence, John's door burst open again as he stood still in his Simpsons pajama top and baggy knee-length cotton shorts. His hair stuck up, as if it had been struck by lightning.

"I'll have bacon and eggs," he said as he tried to force his eyes open more. Liz looked up at him, feeling a deep sense of love for both of them. No matter what else went wrong in the world, she would always have them, and however bad things might be, they always seemed to have the capacity to make her laugh.

"Bacon, eh?" Liz asked.

"Yeah, and egg, and maybe tomatoes, and toast, mushrooms," John replied.

"Anything else? Half a cow perhaps?" Liz asked. John thought of a sarcastic reply, but it was still early and it was the weekend, so he let it pass.

"Thanks, Mom. I'll have it in bed," John said, closing the door slowly.

"Er, no you won't. You can get dressed and washed and come downstairs for it."

John didn't quite close the door. He knew full well he was chancing his luck. "Mom, it's Saturday, do I have to get dressed?" he asked.

"No, but washed and cleaned and downstairs."

"All right."

Patricia smiled at him mischievously, goading him into a response. He ignored her, thinking only of the food to come.

"Mom," John called.

"What?" Liz demanded, more abruptly than she had intended.

"Is Dad back?"

The question made her heart sink again. She had hoped to get the morning out of the way, a cup of tea and rebuild her strength before such questions needed to be dealt with. Given his age, it was hardly surprising her son lacked tact.

"No," was all she said quietly before going down the stairs and away.

Patricia shuffled through the hall door and into the living room. She had managed to pull on a dressing gown, and huge fluffy slippers. Her hair mirrored that of her brother, but she wasn't going out so didn't mind. As long as John had similar hair, he couldn't make so much fun of her.

She slowly walked around the living room, into the dining room, to see Liz standing in the open-plan kitchen area. She was in front of the cooker, dropping eggs into a pan to be fried. "Would you like some breakfast?" she asked.

"Just some toast, please."

Liz could almost feel the tension on the back of her neck, not from herself, but from the need for her daughter to talk. It was an invisible need, but there anyway. Whether it was because she herself wanted to talk, or whether she shared the need to ask, she wasn't sure, but it was like a dam of energy waiting to burst free, and with it unchecked emotions.

Liz turned to look at Patricia briefly. As she turned, she attempted to speak, only to stop herself, realizing she had no idea what she was going to say.

Patricia looked down, not at anything in particular. She knew they felt the same, wanted to speak, but couldn't quite find the words.

The silence was awkward, that anything else said which didn't address the elephant in the room would sound hypocritical.

"Wow, that smells great," John said, bursting in through from the hall. As he rushed in, a cold gust of wind followed, reminding them of the lack of heat.

"John, shut that door," Patricia insisted. He did so, wondering what all the fuss was.

As he quickly sat at the table, feeling his need to eat where no food existed, he looked quickly up at his mother. "So, where's Dad, then?" he asked, without a hint of awkwardness.

"Seriously?" Patricia asked, giving him a serious look, which only confused him all the more.

"It's fine," Liz said, looking at them both. "I haven't heard from your dad. I telephoned his work and they say he hasn't been in. I have no idea where he is, or what he is doing."

"Right," John said, as if he had heard the response but wasn't listening. All he could think of was food.

"So, what now?" Patricia asked, mildly thankful that someone had allowed them to discuss it, even if her brother had done so with all the subtlety of a rhino.

"Well, I did think we were supposed to wait twenty-four hours until calling the police, but apparently that isn't the case. So once we've had breakfast, I will make the call, and we will see what they say and do."

It sounded as if it were a final statement, not intentionally, but none of them could think of anything to add. They would eat, and call, and see. What happened next was impossible for them to know.

Liz filled a large plate with food for John, dropping it onto the table in front of him. It was as if Christmas had come as he sat all wide-eyed and eager. Straight after, she dropped a plate with slices of toast on it in front of Patricia, then sat beside her.

"Are you not eating anything, Mom? You should," Patricia offered.

Liz shook her head. "No, love, I'm not hungry right now. Maybe after, I will," she replied. As she did, she removed the phone from her pocket, pressing for a dial tone. "I just need to make this call." As she pressed the buttons, she felt sicker than she had in her life, knowing that once it rang, things would probably never be the same for any of them again.

6

INVESTIGATION

"Right, I need to ask you a few questions, and just need for you to try to provide as full an answer as you possibly can. While I'm doing that, my colleague would like to undertake a few things while we're talking. Is that all right?" the officer asked. Things had moved quicker than she had expected; from fragile phone calls to struggling to provide information, it had been an intense experience so far, and only threatened to get worse.

Liz, John, and Patricia sat on the sofa side by side, each looking a little lost. Opposite them sat a uniformed police officer, holding a notebook. He looked young, too young to be doing the job he was, but for now he was the only link to anything close to being a way out of the torment. Sitting on a chair nearby was a female officer, liaison, prepared to answer any questions they might have, once it had all stopped. If it did.

The air between them seemed fragile, so delicate that any movement, anything said, might lead to something catastrophic. Nobody wanted to say a word in case they were met with a response they couldn't live with.

Liz looked down at the carpet, noticing a tag on its corner. It had been there since they bought the thing. Jack had chosen it for how hard-wearing it would be, nothing to do with how nice it might look. He had meant to remove the tag, kept promising to do so, but for some reason never quite got around to it. As she stared at it, it seemed to take on a life of its own, where it connected to other things in the house, and her life, reminding her of their joint failures.

Her mind wandered to the kitchen, to the units on the walls, half-built, never finished. She often marveled at the rounded cove he had built, after knocking out the dividing wall between kitchen and dining room. Such a good idea, and so many of them, but these ideas, too often that was all they remained. An idea that never enjoyed the life of fulfillment. The kitchen remained a reminder to her of an unrequited life, where so much was promised, and yet nothing ever quite got there. It was like a mirage, something just at the end of her vision, where a land of contentment and happiness whispered to her, but one that she would never truly be a part of.

"Mom," Patricia said, nudging her mother. Liz looked at her, then to the others, realizing all eyes were on her.

"Sorry, I was miles away. Did you say something?"

"No, it's fine, you take your time. We're here to help," the officer standing before her said. He was young, still bright-eyed, untainted by the effects of too long in a job where human nature and disappointment were eternal bedfellows.

Another man entered through the front door. He was dressed in a long brown overcoat, his hair not a touch out of place, short, slightly graying. He had a twinkle in his eyes, but didn't offer the least bit of humor.

"This is Detective Sergeant Chavards. He will be leading the investigation as it proceeds."

Chavards looked directly at Liz, noted her demeanor and smiled briefly before resuming his stony-faced look.

"Sorry, did you tell me your name?" Liz asked, realizing he probably had, but for the moment nothing was sinking in.

"Of course, my name is Police Constable Dan Trilby, and my colleague here is Officer Sue Danbridge. We work on cases like this, for initial reports of a missing person, and then act as a kind of liaison and administrative officers. We basically gather as much information as we can, and then the team will make enquiries and try to find out what has happened. All of this occurs with some natural urgency, of course, so as soon as we find out anything, we will let you know."

"Is there anything I can do for you right now?" Officer Danbridge asked. She was sitting on the edge of her seat, watching intently. After years in the job, she knew well enough how people reacted, and was waiting for any signs of an emotional breakdown. As much as she could see the sense of loss and desperation on Liz's face, she could also see she had strength, and believed that she could get through it.

"Wouldn't mind a cheese sandwich," John said suddenly, believing he was being asked what he might need too. Sue laughed quietly. She was pleased to see the youngest of them was taking it well enough, so far.

"I'm sure you can manage that, and maybe a cup of tea for your mom," officer Trilby suggested, offering a light smile. He knew the matter was serious, but needed to be empathic to the needs of the family. As he made his comment, he looked at John, then to Patricia, hoping they would get the hint.

"But," John began, but before he could speak Patricia stood up, tugging at his arm.

"Come on, I'll help you," she said, leaning over. It wasn't a request.

"Fine," John said, rolling out of his seat to leave.

As the two entered the kitchen, Trilby looked back at Liz, trying to appear deliberately calm but aware. Often when this happened, he would turn to the person closest to those that were missing, and the look would be almost a signal for the barriers to break down, for the deluge of emotion to come. He could see how much she needed to express herself, but perhaps due to the needs of her children, or that it just wasn't her way, she would never release it, never open up to it.

"Right, let's get this going as quickly as possible, and then see what we can find out for you as soon as we can," Trilby said, flipping open his top pocket to produce a notebook and small pen. For Liz, that provided more comfort than anything else, because it suggested to her that they were taking it seriously. She had visions of making a report and either being fobbed off or them asking for information and then doing nothing. She was experienced enough to know that could still happen, but for now she would go along with it.

"Can you give me some details about your husband, his physical characteristics, maybe a photograph or two, a recent one?"

Liz stood up, feeling the weakness in her knees. She was relatively light, and still felt young enough to engage with anyone and do anything. She felt relatively young, but right then she felt decrepit, as if she had walked a week in frozen air and next day had become crippled with it. She wondered if she would fall over right there on the carpet, to cap it all, being so lost, her husband gone, somewhere, and then she falls over in front of the very people trying to help her. Her mind turned to alcohol, what she could do with a nice drink of gin, but then that last time she had that was Christmas, and none of them were really ever drinkers.

"This is Jack, taken with Patricia and John when they went ice skating a few months back," Liz said, handing a photograph in a frame to the officer. As she did so, she continued to provide various details of his weight, height, and outstanding characteristics.

"That's great, thank you," Sue said, her voice lowered so as not to alarm anyone with what she had to say.

As Liz looked at her, the officer smiled quickly. "If your husband uses a toothbrush, could you possibly get that for us, and put it into this plastic bag?" she said, holding out a clear, square plastic bag with a sealable open top.

Liz looked at it, appearing confused. "Why will he need his toothbrush? I mean, is he going to be locked up for going missing?"

It would have been an easy thing to laugh about, but given the circumstances, and how delicate the situation was, nobody did.

"No, sorry, I should have said. We need to take something of his, which will likely have his DNA on it, so if need be we can confirm identity," Sue explained, trying to sound reassuring.

"Right, but surely you could just ask him who he is, and then he will simply tell you?"

"Yes of course," Trilby interrupted, aware the situation risked getting out of hand. "However, when we come across people, they are not always able to explain who they are, say if they are ill or something."

Liz looked at him wide-eyed, ready to say the thing that those left behind always did.

"However, that is very rare, and very unlikely," Trilby said quickly, before she could allow her mind to run away with her worries.

"It's also best we get this now, so that we don't have to come back again and trouble you for no reason," Sue suggested, wondering if she should move to sit beside Liz.

It was like being in a boxing ring, getting hit from left and right, blows to her sense of self, knocking her belief in what was real and what wasn't.

"I'll-I'll go get that now," Liz said, looking down as she struggled to stand up. As she did so, both officers stood with her.

"No, it's fine, you stay there, I'll go get it," Liz insisted.

"Well, madam," the older detective said, interrupting them all. His voice remained quiet but determined. As Liz turned to look at him, she noticed his clear gaze, his quick eyes looking at her as if she were prey. "One thing we need to do is to search the premises, the house, and the garage, the make sure your husband is definitely not here."

The suggestion caught Liz by surprise. Before she could respond, John and Patricia walked back into the room holding cups. John held tightly to the only thing that mattered to him, a plate with cheese sandwiches on it.

"Are you gonna search my room?" John asked, looked decidedly unhappy.

"Just a quick look, nothing major, so we can tick that off that we've seen with our own eyes that he isn't there," the detective said, looking at John, only now trying to smile, as if he were being reassuring but not very good at it.

"You won't need to go through my drawers, will you?" Liz asked, feeling more than a little lost. The emotion felt like a tornado inside her, threatening to whisk her away until she became hysterical.

"I'll go get the things they want, and show them what they need, shall I? You go get a drink of tea, and keep an eye on John, so he doesn't eat his fingers," Patricia said, gently taking the plastic bag from her mother. Liz continued to look at the ground, a little outside from everything that was going on.

"Hey," John said in mock indignation, deciding to take his sandwiches and sit down. No doubt there would be something better on television than listening to what they were all on about.

"That sounds like a good idea. Why don't you come back and sit with me, and we'll see if you can give me an indication as to what you might think he is doing," Sue offered, holding her hand out towards Liz. Liz nodded, before turning back to make her way to the sofa.

Patricia watched her mother go, feeling more concerned for how she might be coping than for the absence of her father. The moment she was out of sight, she turned to looked at the two police officers still with her. "I'll get that in the bag for you, and then show you all the rooms," she said, turning to begin walking up.

"That's great. We can do it quickly and then get on with our investigation," Trilby explained as he followed.

The word *investigation* felt odd to her, a dual meaning, at once reassuring, but at the same time unsettling—something good could come of it quickly, but also something horrible.

As the three stood at the top of the landing, Patricia again looked at them. "The bathroom is there, and the other doors are all bedrooms, mine, mom and dad's, and John's. Go in them as you like, and I'll go get the toothbrush," Patricia said, for the first time feeling nervous as everything began to sink in.

"You're doing great," Detective Chavards said, mindful of his need to move on. Patricia smiled uneasily at him before going to the bathroom for the toothbrush.

"Right, Trilby, you go in the young lad's room, I'll go have a good look round the room of the missing man. Usual complete search, and any visible signs for anything that might offer clues as to what's gone on," Chavards said, not waiting for a response as he opened the door and went in.

As he went in, the room offered little in the way of character. After many years of dealing with all levels of crime, and so many missing persons he had lost count, he could tell almost straight away about the nature of a relationship. It was pleasant enough, but dim, little to suggest a vibrant atmosphere. The walls were wallpapered, in an average beige coloring, divided by a long wooden baton across the middle of the wall. The paint had yellowed from time, clean but in need of attention. It was clear that the couple had simply lived, day to day, trudging through their responsibilities, without any evident signs of enjoyment from it all.

The double bed was neat, the covers fresh, and even the curtains looked smart enough. It all screamed of being perfectly made without being homely or loved.

Chavards did as he always did, opened a full-size wall cupboard and looked in, knowing full well there would be nothing in there. He went through his routine of opening drawers, more cupboards, peering briefly into things so that at least mentally he could acknowledge he had been there and done what needed to be done. It would be just another of those things, another story that would end bad for some and better for others. The conversation that was to come, later on, would be as difficult as any, but of course it was unavoidable.

"Nothing in here, sir," Trilby said, peering around the doorway. "Just typical for a teenager really, messy, and busy, but really nothing untoward."

Chavards nodded. He didn't need to wait for anything more. As he walked out of the bedroom, Patricia stood nearby, holding the bag with the toothbrush in it. She looked as shell-shocked as her mother, as if she were made of delicate ice and any hint of movement nearby would send her crashing down.

"Try not to worry. I've done a lot of these things, and it's very, very rare anything bad has happened," Chavards offered, looking far more amenable that his demeanor would have suggested of him.

"Do you think you'll find him?" Patricia asked. The moment she said it she regretted it, giving life to a thought she had tried to keep hidden. She really wanted to know when they would find him, but a nagging voice continued to haunt her, whether they ever would.

"There's no reason not to be optimistic," Chavards said, before ushering her downstairs. It was a clever response, one which didn't actually answer her worries, but then that was his point all along. There was never a way to answer what she had asked, because it was what they all asked, and the only real response was their return, or to accept they never would come back again.

As the group found their way quietly back into the living room, Liz sat reluctantly on the sofa, and John sat on the floor in front of her, watching cartoons. Liz looked up, halfheartedly, her attention more on her own feelings than any expectations.

"OK, we have what we need," Trilby said, gently taking the plastic bag from Patricia.

Liz stood up slowly as the officers tried to assure her it wasn't needed. Regardless she would do what she wanted, whether out of expectation or need. At the least it would help her feel better, a bit more normal.

Chavards walked over to her, smiling in a way that none had seen until then. His eyes twinkled, suggesting the look of a man who only new kindness or innocence. Behind them was a maelstrom of wisdom and knowledge, built up from a lifetime of such work, but he had grown good at hiding such things. Whatever he knew, the next steps were never easy.

"We have what we need, and can see he's not here, which we have to do, because sometimes for whatever reason the people are still actually home. We have the brush for a DNA sample, so we can test that against any findings from our investigations."

"Where would he be, Mom?" John asked. It was a sudden request, quite out of character for her son, and a reminder that he was more aware of his missing father than he had let on.

Liz shook her head vaguely. "We have no idea right now, but he'll be home, I'm sure of it."

"The truth is, and I have to say this, is that for now we have no idea where he might be. We have carried out basic checks for any reports, and so far there are none, no sightings or anything connected with him. However, you have to understand that it doesn't always work out well, and there are also instances where we do find the person, but they choose not to return," Chavards explained, listing through all the things that had to be said, because sooner or later they would come asking if he didn't do it immediately.

"No, that's not like Jack, he would be here unless something held him up. I'm sure he's just busy with work, or someone else. He'll be back later, I'm sure," Liz insisted. No one said a word, simply looking at her and each other.

"When you find him, will you let us know as soon as possible so we can go get him and bring him home?" Patricia asked. It was that question, the one that always came up, the one that no police officer ever wanted to answer, but couldn't avoid.

"I have to tell you, that on those occasions where we do find the missing person, and they expressly wish to be left alone, and do not wish to be contacted, then we are not allowed to tell you where that person is."

As always, the sense of shock was palpable, the thought that someone who was a father, a husband of so long, might want to disappear on purpose, and never be found, left the family struggling to comprehend.

"Dad would never do that. He'd come home if he could," John said, refusing to take his eye off the television as he spoke.

"No, I can't see why he would do that," Patricia said, agreeing in part with her brother.

Liz remained quiet, looking at her children, not quite daring to return the look she received from the detective. He could see she was thinking, calculating the probabilities, determining what was to come. He had seen something in her when he first spoke to her. He knew whatever happened, whatever they discovered, life for the family would never be the same, but still, they had her, and she would deal with it.

"We'll be in touch as soon as we find anything," Sue interrupted, aware the emotions were running high, and of the pressing need to move on.

Chavards lifted a flap on his coat pocket, removing a small oblong card, handing it to Liz. "If you hear anything in the meantime, please do call me, and I will answer it straight away. If I hear anything, of course I will come and see you straight away."

Liz took the card, not looking at it, but holding it as if it held a precious answer for her.

The two officers and the detective bade their goodbyes and left, all without saying another word. Liz never heard what they had to say, but she could imagine. As much as she had her own thoughts on things, for now they would remain private.

The moment she closed the door, she felt as alone in her life as she ever had. Things between she and Jack hadn't been perfect, but as she always asked herself, whose relationship was ever perfect? The door signified a cutting off, something absolute, where life would be about her, her choices, for her children, and what she intended to do from that point on for all of them. She reminded herself repeatedly that he would probably be fine, and back soon, sheepish and full of apologies and explanations, but still there was always that nagging doubt, the one that never seemed to be wrong.

As she turned away from the door, she caught sight of Patricia with her hands up around her neck, as if holding something secret, but of course all she held back were the dark thoughts they both shared. Liz gave her a look, an acknowledgement, without intending to, but neither spoke. It was what it was, and for now they had to simply carry on, hoping for the best, preparing for the worst.

7

MOTHER'S VOICE

"Hello, Mom."

"Oh, hello, Elizabeth, that's a nice surprise. I hadn't expected to hear from you until tomorrow."

"Yeah, but—"

"Is everything all right, love?"

"Yeah, you know."

"Come on, tell me, what's up?"

Silence followed. So much for the determination not to cry, no show of emotion, a firm belief that it would be all right. It wasn't, and wasn't going to be.

The afternoon had gone in some ways much as it always did on a Saturday, doing washing, doing lunch, then tea, and a bit of tidying. The usual shopping with Jack would have to wait. John was in his bedroom listening to music, which was fine, because he was happy. When Dan turned up, taking Patricia out for the day, that was the hardest thing to bear, because the one person in her life who understood just enough, could turn away and bury herself in the comfort of someone who would never do such a thing, leave them.

"Oh, love, don't cry," the voice called gently. Until then, Liz had remained calm, promising herself she wouldn't let go, that she was in control. She almost laughed as much as she cried the moment her mother spoke, telling her not to do something, only to be the cause of that same thing.

It felt like a needed relief, to let go for a moment, as tears trickled heavily down her cheeks. She sobbed quietly, unable to form the words that reassured her mother she would be all right. Liz felt an odd sense of truth about it, that she would be all right, because in a way she had expected something like it. What was most odd to her was that she had been expecting it all their married life, until recently. Yes, things were a little stale, not truthfully the best, but they had money, or so she thought, and together they seemed to have turned a corner where in life anything had become possible.

"Do you need me to come there?" her mother asked. It was the worst thing she could say to stop her crying, but also the sweetest. Liz knew her mother was too old and infirm to travel, so the offer to come was so wrought with emotion, in a way it felt like the kindest thing anyone had ever done for her.

"Thank you, Mom," Liz said, still struggling to get a grip on her emotions. "I'll be fine. Just things have changed a bit."

The word *changed* was significant for her mother, she knew it could mean anything but had an idea just what. She wouldn't interrupt, just allow her daughter to have her say, and then help her to deal with it. She was a good mother.

"It's Jack, he went off to work Friday morning, and we've not heard from him at all since," Liz finally said. It felt cathartic to finally say what she had been holding on to, as if by not saying it she could pretend to herself that nothing was fixed, that there was still room for hope. She had found the strength to accept that hope no longer existed in quite the same way.

"Oh, love, you have no idea where he might have gone?"

"No," Liz said, surprising herself at how firmly she spoke. "In truth, I had no inclination that anything might be wrong, that he was unhappy," Liz continued. As she spoke, she found herself deliberately holding back. She had a truth to tell, how she long felt, but she wouldn't burden others with it.

"Are you sure he hasn't been in an accident? Have you called the police?"

"Yes, Mom. They have been here, and confirmed to me that there are no reports of him in any kind of accident. He hasn't been seen at work. The police came and took his toothbrush for DNA, and searched the house."

"Seriously, they came and searched, as if you haven't already done that."

Liz laughed bitterly to herself. "Yeah, I know. Seems daft, but I guess they have a procedure to follow."

"So, now what?"

"Now we wait. They told me that even if they find him, if he doesn't want to come home, they won't tell us where he is."

"That's terrible. You're there worried sick, and anything could have happened, and they simply won't tell you."

"No, well, they will probably tell me if he is OK, but not where he is, and nothing about him or why he left."

"I'm so sorry, love. I know how much effort you put into that relationship, and raising the kids, and the house." It was a small comfort, but still a reminder of how much she had done, and how much over the years she cared. She couldn't help but wonder if it was all going to be in vain.

"Well, you could come spend a few days with me, in Yorkshire. Bring the kids."

"Yeah, I will do, soon, but for now I'll just stay here, keep a lid on things, and see what the police come back with."

Silence descended upon them as they shared a unique emotion that words could not express. Liz felt better, knowing her mother was always there for her. Her mother waited and listened, knowing from her own loss how hard life could be. The very least she would do was everything she could.

"So, how's the weather there?" her mother asked. It was so typical of her, to pick just the right thing to say at just the right moment. Liz burst out laughing, sweeping away any signs of regret or sorrow. For a moment she truly could forget, as she listened to the voice of the woman she had always known, a reminder that some people in life were simply good, that no matter how hard life got, they were there to provide a lift up.

"Well," Liz began, chuckling to herself. "It's a bit chilly, but dry, and smelly as usual."

"Oh, so still as smelly there as ever?"

"Yep, stinking oil refinery nearby, polluting everything in sight."

"Hold your nose, get a peg."

"Better still, if Jack doesn't come back, we won't be able to pay the mortgage, so we'll be off to find a new home anyway," Liz said cheerfully. She reveled in her gallows humor, as much as she knew in time if things weren't resolved there would be a lot more tears.

"Oh, do you need some money? I could try to help a bit."

The offer made Liz's heart sink. It was once again a gesture, but one that held such deep significance to her. She felt the tears wanting to flow again, but she would hold off for her mother's sake.

"Thank you, Mom. I'll be all right for now."

"Mom, what's for tea?" a voice hollered from below. Her short sanctuary in her bedroom was coming to an end, life was once again about to intervene.

"Is that John I can hear pleading for food?"

"Of course, he eats for the three of us." Both laughed at it, as again Liz reminded herself how good it felt to know that for now he hadn't been affected by things.

"OK, I'd better go and sort tea out. I'll call you again soon, as soon as I hear anything," Liz said, feeling better for the warmth of her mother's words. She knew she was lucky to have such a mother, so strong, and having learnt how to be so herself. She would survive it, one way or another.

"All right, love, take care of yourself. Give my love to John and Patricia, and come see us here soon."

The line went dead before Liz had replaced the receiver, and once again she felt alone. She felt as if she were standing before a huge wall, so high she could barely see the top, that she must scale it to find answers, but had no idea how. All she could think of were her children. As long as she had them both, she would cope.

"Mom," John shouted, just as Liz stepped down the stairs in the darkness. Her presence made him jump, as he leapt back, quickly opening the door into the living room. Liz continued to walk towards him, not saying a word, just looking at him, wide-eyed, as if she were haunting him.

"You gave me a fright," John said, looking as if he had indeed seen a ghost. Liz broke up, unable to hold her glare, erupting into laughter. It felt like just the kind of release that she needed.

"Ah, poor John, scared of his own shadow," Patricia said, joining in the fun.

Liz walked over to him, placing a protective arm around his shoulder, looking at him while she smiled.

"Now, now Patricia, don't be mean to your brother," she said, pausing for dramatic effect. "You know how delicate he is," she finished as they both laughed loudly.

"I'm not delicate," John replied, pausing for his own dramatic effect. "I'm manly," he said, stony-faced, as if he meant every word. Patricia and Liz continued to laugh as the problems surrounding them melted away, if only for a short time.

John resumed his sofa duties as Patricia and Liz worked in the kitchen, preparing food for tea. Liz had considered the idea of ordering food to be delivered, but the nagging voice at the back of her mind reminded of the problems with money. It would have to wait, however long that might take.

8

THE BANK THAT LIKES TO SAY NO

"Hi, is that Elizabeth?"

"Well, yes, it's Liz actually, everyone calls me that. Who is this?"

"Hello. I'm calling from Staines Furniture."

The name made Liz's heart jump. It was the last company or people she had expected to hear from.

The weekend had dragged, as if they were living life through a treacle window, where nothing seemed real. Patricia had done her best to be positive, as aware as she was of the situation. John as ever seemed happy as long as he was fed and there was something on the television. The two had woken Monday morning early, setting out bright and early, as if nothing had ever happened.

The moment the two had left, Liz sat down on the sofa, wondering if she would even move again before they returned, as if she were some kind of mannequin that only came alive in the presence of others.

The telephone call had been loud and abrupt, a shock, but nothing quite compared to the voice on the other end, that name, the place where he worked, or did.

"Right, yes," Liz said, stumbling for words.

"Is this Mrs. Cornwell, Jack's wife?"

Again it felt like a stab, his name mentioned, he who was gone without warning. Though she had felt too upset to eat breakfast, she still felt sick.

"Yes, I suppose so," Liz said, her mind a rage of ideas and concerns.

"So it is Mrs. Cornwell?" the voice asked again, sounding like a robot awaiting the correct response before it could continue.

"Yes, yes, I am Elizabeth Cornwell, and Jack is my husband." It sounded forced, as if she regretted having to say such a thing.

"All right then," the voice replied. Liz wondered if whoever it was intended to simply hang up, but before she could speak, the woman continued.

"I am from the Human Resources Department, and we haven't seen or heard from Jack for a few days now, and he hasn't called in sick or to report—"

"Ha, right," Liz blurted out, surprised by her own lack of control.

"I'm sorry, what was that?"

Liz wondered whether to simply hang up, annoyed at their apparent ignorance. She decided not to, for the moment, in case they might prove somehow useful later on, although given the dialogue so far, she seriously doubted it.

"Jack isn't here."

"Oh, right. Well, do you know what time he will be back?"

"You tell me."

"I'm sorry, what was that?" Liz again wondered if she were talking to a machine, something uncaring and unsympathetic. Her instincts urged her to be rude, but it wasn't in her nature, so she remained quiet.

"Hello, are you still there?"

"Yes," Liz replied, so quietly it sounded as if she were far off. In her mind she was, away in a distant place where she couldn't get hurt anymore, or feel such a deep sense of worry. Little voices and ideas whispered to her from the moment she became aware Jack was missing, telling her a kind of truth that she could never cope with hearing. As the woman on the other end of the telephone spoke, it was like poking a fire with a stick, as emotions threatened to erupt once again, out of control.

"Right, well, we need to know where Jack is, as his contract states that he is to be in on time, and if not then to notify us with a good reason for nonappearance. Do you understand that?" The tone was different, that she had grown tired of being polite, and instead offered a more forthright attitude. Ordinarily, Liz would have been immediately reassuring, feeling bad for being so negative. Given what had happened, she wondered if she cared any more.

"Yeah, funny, but I have a contract too," Liz said, her voice firmer, more resolute.

"I beg your pardon?"

"I have a contract too, with him, my husband, only he doesn't seem to have bothered to keep to that commitment either."

"Oh, I'm sorry to hear that. So, when can we expect him in?"

Liz felt like exploding, seriously beginning to wonder if whoever was on the other end really was a machine. It was incredulous that anyone could be so disinterested in the other party in a conversation that they literally didn't hear a single word the other said.

"Who is this?" Liz demanded.

"I did explain, it's Staines Furniture."

"No, a company doesn't pick up a telephone and ask questions, that's like asking a car to go buy a loaf of bread. Who are you, what is your name?"

"Oh, we can't give out that information, for privacy and data-protection reasons."

"So for all I know you could be a complete impostor, pretending to be a talking company, and trying something illegal," Liz insisted, her heart pounding. She never liked confrontation, always one to try to keep the peace, but now she was at her wits' end, struggling to keep a lid on her temper.

"Well, I'm sure there is no need to be so aggressive."

"Aggressive? Do you even listen to anything I say? I make the point about my husband breaking his contract with me, and you carry on as if I hadn't spoken. Then I suggest you could be an impostor, and you respond by calling me aggressive. What planet are you on?" Liz demanded, finally losing control.

The line remained silent. Liz refused to say anything more. The ball was fully in the other person's court, and they could either respond or hang up, whichever didn't matter to her.

"I'm sorry," the woman replied finally, her voice lower. Liz breathed out, releasing some of the pressure. Her head had begun to pound, that she might explode, literally. Perhaps now they could talk.

Again Liz waited for the next step in a proper, understanding conversation.

"So," the woman began as Liz listened, ready to meet her halfway. "Do you know when Mister Cornwell will be in?"

Fireworks erupted in Liz's mind as she screamed internally for something to say, anything that might make the woman see sense. Words never came, except a loud scream, uttered from Liz, loud and proud before slamming the phone down.

She felt better, if only for hanging up on the silly woman, but her mind remained a whirlpool of aggravation. She would need to settle down, which meant a cup of tea.

As she made to stand up from the living room sofa, the telephone rang again. All feelings of release and calm vanished as red mist covered her thinking. How dare they think to call straight back? They would get a piece of her mind now, for sure.

Liz hastily grabbed at the receiver, lifted it quickly, and replied. "What?" she demanded, her voice mirroring her thoughts.

"Hello, is this Mrs. Cornwell?" a polite voice asked.

"Who is this? Is this Staines Furniture again, because if it is, you can damn well—"

"No, it isn't," the voice interrupted, remaining polite.

"Oh," Liz said, slowly returning to the sofa.

"This is Abbey Life Bank, could we possibly speak to Mister Jack Cornwell, please?"

"Er, Abbey, right, can I ask what this is about?"

"We are telephoning about the mortgage on your property. We urgently need to speak to him about it."

Liz felt as if someone were deliberately dropping her into a fire of torment, that somehow they were all cooperating to drag her down. She didn't need it, just wanted to be left alone. Confused, she simply sat, waiting, struggling to know what to think, let alone say.

"Hello? This really is quite urgent."

"I'm sorry, but he isn't here right now, can I take a message?"

"No, unfortunately I can only speak to him, as it is his sole name on the deeds."

"But, what is this about? I'm his wife, I need to know what is going on."

"Well if you could bring in some proof of identity documents, and come and see us, then I am sure we could discuss something with you."

"All right, well, I think I can get in to see you later this week."

"No, I'm sorry, but it needs to be today. Now," the voice insisted. The person on the other end sounded young, a man. He was polite throughout but firm. From the tone, she could tell he meant what he said, without being rude.

"I guess, I guess I'll get there today, then," Liz said finally, her mind a frenzy of thoughts and concerns.

"Thank you, see you later. Bye," the young man said, hanging up. It seemed abrupt, but it wasn't so much, more an example of how serious things were.

Once again Liz stood to her feet, half expecting the telephone to ring. If it did, she made a subconscious decision to simply leave it.

Her mind focused on the documents, then the money for the bus to town, then the time, being back for her children coming home, then what was it about? So many thoughts, so little time, so little ability to cope with it all. She grabbed at what she thought was enough, pulled on a large coat, and walked quickly out of the door. The moment she walked away from the house, a thought struck her—her purse, she had forgotten it. Panic set in as she fumbled around for her door keys. Without them, she couldn't get in to her purse, without that she couldn't pay for the bus. Then she would have to walk eight miles to town in Ellesmere Port.

"Hello Liz, looking a little lost there," a voice said, making her jump. She turned quickly to see Pam, her next-door neighbor. She was standing across the divide between the two properties, looking at her with a mixed view, making it impossible to tell whether she was genuinely concerned or whether she was enjoying the confusion.

"Hello, Pam," Liz said, still struggling for her keys.

"You seem a little out of breath. Out of shape, perhaps?" Pam asked. There it was, that true self, the real person that she would often hide behind a masquerade, a look of innocence, but a sense of the mildest malice.

"No, just busy. Some of us have busy lives, you see," Liz said, looking directly at her. As annoying as Pam often was, there was always the sense of being friendly, even if it wasn't genuine, because with people you lived beside, it simply made sense.

Pam was dressed much as she always was, in stretch trousers that just about fitted her far too large figure. She wore an orange turtleneck jumper that made her look more of a man than anything. Her hair, as always, was tied up in a bun, twisted round, in a kind of bouffant which appeared more of a caricature than any semblance of normal hair. She wore slippers on her tiny feet, and her makeup smothered any chance for her skin to shine. It seemed as if she simply tried too hard to be perfect, but no matter how hard she tried, she could never cover what she was inside; the moment she opened her mouth, that always became obvious.

"I have to go, things to do," Pam said, without another word. Liz regretted what she had said, and how she had said it. The woman was annoying, but harmless. She understood how little her life was, and reveling in the problems of others was her way of feeling better about herself. That never justified treating her badly. She determined to do better in the future. Probably.

A strong wind had descended, with it a coldness that had otherwise been absent. The skies were white, as if all color had drained from around her. Even the grass had given up, showing itself pale and unimportant as she crossed the garden, heading for the bus shelter.

Everything seemed to pass in a blur as she dropped change everywhere for the bus, then struggled to find enough to pay her way, then struggled again to find a suitable empty seat even though the bus was empty. The roads and fields outside were like her mind, leaving no impression, as if they were unreal. The journey into town felt like a dream, that she was drifting along, no longer in her own body, totally out of control.

When she finally met the glass door to the bank, Liz unfolded a bunch of papers, hoping one would be enough for what they needed. She no longer had the courage to even think about what they might want, because the nature of what they were there for, for her, was too much to bear.

Sprawled across the glass window was a banner, which proclaimed in huge letters *We're Here To Help, Make Your Dreams Come True.* All she could think of as she read it was to wonder whether it would be dreams or nightmares. At the very least she was thankful the credit card problem wasn't with the same bank, so it couldn't be too much of a problem.

Everyone inside appeared busy, relaxed and smiling, as if they inhabited a different world, one where things made sense and no one felt like she did. Liz couldn't quite put her finger on it, what she felt and wanted to say, but deep down remained a nagging sense that she blamed herself for what was happening.

The choice was a difficult one, stand outside and feel the recriminations of events, or go in and face up to whatever might happen next. The banner offered some kindness, allowing her to dare to hope that it would be all right. She knew at least that she couldn't cope with things getting worse.

As she swung the door open, a warm draft of air gushed across her, making her shiver for a moment. Until then, she hadn't realized how cold she had grown, but it was another sign that things were never quite so bad as the mind often suggested.

"Hi, how can I help you?" a voice came from nowhere. Liz looked around quickly to see a shorter woman standing next to her. Her hair was a yellowing blonde, fixed up high by copious quantities of hairspray. She was dressed smartly, in a matching two-piece dress outfit, and wore shiny black high heels. Liz wondered what she might look like without her shoes and tall hair, then stopped herself, berating herself for being so negative.

"Oh, hello. I need to talk to someone about my mortgage, please."

"Oh, wonderful, we have a good range of mortgages. Let me get you some literature and see what you need."

Liz felt her heart skip a beat, feeling at once annoyed that she hadn't listened properly, but also embarrassed by what she would have to say.

"No, I need to talk to someone," Liz insisted.

"Of course, well I can help you, I have full access to new mortgages for you, right here. My name is Penelope."

Liz looked down, wondering how loud she might have to shout to be heard. "No, I have a mortgage."

"Oh, sorry, a remortgage, that's fine, I can assist you with that and put you in touch with the right person."

"No, I have arrears on my mortgage, and need to talk to someone about it, now," Liz shouted. Immediately all of the staff and customers in the place turned to look. She felt her face burning as eyes glared at her, hidden thoughts whispered, she was a debtor, couldn't pay, a deadbeat.

"Oh, right, OK," Penelope said, her voice betraying her instincts. She retained her half smile, but the look in her eyes, the tone in her voice, if she had screamed an angry accusation it would have felt the same.

Liz stood looking at the woman, feeling the intensity of the glares around her. She was surrounded by the perfect, those who never struggled, where nothing bad ever happened, and each day was filled with sunshine and roses. All they had to do was walk through the door outside and it would suddenly be summer again.

Penelope fluttered her eyelids, daring to show a disdain towards Liz. "Well, if you could take a seat, I will ask one of our managers to come out and speak to you."

Liz looked around, hoping to find a hole in the ground big enough to swallow her, but instead decided to settle for a small red leather chair in the corner. She walked quietly over to it and took her place. However these people behaved, she would rise above it. As much as some tried to pretend, she knew from experience others went through much the same sooner or later, and had no right to judge her problems.

Time passed, people came and went, business continued. There was no obvious rush to ensure she was attended to, but it didn't matter, because it was warm and comfortable where she was, and besides, for a short while she could pretend she was dealing with issues.

"Mrs. Cornwell?" a strong voice said nearby. The short moment of comfort she had begun to enjoy suddenly washed away as she looked at the man beside her. He wasn't so tall, bearing a sizeable waist to suggest life was good for him. He was dressed smartly in a black suit, with a waistcoat. A gold pocket watch on a chain linked one pocket to another, quite why it wasn't clear. His hair was slicked back and shiny, matching his flat black shoes. He emanated confidence and money, the complete opposite of her.

"Yes," Liz said, looking up at him hopefully. For all her smiles, she felt as uncertain as any time in her life.

"Why don't we go into my office, and have a quick chat about your mortgage?"

Liz smiled quickly, standing up to meet him. She had expected a hand, a quick shake and a welcome, but instead the man walked off, heading back into his obviously plush office. She followed, feeling as if she were walking into the lion's den.

"Take a seat," the man ushered, pointing to a small chair, similar to the one she had been sitting on. He rounded his large deep oak desk, settling comfortably on his thick leather chair. All it needed was for him to light up a cigar and the scene would have been complete, and cartoonish.

Liz gathered herself together, feeling her heart beating harshly in her chest. Still she retained a sense of hope, he would be there to help her, and together they would overcome any problems. That was what he was there for. Ten years they had spent paying off the mortgage, and it was only small, which was comforting.

"Now, my name is Charles Barkley, and I am Branch Manager

here."

"Nice to meet you."

"You have serious arrears on your mortgage," Barkley said, without waiting for her to finish being polite.

"Yes, but I have only just..."

"Obviously this is serious," Barkley again interrupted.

"Yes, of course."

"So we have to act."

"Yes, I know, but I only just found out about it."

"Now you know."

"My husband is missing."

"Now that you know, when can you be out of the property?"

Liz felt sick, unable to fully take in his words. It was like a cataclysmic shock to her system, so harsh that all at once she wanted to cry and be sick. Something about her kept her from reacting, allowing her to show a firm demeanor. To the outsider, it seemed as if she were ignorant of the seriousness of the situation, but from the moment the problems had begun to pile up, she was aware of what was going to happen.

"My husband, he's missing," Liz whispered, so low she barely even knew if she had actually spoken.

Barkley sat, hunched over his desk, hands clasped, looking at her without blinking. He showed no emotion, simply a machine-like stare that offered only one thing.

"But," Liz tried again, but the word wouldn't come.

"We are of course not without understanding. We are here to do all we can to help."

Liz breathed out, realizing she had been holding her breath too long, for fear that she might be spotted by a predator.

"Thank you," she said, holding eye contact with him. "I'm obviously in a situation right now. My husband is missing, and the police are involved, and I only now find out he has run up a large credit card bill without telling me, which is unpaid, and now I find out he hasn't paid the mortgage either."

"That really is awful."

"It is, right now I'm just rushing round trying to find out what has happened, and to buy some time."

"Of course."

"I'm going to telephone the police today to see what they know, and I'm hoping I can arrange something soon for money."

"That's great."

"I just need a little more time, that's all."

"Of course. As I've said, we are here to help."

Liz smiled, feeling a warm sense wash over her. It was a night-and-day difference.

"All right, I'll get to it straight away," Liz offered, feeling reassured.

"Fine. So what date do you think you can vacate the property?" Again, it hit her, knocking the wind out of her. It was bad enough that she had lost her husband, that no one seemed able to offer help, but now they wanted her home.

"But you just said you were happy to help."

"Yes, we are, an extra week if needed to leave the house. We will foreclose on you, and sell the property to try and recoup our losses."

"Where are we supposed to go?"

"Well, I am sorry, Mrs. Cornwell, but we have a duty to our shareholders. We can't simply ignore losses like this." The man seemed interminably unmoved by her plight, his appearance totally disinterested.

"And where are we supposed to go?" Liz pleaded, fully aware that he didn't care, the bank didn't care, nobody cared.

"Well, social housing is available. Quickly go and see your local Council, they will take good care of you."

If he had patted her on the head and shoved her out of the door it would have felt appropriate for how he was behaving.

"We've been with this bank for over twenty-five years."

"Thank you for your custom," Barkley said, standing up and moving around the table. He opened his door and stood, arm out. It was clear the meeting was over.

From all that had happened over the weekend, Liz had little strength to cope with what was happening, so quietly walked out, head bowed, as if she had committed some horrible crime. She was as much a victim as anyone, but it was obvious all the bank cared about was the money.

"Penelope, would you provide Mrs. Cornwell a copy of our mortgage guidelines, and the relevant papers? I believe the property will be vacant possession shortly," Barkley said. Before Liz could turn to look at him, his door was closed and he was back in his closeted world that didn't care and didn't want to know anything of human tragedy or struggle.

Penelope didn't look at Liz, instead walking over to a desk. From it she tapped a few keys on her computer and set in motion a series of printing jobs. As the machine worked, she stood, hands clasped looking through Liz, as if she were a mere apparition, something that had wandered in off the street and shouldn't be there.

A click signified the torment was over as Liz watched the paper settle. Penelope picked up the sheets, folded them over, and walked quickly to her, looking her in the eyes without a hint of subtlety or interest.

"Here are you latest payment statements, and there is a formal letter with them. This gives you due notice under the law concerning your obligations to us."

"Can't I pay the amount now, and end this?"

"Absolutely. The debit is excess three months, and is currently in the total of one thousand, five hundred pounds and eighty-four pence. It will have to be cash only, as proceedings have begun today."

Liz looked at her in stark disbelief. She knew their current account held only a few pounds. Instinctively she withdrew her purse from her pocket, opening it up to see what was in it. She leafed through a few pockets in it, looking around, not thinking what she was doing. Penelope stood looking at her, stone-faced, wondering if the woman had perhaps lost her mind.

"Well, I'll leave it with you," Penelope said, before walking away back to her desk. Liz looked up, her eyes tired and heavy, and she looked around to see others, customers, staff, looking at her, some appearing shocked by what they were seeing, others clearly judgmental. She felt as if she were in court, having been on trial and been found guilty of living illegally beyond her means. Reputation didn't matter now, status didn't matter, anything she might have cared about before was gone. Now all she could think about was losing the roof over her head.

The last thought in Liz's head as she walked out through the glass doors was to wonder if she had enough money to buy food for tea, or even bus fare. It was a long walk home if she was as broke and alone as she felt.

9

A SAD TRUTH

"I have no idea. I don't know what's going to happen."

"Well, do you think we could go and get our own place, and then at least you won't have to worry about what is going on there?"

"What? No, I can't do that."

"Why not?"

"Because my mom needs me, needs us."

The telephone went silent as neither spoke. It felt awkward, because although Patricia had known Dan for a long time, she had never heard him be so dismissive about her family before. She liked him, always had fun with him, but she was well aware there was a streak in him that could be as selfish as anyone. It would never be a problem though, as she knew full well that given time and effort she could change him. To her mind, any man could be changed if you were persistent enough, and they had good reason.

"I'm not leaving mom's, and besides, I'm only just about to turn seventeen. I'm too young," Patricia said, deciding not to wait for him to speak. He could be unpredictable, occasionally thinking only of himself, but there were times when he was kind and thoughtful, which gave her the best of hope that he could always be better, and in time would be.

"No problem," Dan said. From the tone of his voice, it seemed he was all right with things, ready to move on. "How are things in college?"

"Ha, same as always. Dad got me the job in his place as a trainee seamstress, and this college placement came with it, and it's boring. The people are OK, but I don't really want to do it."

"Yeah, but think of the wages when you're fully qualified. Think of what we can do. Not long now."

The suggestion of not being long had a dual meaning for her, that the day was nearly over, but her training had a long time to go, too long. For now she wouldn't admit it, but she couldn't imagine staying in such a place, not with a job sewing material for furniture.

"What time are you finished?" Patricia asked.

"I already am."

"Oh wow, lucky you. So when am I seeing you?"

"Now."

"Now, how, where are you?"

"Outside."

Patricia giggled, placing a hand over her mouth quickly. Thankfully nobody noticed. She often would look around at the class and wonder how so many of them could ever seem as engrossed as they were in upholstery classes. She knew it was wrong to judge, but still, if anything, it proved to her she was in the wrong place. She was never going to make it work.

"I'm not out for another half an hour," Patricia explained, furtively holding her phone. It was a struggle to cope with the situation in her life without the mindless nature of her studies.

"Just come out. I doubt they're going to care about you walking out."

It was a good point, but still seemed far too cheeky, even for her, and besides it was only a short while now.

The final, slow, dragging hour crept by as she watched the white, round clock on the wall flicking by, its black hands seemingly unmoving. She thought of him outside and listened for a moment to the words from the teacher, stitches here, fabric there, technique. It was all too much.

Quietly, without a sound, Patricia pushed her pens into her bag, took hold of her notebook and coat, and stood up. She watched intently as the teacher, back to her, wrote on the board on the wall, occasionally speaking to the class as all listened carefully. All but one.

Ever so quietly she stood up, not a sound, turning to walk to the door.

"Is everything all right, Patricia?" the teacher asked. Mrs. Beacon was no fool, she had been teaching long enough to know when there was a problem.

Patricia turned to the teacher, looking startled as all eyes were on her. "Yes, I have to go to the bathroom," she said nimbly.

"I see, was there a need to take your coat and bag there too?"

It was a good point, one that caused Patricia to hesitate. The longer she waited, the more awkward she felt, as if the teacher could indeed see right through her intentions. She wondered whether to simply take her place back at her desk again, or whether to make something up, however ridiculous. Perhaps she could simply faint, drop down dead to the floor. Then of course they might call an ambulance.

"I'm sorry, Patricia, if you need to go to the bathroom, then please go right ahead. I understand fully."

The response was the last thing she had expected, appearing quite understanding. By now the entire class had turned to look at her, as if she were on trial for something.

"My dad is missing, he's not been seen in a few days, and we're struggling a bit," Patricia said. As the words flowed from her, she felt shocked by her own admission, hearing her own thoughts and feelings on the matter, as if for the first time. Until that moment she had been blunt to it, ignoring any emotion over it. She had assumed her father would find his own way back, with excuses, but deep down she wasn't sure how she felt. The way she had spoken, in front of everyone, proved otherwise.

Immediately Mrs. Beacon walked around the corner of her own large desk towards her. "Patricia, I'm so sorry, why didn't you tell me?" she said, holding her hands out as she approached. Patricia felt a sense of confusion, on the one hand still feeling it wasn't so important to her, but on the other hand a slight sense of welling emotion that threatened to take hold.

Mrs. Beacon stood in front of her, placing one hand on Patricia's arm. She looked at her with a pained expression, showing clear sympathy. "Come on, let's pop out into the corridor and we can chat for a moment."

Without further hesitation, Mrs. Beacon opened the door, ushering Patricia out gently. As they finally stood face to face in the empty corridor, Patricia looked at the woman, continuing to struggle with how she felt. It felt right to simply burst into tears, to express the sense of uncertainty and loss she felt, but something held her back, she just couldn't find the answer.

"Why didn't you tell me? You could have stayed off for as long as you needed," Mrs. Beacon insisted. It was clear how she felt. She was a good person, something you found out about people when you were most in need.

"Thanks," Patricia said, looking down at the ground. She felt a little guilty, as if she had used the situation to get out of a lesson, ignoring the fact that it was true. "I wasn't sure what to do. Things are so up in the air, and the police are involved, and mom is a mess. I guess I just wanted to get on with it, try to carry on as normal."

Mrs. Beacon nodded at her. It was the first time Patricia had seen her in a human light, as a normal person, rather than some stranger trying to teach her things she didn't care about. Emotionally it all just made it so much worse.

"Well I do think it would be better for you being at home, being with your mother. You won't miss much here, nothing that you can't catch up on, but it's up to you."

Patricia felt a sense of confusion. She wanted to go, but it felt so much better knowing there was a decent person here, someone that understood and was able to show compassion. Still, there was no point in continuing if her mind wasn't on it.

"Right, yeah, you're right. I'll go home. I'll call when we know more."

"Well, as long as you need. I'll inform the college, and ensure everything is all right from here. I imagine his employer knows about it?"

Patricia nodded again. She no longer had the energy to talk anymore, wanting to go and get outside, to feel something different, if only for a short while.

"All right, you get off, and I hope things work out for the better soon."

"Thank you, Mrs. Beacon," Patricia said, walking away. She felt uplifted that someone could care, anyone, showing a level of concern she hadn't expected. It wasn't lost on her that this woman, someone she barely knew, had shown her more care and concern than the man she was supposed to be involved with.

As she left the building, she spotted Dan, sitting across his small motorbike. It wasn't anything special, thankfully for her not too fast, but the main thing was it got her out of Elton, a place of few buses and an occasional train from a sleepy station. It never occurred to wonder if she liked him more for being her taxi out of there, or for him.

"Good afternoon. I see you managed to get out anyway. Did you tell them you were feeling sick?" Dan asked.

Patricia looked at him sullenly, her expression blank. "No," she said simply, in no mood for fun and games.

"Oh, right, sounds like it didn't go too well. Did she have a go at you?"

"No, she was very nice. Once she knew my dad was missing, she understood and told me to take as much time off as I needed."

Dan lit up, breaking out into a smile. "Fantastic, well played you."

Patricia stopped and looked at him, her eyes burning into him. It was obvious he had badly misread the situation. "I didn't tell her for sympathy, I just told her the truth. It's not a game, and none of us are happy about it," she snapped.

"I'm sorry, I just thought you and your dad didn't get on," Dan replied, wondering whether he had a right to be annoyed or not.

"It's complicated. He's not great, but he's still my dad, and what really matters is mom, and my brother."

"Your brother barely knows he's even gone."

"No," Patricia shouted, feeling at the end of her ability to cope. "He knows, he just doesn't show it."

Dan declined to respond, realizing no matter what he said, it was going to be wrong.

"Things are a mess for all of us, and we don't need to joke about it. I think it's too late for that."

Silence descended upon them. Dan lifted his helmet up, toying with the face straps, waiting to put it on, but wondering what her next move might be. It was obvious who was in control.

Patricia picked up her helmet from the side of the bike, almost copying his stance, toying with the straps without actually putting it on. It was like a dance of two birds, each prancing around the other, trying not to interrupt the delicate flow between them, seeking to ensure the fragile detente between them remained so.

Dan, being typically impatient, could only wait so long before he felt the natural male instinct to take control, to fix things, in his eyes.

"Do you want me to take you home? I'll shoot off then if you like?"

Patricia looked at him. Her first thoughts were that he was being awkward, making his usual silly point which solved nothing, but proved he was right. The moment she saw the look on his face, she could see he meant no such thing, and in fact had no answers to give. In that respect, it was obvious they were both right, and both wrong.

"Yeah, if you like," Patricia said quietly. It wasn't what she wanted, but she couldn't think of anything better. Dan returned her look, crestfallen, so sad in a way in which she had never seen from him before. He was never the emotional type, but to see him in such a way hurt. He would never go so far as to actually shed a tear over her, if he ever could over anything, but she knew he cared about her, in his own unique but limited way. She would convince herself that it was something she loved about him, but in reality she simply tolerated it in him.

Nothing else was said, as Patricia gave in to her own emotions, walking over to him and placing a caring arm around his waist. It was unexpected but welcome. There were emotions to be shared, things that needed to be said, but never would be. In that tiny instant, they shared all they needed to, and gained a greater acceptance for each other's moment in life.

"You can take me home, but first of all, how about we stop in for a takeaway meal to take home with us?" Patricia asked. The look on his eyes said it all as he sprang into action, placing the helmet quickly on his head.

Together they climbed on the motorcycle. As the engine roared, for the moment their spirits lifted with it, heading off to a darkening situation neither of them could ever expect.

10

THE SCHOOL BULLY

"So, are you coming or not?"

"I can't."

"Why not? You said the other day you could come, and we could play this new game I've got."

"Yeah but—"

"Yeah but what?"

"But—"

"But what?"

It was as awkward as anything could be. There were choices, and there were facts of life, and in the life of a young boy, about to become a teenager, realizing that the two rarely coincided made for a tough life.

"Well, I want to go, but I can't get home again," John said, picking at a hole in his trousers. As he had been out in the grounds for break time, he had fallen, clipping his gray school trousers, tearing a clear hole in the knee area. Obviously his mother would be angry, but there was nothing he could do about it, so like him, she would just have to accept it.

"Yeah you can, your dad can pick you up." The words sounded as if they were coming from someone who was a mirror image of himself. The boy opposite looked entirely different, with huge tufts of reddish hair and equally bright freckles covering his rounded cheeks. He was shorter than John, which in school was rarely a desirable quality. His black satchel dragged on the floor as they walked and talked. He looked at John with lost eyes, as if all the fun in the world had been torn from him in that moment.

John stopped walking, turning to look at him, as if somehow solemnly. "Dad's not here at the moment," he said, without a hint of emotion, as if he has simply told him the times of the next bus.

"Oh, right," the boy said, sounding as equally uninspired by anything except the impact it would have on his premade plans.

John liked his friend, he had been fun, but not too close. They had similar outlooks, even sharing the same interests in comic books and video games, not to mention films. Such was their shared passion for comics that John had given him the nickname of Digby, after a character from comics long gone. His real name of Jonathon Myres always brought with it smirks and comments from others, as when spoken it made him sound posh, not something particularly popular in a British Comprehensive school.

It never occurred to his friend to ask why his dad couldn't pick him up, his thoughts were far too focused on his own needs.

"Well, you could cycle back home again," Digby said, pleased with his own imagination. He could always be relied on to come up with solutions.

"Right," John said. Digby smiled briefly.

"But what am I gonna cycle home on?" John asked. He was rarely one given to great ideas or quick to notice problems, but even he could immediately make out the issue at stake here.

Digby looked at him as if he had lost his mind. "Well, what else could you cycle home on? A bicycle!" he exclaimed proudly.

John slapped his hand to his forehead, more a gesture than anything else. He thought about explaining it, but as he was about to, the bell rang for classes. Like a pair of Pavlov's dogs, they both quickly turned and headed off. The noise was all consuming, as each student quickly filed into the packed room, taking a place at a small wooden desk, sat on a wooden seat, pens and books out, bags dropped loudly to the floor.

As the tumult continued, a cacophony of noise moved around, like a chaotic symphony playing out a youthful energy desperate to express themselves.

A tall, thin man strode into the class, not bothering to look at anyone. He wore a faded brown two-piece suit which matched his demeanor, along with thin but scruffy black shoes. He held on to a briefcase, which as he approached his desk he slammed down hard. The racket stopped as all eyes focused on the teacher. It was Mister Bently, known for being strict, if a little useless as a teacher. He stopped and stared at the class, as if his gaze was enough to elucidate and educate them, without the need for mere words.

As each took their place on their seat, all voices quietened, and noise abated. John took his place in the middle, as always of any class. Not too close to the front that he might accidentally appear too interested to volunteer answers, but then not at the back either, for fear that he would be focused upon, asked annoying questions and accused, rightly or not of being a troublemaker.

Along the left side of the class all the way along sat a row of girls, as if their chairs had a female genetic stamp on them, and any boy sitting in such a place would render themselves open to ridicule. Along the entire right side of the class sat those who saw themselves as too good for the rest, too clever, and simply those who might cause mischief or bullying. It was as if they inhabited a zone where teachers dared not stray, where protected pupils of teachers' children might sit, or those who would gladly stand up to a teacher for all their worth, so proving not worth the effort to control.

Which left Digby, struggling to find a desk, and when he did, struggled to find a chair, which eventually he did, beside his good friend, John.

Silence befell the class. Not even a sound of breathing, as each did so in fear of being the cause of Mister Bently's need to prove he was in control, not they, and that he was right, always. In truth, he was a simple bully, someone who gladly did his job because it was easier to stand up to young, impressionable people than it was to stand up for himself in the outside world. Every other teacher in the school thought such of him, but their meek response to such behavior was to ignore, rather than confront, and so on it went, the bully and the children, and the poor learning they suffered as a result.

"Right, now you rabble have calmed down, stopped acting like a pack of wild animals, perhaps we can get on with trying to eradicate your ignorance, and instead instill a worthwhile sense of purpose."

Nobody argued, nobody ever dared, because it simply became his excuse to be even more abusive. The only lesson he taught seemed to be the disillusionment in the profession, from a young person's perspective, than a sense of enjoyment of what mattered in his lesson, which was history.

"Right, open up your textbooks. at chapter five. We will discuss the involvement of Roman occupation on the sheep population in the Outer Hebrides."

A collective groan was felt by all in the class, rather than heard, as each knew they were about to enter a pit, a morass of dread, where imagination and thought about the wonders of the past would quickly sink into the oblivion of boredom.

John looked up at the teacher as he shuffled his satchel wearily around the desk and sat heavily back on his chair. It was clear nobody wanted to be in there. Until that moment he had felt neutral about so much that was going on, but for the first time in his life he felt an innate desire to do something different. It no longer seemed to matter to him that he should fit in, only what he thought was right.

"Sir," John said, leaning back in his chair. All eyes were suddenly on him. He was the last person anyone expected to speak up in any class, let alone this one, with such an unpredictable and volatile teacher.

Bently looked up, searching around with his eyes to see who might dare to interrupt his ambivalence towards his work. He couldn't quite comprehend that it might actually be a student who he could never recall ever speaking to before.

Finally he focused on the beaming spectacle that was John, sitting there looking proud, as if he had an almighty need to open to the world all of his claims.

"Yes, Mister Cornwell. What is it?" Bently asked tersely.

John didn't bat an eyelid to the response; he was used to such things and had expected no less this time.

"Are you sure there were any Romans at any time in history, in the Outer Hebrides?" John asked. To his mind it was a fair question, because regardless of how little he knew of anything of history, his mind refused to consider the possibility that such a thing could be true.

Bently stood up, straightening his back, as if he were up for a fight. His eyes glimmered as his face contorted, like a bull raging to charge. "Yes, of course, otherwise I wouldn't be here ready to teach that, would I?

John didn't move, declining to give way to what he saw as an utter absurdity. "Yeah but, I mean, can't we study something a bit more interesting? Like how they gave us roads, and murdered Caesar?" At the last a girl giggled, too loudly, unable to stop herself from the sudden surprise, not only that John dared to argue, but that he should pick such unlikely subjects for his opposition to sheep.

"Look, just who is teaching this class?" Bently stormed, shouting so much that spittle flew from his mouth. A collective gasp was barely audible as the class held their breath, as if the raging teacher might climb quickly over desks and charge at the boy.

John knew very well the teacher wouldn't put a hand on him, none of them ever did, because it would be the end for them in that and every other school. Given such a truth, he had nothing to lose by being honest to himself. It seemed to him that if his own father could do as such, living his life according to his own whims and needs, then why shouldn't he?

"It just seems a huge waste of our time, learning about sheep in the back of beyond, when there's so much other history we could learn, that matters, that we care about, that can affect our lives and shape who we are," John continued, still sitting back, his hands on his desk, not moving an inch.

His friend Jonathon sat staring at him, almost leaning away, wondering how to react. He was as wide-eyed as the others, shocked that this person he had known so long, known that he would never care to say a word out of place, let alone argue with a teacher, might actually be sitting beside him, doing just that.

"Who are you?" Jonathon tried to say, but the words refused to come out.

It was like a final salvo in a war of attrition, where one side had just used a weapon the other could not refuse to acknowledge. Regardless of anything else, it felt like a personal insult to Bently, that someone such as a young boy should dare to question what he chose to do. In a surge of rage, Bently leapt around his desk, surprising John. He had expected him to shout, but to react in such a manner. Before he could adjust his position, Bently was standing beside him, leaning over, shouting and raging at him.

"Stand up, boy, stand up," Bently screamed as John looked at him in shock. He had expected him to be angry, because he always seemed to be in a natural state of either anger or disinterest, but never as he was now.

John tried to stand, but with the man standing over him, it was difficult to do so without getting too close. Bently wasn't moving, just leering at him like a dog about to attack a bone.

"I said stand up," Bently screamed even louder, if such were possible, only now moving away a little, as if for all his anger he knew full well he was in the way.

As he moved away, John stood, pulling his chair out a little behind himself to create distance to move. He couldn't imagine the teacher actually becoming physical with him, but given how his life had been lately, nothing would surprise him. For all his refusal to say much, he was becoming accustomed to the fact that he felt much more than he showed.

Nobody in the class said a word. At first it seemed like something of a joke, where whispers shared and giggles were heard, but now it was all too real, the two were squaring up, anything could happen. No one wanted to get involved. Even his friend remained silent, not daring to look at either of them.

John finally stood up, hands by his side, looking at the teacher, struggling not to shake. Deep down he knew he was right in a way, that he had the right to say something about a subject that had no value, and everyone agreed with. He also knew the teacher was wrong, and had no right to respond in such a manner.

"What do you think you're up to?" Bently shouted again, his expression one of anger, rather than an interest in what the answer might be. His face had become visibly red, his demeanor clearly suggesting he was considering doing more than just shout.

"Nothing," John said, trying his best not to provoke him further.

Instead of a release, it showed the boy couldn't stand up to show the courage of his convictions, that he wasn't prepared to fight his ground, figuratively or otherwise. To the bully, this was as much an invitation to carry on as anything else.

John had expected more shouting, but he was wrong, as Bently moved once again to him, standing right beside him. He leaned over the boy's desk quickly, slamming his open hand on it. It gave out a huge cracking noise, making the entire class jump. John jumped with it, feeling more nervous than ever, but still he knew he had a right to ask, and had done nothing wrong. All of his life both of his parents had taught him to stand up for what was wrong, to not be afraid to have his say, because he had as much right to be heard as anyone. Right on that moment, he wondered if such were true, then why wasn't anyone listening to him.

"What are you up to, boy?" Bently screamed. The situation was close to getting out of hand. All John could think was to sit down and withdraw into his shell, something he felt the entire class would welcome. Sadly for him, it would not be an option.

As John looked towards his seat, Bently glowered at him like a nuclear furnace about to go into meltdown. His eyes were bulging, his skin bright red as if he might blow his top any moment. As John hesitantly placed a hand gently on the back of his chair, he began to lower, as if to half suggest he was taking his seat and half show the teacher his words of dissent were quickly over.

It wasn't enough, it would never be enough. Bently grabbed hold of his shoulder, taking a firm grip, before dragging him away from his desk. At first John simply wondered if it were a dream, or a prank, that something like it could never happen, but as the teacher struggled to lead him away, it became all too real. Without any hesitation, Bently reaffirmed his grip, before lifting with all his strength. John was no longer quite so small, but his level of trust in teachers had always remained strong. He let it happen, unable to cope with the thought that it truly was. Bently lifted the boy as much as he could, before swinging him, throwing him to the front of the class. His rage consumed him, as daggered thought constantly reminded him he was in the right, go ahead and do it, do it, do it.

John lost balance, feeling himself tumble over as he crashed onto the floor, into the leg of Bently's desk. As he hit it with a thud, Bently stopped a moment, like a barking dog taking a breath to think its next step. The class was no longer silent, as others around him gasped in shock. Beyond it lay only the muffled sounds of a boy crying.

Anger subsided, as realization that he had gone too far dawned on him. It wasn't the first time, and in the past no one had spoken of it. Young people it seemed were a breed apart, far more inclined to accept the wrongdoing of someone in such a position of trust, that when something like it happened, it was quickly forgotten, accepted as if it were the way it should be.

John was different, he had been raised in a different way. As he turned over, struggling to stand up, he turned to look at Bently. As the teacher noticed him, making eye contact, it was obvious the boy was crying. It was unusual for him, someone little inclined to show emotion, but this was too much, it hit home, physically as well as mentally that he had been wronged. Worse, he felt betrayed, that his deep sense of belief in what was right and wrong had been affected.

"Come on, get back to your seat," Bently said, his tone softer, an arm out as if to suggest he was there to help. The absurdity of it almost made John laugh, more out of nerves than anything else. How one moment he could be in a maniacal rage and the next helpful and kind, it said something of the man's character, and his suitability to be a teacher.

Ignoring the outstretched hand, John stood up, still looking at the teacher. Come what may, it wouldn't happen again. As he stood, he noticed his left hand bleeding slightly, more from scratches than anything else, but it was painful.

"Go back to your seat, boy," Bently said, firmly but quietly. He was all too aware that if he did not assert himself, and ensure control right now, he may never get it back again. He was aware too of the need to ensure the pupils didn't gather together and stand up to him, nor discuss it at all if possible, such was the need for him to be firm.

John turned, looking away, before moving for the door.

"I said take your seat," Bently said, sounding more agitated. It was obvious he might well become violently angry again, but it was a risk John was willing to take. Whatever the teacher decided to do, nothing was going to change the outcome.

Murmurs of discontent grew around the class, sufficient that Bently turned to look at them. None were brave enough to challenge him, but it was fast becoming a standoff, a battle of wills over who was in control, of the situation as well as their minds.

The door to the class thudded as John walked out, as once again all eyes rested on him. Bently turned quickly, walking fast after him. He swung the door open, looking out into the corridor, in time to see John walking away, towards the outside door.

"Get back here," Bently shouted, as loud as he dared without potentially alerting other teachers of the problem. John ignored him, taking a hold of the main door, swinging it open before turning to look at the man one last time.

"If you don't return to class, you are expelled," Bently shouted, wondering if he should go after him, to drag him back if need be. What little common sense he had restrained him just enough that he chose not to, instead simply walking back into class to deal with the students he could control.

John stopped the moment he was outside, felt his emotions overwhelm him, whether because of the situation over his missing father, or because of the failure of a teacher to do the right thing, he wasn't certain, but it was all he could do not to burst into tears. It wasn't the done thing, not in school, never show emotions if you were a boy, because you would get ribbed for it endlessly.

A few seconds, a deep breath, and once again he was his old self. He walked again, at first towards the head teacher's office, but then it was obvious, he knew full well it would be brushed off, that they would club together and ignore his pleas. No, there was only one thing to do. He walked ahead, ignoring the cold air, the threat of rain, the white deadness of the skies, heading out of the school gate.

As he walked off down the street, his mind wandered, at first to images of his missing dad, then to the incident in the class. He stopped, looked left, towards town, then right, back to home. Home, however, was over ten miles away, a long old walk down a very long road, then another even longer walk along a road past the stinky oil refinery. No matter, it beat being in school, and would give him time to come up with a plan of what to say to his mom. One way or another, someone was going to get into trouble.

11

DON'T MESS WITH MOM

It was as if fate had intervened, that the moment was set to occur without any intervention from others. As Liz stumbled along, trying to ignore the pain in her legs and feet, the sight on the opposite side of the road to her seemed so improbable, it was almost surreal.

As she had left the bank, she had walked into a supermarket, looked at foods, decided what to get for tea, and then gone to the till. After placing several items on the conveyor, she had opened her bag, withdrawn her purse, opened it, and noticed only pennies inside. No notes, only coins and her usual cards. It was the first time she had thought of money in hand, or felt the need for it, and had expected a sum of money, notes, twenties and tens, only to find them missing. She had cards, but they were useless; obviously the bank had stopped it all. So there she was, standing in a shop line, items ready to buy, and no money.

She had thought to apologize, to ask them to replace the items, that she couldn't afford them. It wouldn't have been the first time it had happened, such as when Jack had been out and bought himself something nice with the week's shopping, but this time was different, now they were in trouble. As the conveyor belt slid along, so went Liz's imagination, as she wondered if that belt took with it her pride. As low as she felt, she was a woman, born and bred in Yorkshire, a place where there was no room for being soft. Deep down she always had it in her to be much stronger than she showed, but until then had never felt the moment right for it. Life, it seemed, no longer gave her a choice; she could either give up and wither, or fight for some reason to be happy.

At first she thought to be bold, to call out loud, *take these back, I don't need them*, but for now it was just baby steps, one thing at a time. She had looked up, trying to remain aloof, above it all, before tripping on the pile of baskets as she walked away. She regained her balance before walking quickly out, ignoring the calls for the items she had left.

Her mind had quickly become a maelstrom of concerns and worries: where was Jack? Where would they live? What happened to the few bank notes in her purse? It was all too much, making her mind dizzy, but she had one answer, that she wouldn't be getting the bus back home again, not with the few pennies she had left. So she began to walk, from Ellesmere Port to Elton, over twelve miles, the long trek.

As she trod along, occasionally walking on grass where no path existed, in a way to her it seemed like a metaphor for her life, where sometimes it got bumpy along the way, and sometimes it wasn't always pleasant, but no matter what, you had to keep believing, and keep going, right to the end, because for her it always worked out for the best. So far in life, it hadn't been perfect, but together they had all worked it out. The fact that there wasn't an *us* anymore affected everything that she believed in, making every step a walk to an uncertain future. Her mind ached as much as her feet.

All sense of struggle went out of her mind the moment she looked across the road, at first looking away, refusing to believe her own eyes. She couldn't ignore it, so again looked, right across the road, to see a young man, stumbling along, wildly kicking here and there, sometimes at a piece of debris, sometimes at nothing. He had his hands in his pocket, and walked airily along as if without a care in the world.

For fear that it might not be who she thought it was, Liz looked away again and carried on walking, but she was certain it was who she thought. There was only one thing for it, to cross over and see for herself. She stopped, looked both ways until no more cars passed, then hobbled across as best as her feet would allow.

The person ahead was mumbling something, half song, half muttering. Whoever it was looked well away, enjoying themselves. Far more than she was. As she hurried to get closer, it was obvious the person was wearing a uniform, one she recognized.

"Hold on," Liz called, looking like a crazy woman in an egg and spoon race. Whoever it was in front ignored her.

"Stop a moment," she called again, much louder. This time it worked, as the person turned briefly without looking, then stopped.

Liz caught up as the person turned. "Mom," John called. He couldn't quite believe his eyes, he had only been out of school walking ten minutes, just ten short minutes, had barely walked a mile, and there she was, his mom. He wondered if she were psychic or something, somehow watching over him, the moment he tried to get out of school and there she was, magically swooping down from on high to ensure he got back to studying again.

The two looked at each other, both completely confused.

"What are you doing here, Mom?" John asked.

Liz frowned. "Er, excuse me, but what are *you* doing here?" she insisted.

"Walking," John said. It was typical of him, never really grasping her questions, or much of what was said to him.

"Funny. Why aren't you in school?"

John rubbed his hand instinctively, not having thought of it until then. As he did, Liz noticed the abrasion.

"Have you been fighting?" she asked, sounding stern but feeling only concern.

"No, Mom," John replied sullenly. His head dropped, as his mood reflected his feelings.

Liz naturally sensed his unease. She walked closer, placing an arm around his shoulders high up and hugged him. As awkward as it felt for him, in public, it was welcome. He welcomed that she could comfort him, and would do so regardless of what was going on, that she was always there for him, and always would be. She was a good mother, of that he had no doubts, and knew how lucky he was for her.

"So, where are you headed?" she asked, deliberately refraining from being confrontational.

"I was going home."

"Why, has school finished?"

"No."

"Oh, so that's why no school bus?"

"Well…" John said, his words trailing off.

"It's OK, you can tell me, I won't get annoyed," Liz said, turning to look directly at him.

Without looking at her, he felt the need to be honest. No matter what he said, there was going to be trouble, and if he didn't say anything then he would be in trouble. He certainly wouldn't take the blame for the actions of someone else.

"The teacher, he was pretty angry about things, for history class, and he just went a bit far. So I left." It was as much as he could manage, disjointed, stumbling with his words, but there were enough indicators in there for her to get the idea.

"History, did you say? Isn't that Mister Bently?"

John looked at her, eye to eye. "Yeah."

Liz's eyes lit up as her expression grew pointed with anger. "Yeah, I've heard about him, and what he's like, from others."

"Oh," was all John said, wondering if they would be going home after all.

"Come on," Liz said, turning away from him and walking off. She didn't give him time to consider what was going to happen next, simply trudging off in search of something. He still had no idea what was going on.

"Come on," Liz repeated, barely looking around, but she knew very well he was standing there looking daft, because it was what he always did. He lifted his legs, broke out into a weary run, and caught up to her.

"Where are we going?" he asked.

"You'll see."

"Are we going to town, get something to eat?"

"Nope."

"Oh, right, where to, then?"

"Back to school."

"Oh no, I don't wanna go back there again, not with him."

"No, we're going to be see the headmaster."

"Oh," John said again, occasionally breaking out into a trot, struggling to keep up. Liz was on a mission, clearly determined to do something.

As they approached, a woman stood at the gates, as if they had a signed invitation and were being welcomed. John immediately recognized her, Deputy Head of School, Mrs. Tressel. She looked as stern as his mother did, but she was dressed all in black, as if ready for a business meeting.

"Mrs. Cornwell, how nice to see you," Mrs. Tressel offered. Her voice sounded pleasant, where her face looked like thunder. She was such a contrast in appearance, but everyone knew how strict she could be.

"Not today," Liz said, feeling her anger, but still wanting to remain reasonably calm—for now.

"Oh, I'm sorry to hear that, is everything all right? Is John OK?"

"No, I need to see the headmaster, right now."

"Oh, well, I think he might be in a meeting. Is there anything I can do?"

"Yes, you can get me the headmaster, *now*," Liz insisted, sounding firmer than even she was used to. John looked at her, shocked. He had never quite seen his mother react in such a way.

Mrs. Tressell's face dropped like a stone, her mouth open in surprise. Parents were rarely so abrupt, and certainly never someone as quiet as his mother.

"Well, I will see if he is around," Mrs. Tressel said quietly, turning slowly.

"Well, if he isn't, then we will go to the police, and ask them to help," Liz said, feeling emboldened by the lack of serious response from the deputy head.

The three walked silently, Mrs. Tressel out in front, Liz behind her as John straggled along behind. They looked like a trio of differing individuals, off in search of the truth. They walked through the old glass doors into the school reception, then through a corridor. Further down was the headmaster's door, which offered light out into the hallway, suggesting it was open.

As they approached, it was obvious there were people in the room, shadows reflecting with movement as they talked and moved around.

Mrs. Tressel approached the doorway before stopping, looking in.

"Headmaster, I have a parent here who needs to have a word with you, if you're not too busy?" she said pleasantly. As she finished her sentence, she turned to look at the approaching mother and son, her face no longer so pleasant as she looked at them both. Her disdain slight, but obvious enough.

"Right, I'm just in a discussion for a moment," the headmaster suggested, responding in an equally pleasant manner.

As Liz walked around the woman, she looked into to see two men standing beside each other. One was the headmaster, Mister Bellows, a portly man with rosy red cheeks. He was fairly short, wearing a light brown waistcoat, and a tweed jacket to accompany it. His dark brown trousers completed the look, that he might better suit being out in a field than heading up a school. He had thick, bushy sideburns and a glint in his eye, well used to the challenges of school life, not to mention handling parents. He was all smiles as he made eye contact with Liz, and she returned the look, smiling briefly, until she caught sight of the person beside her.

As she walked into the room, past Mrs. Tressel, John followed, ensuring he kept this head down, but looking up enough that he could see the other man was Mister Bently.

"Oh, perfect timing," Bently said loudly, looking directly at John.

Liz waited, looking at him directly, refusing to look away. She would keep her powder dry for the moment.

"Yes, Mister Bently was explaining to me that John was obstructive in class, and eventually walked out, in anger," Bellows explained, trying to sound reasonable but firm.

"Oh, I see," Liz said, deliberately restrained in her manner.

"So what was the problem?" Bellows asked, looking at the boy, who had crept ever so slowly behind his mother.

"He's like it all the time, a real nuisance," Bently insisted before John could reply.

Whatever he was normally like, in some respects he was like his mother, completely quiet unless properly provoked. This was just such a moment, where pride as much as anything demanded he do something.

"Er no, that's not right," John said, feeling his mouth dry as all eyes were on him.

"You see, quick to react, and never nice," Bently said, his chest puffed out, bold in his claims, knowing he had the backing of those that mattered. He always did.

"That's not fair at all," John said, suddenly at the mercy of his emotions.

"Well, what was the reason for the problem this morning?" Bellows asked.

"He's just trouble, plain and simple, he needs dealing with," Bently insisted, determined to control the outcome. John looked at him, remaining silent. Bently eyed him firmly, feeling confident in his control, and the outcome.

Liz quietly turned to look at her son, once everything had settled. She had waited her turn, understanding her son well enough that he needed something from her.

"It's OK, John, you know I'm here. You know I'm not going anywhere, so you can say what you need to," she said. In some ways it didn't help, not with his nerves, or how he struggled to cope with the thought that no one would believe him anyway, but still he felt wronged, the need to say something, even if it made no sense.

"All I did was ask you a question, and all I did was to ask why we had to know about the effects of the Romans on sheep. That's all I asked, and you got so angry, started shouting, screaming at us, slamming the ruler down, really going off on one, like you always do," John said, like a dam bursting its banks, flooding the room with emotion. It was too much, as tears rolled down his cheeks.

The room was frozen by the outburst as all eyes turned to Bently.

"Yes, well, you shouldn't be so much of a problem, asking questions incessantly, and winding everyone else up," Bently said, beginning to sound flustered as he struggled for a response.

"Aren't children supposed to ask questions in class?" Liz asked, wondering if she might be told off for asking something. She thought of saying so, but decided to keep calm, hoping to find a response to it all.

"No, but—" Bently said.

"Yes," Bellows said decisively, as the deputy head nodded sagely.

As the three discussed the matter, John stood, looking down at the ground. Liz looked at him quickly, noticing his agitation.

"Are you OK?" she asked quietly.

"Yeah," he said, wiping tears from his face. As he did, she noticed the abrasion on the back of his hand.

"How did you do that?" Liz asked. John rubbed his hand, trying not to make it worse.

"When he grabbed hold of me, and threw me across the class, I fell and banged myself, and scraped my hand on the floor," John replied, offering no malice, nothing in his words other than an explanation, but it was like a flame to a rocket, as the room erupted.

"Er, no, that is not what happened, don't lie," Bently shouted, reminiscent of the class earlier.

"You did," John insisted, turning to look at the headmaster. "Go ask the others in the class, any of them, they'll all tell you what happened," he continued, tears now flowing again.

"You hit my son?" Liz shouted, struggling to hold herself back. She never had it in her to be physical with anyone, but her rage brought her to the brink.

"No, I didn't touch him," Bently snarled, finally losing his short-lived temper.

"I think we had best investigate this," Bellows said, at which the room went quiet.

"I think we had best call the police," Liz offered, now loud and clear, firm in her response.

Bently shrank away, suddenly aware that his world had collapsed in on him. Everyone looked at him now, waiting for yet more flashes of anger. None came.

"I-I might have made a mistake," he said quietly, no longer so boldly in control.

"I think it might be best if you consider yourself suspended from duties, Mister Bently," Mrs. Tressel finally interjected. Mister Bellows nodded. Bently looked down at the ground, suggesting a mixture of anger and fear. He knew when he was well beaten, slowly walking away.

As he walked to the doorway, he had little choice but to walk immediately past the boy and his mother, the source of his downfall, in his own eyes. He looked up at them, and finally back at Liz, offering one final show of dissent, to show his true feelings on the matter. It was fleeting, but she noticed.

Without hesitation, looking directly into his eyes, she abruptly lifted her arm, slapping him firmly across the face. The sound gave a harsh rapping noise as his face shook sideways. He stopped, looking at her, mouth wide open, in complete shock. John looked, barely able to take in what had happened, but he couldn't help but feel brighter for her strength.

"That's for hurting my boy. Nobody hurts my boy," she said, before taking John's arm and barging past. "Come on, Son, let's go home," she offered without looking back. Whatever happened, he had a feeling he would never see the man again, which was the best thing he had heard in a long time.

As the two walked out of school, John caught up to his mother. "So, now what? Should I go back to the rest of my lessons?" he asked.

As she walked, Liz turned and looked at him, wanting to smile, but unable to, as she was shaking too much with nerves. "No, John, you can have the rest of the day off."

"Oh, great," he said, before realizing what came next. "Are we getting the bus home, though?" he asked, no longer looking quite so happy.

"No, love, we're walking," Liz said, before walking away quicker.

"Oh, Mom," John said, but he knew better than to argue with her. He knew she wouldn't have any messing from anyone. Not anymore.

12

LIFE MOVES ON

It was never ideal travelling in England on a motorbike, usually because of unpredictable weather, but more so when the seasons changed and cold came in. Patricia held tightly to Dan's leather jacket, trying to lean into him to cut some of the draft. He seemed to love it, not caring how cold or wet it was. For her, it was just a good excuse to get away from the cosseted nature of a place like Elton, cut off from surrounding towns and cities, as if it had been forgotten by the outside world. As much as she clung to the man, in some ways how she was mirrored how she felt about him, because he was there, and because he was useful, but not because they were particularly close.

As they sped along the long, boring road past the refinery, she looked out, seeing trees go past, feeling each bump. The smell from the place was like a kind of gas blanket that divided the two worlds, the outside to the in. With each mile she would feel less happy, more apprehensive, as if her happiness were draining away, refined away, until when they turned into the street where they lived, everything seemed bland, dark, and empty. It never occurred to her to wonder if she might ever be happy anywhere.

As they drove on, down School Lane, they passed two stragglers, looking for all the world as if they might collapse any moment. At first she thought it looked like her mom and John, but of course it couldn't be, John was at school, and her mother wouldn't be walking that way if she had been out. She forgave herself for thinking so foolishly, and put it out of her mind.

Dan brought the motorbike swinging round, up onto the empty driveway. Even if Jack had a car, he wasn't there, now it was different, empty, perhaps forever.

As he turned off the engine, silence fell between them, as if it suggested talk must begin, that something must be said. He felt like saying sorry, but wouldn't, because he never did.

Patricia stepped off the bike, removing her helmet. It felt like she was awakening from a slumber, where for a moment she could cut herself off from the outside world, only now she could feel the biting chill in the air around her neck and see the whiteness of the sky which always threatened snow that never came. It was a kind of life where theirs had stopped, but movement continued in a slow, sad charade, a pretense at what was supposed to be, but in some ways she knew never would be again.

Opening the door felt better, as she turned the key, expecting to see the usual face when finishing work and stepping up into the living room, there would be mom, sitting watching television, and likely John, back from school, still in his uniform, looking a mess but glued to the television. He may well be annoying, but he was always happy, a positive even when there was doubt. Then later on dad would get back, and they would all have tea together, and whatever else was going on in the world, this was their home, and nothing could change that.

There was no warmth, only the same chill air inside. It was dark, no lights, no movement, no sounds. She couldn't remember the last time she had entered into the house when empty, because when she usually did she never had to care about anything being wrong, only what she wanted or needed.

As she stepped in, she noticed letters on the floor, and a folded note. Opening letters were part of her mother's routine, nobody else dared do it. There was no real reason why not, just that bills she would pay, and anything else she would deal with, and nobody ever dared argue with that. So to see such letters, ignored and unopened, was a sign of the change that was occurring. It disturbed her, like another chip in the wall of her life, that safety net that was tearing open and bit by bit things were dropping through.

"What is it? Anything good?" Dan asked as he stood behind her, waiting to go in.

It annoyed her, but she didn't know why. Perhaps because of how he had been before, so disinterested in their problems. Perhaps she was still angry with him.

Ignoring his fatuous behavior, she bent over, picking up the letters and note. As she stood up, she unfolded it, looking at its small but neat writing.

'*Hello, Detective Sergeant Chavards here, could you call me on...*' the note said, reeling off a telephone number.

Patricia's heart pounded, that they had called, that there might be news. Try as she might, she couldn't allow herself to be positive about it, it would be bad, they knew something.

"So what is it?" Dan asked again, sidestepping her. Patricia ignored him, barely able to find the strength to deal with the note, let alone letters, or of him being annoying. The last thing she needed was him being immature and unable to comprehend emotions when all of theirs were such a mess.

Little would ever affect his mood, even if Patricia seemed off, as he saw it, for some unknown reason.

"I thought I saw you going past."

Patricia turned quickly to see Liz walking in through the still open doorway as John plodded in, walking heavily, head down, looking as if his world was ending.

"Mom, I didn't see you there," Patricia said, feeling a deep sense of unease in her stomach. Before she could say anything, Liz focused on the note in her hand.

"Are you off sick again, lazy?" Dan asked, looking at John. A collective sigh signified their disdain for his remark, as well as his attitude, as the tension in the room sailed entirely over his head.

Ignoring the comment, John simply dropped down onto the welcoming sofa, ignoring the beads of sweat running down his forehead, as well as Dan.

Liz and Patricia looked at each other, neither wanting to be the first to speak. Instead, Patricia nudged her hand outwards, as if to give away the poisoned chalice, that she may pass the burden on to someone better able to deal with it. She knew full well her mother was struggling, but no way could she cope with supporting everyone and dealing with the police.

"Is it from…" Liz hesitated, trailing off. She never finished her sentence, never wondering if it might be a note from Jack, but as she took hold and opened it, a new problem arose, not from knowing once and for all his intentions, but that the sense and loss might continue, and perhaps grow much worse in the short time to come.

"I guess I had best call them," Liz said, her voice weak, as if any last vestige of life were releasing from her. Any sense of innocence she may have held on to as a person died in that moment. No matter what was said when she called, there would be no more pretense, no going back. It was truly over. If she had been alone, she would have gushed tears, released it all, allowed herself the need to vent all her emotions. For John, and Pat, she would hold on, and do what she always did, thought of others before herself.

Without another word, Liz took the phone from the base and walked to the dining area table. She pulled out a chair, sitting with her back to the others, unsure whether she could hold it together if the news was bad and they were all looking at her.

Patricia took it as a sign, choosing to simply go out of the room, up the stairs and wait for the cries, or the anger, whichever might come. She would know then, and be able to have a moment to compose herself, to try to be the strength that was most needed.

Dan looked around himself, wondering what was going on. He couldn't decide whether to follow Patricia upstairs, or get something to eat. It was a difficult choice, but his stomach made it clear what it would be. She could wait.

"Er, hello, this is Elizabeth Cornwell, I received a note through my front door earlier today, asking for me to call you."

"Oh, hello, Mrs. Cornwell, this is Detective Sergeant Chavards here," the voice came back. It was slight, as if the line was poor, but she could hear traveling noises, as if they were in a car going somewhere.

"Hi," Liz said. She wanted to say more, wanted to ask questions, but her fear of what might be said haunted her. Sitting at the table, one hand pressing the phone to her ear, the other holding the side of her head, leaned over, she felt as old as she ever had. She wondered if she would ever feel right again.

"Hello. Well, all I am calling for is to update you on our progress. We have spoken to a number of people from his place of employment that know him, and we have also posted a missing-persons alert with the usual organizations. There are a number of other lines of enquiry we're looking into, but at this moment, we still have no concrete news on his whereabouts."

Liz felt like collapsing on the table, but just about managed, more from not wanting to appear melodramatic than from her inner strength. She breathed in deeply, struggling to find the words.

"How are you coping? Are you all right?" Chavards asked, now quieter, aware of how every such statement impacted on those he worked with, those left behind.

Tears threatened for form in Liz's eyes again, but even if it were just for John's sake, she wouldn't allow emotions to dictate to her. "I'm fine, we're fine. We will probably have to change things here, but I will let you know where we are. If you hear anything certain about him, then please let me know, otherwise."

"I understand," Chavards said, and he did. Few could stand to hear every detail of their investigation. It was better dealing with a missing adult than a missing child, but it was still difficult, with such strong emotions, and terrible changes people went through.

"Would you like a Support Officer to visit, to have a chat about things?"

"No, that's very kind of you. Just if you hear anything for certain."

"Of course. Thank you, bye."

"Bye," Liz said, before clicking the off button to end the call.

As she looked up, she saw Dan standing beside her. She expected he might place an arm around her shoulder, or perhaps offer some words of encouragement. He was poor at doing such things, but his heart was in the right place.

"Hungry, Liz?" he asked, struggling to speak with a thick cheese sandwich stuffed in his mouth.

Liz laughed. It was a slight relief, but enough to pop the bubble of trauma which had hung over her. She smiled as she looked up, not feeling the least interested in eating, but she knew she liked Dan, for all his failings.

"No thanks, love," Liz barely managed before John suddenly appeared from behind the sofa.

"Yeah, I'm starving," he said, holding on long enough to provide a look which backed up his plea.

"Come and get it yourself, then," Dan insisted, struggling to talk and eat at the same time.

"Aw, come on, you just offered."

"Nope," Dan said, before turning to prepare him a monster sandwich.

Before any more protestations could be made, Patricia interrupted them. "Any news?" she asked understatedly.

"No, just they are still following up, and nothing else to report. I guess we keep on waiting," Liz replied, feeling mixed about it. In some ways better that it wasn't bad, but in others frustrated that she was still left wondering. As much as she wanted answers, she was aware it might be better not to know, or which outcome might prove the most upsetting. For her, only time would tell.

"So, what's next?" John asked, wondering when he would get fed.

"Well, next is that we pack," Liz said, feeling resolute. However difficult things would be, she was always one to face up to the truths of life, and now this was one that couldn't be avoided.

"Pack? Are we going on holiday?" John asked as Dan handed him a plate filled with sandwiches. The moment he saw them, his eyes lit up, his mind no longer caring what the answer was.

Patricia stood close to her mother, the look on her face saying more than she ever needed to.

"I went to the bank, and they said the mortgage hasn't been paid in so long that it's too late now to do anything. Legal proceedings are at the stage where we have to move out, or I guess someone will come and do it for us," Liz explained.

Even Dan had latched on to what she meant. He was rarely one to take things seriously, but he accepted that at times even he couldn't avoid responsibility. "You need a van. I can get one," he offered, wondering if he should even be listening.

"Thanks, Dan," Liz said, smiling at him. It was a small thing, but welcome nonetheless. "We'll need some boxes too, to pack up our things."

It was a sledgehammer to Patricia. Until then she hadn't thought for one moment that something so drastic might happen. "You're saying he stopped paying the mortgage?" she asked.

"We can discuss it another time," Liz said, looking over at John. He was lost in his food, while watching television, but she knew full well how he had a habit of listening in to things. The last thing she wanted was to burden him with such problems.

"If you can get some time off tomorrow, then maybe we can go to town again, and we'll have to go to the Council, and see if we can get a house or something from them, as an emergency," Liz explained. The way it sounded, how she appeared, few would ever appreciate the level of hurt and suffering she was going through, after so long married, so long building a life for herself and her family. It no longer mattered, it couldn't, because worrying wouldn't help, nor would crying, not for now.

Patricia nodded.

"Yeah, I'll get the van, and try and get some boxes," Dan said. He had his moments, good and bad. It was obvious what a mess they would be in without him.

Liz nodded, smiling again, before turning back to Patricia. "One slight problem," she said.

"Another one," Patricia said, wondering if she could take any more.

Liz laughed quickly, before frowning again. "Yeah, I don't have any money. The account is frozen, and I have nothing in my purse."

"Oh, right, I see, that's why you were walking," Patricia said.

"You walked all the way from Ellesmere Port to here, you two?" Dan asked. Liz nodded.

"Don't worry, Mom, I have a bit left over from my wages. It's not much, but enough to get us by for what we need."

It was a small comfort, but something. There were many things Liz felt like saying in the moment, but wouldn't. There was no time for sentiment, only action. Now would be the time to do things, and later on time for thoughts.

"I'll get the suitcases out, and Dan, please look up in the loft and get the flat packed boxes out. Might as well get started, because things will probably move quickly," Liz said, looking a world away from the lost woman that had been moping around for days.

"Wow, Mom, what's gotten into you?" Patricia asked.

"Nothing, though perhaps I've finally rediscovered the Yorkshire woman in me."

Patricia smiled, looking at her mother, feeling a sense that things were indeed about to become complicated, but for all that, they would cope, together.

13

BARE CUPBOARDS

"Well, I've not seen him around in weeks, and they hardly speak, and I think something is up, but you never know, but I bet it's bad."

"Yeah, well, she was always a funny one, I mean they came from down south, and always seemed to be spending money I'm sure they never had, and the kids, well look at them."

"And look at the house, I mean everything in there is half finished, kitchen half done, living room half done, and the place is always such a mess."

"Compared to yours, Pam, yes, such a mess."

It never mattered how cold it was outside, when it came to gossiping it would never hold back Pam and Elsie, two neighbors beside Liz and the next house down. Pam's house was large, four-bedroom, much like theirs, but Elsie lived in a bungalow beside Pam. The two seemed to inhabit a little world of their own, where everything was perfect, and anything outside of what they viewed as perfect was simply not good enough.

Pam stood in her light knit pale purple cardigan, half unbuttoned, wearing checkered pants that looked two sizes too small. Her hair was bouffanted up, in a tight curl at the front. It looked so perfect, anyone might mistake it for a wig, but it was all her own, tightly arranged and full of lacquer, so that nothing might spoil her look. She wore a full smear of makeup, all finely detailed but plenty of it. If she were on display in a shop window, passersby might look in and wonder how it was ever achieved without hours of effort. Only Pam knew how she did it, but getting up at five o' clock in the morning certainly helped.

Elsie was much older, white hair but always well permed and clean. She too wore a cardigan, and for someone so late in age she did well to stand the cold air around them, but the hot gossip kept her warm, and interested. She too wore a pair of brightly colored slacks, only spoiled in their impression by her fluffy fronted slippers. She may well have standards to keep, but cold feet would never do.

The two stood on each side of their properties, arms folded, looking around as they conducted a thorough verbal investigation of everything that went on in the close. Each neighbor had their lives dissected, each were judged and opinionated. None would be spared.

"Well, I tell you, Jack, I think he was always up to no good. I mean, how could they afford a house like that on his salary? And why would he be—"

"Morning, ladies."

The voice was calm but clear, firm without being aggressive. Both women looked up quickly, confused as to whom it might be. Pam looked behind herself, half expecting the postwoman to be delivering mail, unsure of who it was because the voice sounded different to any she was used to.

"Morning , everything OK?" Elsie asked, smiling innocently.

"Yes, thank you," Liz replied, standing at the doorstep in her dressing gown, bare feet, hair wild and woolly.

Pam struggled to focus on who it was at first, finding it difficult to match the voice with the woman. She had always had a fine relationship with her neighbor, on the surface, except when she wasn't the center of their discussion.

"Do you have a cold, Liz?" Pam asked, attempting a pleasant smile but instead looking as if she had lost a tooth.

"No, love," Liz replied, at first intending to say more, but quickly deciding it would be a waste of time even trying. She knew what was coming in the days ahead, and so after that, any conversation with them would never matter again.

"Oh," Pam said, unsure of what to say next.

"You sound different today," Elsie suggested, more a question than a statement. Liz refused to bite.

"I'm feeling good today, ladies," Liz suggested, and she was. It seemed the more turmoil she felt, the stronger she reacted.

Both of them looked at her, half smiling, wondering when she would go back indoors so they could get to discussing what they so urgently needed to discuss, mainly her.

"How's Jack?" Elsie asked. Pam almost jumped at the comment, immediately wondering if she should go back indoors to avoid any trouble. Before she could react, Liz simply turned away and closed the door.

Pam looked back around at Elsie, to see a mischievous smile

written across her features. She didn't say anything, but still, to them it was fun.

"See, I told you. I bet he's in prison," Elsie said quickly, in a hushed secretive voice.

"Oh, well, you could be right. I mean, there were police officers in there the other day, and then again I saw them trying to get in yesterday. I wonder if she's involved," Pam replied.

Once again they pulled their cardigans closers, leaned closer to a huddle, and got back to their gossip. It didn't matter if it was true, only if it was interesting. To them, anyone else suffering was a good thing, because it made their lives seem so much better in comparison.

"Anyway, have you heard about Mike, over the road?" Elsie asked, at which Pam's eyes lit up, and so it continued.

The moment Liz retreated and closed her front door, it no longer mattered. She had shut off the outside world, and all that mattered was her family. Except the reality was never like that, she was as much human as anyone else, and subject to all the same frailties. She stopped a moment, leaning her forehead against the solid brown door, sure the frosted glass would keep her private suffering away from prying eyes. Tears threatened, but it would become a cascade, and one that she knew none of them could afford right then and there. Any sorrow would have to wait for another day. Maybe never.

Liz began to turn around, but as she did, a large presence behind her made her jump, almost to the point of shrieking. She held her hands to her mouth quickly as her eyes struggled to adjust to the sight before her.

"What's for breakfast?" John asked. It was only at that point that she realized just how tall he was growing, and how fast. Little did she know how much of a problem it would be, when he needed to eat more to cope with it.

"John, don't sneak up on me like that," Liz insisted, gathering her dressing gown around her. She could feel herself shaking, such was the fright he had given her.

John looked at her, as if her words were some kind of alien language. Whatever she had said clearly did not compute.

"What's for breakfast, Mom?" John asked again, as if that time of morning his brain could only handle one sentence.

"I don't know yet, love, I'll go have a look."

"I'll have eggs, and bacon, and some toast, and juice," John said, as if his stomach had informed his mind that he was allowed to expand his vocabulary to offer guidance on what it needed.

"Sure, how about grapefruit first, and some sugar on top, and maybe mushrooms and tomatoes and black pudding?" Liz asked, looking at him as she walked to the kitchen. Her expression should have said it all, but for John, that early in the morning, all wasn't enough.

"Yeah, go on then, skip the grapefruit and sugar, but I'll have the rest," John replied, yawning immediately after he had given her an update on his needs. She couldn't quite tell if he was serious or not, because as much as he enjoyed a joke, when it came to food he was always serious.

Liz proceeded to the kitchen as John collapsed onto the sofa. He was still in his baggy pajamas, barefooted, looking as if wanting to eat might be enough of a challenge, let alone thinking about getting dressed. Quickly, she endeavored to find something that he would approve of, ignoring her own needs. She had long forgotten the art of caring for others while doing the same for herself, almost ceasing to exist mentally, as the family came first.

"OK, love, your feast awaits," Liz called as she placed his breakfast on the table.

John's eyes lit up. Nothing quite woke him up like a hot cooked meal. He leapt over the back of the sofa, dropped to the floor, and raced over to the table. As he went to sit, his heart dropped at the sight as a small bowl of cornflakes met his gaze.

"Er, Mom, have you forgotten? I asked for bacon, eggs and—"

"We don't have any," Liz insisted, quietly but firmly.

"Oh, Mooom, but—"

"I said we don't have any," Liz finally snapped, staring straight at him. As soon as she did it she regretted it. She had never raised her voice to her children, but opening the cupboards brought home a certain reality to their lives now that didn't exist before.

John stopped instantly, shocked by her response. He was speechless, unsure of how to react to an angry mother that he no longer knew so well.

"I'm sorry, love," Liz said, quieter again. "I haven't been shopping. I'll get you some soon," she said, knowing in the back of her mind she couldn't do it, but couldn't be so hard on him by telling him the truth. She suspected he knew and full well understood what was going on, but like so much in his life, good and bad, he just brushed it off and got on with it.

"OK," John said, looking down at his bowl. It was half full, but looked dry, as if she had forgotten to put milk in. "Is there any more milk in?" he asked.

Liz opened the fridge door, knowing what to expect, but as if she were forced into a kind of charade she had to go through the motions of trying to see, hoping. The fridge door swung open just enough for her to see, but she wouldn't trouble him over it, seeing how bare it had become. It was amazing to her how quickly things broke down when life wasn't working right, how quickly it all fell apart.

"No, love, I'll have to pop out later and get some milk and things."

John shrugged without saying another word. He lifted his spoon and dipped in, before taking a crunching mouthful. At least they were fresh, he thought.

Liz took a deep breath, leaning on the kitchen counter. She looked at the place, the half-finished units, the archway dividing the kitchen and dining room. It was like so much about Jack, that he had such wild plans and dreams, but as soon as he got stuck into making them a reality, he just gave up. He was a fad-driven man, truthfully. In all of their years of marriage she had such trust in him, it had never occurred to even think badly of what he was like, such were the signs of change between them, now the rosiness was gone, she began to wonder who he really was.

"Hi."

Liz looked over to see Patricia.

"Oh, hi. Been there long?" Liz asked.

"Long enough, Mom," Patricia replied, looking pensive.

Liz smiled gently. "It's all right, lots to get on with today." Patricia nodded.

"I don't want any breakfast, thanks."

Liz instinctively thought to argue over it, to insist that she ought to eat breakfast, but she knew too what little there was. She couldn't help but be thankful for her understanding.

"Am I going to school today, Mom?" John asked, providing a welcome respite from the building tension.

"No, not today. I'll call in later and tell them you're sick. We have too much to do around here for that today."

John smiled broadly. "Yes," he said in a fake deep voice. He was neutral about school on the whole, when others didn't make his life difficult, and he liked his friends, but a day off was always welcome.

"What time did Dan go home?" Liz asked, turning to Patricia.

"Late, he needed to go so he could go into work and see if he can get us a van."

"That's good. I don't know what I would have done without him," Liz said.

"What's the van for?" John asked mockingly.

"Seriously?" Patricia asked, feeling her temper rising. Liz laughed briefly, fully aware of what he was like, and intended. She was more thankful that he could still show a sense of humor during such times. Wherever they ended up, she prayed he would never lose it.

"Come on, then, let's get dressed, and get stuff done. Pat, you and I will have to go to town, and go to the Council and see if they can get us emergency accommodation," Liz said, walking around towards the stairs as she did.

"What about me?" John asked, hoping it might involve him watching television or playing a game.

"You can get cleaned up, get dressed, and start sorting your room."

"Sort it how?"

"Well, for a start, take down all your posters, and collect all your clothes. I'll put a suitcase on your bed, and you pack as much as you can fit into it."

"Why, are we off on holiday?" John asked, looking directly at his sister. The moment he finished his sentence, her eyes lit up as she went to swipe at him. He was always fast, always one step ahead of her, as he fled up the stairs like a gazelle. Patricia turned and chased after him, calling out.

Liz stood for a moment, watching them go, before starting up the stairs behind them. She knew then that they would cope, together.

14

LIZ DISCOVERS HERSELF

When Jack had driven up with his works to find a suitable place to
live, he had gone alone, leaving Liz and the children at home while he
dealt with it all. The moment he was out of the door, all things
changed, with considerations of schools and shops secondary to his
needs for work and what he liked. To Liz, it was typical of the worst
elements of her husband, but like so many, she allowed herself the
right to just deal with it, to get on and go along. It was one of the
many compromises that couples made for the sake of their marriage.
At the time, Liz couldn't help but think of how she was the one
making all the sacrifices, all the compromises, simply to avoid an
argument for what was often something petty. As the years passed
by, Liz found herself more and more the one to maintain her silence,
even if she was the one being wronged, simply to ensure peace. It
was only now that she came to think of such things, and for the
difficult nature of their circumstances that she began to see how
wrong she had been, for far too long.

At the top end of Elton sat a small railway station, nestling
between high embankments, with trees lining one side. The train
traveled to many smaller towns and villages, before getting to
Ellesmere Port, and most importantly for her, Chester, where the
closest Council Offices lay.

As she walked alongside Patricia, down the gray tumbling tarmac
road towards the station, her mind began to wander. Until then she
had so much going on in life, things that always seemed to matter,
but now they reminded her of their insignificance. There would be
the need to do the work clothes for Jack, John's school uniform,
Patricia's clothes, and last, always last, her own things, if she had time
of course. There would be food to prepare, the house to tidy, and
always something else to think of. It was only as she walked then,
knowing she was relying on her daughter to pay her train fare, that it

brought home what a waste it had been. She chastised herself mentally for thinking that raising her children and running a house had been a waste, but she couldn't avoid the sense that so much of it had been for nothing, that all she had done, for Jack above all, didn't matter. Jack, it seemed, didn't really care. She wondered if he ever had.

Rain began to lightly fall, reminding Liz that she hadn't brought a scarf. She expected it to be cold, so wrapped herself well in a long beige Macintosh, as well as some decent boots for walking. She knew she may not look great, but she would be warm.

"I guess my hair is going to be a mess," Liz said, looking ahead.

"You're fine. Everyone is going to be wrapped up in town, so we won't look out of place," Patricia said, aware of how low her mother's spirits were. As always she had dressed however she wanted, in a black leather jacket and a long skirt with boots. It was never going to be an ensemble, but she didn't care.

The railway station was a small place, unmanned, with a large Victorian-style building that had once served as a ticket office and place of residence for the Station Master. The place was clean and well kept, with perfectly painted white lines along the edge of the platform. There were only two lines, one with the return train before the depot, and the other off to Chester. Trains were few and far between, but much cheaper than the bus. Patricia had tried to insist that they pay for the bus, but Liz refused, knowing how difficult it was going to be for money in the days and weeks ahead.

The two stood, side by side, a few feet away from the only other person waiting. It would be a long, interminable wait, full of thoughts and emotions, as if waiting for a sentence that would heap misery on an already fraught situation.

"They reckon it's going to be nice today, sunny," Patricia said, turning to look at her mother. Liz looked back at her as heavy rain ran down her face. They looked at each other a moment, just as the heavens opened and rain poured. It was as if she had spoken at just the right moment, and a higher power had switched on cue the effect she needed. Liz smiled at first, before laughing quietly. Patricia followed suit, giggling at her. It was a miserable day, and would no doubt get worse, but they could still laugh.

The train arrived, an old two-coach electric thing. It often got packed, but the conductor took his money, cheap with it, and they clattered along. With each rattle of the rails Liz felt a tug inside, as if she were drifting away from her life, the one she had planned. Now she felt sick inside, that something truly inevitable was coming, that she would have to accept the kind of change in life which few could ever want at her age. She was approaching forty-eight years of age, too late in her mind to start over again.

Chester train station appeared huge. She had seen bigger, in London, but not for a long time. It had an Old World smell to it, typical of stations of the past, full of diesel fumes and oil all over the track area. As dark and smelly as it was, it still reminded her of the past, of traveling with Jack when they were younger, and good times. It was a portent of things to come, a ride that stopped at a station where the ride of her emotions never seemed to.

"Do you know where this place is?" Patricia asked.

"Which, Chester? Yes, here," Liz said, looking around as they walked along the station.

"No, Mom," Patricia replied, laughing briefly. She could see her mother was nervous, struggling to cope, looking all over as her eyes glazed over.

"Oh, right. Well, I have an idea. It's in the town center, near the market."

"Well, that's good. Maybe we could look around, there are a lot of shops here," Patricia offered hopefully. She didn't have a lot of money, but could never resist the chance to buy some clothes.

"No, we can't afford it. No."

Patricia felt the urge to say something, to remind her that they were there on her money, and it was up to her to decide what she would spend it on, but it was obvious how fragile her mother was. She would just have to bite her lip.

The roads and paths around the canals from the station to the center were long and winding, as if they were being tested, to see if they could stand the pace. The only time Liz could remember having contact with the Council was to pay local taxes, and Jack had mostly handled that. It seemed he handled so much, that everything was a mystery to her.

Chester center was bustling, buses, trucks, and cars all around, with the narrow Roman paths packed shoulder to shoulder as people went about their business. Liz wondered how many of them were in a similar state to her, how much desperation there was. From the looks of the fine coats and bulging shopping bags, she doubted it was many.

As they passed the library, the building changed, the bricks and coverings looking different, darker, dirtier, more affected by time and less cared for. A sign pointed in the direction they needed, down a side alley between the tall buildings. A man passed them, wearing a denim jacket and jeans, worn shoes that looked as if well past being ready for the bin. It was as if they were stepping away from the bright lights of a major city, into a hovel where only the downtrodden and desperate lived. She knew it wasn't truthfully the case, and how important the function of the local Council was to their lives, but for all that it shadowed her, as if she were walking beside a future personified, in a way she didn't want.

Two glass push doors led to an elevator, and concrete stairs beside. The elevator had a sign across it, written in black marker: Out Of Order. It was no surprise. Reluctantly they both pushed on, going up the stairs, looking at each sign on each floor. One mentioned Social Services, the other Rents, another Pensions. It seemed a catch-all building where all the needs of those without were taken care of. Finally, near the top the sign said in large black letters: Housing.

Liz pushed open a door and walked through, to see a fixed desk on one side, with several women standing behind, looking busy. Fixed chairs were laid out in rows facing towards them, as if the ladies might put on a show any moment and they could all enjoy the fun. A man stood across near a tall window, his hair a fuzzy gray mess, an unlit cigarette hanging from his mouth. He wore dark brown trousers that were too short for him, not covering worn baseball shoes with no laces. His baggy T-shirt offered a kind of street wisdom, but Liz tried not to look for fear of engaging him.

Patricia looked around at two others, a young couple sitting, huddled over. Beside them was a large pram, likely secondhand, but it did the job. They looked up at her, eyes focused, as if to ask what did she think she was looking at? She looked away. The air was dank, as if windows were never opened, a kind of musty smell which tugged at their mouths as they breathed in.

Liz struggled herself, wondering if it might simply be better to go home and return another day. As much as she wanted to about face and go, she knew she couldn't, she was at a dead end, voices were screaming at her, letters piling up, telephone ringing all the time. It was endless, and would get so much worse until something broke, probably her. She looked up at the counter, the women behind it. One glanced at her, then away, as if they had no interest in anything she wanted. She had never felt so meek.

Hesitantly, feeling herself tremble, but knowing she had to go, Liz walked slowly over. She looked hard ahead, wide-eyed, no longer able to swallow. It seemed as if the place was too hot, her mouth dried out with it. The shaking grew worse, making her wonder if she might simply collapse. She could feel Patricia's presence beside her. For her she would do it, for John, her children.

"Hi, can I help you?" one of the women finally asked, looking at them both. Liz stood directly in front of the counter, placing one hand on it, as much for support as anything else.

"Ye-Yes, I'm, here," Liz began, as her throat closed up. The woman waited, in a manner which suggested she was being patient, but her expression said anything but.

"Do you need some water?" Patricia asked, looking at her mother with concern. She knew she was nervous, but had no idea what to do. It was as new to her as her mother. All she could do was try to offer some kind of support, simply by being there.

Before Liz could reply, the woman at the counter interrupted. "We can't afford any fluids here, I'm afraid, we are not allowed to do so, but there is a cafe across the street," she said, leaning on the counter, hands clasped. It was less a polite explanation than a curt instruction.

Patricia looked at her, wondering to say something, but they were there to ask for help, and so the last thing they needed or wanted was an argument before they had even begun. Again she bit her lip, focusing on her mother.

The woman behind the counter was average height, her hair pulled tightly back, dark brown with more than a hint of excessive dye in it. She wore just enough makeup to achieve the austere looks she wanted, and a silk-style blouse the color of which matched her hair. She had a cheap pen in her hand, rolling it over, looking directly at Liz, as if she had such disdain for her that she might prefer she simply left.

Liz coughed once, then again, loudly, before pulling a wrapped mint from her pocket.

"I'm sorry, but no eating..." the woman behind the counter began.

Before she could finish her sentence, Liz popped it into her mouth, and the disagreement became moot.

"I'm here," Liz finally began, feeling a shiver of ice down her spine the moment she gave birth to the idea of all that was about to happen to them. It had been there, in the back of her mind, like a prisoner of conscience demanding to be let free, but she had ignored it, until then.

As Liz struggled to speak, she noticed a badge on the woman's lapel, giving her name. It said *Margaret Fincher, Housing Officer*. At least she could draw comfort from knowing she had the right person.

"We're, we're, going to be homeless, and need help," Liz finally said, finally managing to unblock the mental dam which had been holding her back so long. She had half expected some great release of all her tension, to rediscover herself from the pit of depression she had been sinking into, but no such change occurred. The skies outside continued to look black and white, the room inside where she stood still cast shadows, reflective of her mood. Everything now hinged on the woman opposite.

Both looked at the woman, waiting patiently, silently. They had expected a formal response, even if bureaucratic in nature. Instead she simply looked at Liz, a kind of withering look which would drain the essence of anybody.

It suddenly felt too warm in the place, as if a surge of heat had blown her way, that she was somehow being punished for having the temerity to ask for some kind of help. All she could think about was the need to sit down. She could murder a cup of tea, but knew full well from the woman's look that she would never be offered one.

"Well, the waiting list for a property of any kind is extensive, and you will have to join at the back of the line. You can expect a wait of up to two years before being offered a property," the housing officer suggested. As she spoke, her mouth seemed tight, as she forced a slight but obvious grin, her way of being polite but appearing more to enjoy the moment.

"What?" Patricia gasped, looking at the woman sternly. Another woman behind the counter looked at her. She had a full head or purple bouncy hair, and wore a long beige cardigan. She wore dark brown trousers several sizes too big and heels on thick shoes to improve her height. She looked at Patricia disapprovingly, as if annoyed at being disturbed. It was more like a library than a housing office, where nobody dare speak for fear of being told to be quiet.

Silence befell them all as each looked at one another, none sure how to respond. Liz looked at the woman, her eyes boring into hers.

"I'm sorry," Liz began, as she struggled not to break down in grief. She refused to, more out of certainty that the woman wouldn't really care, and besides, it might make her worse. "We have an eviction notice from the bank, and because it is late in proceedings they say bailiffs will be brought in any day to force us out."

A glimmer in the woman's eyes suggested she might have struck a chord. Her expression remained the same, but something in her reaction, a fleck of change in her eyes, gave some hope.

"Well," Fincher began, shaking her head as she spoke. Liz felt her heart sink as images of sitting on suitcases outside their home filled her mind. "You will have to fill out this form," the woman continued, her tone softening slightly.

"Why have you left it so late?" the purple-haired woman asked, moving to the front of the counter, as if she had sensed a weakness in her colleague and was charging to the front to ensure their blockade wasn't breached.

"My dad left, never told us anything, just disappeared, after not paying any bills for months. We don't know where he is, and now all of us are going to be on the streets," Patricia said. It even stunned Liz, who knew her daughter could be feisty, but never quite like this.

"My name is Gemma, Gemma Scott, and I am a Housing Officer here, along with my colleague Margaret," the woman began. Her composure, the words that she spoke, lifted them both, as if finally they had made a breakthrough.

"However, there are no properties available, so you will need to fill out the form and then we will be in touch," the purple-haired woman explained, sounding like a soulless robot. The moment she finished her sentence she turned away, as her colleague took leave to do the same. They began rifling through papers, as if to mock collect what was needed, slowly, in the hope that the nuisance would simply go away.

Liz looked away, stunned, feeling her heart beating so heavy she wondered if the entire room might rock with it. Patricia felt tears well in her eyes, the absolute hopelessness of it threatening to overwhelm her.

"'Scuse, love," a bleak voice whispered. Liz had no time for it, shuffling aside as she looked around in bewilderment. She noticed the square linoleum tiles were white but worn, having shouldered the footsteps of countless thousands of others, each one being told the same thing, they don't matter, go away, stop bothering.

"Hey," the voice came again, more persistent, but not so loud that the housing officers might hear it. Liz finally looked up. It was the fuzzy gray-haired man, leaning towards her furtively.

Liz shook her head, as if shying away from a vagrant. Then the thought dropped into her mind that she might well be a vagrant herself if she got no help soon.

"Tell them you are classed as an emergency, about to be made homeless, have children, and need rehousing immediately. If they refuse, tell them you will make a written complaint there and then," the man whispered. As he looked at her, he had a glint in his eyes, and a brief smile, showing there was life in the old soul yet. It was a cheeky look, full of mischief, as if he were enjoying the moment.

Liz continued to look confused, struggling to make her mind work. It was more than she was ever used to, more thinking for herself than she had done so for a long time.

Patricia nudged her, gently pushing her to go back to the counter. Liz turned to look at her, then back to the women shuffling papers. There was no way out, she would have to do as expected. She couldn't disappoint her daughter, that was too much.

"Excuse me," Liz said, her voice breaking as she leaned gently on the counter, more fear of falling in a dead faint that anything else. Neither woman looked at her, as if she wasn't even there.

"I said excuse me," Liz said, much louder than she had intended, shocking even herself. Now everyone looked at her. In for a penny, in for a pound, as her mother used to say.

"I, we are an emergency case, and as we, my children and I are about to be made homeless, by no fault of our own, I must insist you help us and rehouse us as soon as possible."

Both housing officers looked at her, finally at a loss for words. It wasn't what she said, so much as how she had said it. The pause was unbearable, as with each second Liz wanted to turn away, to walk out of the door, full of apologies for daring to be so rude.

"Can't you put your children in care, and then we can offer temporary bed and breakfast?" purple-haired woman asked, looking as if she had just offered gold to a beggar, expecting her to lap it up with joy.

A fire lit in Liz's stomach, her mind erupting with anger. She struggled to find the words, looking from the woman to Patricia, then she spotted the man again, looking so scruffy, so out of place, his hair wild and distorted, that same cigarette hanging from his mouth. He was shaking his head, slowly, deliberately, his face a picture of seriousness, *no, no, no* he mouthed.

Liz turned back to the woman. "No, I will not break up my family, I will keep us all together, and I am entitled to help from you, I need a home, we need a home, it is an emergency and you must help us," Liz almost shouted, her words like a chorus of begging.

Fincher took in a deep breath, as if Liz had somehow taken all the air in the room, leaving little for anything else.

"I will make a complaint, I'll go to my local MP, my local councilor, anyone and everyone, a lawyer if need be, but I will not break up my family," Liz continued to exhort, breathless, tears obvious in her eyes. She was at the end of her tether, barely able to think now.

She had no way of knowing, but the first thing she had said had worked, they knew it, they were simply delaying, trying to avoid providing what they knew was her legal right.

A large white form was slapped on the counter, and beside it a pen. Liz almost jumped at the noise, but she could tell it hadn't been done out of anger, more out of haste, to get it done, to give her her rights. The man in the corner took hold of his cigarette and smiled broadly. He knew it would make problems for him, but it didn't matter, he couldn't help but do the right thing.

Patricia didn't wait, instead grabbing it and walking away to a set of small chairs surrounding a table. She pulled one out and sat quickly, looking up at Liz.

Liz felt lost, unsure of herself, but deep down wanted to shriek with joy, to show her elation that she had won. Fear stopped her, aware of human nature and how fickle people could be. Instead she kept her head bowed and took her place beside her daughter.

"Here," Patricia said, offering the pen.

"No, you do it, I'll mess it up," Liz replied, feeling herself shaking with nerves. As low as she felt, it was the first time in weeks that she had felt any sense of hope of what was to come.

Together they worked away, filling question after question, often the same thing asked in a different way. It was obvious the form had been designed by someone being paid too much, doing a job they didn't like, purely as a means to ensure they were caught out. The final page was all white, a large section for own comments to finish. Liz looked up at her daughter, thinking it was enough, hand it in and go quickly before they changed their minds.

"Add something, write to say it wasn't your fault, that you were abandoned through no fault of your own, and make it clear you need a house as you have children. Write that and other bits like that, lay it on thick. That way if you have to appeal, if they refuse, then you can say that is why you're so desperate." Both looked up to see the scruffy man standing over them, looking at the form. Now he was like a kindred spirit, akin to their needs, as if he too shared the burden, their sense of loss.

Liz didn't speak, she was lost for words, unable to link the image of the man with his manner, how kind he had been. She knew she should never judge a book by its cover, and he was living proof. Instead she just nodded, before taking the pen from Patricia, scribbling in notes and comments, anything she could add. Before she knew it she had filled the page, a mass of tiny words, adding every single thing she could think of, full of emotion, almost pleading for help. If that didn't help, nothing would.

Patricia took the form once she knew it was complete and the pen and quickly dropped it onto the counter. Both women had been standing in silence, waiting and watching, aware of how little real power they had. It was never a position where anyone should be able to exercise such against another, but still human nature being what it was they sometimes tried.

Fincher picked it up and began leafing through it. Patricia stood looking at her as her mother sat waiting, unsure if her legs could support her.

After what seemed an interminable age, the woman folded the form, read the entire back page and looked up, once again offering the same sneer of a look, as if she were ready to dismiss them out of hand. Patricia felt nerves of her own, thrust into a situation that even she didn't think she could cope with. Still she stood her ground, waiting and watching. She was ready, the moment they refused she would request an appeal, whatever that meant.

Purple-haired woman took the form, leafing through it as her colleague looked on. Finally they looked at each other, neither speaking.

"Right, I will process this form, and put you down as an emergency, and we will telephone you as soon as something comes up," Fincher offered. Liz almost jumped up, wanting to shout and holler with joy, but she just couldn't allow herself to believe it, not yet, not until they were through the door and away, so she could believe in something, even if at the back of her mind she knew anything could happen.

Liz stood up, smiling at Patricia, before turning to the man. She mouthed the words *thank you* towards him, smiling so much her eyes threatened tears again. In a way it was a hollow victory, one that she should never have had to fight and she knew it, but also because it was a place to live because they had been abandoned and left likely homeless. It was a victory based on the destruction and loss of her life, which as she saw it, at her time of life should never have happened.

Together they both walked to leave.

"Don't forget," the man said, as they both turned to him. "You need a receipt," he continued, still offering that cheeky smile.

Without needing further prompting, Liz walked back to the counter and looked at them both, finally offering her own thin-lipped smile, a look full of emotion and satisfaction, "Could I have a receipt for my form, please?" she asked, doing her best not to laugh.

Neither looked at her as Fincher took a small square pad from under her desk. She scrawled a few words on it, dated it, and dropped a heaving thudding stamp on it, before dropping the piece of paper onto the counter. Liz snapped it up, turned briefly to smile at the man, and walked away.

Whatever happened next, however it turned out, she had the satisfaction of knowing she still retained her pride.

"One moment," Fincher said. Too quick, she had said it, before they could escape. Liz wondered if she too were playing a game, had been waiting till just the right moment to spring it upon her. "You haven't put a telephone number on here, we can't contact you."

Liz turned to her, looking solemn, not quite so joyful. "I'm sorry, it's going to be cut off, I don't have a number," she replied meekly, wondering if she had placed her head inside the lion's mouth.

"You'll have to telephone here then, check tomorrow, and we will let you know if anything has come up," Fincher explained. It was more than Liz had expected, thinking she had been dealing with someone who thought nothing of loss or struggle. It was a small victory, enough of a change that she could appreciate the gesture, no matter how small.

As the two walked back down the stairs, things felt different. It wasn't much, but it was something. As they exited the building, they looked at each other, as if to say, now what?

"I've got five pounds left, which is two pounds eighty-five pence for the train home, and two pounds fifteen left," Patricia said.

Liz looked at her, feeling sick that she had to rely on her own daughter for anything, let alone the fact that it was the last money she had.

"Shall we go splash out, buy a meal?" Liz asked, aware she was being cheeky, but unable to resist the urge to object in some way to it all.

Patricia laughed. "Yeah, how about fries?" she asked, at which her mother nodded. The two headed off to find a food shop, feeling good about themselves finally. They had done something together, made some kind of progress, and learned something about themselves in the process. Whatever happened, they would fight together, all of them; nobody would separate them. Patricia learned that much from her mother, that nobody would ever tear them apart.

15

THE WEAK MAN

"Hello, Mister Laker?"

Silence...

"Hello, is that Mister Laker?"

"Who's calling?"

"Hi, I am Detective Sergeant Chavards, of Cheshire Constabulary. I'm calling in relation to the disappearance of a Mister Jack Cornwell."

"Oh, right, OK."

"Well, I was given your details as being a close colleague of Mister Cornwell's. Your employer gave us your details, and we're traveling near to you. I was wondering if I might come and ask you some questions?"

"What sort of questions?"

"Well, it would be much easier to explain in person, if I could?"

"I'm sort of busy right now."

"It won't take long, we're very close to yours right now."

Silence...

"Are you there?"

"Yes."

"Oh, that's great, we'll be there in a few minutes. Thanks, bye."

"No, but hold on. Damn."

Silence...

*

"Good morning. We just spoke on the telephone. I am of course Detective Chavards." He held out an oblong card inside a leather wallet with a clear face. It had a picture of him on it, with his name written beside, and a circular stamp across, under the heading Cheshire Constabulary. Beside him stood another man, tall and thin.

He looked immaculate in his dark PC uniform, and smiled as if to offer a positive welcome. Neither man appeared to suggest any kind of threat, their demeanor more of a family gathering where all were trusted and welcome. It was a well-worn theme, deliberate and designed to put people at their ease, to ensure better cooperation.

"I didn't, I mean I wasn't," Laker began to say, struggling to utter the words his brain insisted he say. Nerves blocked him from being persistent, not used to the presence of police on his doorstep.

"It's fine, we won't be more than a few minutes, and we will leave you in peace," Trilby offered, his smile unwavering, the look in his eye as if they were planning a day of fun all of them, that it would be great, even if they arrested him, it would be amazing.

Unable to express himself further, and fully aware than they wouldn't leave without him appearing suspicious, Laker moved aside, beckoning them in.

Both officers glanced at him before walking in through the front door. A strong smell of tobacco met their entry, suggesting he was a heavy smoker.

The hallway led down to the right, through a door into the living room. The walls were of a beige color, worn by time and smoke. On either end of the long room were large windows, to the right an open-plan kitchen. Both went in and turned, waiting to be invited to either sit, or simply speak. Laker followed them, barely looking them in the eye.

No invitation to sit was offered, so all three stood looking at each other.

"I'm sorry, I don't know anything," Laker insisted. He was an average man in many respects, a quiet person, short trimmed graying hair, wearing a thin, light cardigan and deep brown trousers. He wore slippers, equally worn, as if his clothes mirrored him, old before their time and neglected.

Chavards looked him up and down fleetingly. He had long grown accustomed to sizing people up quickly, to avoid their becoming defensive, as well as ensuring he had a good take on who he was dealing with. A simple look could give so much away, and often did. Now all he could see was a man tired with his mundane life.

"Well, you see, often when we ask something, it can prod the memory, and where people often don't realize they know something that might be useful to us, until we ask and talk, we can't tell," Trilby explained, his smile unchanging throughout.

"So if we can just ask one or two things, then we will let you get back to your day," Chavards said, his words almost meshing with his colleagues, like a double act working in sync, not missing a beat as each looked at him as if he were a child at Christmas and they were simply there to give presents.

Laker shrugged, sort of nodding, but unwilling to commit himself too much. "What do you need to know?"

"Right," Trilby said, at which point Laker expected him to pull out a pocket book to make notes. Neither did, which confused him. He couldn't tell if it made him less of a suspect in any wrongdoing or more, whether they doubted his being useful, or were simply lining up to arrest him.

"Are you single, sir?" Trilby continued.

"No, my wife is out shopping. She's going to her sister's afterwards, and home for tea," Laker explained, feeling the need to smoke.

"That's nice. Does your wife know Mister Cornwell at all?" Trilby continued. Now Chavards simply stood, continuing to smile, no longer sizing the man up, just listening. He had what he needed, knew as much as he wanted, now words mattered. He trusted his colleague would gather what was needed.

"No," Laker replied. He was clearly a quiet man, uncomfortable in such circumstances. He looked at the officers as if he were beaten at their game. Finally he shuffled over to a large flower-patterned armchair, ready to sit. He knew he couldn't be so rude as to sit and leave them standing, so he waved his arm, beckoning them to sit. It occurred to him that if they continued to stand, that they might mean more than they had shown, they could be a problem, but if they sat, then he could relax, they simply needed information. He would never consider himself a student of human nature, but he was aware enough to know that much about people. His instincts weren't completely dead.

To his surprise, both men nodded at him and sat on an equally flowery sofa opposite him.

"Could you tell us again what you told the officers earlier, about the circumstances of the day Mister Cornwell went missing?" Chavards asked.

"Well, I always pick him up from his place on the morning, and we share the costs. It was his idea, bit of a nuisance for me because it's out of the way, but he could always be persuasive like that, Jack could."

"So was it a usual routine kind of thing, you picked him up every morning?" Trilby asked, appearing more interested now, less of his smiles.

"Yeah, pretty much. I'm fine if there's a routine, I like that. I would always pick him up, and we would go into work, and then see each other from time to time during the day."

"So, was he your boss?"

"No, different areas. He was, *is*, I mean, sorry, is factory manager, shop floor, I'm up in the offices, work between there and other management."

"I see," Chavards said, picking up the thread. "So could you just tell us again what you can about the last time you saw him?"

"Yeah, I did say this several times to different people over it."

"Of course, but the reason we ask several times is if in case you either remember something not thought of before, however little, or that we pick up on something you have said, but others have missed. As things change and we find new leads, then what you or others say can change what questions we ask or what we pick up on from things discussed," Chavards explained. It was the most anyone had said to him about the process. Where others had simply asked questions and left, now he had an understanding of what was going on. He appreciated being informed, and smiled briefly at them.

"That makes sense, I get you. Right, well we usually go straight into work, though sometimes we do go call at the local shops in Elton, and get newspapers or something. He mentioned going there that morning, and so I drove us there."

"How did he seem to you, any different than normal?" Chavards asked, looking directly at Laker.

"No, we… Now I think of it, yeah, a bit," Laker said. His response clearly made an impression, as both officers looked at each other.

"How so?" Trilby asked.

"Well, he's one of those people, I guess typical management style, efficient, and he just got on with it, as if he was on autopilot most mornings. You could say he had a bland style, as if he were not really interested in what he was doing, but going through the motions. He was pretty good at what he did, so could get away with being halfhearted."

"So, what was different that day?" Trilby asked.

"You seem this is what I was referring to, because I don't think you mentioned seeing a difference before," Chavards interrupted.

"No, I guess it wasn't until you said what you did that I realized that, made me think, what else was there."

Chavards smiled, acknowledging his understanding. "Please, carry on."

"So that morning, thinking about it now, he seemed quite a bit more lively, focused, as if he were alert to something. In work he often would laugh with others, and you would see more of him, but you wouldn't see the real him, nothing personal, just the kind of things managers say and do with each other, back slapping because they're in charge."

"You make that sound like you're not part of it," Trilby suggested, at which both officers looked intently at him. Once again the mood appeared to change, as if it wasn't just a question, more a comment designed to elicit a certain answer, spoken or otherwise.

"No, no, not at all, that's not the case. I just wasn't part of that, their clique, but I'm good at my job."

"So you're not left out of his circle?"

"No, I have just been advised I am being given a promotion."

"You're getting Mister Cornwell's job?" Chavards asked pointedly.

Laker laughed, looking at him, aware of this mischief making. "Nice, but no, his job as far as I am aware is still there for him. The job I would, or will be getting, would be his superior, his boss, so to speak."

"I see, was he aware that this might happen, that at some stage you might get promoted above him?" Chavards asked, leaning closer now.

"Maybe, I'm not sure. It wasn't an issue for me, really."

"But it might have been for him?" Trilby asked. Laker nodded, at which again both officers looked at each other briefly.

"So he seemed a little different then, on that day?" Trilby continued.

"Yeah, but not angry, he seemed chipper, upbeat, as if he was happy about something. I couldn't tell if it was a forced positivity, sort of through his teeth happiness, but it was certainly different."

"I see, and then what did he do?" Chavards asked.

"He mentioned going to the shops. We drove there, and he said he wasn't going into work, or something like that."

"Did he say why, or anything else?" Trilby asked, sounding more urgent.

"No, he just seemed as if he was relaxed all of a sudden, that he had decided on something, and he was going to go do it."

"Perhaps, take his life?" Chavards asked. It was a difficult thing to discuss, but had to be asked. Laker responded as he had been expected to, looking shocked at the suggestion.

"I, I don't know. Until you said that, it hadn't entered my mind. I would really say no, but then I know managers can struggle sometimes, and never say anything."

"Why don't they talk about it?" Trilby asked, aware of the likely answer, but it needed to come from him.

"Because weakness, well, it can stop you getting on, stop promotions and the like. Doesn't matter how trivial your job, you show weakness and people look at you differently."

The conversation had gone better than they had expected, but left more questions than answers.

Chavards stood up as Trilby followed his lead. "Mister Laker, I want to thank you for sparing us some of your valuable time."

"It's fine. I hope he turns up soon," Laker explained as he led them out.

"We can only hope, and keep looking," Trilby agreed as they followed on.

Laker opened the door, showed them out, and closed it without looking.

"What do you think, should we look more into Laker's background?" Trilby asked.

"No, I don't think he's involved, and doesn't really care. With Cornwell gone he gets a promotion, but I get the feeling this was only down to one person, and until we find him, we won't really know," Chavards replied.

"You think he's still around, Cornwell?" Trilby asked, opening the car door.

"Could be, but if he's no longer alive, I get the impression no one else is to blame."

Trilby nodded before sitting on the driver's seat. "Should we keep looking, now?"

Chavards shook his head. "No, we've spent enough time on this. Given what we've heard, let's place it on the back burner, and get on with the next case," he said, at which they drove off.

Laker lifted the curtain to his lounge window, watching them go. He smiled, simply at his satisfaction of the promotion to come. Far from being angry with his colleague, he couldn't help but be thankful, because due to his actions, his own life just got a whole lot better.

16

LONG NIGHTS ALONE

Nights were sometimes difficult. They could drag, be a source of struggle, the long darkness, and time alone. All of that was when she was next to her man, beside him, listening to him sound asleep, without a thought or care in the world, while she lay thinking of all of life's problems, all of what was to come with the daylight.

Liz rarely enjoyed peaceful sleep. It was too long for her to remember that last time she slept well. Being alone now, in that large bed, the solid mattress more like a sheet on a stone floor, she felt no different. The night still dragged, but with each ticking moment going by, the tumult of the coming day wouldn't bring her children to school or college, or her husband to work; instead, it would mean packing, sorting, emptying. Every second closer to leaving their home and out into uncertainty.

The walls felt as if they were closing in, as the warm air felt empty of life, almost as if it were dead around her. She could hear the sound of the old clock ticking nearby, counting seconds, almost in rhyme with each breath she took. A sound downstairs broke the tension, the letterbox, but with it new worries. Her heart beat harder as images flooded her mind over what might have come, what new threats lay in store for them all, what next?

It was like lying in a prison with no lights, where each way she turned there would only be accusations, shame, for debt, for failure. Each thought brought with it a new sense of wrong. Where was he? What did she do to drive him away? Something tickled her cheek before she realized it was tears; she was crying and didn't even know it.

Then there was the question which had been in the back of her mind all along: did she really force him away, or was he hurt, lying somewhere in need of help? No matter what, she couldn't allow herself to think about the worst, that he might no longer be...

A door clicked, suggesting someone was around. For a second she wondered if he was back. The thought in her mind brought confusion over her emotions, as in part she felt happier, because they would be safe again, in their home, with someone to pay the bills and sort all this mess out. Then her conscience kicked in, not so delicately reminding her that her main concern was keeping her home, paying what was owed, not being back with him. It was a consideration she had never allowed before, perhaps that she no longer loved him, but still needed him.

Twenty-seven years of marriage, so long, two children, their own home, and so many plans. Had he thought what she did? That they were no longer in love? It couldn't be, things were poor between them, but it had been like it in the past and they had always rediscovered their love. She was wrong, she was a fighter, in life for her family, and for her man. She wouldn't give up.

A flushing sound brought her back to the here and now, a shuffling to follow, as John returned noisily to his bed. The same trickling sense of unease returned to Liz, her mind feeling sick with it. It was as if it would never go, never leave her to her senses, that she was trapped in a sense of sickening unease and unhappiness that would define her, and possibly her family like some kind of stain.

A heavy thud in the next room followed by an oof sound forced her to open her eyes. She looked, holding her breath, waiting for signs of movements, calls, anything. Nothing. It was probably John in his room, getting lost among all the stuff he kept in there. That was going to be the hardest part of it, what to do with all of their things. Tough choices were coming.

No matter what she thought, nothing would lead her to feel optimistic. Liz searched her mind, trying to force herself to think of something positive ahead. Could there be a release she was looking for? Was there something in her life which would improve without the man she had devoted so much to? The rest of her life beyond Jack was like a blanket, smothering everything. Her children, her home, the life around her they had built together, it was oppressive, the thought that so much would be out of her control. She could find a job, but hadn't worked for so long. She could get a new home, but would be alone for the first time in so long, and everyone in her life would be looking to her to make it all work. The pressure was unbearable.

Tears again, only now met with silent sobbing, her face buried in the covers. She felt rock bottom, as low as anyone could go, but for all her fears and pain, she would never think to share it with her children. She was too good for that.

The night ticked on, as if the rhythm shared between her sobs, the clock ticking, and her heartbeat. She could cry it out, let go of the anger and emotion for now. After that, she would double down, grit her teeth, and put up with whatever happened. Whatever was to come, she would deal with it.

17

DEBT COLLECTORS

"Mom," John called, standing over his mother's bed like a tall tree waiting for rain. She looked so sound asleep, he wondered if he should simply join her and go back to his own bed. It was such a good idea, and so kind of him, he turned to walk out of her room.

"Is she awake?" Patricia asked the moment he placed a foot out of the bedroom door. It was as if she had been waiting there to pounce, just for that exact moment.

"No, she's fast asleep. I didn't want to disturb her, she looks peaceful," John replied, the look on his face giving nothing away.

Patricia felt torn, wanting to berate her brother, even in times when he didn't deserve it, but also touched by his consideration of his mother. He was always so immature, and with it never caring about others, but given all that was going on, she wondered if he was growing up a bit.

"Well, there are two letters here, and I think she needs to see them, so hard as it is, we'll have to wake her up," Patricia insisted, her tone reflective of her changed nature towards him.

"OK, I'm going back to bed then," John said, wandering off to his room. So much for his growing up or changing. Patricia felt infuriated, but before she could vent, he was gone, door closed and back in his cozy little world. It was never that he deliberately ignored what was going on around them, just that in his mind he had more important things to think about.

"Mom," Patricia said, sitting on the side of the large bed. She rarely had cause to go into their room, but it was the largest of the bedrooms, well-tended, a dressing table, king-size bed, and large dark-brown wardrobes along an entire wall. Though it was wallpapered quite brightly, the room always seemed dark, as if there were a large shadow hanging over it. She could never tell if it was the room itself, or the window size, or simply how the place made her feel while in there. Whatever it was, she would never say, not wanting to sound so negative about her parents' room.

"Mom," she said again, still softly, for fear of making her jump. The last thing she needed was a shock to wake her. Nobody had suffered more than her mother, she could see it in her face every day. It obviously wasn't all worry about her father, as much about what to do next. Some things just had no answers, and as strong as they had tried to be with the housing, unless they came through, what came next would be catastrophic.

Patricia turned, looking away at the windows, wondering what to do. Her choice was made for her as she turned back to see Liz lying in the same way, only now eyes open, staring at her, as if she were awake but empty of thoughts. For a split second she envied that look, the same one John had somehow perfected, the ability to take a moment and think of nothing, to give the mind and body time to gather together and function without stress.

"Sorry, I didn't want to wake you," Patricia explained gently.

Liz looked at her, thinking to ask why had she then, if that was the case, but it would be callous under the circumstances, so she smiled instead. "It's OK, love, I need to get up anyway."

"I'll go down and make some breakfast for us all," Patricia offered, struggling to provide a positive feeling between them. She could sense the overwhelming depression hanging over the house, but like her mother, saw herself as something of a fighter, and whatever happened, she would never give up.

"OK, not too much for me, please. Some toast or something. I don't feel great," Liz said, slowly pulling herself up as if she had been asleep for weeks. As her daughter left and her mind opened up for the day, she began to ask questions of herself. What could she do? Was there any point? Each time she thought of such a question, an image of her family presented themselves to her, as if she were having a conversation with her own mind. At least she had something to live for, to go on for, for her children. She knew if they hadn't been there, things may have well been different. She could never imagine going back home, to her mother, to where she grew up. It would never be the same, and besides would in itself be an admission that her life was over. She might as well get it over with there as anywhere else.

Liz forced her cold feet into her fluffy slippers and wrapped herself in the gown that Jack had bought her a few years ago. At the time it was a lovely gesture, but now it just seemed empty, devoid of any emotional connection, as if it were a used garment she had bought from a charity shop. It didn't matter, it served a purpose, and she was never one to look a gift horse in the mouth.

The air was chilly, not only a sign of the changing season, but the fact that there was no heating. There were no fires to light, no gas to power the radiators because there were no radiators. All they had was electric under-floor heating, which took days to properly kick in. Another of Jack's fine discoveries: a house with no heating.

As she looked through the window, she noticed Pam standing outside, talking to a man she didn't recognize. She had the same old look, coiffured hair, and tight checkered pants, wrapping a slight cardigan around herself. She was chatting away, no doubt gossiping, as she occasionally furtively looked around herself, as if what she was conveying was a state secret that nobody knew of until she told everyone of it.

The skies were ever white, signifying the bitter cold outside, and the onset of winter. Leaves had long fallen to the ground, as plants and trees had withered away and flowers died back to black. It was as if her life had diminished subtly, and everything around her reflected that, decaying and turning to ash, becoming nothing more than dusty memories of a better time. She wondered about those times, trying to imagine a happier moment, but for all she did, they were always tainted by something bad happening, however minor.

It was too much, too much feeling sorry for herself. All it would take was a deep breath and a determination to move on, to carry on and do something about it all. So that was what she did, breathing in deeply, mentally sweeping away all of the debris of sadness that surrounded them, and out she went. If there no brightness in the day, it didn't matter. If her family was unhappy and depressed, it didn't matter. She would be the sun, the smile, the effort in anger if necessary, she would drive them on and they would not give up.

Bang, bang, bang she thudded loudly on John's door. She knew she could go in hard, kick his door clean off its hinges shouting *this is a raid* at the top of her voice while banging a drum and it wouldn't make a difference. The side of the house could fall off, the world could be ending, and John would sleep through it. As long as nothing affected his bed or his warm covers, then he wouldn't move an inch, lost to the world of slumber.

She pushed the door open, looking in, to see his curtains half-open as bright sunshine broke through the clouds. It seemed as if it happened just at that moment, to remind her of the love she still had for her family. For a second she felt a great urge to cry, to release it all, but it was hardly the right place and time. She was a mixed, confused cauldron of emotions, but her son gave her all she needed in that moment. For that split second he gave her a reason to smile, lying there looking like he had simply flopped down and not moved an inch since.

Liz knelt beside his bed, on the floor, looking at him as he snored lightly. She envied his ability to switch off from it all. She hoped it would last, and would protect him for as long as she could from how life could be, and how tough the world often was.

"Morning, love," she said lightly. She knew banging and shouting wouldn't wake him, and pulling his covers off or spraying water on him would just make him grumpy, so different tactics were needed.

"That girl you like from school is here, love, she's waiting downstairs for you. Looks very nice," she said, struggling not to chuckle.

"Uh, what?" John murmured.

"As if," she continued, only now whispering so slightly nobody could hear it. If only, she thought, but he was too busy having fun to bother with girls yet.

"Yeah, get up and come see," Liz continued, doubtful it would work. It was worth a try.

"OK, all right, I will," John said, mashing his words as his mouth refused to wake up with the rest of him.

"Plus I'll make you a nice breakfast," Liz offered, the final temptation to lure him out.

"Right, I thought we didn't have anything," John said, sounding clearer as he opened his eyes blearily.

"Oh, I'll have a look. I'll find something."

John nodded, turning over to signify his intent. Liz stood up, feeling the ache in her limbs. She wasn't the only one who had slept heavily, only for her the aches signified a weariness of life. She dismissed it, filing it to the back of her mind under "deal with later."

Or never.

"Well, there's not much in, I guess we're running out of things, so we'll need to go to the shops and get some food," Patricia said, as if nothing in particular was going on around them and all was normal.

"Oh, that's fine. One slight problem, we don't have any money to get us to the shops," Liz said, sounding lighthearted, but the intent was obvious.

"Well, we can walk to the local shops here," Patricia insisted, holding the near-empty fridge door open.

"Right, then I guess we can pick up a few things, and then put them back because we have no money."

"I have some, not much, a few pounds, but it can get us some things in."

"No, I can't keep asking you for money," Liz insisted, her tone no longer so sarcastic, but serious.

"It's my money, I don't mind," Patricia said curtly. The discussion was fast turning into an argument, interrupted as a hard thud at the front door broke their engagement.

Both turned to look at it but waited, as if for the other to get it. Neither wanted to go, more out of concern for who or what it might be. Feeling a sense of frustration, Liz looked at Patricia, then back to the front door, before walking over to it. Just as the thud, thud, thud came again, she opened it to see Dan standing there, holding on to his motorcycle helmet.

"Morning," Dan said, looking up at her, smiling cheerfully.

Liz turned away from him. "Patricia, It's Dan," she said, standing back with the door open to let him in. "Morning," she said, smiling briefly.

As he walked through, he looked at Liz before stopping. "Oh, there's someone here for you," he said, shuffling his arm out as if to point the way, but not wanting to be involved in it. He knew clearly there were problems, but the last thing he needed was something to interrupt the whole point of his being there: Patricia.

It was obviously going to be messy, so he preferred to stay out of it. That was best all round, especially for him.

Liz turned quickly to see a man at the door, wearing a long gray raincoat. He held a smart oblong leather briefcase in one hand, and in the other a slim white oblong envelope. His hair was thin on his head, but what there was of it was light brown and slicked back by grease. He looked smart, as smart at his shiny shoes, which betrayed his intent, as serious as his demeanor.

"Good morning, are you Mrs. Elizabeth Cornwell?" he asked, his voice sounding as if he had taken elocution lessons.

She wondered whether to simply slam the door and go in, yet another debt collector, but she knew she couldn't, because it could be about her husband.

"Yes," she said meekly. The cold air made her feel worse, but the look in his eye gave her a greater chill than the effects of any season could.

The man swiftly lifted the white envelope up to her, holding it out close enough that she may take it. It looked to her as if it were some kind of portent, that if she touched it she would become involved in something she had no desire to be a part of. She hesitated, reluctant to take hold.

"It doesn't really matter if you take it, I am simply holding it out for you to take as a matter of courtesy," the man explained, his eyes entirely focused on her, but his lips betraying a mild smile, as if he were trying to be decent towards her.

Before she could take a hold of it, she noticed another man standing back, behind Dan's motorcycle. He looked different, dressed all in black and much larger in size. He wore a smart suit and a white shirt, with a thin black tie hanging loosely from his neck. Beside him but further back again was a police officer, dressed in uniform. For a second Liz felt a fleck of warmth as she noted the presence of police, before realizing they were not there about her husband, simply about the letter.

There was no choice, she was at a dead end, one of many in recent weeks, so she took the envelope slowly, for fear of detonating something inside of it. The man continued to stand, looking at her pleasantly, as if waiting for her reaction to it.

It was fine paper, clearly expensive, with a crown stamp on the front, and black letters depicting the name of Jack Cornwell. She wanted to look back at her children, to take comfort from them, but even then she wouldn't put them through what she was going through. She slipped a fingernail under the back edge, which moved easily. Flipping it open, she pulled out the bright white paper and unfolded it. The technical aspects of it didn't matter to her. It mentioned her husband's name again, and right there, in large bold red letters said the word which she knew of, but confirmed legally, *eviction*, Friday, the date, this coming Friday.

"My apologies if I have upset you with this, madam, but you have been served, and have forty-eight hours to vacate the property in full. If you are not out after this time, court-appointed bailiffs will force entry and remove all of your possessions, leaving them for you to deal with," the man said, determined to finish his words. She stared at him as he spoke, aware of how uncomfortable he was in doing it. She could see the large man in the black suit was there to ensure there were no problems, and that police were there to ensure no one got hurt, but no matter how good he was at his job, nothing could stop her feeling as hurt as she did then.

Liz closed the door as the three continued to look at her, as if the world outside was closing in on them and the moment it shut they no longer existed. If only life were so easy.

"So that's it?" John asked, standing at the door to the hall, still wearing his pajamas. She had tried hard to protect him above all else, but now the truth was there for all to see.

It wasn't the end, not for Liz. To her, it was the beginning. Not an end to their home or her marriage, but a beginning of dealing with it, and preparing for what was to come next.

"We will go to the local shops, Patricia, and we will gather as many boxes as we can to pack. Dan, I need your help, I need you to go get us that van, as big as you can, from work, or friends or anyone. John, get dressed, I will find something for breakfast, and then together, all of us will pack, and before that deadline we'll move. I don't know where, or how, but we will, and we will deal with this," Liz said, before screwing the letter up, throwing it as a ball behind her. She didn't care where it landed, all that mattered was that they were going to act, all of them, together.

18

AN UNCOMFORTABLE SILENCE

"So what do we say?"

"The usual, nothing."

"Not a word, not a single thing?"

"No, because our duty isn't just to the one person, or to the family, it's to both sides, to everyone, and the rules restrict what we can say and do to any of them."

"Sounds like the law is an ass."

"Funny, we're here to enforce it, so what does that make us?"

Detective Sergeant Chavards and Constable Trilby both stood up together, as if they had a synchronized mind, as well as movement. Chavards had been here before, this kind of situation. It was difficult knowing the facts behind a case, but actually imparting such information to loved ones or family was far and away the toughest part of it. To him, it was like breaking the news of a bereavement, but only now there would be no comforting truth behind it, no solace as to anything they needed to know, simply a bland statement about how it was and how it couldn't change.

"So who's going to do the informing, then?" Trilby asked, pulling on his dark gray overcoat.

"Well, you're the one attempting to get into detective work, so I guess you can do it," Chavards responded, not a hint of a smile on his face.

Trilby looked at him, expecting a grin, but quickly realized he meant it. He was right, he had wanted more from his career, but knew some of it wasn't as glamorous as other parts. Still, he would have to just get on with it.

"Shall I get Sue Danbridge? To help with Liaison?" Trilby asked.

"No, this isn't a matter for Liaison now, it's just wrap it up and move on."

Trilby looked at Chavards, the harsh look on his face. Of course he was well adjusted to what was to come, and the different scenarios behind it all.

"How did we find out?" Trilby asked.

"Just a phone call from that man, Laker, enough information to kill it, and here we are on our way to close it down."

"Sad, really sad."

"It's life. You'll get used to it."

*

"I'm sorry, but it's store policy not to give out cardboard boxes anymore. We recycle them." The woman looked tired, dressed in her long blue and white checkered dress as part of her Kwik Save uniform. She looked at Liz as if she were just another customer, that to her the decision didn't matter, she was only doing her job, looking forward to clocking off time.

"But we really need some, I have to move, quickly, and you have a big pile of them there," Liz explained, realizing it was a losing battle.

"I'm sorry, but it's store policy not to give out cardboard boxes anymore. We recycle them," the woman said again.

Liz looked at her, astonished, wondering if she were in a time warp where the most idiotic things kept reoccurring. She thought to try again, only saying something different, or to plead with her some more, but it was obvious she wasn't listening. The long row of ten shops combined everything a neighborhood might need, including a newsagent, an off license, and other minor stores. Kwik Save was the only store for miles that had boxes big enough for their needs.

Liz looked lost, turning to Patricia, looking as if she were ready to give up.

"I guess it's been a long morning, a long week. I know that feeling," Patricia said, looking at the woman. She looked at her name badge; Ethel it said. "Not too long now till home time, Ethel," Patricia said, smiling at the woman.

"No, well, it's not great, but it pays the bills. Some silly rules, you know, but what can we do?" Ethel explained. Her visage relaxed, suggesting she was a little kinder than her exterior had otherwise suggested.

Leaning in, as if to whisper a great secret, Ethel looked from Liz to Patricia, eyes wide open. "If you go outside, and go round the back of the store, there are big trolleys full of these boxes, flat packed. If you grab a few boxes, I don't think anyone will say anything. Just make sure no one is around and don't take too much."

Patricia smiled at her broadly, thankful for the small but kind gesture. Before she could express the words to show her gratitude, Liz suddenly took hold of the woman, pulling her in, hugging her tightly. The look on Ethel's face said it all, sheer surprise, as if she had been hit on the head with a huge water balloon. Patricia laughed as Liz repeatedly thanked her over and over.

"Oh, thank you so much," Liz said, tears in her eyes. The last thing she wanted to do in front of her daughter was cry, but some tears of happiness were fine.

Ethel finally stood back, smiled awkwardly, and nodded. "You're very welcome," she said, before picking up a box of something, anything as an excuse to carry on, away from the crazy woman.

The moment Ethel had walked away, both Patricia and Liz scampered out of the shop, trotting off around towards the back of the buildings. It suddenly occurred to Liz that she might not have been telling the truth, simply fobbing them off to get them out of the store, but no, she was being daft, no one could be that mean. Besides, if she was, she would certainly be back in there to have her say about it, she was in just the mood.

The two slowed to a walk as they came upon a dozen or more high-level silver metal cradles, all full of packaging, plastic debris, plastics bands, and cardboard. Some of it was damaged, ripped, but two of the stacks appeared intact, tied down with string, but lots and lots of boxes. It was like Christmas, a simple thing, but so important to them. It wasn't all bad in life, and proved to them the importance of appreciating such small things.

"How many shall we take?" Patricia asked, looking eagerly at her mother.

"All of them," Liz said boldly. "You take one trolley, I'll take the other."

"Really?" Patricia asked, shocked at her mother. She had never heard her talk like it, or behave like it, but whatever it was, she liked the improvement.

"No, silly. Well, I would if I could, but there's no need for all these, because the van probably won't hold it all anyway," Liz explained.

"That's if he can even get a van," Patricia said.

"He had better, because otherwise we're literally on the streets. We don't even know if we have a place to go to yet," Liz said, pricking the balloon of happiness they had enjoyed all too briefly.

Liz grabbed a big armful of flat boxes, pulling away as she waited for Patricia to do likewise. "Make sure to get as many as you can carry, we don't have time to come back again." The two took their stash, almost more than they could manage, walking back around the front. Liz deliberately avoided going near to the front of the store. The last thing they needed was to be seen by someone in charge with demands to put it back.

Within a few yards of walking up the slight hill from the store, Liz slipped a little, as the boxes slid sideways, slipping from her grasp onto the floor.

"Hello," a voice said, interrupting her annoyance. If nothing else, at least it was an opportunity to stop for a moment. If anyone saw them from the store, she would simply deny they ever came from there, and if that failed, she would simply run.

As Liz looked up from the fast collapsing pile of cardboard in her arms, she noticed two men stepping from a car.

"Fancy meeting you here," the voice continued. As Liz focused, finally giving up on the boxes as they slid down, she noticed it was Officer Trilby as Chavards withdrew from the other side.

"Oh, hi," Liz said, feeling her heart pounding again. She knew it was more than just a little coincidence, but refused to say anything for fear of tempting fate. Emotionally, she was so brittle that she feared anything might push her over the edge. Right now all she wanted to do was act, and think as little as possible.

"Where are you off?" Trilby asked, looking at the boxes. Both Liz and Patricia looked at him, wondering if it was a trick question. The two of them, in the situation they were in, carrying boxes, it seemed obvious. It was certainly a concern that a police officer might not know from the look of them what they were doing. Liz bit her lip. In other circumstances she might have said something, but she simply didn't have the strength.

Patricia looked at her mother, aware that she was struggling. "Well, we're packing, to move as you might guess," she said, turning back to look at him.

That was it, as if a light bulb had appeared in his mind. Chavards stood looking at him, trying not to smirk, given the difficult circumstances.

"Perhaps we could offer you a lift home with your boxes?" Chavards asked.

Liz was of a mind to refuse, considering her desire to rely on men was at an all-time low, it annoyed her to think that she would even think of agreeing.

"Oh yeah, please," Patricia said. It wasn't obvious if she knew her mother wasn't interested, but she didn't relish the walk back carrying a heavy pile of boxes. Liz just looked at her, deciding it wasn't worth arguing over.

Trilby quickly popped the boot of the car, at which both dropped their piles of flat boxes in. Together they got into the back of the car, immediately aware of how nice and comfortable it was.

"It's a bit better than anything we've been in, this car," Liz said, not entirely interested in idle chatter, but at the back of her mind was the need to ask what, if anything, was happening. It could wait.

As they pulled up into the driveway, short of the motorbike, they stopped, quickly jumping out to empty the car. As Liz walked behind to grab some boxes, Chavards looked at Trilby. It was enough of a nod for him to know what to do.

"Patricia, how about we get these boxes and take them where they're needed?" he said, smiling at her pleasantly. She smiled back, appreciating the kindness.

As they walked away, into the house, Chavards stopped in front of Liz. "Is there somewhere we can go to have a chat, just the two of us?" he asked, aware that the house was open plan, and not wanting to talk in the open.

She knew what he meant immediately, but the moment he began to talk she felt sick, into the pit of her stomach, as if all hope had dropped out of her and was sinking with her life.

"We, we can go into the garage," she said, looking towards the large white door in front of the house. It was built into the place, another space which Jack had often suggested turning into a room instead. Another of his dreams which came to nothing.

Before Chavards could agree, Liz strode over to the door, leaning over to grab its metal handle, and pressed a button, swinging it up and in until it opened. It was empty, save for walls of dusty and barely used tools. As Liz flicked the single hanging light bulb on, Chavards entered, walking closer to her.

This was it, the moment she would find out, one way or another. She wasn't sure she could cope with knowing if he was dead. Her husband, for all his faults, was still the man she had children with, and had spent the best part of her life with. It was all she could think of as she stared at the man who held her future in his next few words. It was intoxicating, but overpowering, the sense of powerlessness, that she was about to be finally swept away in an ordeal of emotion which she would never recover from.

"Right, we have had some conversations with people your husband knew, and as many people as we can. We have traced his whereabouts from the village shops as best as we could, but there are almost no operational cameras in Elton, or the shops, other than in those shops, and he didn't go in them, he went around the back and to all intents and purposes, disappeared."

It was much more than she had expected to hear, more than a simple gesture that he was no longer alive. A thought occurred to her to wonder where the other police officer was, the one she had seen before, Police Liaison. If she were about to be informed of his death then surely she would be there, to comfort her, to provide support for the family.

"Right," Liz said, feeling more than a little confused.

"The problem we have, is that in some circumstances, we are limited in what we are able to do," Chavards suggested, looking at her warily.

It was like a red flag to a bull, the idea that they might actually be giving up on them. "You mean to say," she began, as Chavards raised his hand gently.

"What I mean to say is, in some circumstances we can't say what has happened."

Liz looked at him, as if it were some kind of dream, that in this particular dream he could say something in jest, while discussing the disintegration of her life.

"Is he alive or not?" Liz demanded, out of patience with the metaphorical dance they had played for too long.

"Well, the thing is—" Chavards struggled to say.

"The thing is," Liz mimicked, anger clear in her eyes.

"The thing is, if we knew he were dead, then we would say so, but it isn't such a simple matter. The reality is, some people just don't want to be found, and we as a rule are required to respect that."

Liz felt furious. She knew if he hadn't been a police officer in front of her, she might have finally snapped, and reacted in pure anger. She held on to her anger but wouldn't hold on to her bitter tongue.

"You're useless, it's pathetic. What are we supposed to do with that?" she seethed through gritted teeth.

He knew it would happen, it would come to that. There was always anger and resentment when they told those left behind the news that there was no news. It was difficult enough telling someone their loved one was dead, or that members of a family were gone in an accident, but when you couldn't say what you knew, it felt like you were part of it, some corrupt conspiracy to cover up the indecency of it all.

"I'd say sorry, but I know it's not enough. I'd explain our thinking, but then that might suggest we know something, and we can't do that, because it would in some way explain what we're doing, and thus tell people what we're not allowed to. It's a kind of taking sides, and we can't do that."

"So you're saying you can't tell me where he is, or even if he was alive or not?"

"The way it is, I can't say anything, other than we do not suspect foul play, and that we can no longer proceed with our investigation. I am so sorry, I wish I could do something more, but as a senior officer, I can't."

"What about the others, can't one of those tell us? Anything, just a clue for us?"

Chavards looked down, shaking his head. "We can't, I'm sorry."

"Sorry won't get us anywhere, it won't give us a roof over our heads, it won't give us our lives back, it won't bring me him back, even if we—" she began to say, but refused to finish her sentence. She was angry with Jack, even if it were possible it had happened through no fault of his own, he was still the father of her children, so she would stop there.

Before the inspector could say anything else, she turned to walk away. Instead of walking through the internal door and through the hall to the living room, she walked out of the metal garage door. It was deliberate, so that she wouldn't invite the man into her house, even if it wouldn't be for much longer.

"Thanks for everything, we've got it now," Liz said the moment she saw Trilby. Her voice betrayed her act of trying to hold on to her emotions, but she wouldn't give them the satisfaction of seeing it from her. She knew full well they wouldn't take actual pleasure from the situation, but she needed to express her anger in some way, and Trilby was the focus of it.

"That's fine, I don't mind," Trilby began to say, sounding happier than she was prepared for.

"No, bye, you can leave," Liz insisted as she stood in the living room, arms half folded, unsure of what to do with herself.

Chavards stood outside the door, aware of the tension. He didn't speak, but knew it was time to go. Trilby looked at Liz, then at his colleague. He still wasn't the quickest on the uptake, but even he could see the problem. She had been told. It was time to go.

Trilby briefly looked at Liz, then to Patricia and the others. John was at the table with Dan near him, all looking and waiting, unsure of what was going on. Without another word, he walked across the room, met the gaze of his colleague, and stepped out. Liz quickly followed them until the moment they were out of the house, and then she slammed the door.

"Mom," Patricia said, shocked at her actions. "They were being nice."

Liz hesitated, pausing so that she could control how she felt, but also what she might say. She thought of not saying anything, just leaving it that they had no news, but then that would be worse, because if there was a lie being perpetrated, then she would become a party to it.

"He said they don't know anything, and that the investigation has ended. He said that some people just don't want to be found."

"So he's out there, but doesn't want us to know where?" Patricia asked, looking at her mother incredulously.

"They won't say anything. They say the rules don't allow it, and that they have to stop now and it's ended. He didn't say anything else, and we're on our own."

The silence enveloped the room as each thought about things in a different way. Liz had felt it would be over early on, but still kept hope that he would come back, if only for his children. Patricia was aware of the problems in her relationship with her father, but still he was so important to them, as if his presence held it all together. Dan felt concern, but mostly for himself, if it might cost him. He wanted Patricia, but the last thing he needed was a big family that wasn't his own, or anything approaching responsibility.

"So what's for tea?" John asked, expressing his view on it all. He could be sitting in a tent in a field, surrounded by cows, utterly broke and alone, and his only thought would be food and sleep.

Liz laughed, lightly at first, then more, as the tension they all felt got to her. She shook her head gently, thankful she had him. She envied his innocence, and if that wasn't it, she envied his strength to deal with it all. If she learned nothing else from their ordeal, the very least she would learn from him was to be resilient. It was a good way to be.

19

PAIN AND LOSS FOR FREE

It took two more trips to the Kwik Save for boxes until they had enough for what mattered. Dan had left to pick up a van, and returned with a white Ford Transit van. It was the biggest he had been allowed to borrow from work, but simply not big enough.

"What are we going to do with all the rest of the furniture, and the carpets?" Patricia asked. She was sitting on a box, which sat on top of others, all full of things, taped up well.

"I guess we will either have to offload it, or it will stay here and they can bin it," Liz said. It sounded disheartening for them to hear. As much as they would need new things in wherever they ended up, if it couldn't get there it had to be left.

"Where are we going?" John asked, showing a rare sign of interest in events.

"I guess I will go to a local telephone box, and telephone the housing in Chester, and see what they say. If nothing, then I think we'll be sleeping on the streets," Liz explained.

John looked at her, but the look he gave was difficult to determine if he was being serious. His eyes were lit up, his mouth hanging open in shock horror. Even his sister looked at him twice, second-guessing herself over whether he was being serious.

Liz looked around, as if she were struggling to find her keys, then stopped. She looked ahead as her eyes glazed over. Patricia pulled a chair out from the table before sitting down. The room fell silent, as each in their own way contemplated the coming hours and days.

Without saying anything, almost as if on autopilot, Liz walked out of the room. Even she had no mind over what she intended as she walked up the stairs, oblivious to what was around her. She walked into her bedroom, the one she had shared for so many long years with Jack. Glancing around, she noted the absence of important things: photographs, ornaments, personal things that made a home special, and what made a room in a home their sanctuary. They weren't even out of the door yet but already she felt homeless.

All that remained were the biggest things, the rest either out in the back garden or in boxes. There were the wardrobes, full of clothes which she knew she would never wear again, the drawers likewise, and the bed, looking unkind and far from welcoming. That last night she would sleep on the downstairs sofa rather than be in there, because even if by some miracle he came back, and all was well, she knew it would never be the same again.

The large clock on the wall downstairs struck, chiming loudly, bringing her around a moment. She listened, counting each chord as it struck, three, four, five, six, then stopped. It was six o' clock, getting late, the hours and minutes ticking by and so much to do. Quickly, as if someone might hammer on the front door any moment, she pulled open doors to all of the wardrobes one by one, then the drawers until they were sticking out. She thought of grabbing all of the clothes, hers, Jack's, everything, and opening a window, throwing it all out. A better idea struck her, one that would be an ideal way to say goodbye to it all.

Liz grabbed a handful of Jack's socks and vests from a drawer, bundling them into her arms. She walked out of the room, rushing down the stairs, uncaring if she dropped some along the way.

"Mom, where are you off to?" Patricia asked as Liz burst through the door into the living room towards the front door.

"Don't you mind me, I have an idea," she said, struggling to open the door. She stepped out into the chill air as the orange streetlights threatened weak shade across the gardens. Of course, there was her neighbor outside her front door, talking to someone she didn't recognize. That didn't matter, because she knew Pam would talk to anyone, even a lamp post if it was willing to listen to her gossip.

"Pam, Pamela, darling," Liz said, sounding brash and full of herself.

"Oh," Pam said, looking at her in sheer shock, unsure of what was to come.

Liz walked closer to her, still holding all of Jack's underwear and socks. "I was wondering, would your husband like some of Jack's pants and socks?" she said, without a hint of mocking.

Pam looked at her, as did the woman beside her, both appearing to wonder if the lady had gone mad.

"No?" Liz said, aware that they weren't following her. She dropped the garments in a pile right onto her neighbor's lawn, before grabbing Pam by the arm. "Come with me," she insisted, half-dragging her.

"Well, I'm a bit—" Pam began to say, but Liz refused to give as she tugged her neighbor to follow.

The two went into the house to see the lights were all on, Patricia, Dan, and John sitting around the dining room table, as if in a war conference over what to do about their newly mad mother.

Pam quickly noticed how empty the room was, except for boxes littered around. "Oh, are you decorating?" she asked, still in shock.

"Nope," Liz said calmly, still pulling her along. The two went up the stairs, into the large bedroom.

"Oh, I think I—" Pam began to say, unable to break free. Again she noticed the sparse room, the gaps on the walls where pictures might have been, no sign of the minor things which gave life to a room.

Liz stopped in the middle of the room, released her grip, and looked directly at Pam. "Well, I no longer need or want any of this, so dresses, trousers, blouses, whatever, you can take it. I have jeans, T-shirts, basic clothes all that I need, and what is left here, you can have."

The look on Pam's face said it all, a mixture of confusion and shock, but she would never lose her basic instincts. Liz simply watched, no doubt at all in her mind what the ultimate outcome would be. She expected scorn, even if unsaid, and greed, because it was simply how some people were, and they were poor at hiding it.

"Well," Pam began to say, and Liz smiled. She knew, she just knew. "I guess I could have a look."

Liz simply waited, wondering what to do next as her so-called neighbor leafed through her entire set of clothes, a part of what defined her and who she was, or at least, had been.

As Pam looked through, umming and aahing, enjoying herself, Liz walked out quickly back down the stairs. She had had another idea.

"Mom," Patricia tried again.

"It's OK, love, I know what I'm doing."

"What are you doing?"

"Well, no point in leaving it all here, might as well let others make good use of it."

"But," Patricia said, the sound in her voice finally catching her mother. "What if," Patricia began, but it didn't matter. She could tell from how her mother looked at her that it was over, even if he walked in then and there, the damage was done, even if he was hurt or worse, thing had to change. At least it was obvious her mother was fighting for it, for them. Some would have given up, or sat and waited, cried and complained about how unfair life was. At least she had a mother who would fight for something.

Liz turned and walked out again, walking off down the street. First there was Mrs. Arby, hers was a bungalow, everything nice and prim, an elderly lady prone to occasional gossip but not so obvious with it. She was elderly, white-haired, something of a mystery to others around her, but worth a try. Liz knocked on her door, waited for it to open, and then explained, open house, free clothes and furniture, go see. She didn't wait for an answer, too much to do.

Next up was the Johnsons, a nice enough couple, hello here and there, a son about John's age, but they loved a bargain, or even better, a freebie. Liz recalled a time when Jack had thrown a small party for neighbors and friends, and her kind neighbors had been caught red-handed bagging some of the bottles of drink up. The next day they acted as if it never happened, but Liz never forgot. She often laughed about it, but Jack always bore a grudge. He would never let them in the house again, but of course he wasn't there now. Nothing mattered to him anymore. She felt a sudden pang of guilt; it washed over her as a reminder that she was still married, and he could be dead somewhere. However she felt about that, she still had to deal with what was coming right now, and madness.

"Evening, the house is open, and all of the furniture and clothes in the main bedroom are free. Go have a look," Liz said, struggling to stay cheerful as she spoke to Mrs. Johnson. The response from her was like a large sale sign going up in her favorite store. She could see she was hooked.

Liz didn't wait for an answer, she had more doors to knock on. There were Mr. and Mrs. Climby in the other corner, before those several small houses of people she never spoke to. She called on them all, gave each a few seconds to tell them the sale of the century was on, and all free, and then on to the next, until two dozen houses later the house was filled with people almost fighting over each other to get in, to get access, to get what was free.

One after the other people piled in through the doors, up the stairs, picking and grabbing at things.

Suddenly the back door opened as Liz stepped in. She looked over at her children, and Dan, aware of how distressed they were at the vultures picking at the bones of their lives.

"Don't worry, loves, we'll be gone by tomorrow and soon we'll have our own home, and no one will ever take anything from us again," she said, struggling with it all herself. As difficult as it was, she feared a full final bill for house clearance when they repossessed the house the next day.

"Everything has to go," Liz said, loud enough for everyone to hear.

Without even speaking to her, a young couple approached, each taking one of the dining chairs. "Has anyone asked for the chairs and table?" the young man asked. He was short, with equally short blond hair.

"No, it's there if you want it," Liz replied, at which Dan and her children all stood up, preparing to be left with nothing.

"What about the beds? Can we take the beds?" Mrs. Johnson asked, poking her head around the hall door.

Liz was shocked, she didn't think anyone would take beds in a place such as where they lived. They weren't the richest of people, but nobody was poor. She shrugged her shoulders. "We need those for tonight, but you can get them in the morning if you want them."

Mrs. Johnson nodded, smiling briefly. "I'll stick something on them to say they're ours."

"What, all of them or just mine?" Liz asked.

"All of them, please," Mrs. Johnson said, before disappearing again to see what her husband had poached.

Liz, Patricia, Dan, and John all looked at each other, astonished. None of them spoke, instead simply watching on in awe.

"Have you noticed?" Patricia finally said, breaking their focus.

"Noticed what?" Dan asked, looking as bemused as any of them.

"That no one seems to have asked any of us what's going on. No one has asked why we're giving it all away, or anything," Patricia said. Liz smiled at her truculently.

"Last chance, closing up soon," Liz shouted. She had had enough, they all had.

It only made matters worse, as everyone felt like it was last orders, so they made the most of it. The rats were scurrying, hollowing out their home, and their memories, with things they would never forget. To Liz it was a damned necessity, she just wouldn't give up, because if she did, they might break apart and never recover.

Eventually the pack dwindled, until one or two stragglers carried out lamps, bedding, small tables, odds and ends. It was amazing how quickly a house could become empty, how many dreams built up over the years could vanish like magic, only without the smiles.

The four were finally alone, without even a rug to sit on. The walls, floors, and cupboards were stripped. All that remained were lights, no shades, white and bright, shining on them like a spotlight as if they were on stage. Patricia walked out, up the stairs to her room to see it laid bare. All that remained were the beds, but nobody had thought about anything on them. Far from being covers or quilts, there weren't even pillows, or sheets.

"Mom," Patricia called. Liz followed up, along with John, as Dan remained, pondering whether he could get away with going back to his flat, back to his comfy bed. His only concern that of whether his girlfriend would follow him, or even if he wanted her to.

Liz followed up, feeling hurt but satisfied. She knew what was needed was all safe in the boxes, taped up and protected. As she got to the top of the stairs, she saw her daughter through the open doorway, sitting on her bed. It was obvious she was crying, but trying not to show it.

Without saying anything, she walked in and around the bed, sitting beside her. She placed an arm across Patricia's shoulders, hugging her gently, determined not to let go of her own emotions. There would be a time and place for it, but for now she needed to look after her children.

"I'm sorry it's come to this, and it happened like this, with you and John here," Liz said, quietly and calmly. Patricia continued to cry gently, holding her hands to her face, head bowed, no longer able to keep up the pretense of strength in the face of it all.

"We just have to face up to it, what has happened, and fight to get what we can now," Liz explained, feeling unusually devoid of sentiment.

"I know," Patricia struggled to say. "It's just, until that moment, until right now, I kept hoping he would come back, just turn up, and everything would go back to how it was."

"No, well."

"You didn't think that? Want that?"

Liz shook her head, something she found herself doing more and more lately, whether in response to someone or simply to her own thoughts.

"I knew he wouldn't, but didn't want to say anything. I don't want to burden you or John with anything."

"You need to tell me, even if not John. I'm old enough now to know, so I can deal with it."

"Your dad, it just looks like he left us with lots of debts, and didn't pay anything he needed to. I have the worst feeling for him, for what he might have done."

"You mean, like," Patricia asked, looking up at her mother, almost as if she were holding her breath for what might be said or even thought.

"I honestly have no idea. I don't know anything now. All I can see is we're homeless, and I have two children still living with me, and I need to sort it."

"You didn't ring the housing."

Again Liz shook her head. "No, but if they give emergency, it won't be in time to leave here."

"So, now what?" Liz could feel the tremble in her daughter's hand. It made it so much worse. She was on the threshold of becoming a woman, ready to live her life in her own right, but for all that she was still fragile, still her little girl, needing to be protected.

"Well, I think now we try to get to sleep. Dan needs to go get that van for us, and then in the morning while you three are loading it, I'll go call the housing, and I have another idea or two. When I'm done with that, I'll come back and we'll set off and see where it takes us."

Patricia felt lost by it all, but it was late, and cold, and all she could think of was sleep. They were tired, hungry, and had nothing to look forward to. It was going to be a long night.

"Come on, let's go see Dan, let him know what we need and get John settled."

"There's no bedding," Patricia said, almost daring to laugh about it.

"Yeah, I noticed. We'll have to just pull our coats over and make the best of it," Liz said as she stood. She tried to offer the suggestion that she was in control, certain of what she was doing, but inside she was in turmoil, sickness washing over her, the feeling that she was hanging on by her fingernails. It was as if any moment it could all fall apart.

The two made their way downstairs, going into the living room to see John on the dining room floor. It was obvious he was tired, simply wanting to go to bed, but he still had other ideas.

"What's for supper, Mom?" he asked, as if nothing had happened.

Liz laughed quietly to herself. "Let me look," she said, as if she didn't know the answer. Nobody had taken the electrical equipment, thankfully, though she couldn't help but notice someone had still gone off with the large, round, concrete grass roller from the garden. She could just picture it in her mind, as whoever simply rolled it away down the street, feeling pleased with themselves that they could roll some grass.

"Where's Dan?" Liz asked, looking around.

"He went to get the van," John replied as he leafed through a comic book he had pulled from one of the boxes.

"Oh, he could have waited to go for that," Patricia answered, feeling happier that he was so involved.

"He said he's coming back with it in the morning," John continued, still engrossed with his reading, completely unaware of the impact his words had.

Patricia's eyes lit up, but her mother just looked on, fully aware of how he could be. It was no surprise.

"Right, come on, let's get to bed. Got to be up early in the morning," Liz offered, ready to do just that regardless of what they chose. John didn't say a word, simply standing up with his nose pressed to the comic. She watched him go, envious of his ability to adapt to so much, without a hint of discord or sadness. Patricia was different, but at least she was angry with Dan, rather than dwelling on how their lives were failing around them.

The three went upstairs as Liz clicked off the lights. The air had grown cold and the night grew long. None of them spoke other than to say goodnight, as each took coats and clothing still hung up on the hall rack. It was obvious it was going to be a long night, for all of them.

20

NO PLACE LIKE HOMELESS

The door shuddered with the weight of the knocking, sounding so loud it seemed as if someone was trying to break off its hinges and barge in. John still didn't stir, enjoying the warm autumn sun flowing through his windows, onto his sleepy face.

Liz reacted differently, suddenly lifting her head so quickly, she felt dizzy as her vision spun. Her head ached, sick with the noise of her worries and concerns.

A voice interrupted her pain, forcing away the ache in her limbs from the cold night as her coat did little to maintain her comfort on the empty bed. She didn't have time to think about how naked her room looked, or how alone she was. Now all she could think of was the banging downstairs, as a voice in her head reminded her it was here, the day, the moment had come, they were out, with nowhere to go.

Bang, bang, bang, the door went again. It was obvious it wasn't going to stop. Liz shifted her legs over, off the bed, trying to ignore the immediate pain in her knees, as she felt every second of her age. She dreaded hearing that sound, so pushed herself to move, struggling to open her eyes. For all the fitful nature of it, she had still fallen soundly asleep eventually, drifting off, whether from sheer tiredness or a need to blank it all out. It had left her feeling so drained that every move required huge effort, but again she reminded herself, if it were even necessary to get up and go, that every single thing she did was for them.

"Mom," Patricia called again, now standing by the bedroom door, rubbing her eyes.

"Yeah, I know," Liz said as she plodded wearily down the stairs. It wasn't as cold as she had felt, an unusually warm air around them, a minor intrusion on the natural apathy the season brought, but welcome nonetheless.

As she entered the living room heading towards the door, a large shadow loomed by the side window nearby. It was frosted, so no one could see in, but still it felt ominous. She had visions of opening her door, only to see it crash open as burly men in dark suits rushed in, shouting and screaming their demands. She knew it wouldn't be quite so bad, in her mind, because it was a repossession, not a raid, but still, it didn't stop her from feeling sick.

Breathe, one, two, three, turn the latch, open, accept what is to be. The door opened as Dan stood right on front, peering left and right, looking far more cheerful than anyone should on a day such as this.

"Seriously?" Liz said, louder than she should but quieter than she wanted.

"Morning," Dan offered, smiling. She wondered if he was just a little bit too much like John, lacking where it mattered. At least her son had the excuse of youth to explain his attitude; she wondered what Dan's excuse might be. She could see the van on the driveway, so for all he could be narrow-minded and occasionally useless, she was still thankful for him being there.

"You can come in, but there's no food, I'm afraid."

Dan shrugged his shoulders. "That's fine, I had egg and bacon at home." The statement wasn't lost on her, but she wouldn't waste any more time trying to improve him as a person, she would leave that for her daughter to waste years trying to do.

"Should I open up and start loading?" Dan asked.

"Might as well. It's quite a big van, isn't it?"

"Yeah, bigger than I had expected. I should be able to get everything in, washing machine, cooker, etc., and all the boxes."

"What about us, though?" Liz asked, feeling a moment of unwarranted levity.

"Yeah, no problem," Dan replied. She had at least thought he might pick up on her tone and reply somehow in kind, but of course he was never the sharpest tool in the box.

"All right, love, you get doing that, and I'll get those two up, and we'll sort everything out."

As Liz walked back into the living room, Patricia was heading the other way. They never spoke, but it was obvious things were going to be said. Liz smiled a little, enjoying the moment as short as it was going to be. She thought to suggest she go easy on him, because he was there, but it didn't matter, it was water off a duck's back. Dan would listen to her, not hear a word of what she said, and then carry on loading the van.

"John," Liz shouted from the bottom of the stairs as loud as she could.

John peered over the banister, looking at her. "No need to shout," he said, before sliding away again silently. At least they were all up, with nowhere to go. Now it was up to her.

"I'll go phone the council," Liz said as she struggled to put on some shoes. She thought about sitting on the floor to do it, but wasn't so sure she could get up again, so bent over, regretting her decision.

Patricia walked in through the front door, continuing to carry small items back and forth as Dan tugged away on the cooker, wondering why it wouldn't come loose.

"Er, Dan, that needs removing from the socket," Liz insisted as Dan gave it an almighty tug, pulling away the cooker, wire, socket, and part of the wall.

"Sorry, Mrs. Cornwell," Dan said, dragging the thing away with a large screeching noise.

Liz picked up her purse, opened it, half hoping some money might have magically appeared, and leafed through the back. There were coupons, old bus tickets, and a small pad of numbers. As she flickered through the purse, she came across what was obviously a photograph. The faded white background stuck out to her, but as she flicked it over, she could see a picture of what were supposedly happier times. There she was so many years ago, with John and Patricia much younger, and Jack, looking unusually happy. It was the first time she had taken the time to properly look at a photo of her husband, having handed over pictures of him to the police without even looking. She knew at the time she just didn't have the strength to do it. Now, somehow she had that in her, to look, to think of him, how he was then, how he looked, and how perhaps he might have changed since. There were too many questions that she couldn't answer, but something inside her, the good part of her, the biggest part of her, needed to know.

Quickly dropping it all back into her purse, she went back up and changed. She knew time was a burden, any moment things could be taken out of her hands, so she needed to act.

"I'll be back as soon as I can. If anyone comes, just load up and wait…" Liz said, trailing off. Patricia stopped a moment to look at her, concerned at the way she was behaving. She didn't have the words to express herself, what to say to make a difference, so remained silent. It would be a difficult day for all of them, and nobody had any answers.

The skies were clear blue outside, as if you could dip into them and feel not only reinvigorated, but reborn, so clear and pure that it would wash away your sins. The sun was warm enough so that it kept the chill at bay, and it was dry, so easy to walk. It was the same old road, out of the close, along the rows of charming, polite little houses, the same ones with the same people living the same lives that they were. For a few moments more, anyway.

If anyone spoke, she didn't hear it—she could barely hear her own thoughts. A lady looked at her. She was wearing a light blue raincoat, and had curly white hair. She stopped to look at Liz as she walked, almost in a trance. Liz stopped, lifted the photograph up, and asked her, "Have you seen this man?"

The kind, white-haired lady shook her head. "No. Isn't that—" she replied, but all Liz could hear was *no*. She moved on.

There was Mister Traishaw with his dog, walking several times a day, as much for himself as the dog. "Have you?" Liz asked, not hearing the rest of her words, but the thin, frail man shook his head, and asked, "Isn't that—"

Liz moved on.

There was a young lady with a little girl. They looked happy, if that was what happiness was. "Have you seen this man?" Liz asked, and they shook their heads. He had vanished, but it seemed as if he did so long ago, so much she wondered if he had never even been there, that she only imagined he was there, a ghost who comforted her in her loneliness.

Liz stumbled, almost falling, but not quite. Her head was a mess, out of sorts and struggling to keep it all together. Images flashed in her mind of times with Jack, when they were young. He would be so funny, so handsome, but not always happy. She tried to picture in her mind how he looked when she told him she was pregnant with Patricia, only no smiles came forth. All she could see was the last morning they were together, that unhappy look, the frown, the sense that he had been gone long before he did. Again she felt guilty, feeling he had simply walked out when he may well be injured or dead. He was the father of her children, she wouldn't forget again.

As if she were floating along on mindless air, Liz came back to the shops. There was the phone box, to make the call, or calls. First she would go into the shops to show the photograph and hope.

The newsagents shop stood out at the side of the alleyway he had gone through and disappeared into time. Walking to the door, she stopped, looking around, trying to imagine what he might have felt. Tears ran down her cheeks as she felt numb to the pain. She walked ahead a little, looking at the small waste ground behind, way over a row of houses, a small road for deliveries. There were cars, and signs that life existed, but no people. This was a place where people didn't inhabit, instead a place where they went to enter nothing, become just a memory, and when they were gone, not even that. He wasn't there, and no sense of him being there.

People were kind, the platitudes, the reassurances, the arm around, the smiles. People did care, they tried their best, but they all had their own lives, as difficult in different ways to hers. No one knew anything.

Without noticing, she came upon the telephone box, as if it had moved, and waited to be near her, so she could get on with her life. It was like a doorway to where she had to go, and all until that moment had been deliberations, procrastination, designed to ward off the inevitable. She had coins in the pocket of her coat, as if they too were part of an inevitable cycle that was developing itself. She gave herself up to it.

Coin in, number dialed, everything automatic, including her.

"Good morning, Chester Council, Housing Department, can I help you?"

"Hello, my name is Elizabeth Cornwell. I came in the other day to apply for emergency housing. I was told to telephone to see if you could help me. I'm going to be fully homeless today." How she spoke, what she said, surprised even her, how clear she had been in contrast to how she felt, but it reminded her again how strong she was, how she could be when there was a need, for her children, if not herself.

"All right, let me check." Music interrupted as she was placed on hold.

Liz waited, looking around, flashes of thought that she might see him, he might drive up, back from work to call in for something before going home. It was like losing a limb, he was the phantom limb she could still feel, next to her, a part of her. She couldn't be sure if she even wanted him back now. If he were to show up, she knew she would be angry, but she would give in, even so late as it was. They were moving out of their home, and had nothing left of value, so deep in debt, and she was so hurt, and yet she would forgive him. That was the worst of it, because she would forgive him for failing her, and their children, but when she did, she would never forgive herself for accepting her own weakness, her own failings, her acceptance of their joint failure.

If only. If only that were an option, it was like the dreams of scratching a ticket, or watching numbers appear on the television and hoping they would match hers, to give the money to release their dreams, as if it were some kind of doorway to happiness.

As she waited, listening to the faint classical music on the other end of the line, her thoughts drifted to her mother, and to the things she had seen and heard growing up. She suddenly remembered the optimism her mother had for her when she was so young, a profound belief that she would amount to something, but whatever it was, the most important thing was that it was a life of happiness. When she thought of her children, she thought of love, and she smiled, of happiness too. When she thought of her husband, the man of her life, of so many years, she felt love, and passion, and friendship, and respect, all the elements she was taught were needed for a relationship to work. Still, she asked herself, she finally allowed herself the question: was she happy, with him? She had gotten that far, to be able to ask the question, but the answer might take a bit longer.

"Hello, Mrs. Cornwell?"

"Yes, I'm still here," Liz replied, her voice breaking as she felt a dryness in her throat.

"Right, you've applied for emergency housing, for yourself and your children."

"Yes, that's right."

"Right. We have nothing available."

"What do you mean? You're the Council, you're supposed to help the homeless. You have a legal obligation to help us." She was only guessing, desperately torn between crying or screaming at the woman on the other end. Moments of silence passed.

"Hold on please," the woman offered. Liz almost laughed, unable to bear the tension, the worry. There would be no miracles, no happy endings today, but this, this was too much. An image presented itself to her, of them sleeping in the van. She could picture setting up a tent in someone's beck garden, it was all so surreal now.

"Hello."

"Hello," Liz said, gripping the phone handle tighter as she put more coins in. "Look, I know this isn't your fault, I have two children, and I'm desperate because my husband has just disappeared, and nobody seems to either care or want to help us. Please..." she said, trailing off as the hurt finally took hold of her. Tears rolled down her cheeks as she trembled, both hands on the phone handle, finally out of hope.

"Hold on again please," the woman said, her voice slightly different, lower, as if she were sharing the moment. Liz didn't speak; words refused to form in her mouth as she let it all go, a flood of sorrow for the loss of everything that mattered in her life.

The line crackled as the woman returned. Liz listened intently. Surely they had a heart, surely being there someone would care.

"Can you not split up, put your children into care, and you go into bed and breakfast?" the woman asked.

To Liz the suggestion was so profoundly awful that it took her breath away. Her mind reeled, looking not only for a response which would give a strong enough answer, but one that fully conveyed her horror at which she felt, the revulsion she felt for such a terrible question. She wanted to ask what kind of person could even utter such a thing, what kind of person would want that on another, but as much as she struggled to come to terms with it, she couldn't find an opening to what was needed.

"No, no, I won't split up my family. We will stay together, and even if you won't help us, we will fight to be together. I'll do what it takes for my children, and we will have a home," Liz said, tears giving way to anger, as she felt the difference within her, not an awakening, but an acknowledgment that she was always strong enough to deal with the problems of life, she had just not tried until now. Now she had no choice.

Silence resumed, which felt like a needle pressing into her temples. She felt that anything she said from that point on would be futile, and that there would have to be a plan B.

"Ring us again please, in a few days, and we will let you know what we can do. It's the best we can do at this time." Liz thought for a moment to fly off into a rage, to let loose on this unforgiving woman everything she felt, but now wasn't the time.

The line went dead, whether due to lack of money paid in, or someone hung up. Whichever didn't really matter, all that was left was her holding on to the handle, as if it were her last thread to normality. When the chips were down, when she and they had nothing left, not even hope, everything and everyone had failed them. It would be the lowest she would ever go. At least from this point on there could surely only be better.

Liz fumbled around in her pocket, feeling the last of the coins. A thought struck into her mind of a time when she had been out with her sister, they had found a purse, and in it were pennies. When opened, they both felt as if they were rich, they could own the world, and anything was possible. They took out the small coins, worth little, and took them to the local shops, and bought sweets, a bag of sherbet sweets and some licorice each. They shared a bottle of fizzy pop, and walked home in the sun feeling closer than they ever did after. Then they got home, and mom saw them, and asked where it had all come from. The truth hurt, and they paid a great price, early to bed, no sweets for weeks, no radio. Mom was their rock, always was, always would be.

Liz knew she could trade those last few coins she had now for another plea for help, but it became clear in that moment who she might go to in her moment of need, the one person who would give her anything, and do anything for her. She picked some out, pressed them into the slot and dialed the number she knew so well, then waited.

"Hello."

"Mom."

"Liz, oh, I've been so worried about you. Where are you?" her mother asked. Her voice was a little more distant, softer, but still that same love and warmth. That voice was the reassurance she needed, there was somebody else in the world that would be with her, without question.

"Mom, I need help."

"Ohm Liz, tell me, what's the matter?"

Liz stuttered, struggling to hold on to her emotions, mindful of the call time running out, and she had no money left. She imparted what she could, and waited.

"So, that's it. You're putting what you have left into a small van, and don't know where you're going?" her mom asked, sounding pained in a way a mother does over her child. The distance between them wasn't huge, from Elton to Yorkshire, only a few hundred miles, but in such a time, with so little left to hold on to, it might as well have been on the other side of the world.

"Yeah, well, we have each other. But I don't know where to go," Liz replied, her voice mirroring how she felt, tired, defeated.

"Who's driving it?"

"Dan, Patricia's boyfriend."

"Can you not ask him to bring you here?" Liz felt herself deflate even more, if it were possible.

"I, well, I don't want to go back home. It feels like I've failed."

Her mom laughed softly. "No, love, you haven't failed. Other people have failed you. You're there fighting for your family, and your kids. Come back, for a short while, and then work out how you'll get going again."

Liz nodded to herself. She was out of ideas and out of options. "All right, Mom," she said, breathing in deeply, a glint of change, something to offer a way forward. "Has Brenda told you—" she began to ask.

"Yes, a little. It's OK, we can talk when you come here."

"Thanks, Mom," Liz offered, those selfsame words she had spent a lifetime saying. Her own mother had been through difficulty and adversity, and now she had hers, and they would learn how alike they truly were.

"See you soon."

"Yeah. Bye, love."

"Bye."

Liz hung up, walked out of the telephone box and away, her mind absent of much thought, other than what was needed. She never looked back, knowing she never wanted to see the place ever again.

As she rounded the corner to the close, she had expected to see either nothing going on, or perhaps with luck at least Patricia and

Dan doing something. Instead the van was closer, with the two of them in the front, waiting.

"Where's John?" Liz asked. Patricia wound the window down as her mother walked up.

"He's in the back, squashed between boxes," Patricia replied. There was a space beside her, ready for one more person.

"Have you done it? Have you really emptied it all out, all the stuff?" Liz asked.

"Yep, we had to be quick. Didn't have much choice," she replied, briefly looking over to the front of the house before looking back at her.

Liz quickly turned to see a white poster stuck on the front door of the house, covered in red writing.

"They changed the locks, front and back, while we sat here," Patricia explained. She sounded muted, as if she felt no emotion over the matter.

Liz didn't respond, aware of the twitching curtains from the window next door. She could feel a sense of eyes on them, and interest that had no care to it. No one would come out to enquire of their problems, nobody would say a word in support. It was the nature of the place they had lived, and of the people who lived around them. She wondered if it might be a reflection of who they also were, uncaring, thoughtless to others, no better. She promised herself in that moment that in their new life, they would do better. *She* would do better.

"Right, Dan, I need you to drive us, no questions asked, and help us with this stuff. All right?" Liz explained. Dan felt it was mildly ominous, but he knew he couldn't argue. He could see how bad things were, he wouldn't make it worse.

Liz pulled open the door, stepped in, and beckoned they drive. Dan put the van in gear, backing out before turning slowly to drive. John couldn't see a thing, but he was laid well enough, comics in hand, drinks at the side, and was happy. Patricia looked slowly at the house, the place she had grown up in, watching every second as Dan pulled gently away. Liz looked ahead, empty, devoid of any emotion towards the place. She saw nothing, and cared about not one bit of it. What she cared about moved away in the van with her. She left Elton, determined never to go back. There was nothing there for her anymore.

21

MOM KNOWS BEST

Bessie replaced the dark red-handled receiver of the telephone. It was an old circular dial type, but one that she liked and had been reliable enough, so she wouldn't change it. She had lost count of the amount of times that her other daughter Brenda had called to enquire what she knew of little sister coming up. All she knew was it would be any time now, and likely would not be for long.

Outside was dark, but not too dark to see, as orange sodium lights flooded the back alleyways. She had lived in the house longer than she could remember, since The War, and seen so much change and things happen. One thing that never changed was the whims and mercies of people, the ones she loved and the ones she knew. People had come and gone, moved near, moved away, become close and died, but her daughters always remained there for her.

As she sat, the television played in the background, Coronation Street played its signature tune, a pleasant enough note that her favorite program was beginning, but still also a welcome distraction from being alone. Bessie took a poker and prodded the small open fire, sparks flying around from the brittle coal as it became engulfed in heat. It was a nice home, comfortable and warm amidst the chill weather creeping in. Yorkshire was rarely known for being particularly sunny, but with winter approaching, direct heat was always a welcome guest.

As much as she felt happy at the thought of seeing her

grandchildren again soon, and Liz, she couldn't help but feel saddened at the prospect of what was happening to their lives. She had been all too aware of the problems life could throw up, remembering the bitter heartache of an accident on the local steelworks, and the months dragging out as her husband struggled to cope with the serious injury, and live for them. They were hard times, no money coming in, no future, children to worry about. At least she had the experience of knowing she could survive it, come out the other side and find a life still full of love and reasons to be happy.

It would also help her forget the pain, as she rubbed her arthritis-wracked wrist. Her knees ached so much that the pain had become part of her, as if it were a normal part of existence. It didn't matter, it wouldn't have to, because she had other things to be thankful for.

Bessie looked at the clock, wondering how long they might be. Nine would be the time she would usually crawl up the stairs of the old terraced house, climbing slowly into bed, and then sipping from a lovely small glass of whiskey. It was a small treat, but a necessary one, and which made life just a bit more bearable.

As the television blared out once again the end of her program, the clock began to strike, seven, eight, nine. Dead on the strike of nine, a thud in the hallway, a commotion, voices and cool air coming through the gaps in the door from the hallways.

As Liz pushed the door open, light spilled out onto her, the same kind of off-white light she remembered all her life, growing up in the place. Somehow it all felt natural again, as it always did when she returned. That feeling of being home would never last; as days passed, she would feel the urge, the bug, as if having been bitten by a beetle, leaving her with a nagging sense that it was time to go back to her real home. That she always did, but not now.

"Mom," Liz said, dropping a handful of carrier bags to the floor. There she was, her mom, sitting there in a small wooden dining chair, next to the fire, beside the television which was always on. It looked and felt like a scene from a Christmas card, with a kindly old lady sitting there. All it needed was a cat to set the perfect scene, but of course she knew her mother couldn't cope with it. Her mother had those eyes, behind faded pink glasses, but still, those eyes which were so full of kindness, and suggested a naturally happy smile, pleased for company but so pleased to see the people she loved the most.

They hugged, mother and daughter, but it wasn't a welcoming

hug, a natural hello, but one that felt different, an obvious need, as if her daughter might collapse any moment in her arms, so weary and lost.

"Hello, Liz, are you all right?" Bessie asked, doing her best to cuddle her daughter, but her arms were weak and aching from unending pain.

"I'm OK, Mom. We're surviving just," Liz said, determined to hold it together, until they might be alone. She was the little girl in mother's arms, needing a hug to make it all better. It seemed that would never change. "Don't know what I'd do without you," Liz continued, wanting to say more but not wanting to see her mother cry.

As she backed off, trying to regain some sense of composure, Bessie looked at the children, both grown so much, looking so different, even though she knew it was only months since she had seen them.

Patricia stood, looking more a woman than ever, a beaming smile on her face, clearly happy to be there. Then there was John, looking as grumpy as ever, but then he obviously needed a hug, not to mention food. Patricia went first, quickly but gently leaning in to hug her Gran. For her, there were no regrets, just happiness to be there. She was too young to dwell on things, too strong to worry about it—she had confidence and belief in coming through, and it showed.

"Hello, Gran."

"Wow, look at you, so grown up," Bessie offered, sounding so cheerful that her voice broke.

Patricia stood up and back a bit as Bessie looked at Dan and smiled gently. He returned the smile, feeling awkward, but they had met, and it was fine. Bessie looked for John, expecting a hug from him, but he was looking away, into the kitchen, as always.

"What's for supper?" John asked. He didn't have to worry about convincing anyone of how hungry he was, his stomach did that for him as it rattled away, gurgling its empty displeasure.

Bessie laughed to herself, looking at him. "Every time I see you, you seem to have grown a foot taller," she said as everyone laughed with her. Everyone except John, who was sure he was going to pass out from hunger.

"I'm hungry, Mom," John insisted, as if he needed an intake of life essence simply to exist.

"I'll get you something in a moment," Liz insisted.

"Go feed him, he has a lot to fill. It's those hollow legs of his, food goes all the way down," Bessie replied as again everyone laughed. "There's bread, and cheese, and I've done some baking, some Cornish pasties, so let him get what he wants."

The thought of pasties almost made him pass out. She made the best he had ever had, full of potato and carrots and pieces of meat. It always tasted so sweet, and with that fresh-baked pastry, he always ended up eating all that she had. It only then occurred to him that he could smell them, and without waiting went into the kitchen to see trays of food all over. Bessie had been a baker, and Brenda was a baker. It was special to them and showed. Without asking, John grabbed one, stuffing it into his mouth.

"Pig," Patricia said, aware of how she was sounding. "Umf," John replied, unable to speak with his mouth being so full.

"Cut it out, please," Liz said.

Bessie again laughed. "Some things don't change," she said, looking at Liz.

"No," Liz said, frowning.

"Erm, what should I do with all the stuff?" Dan asked politely. As ever, in the back of his mind was the desire to get away. He was happy to help, to a degree, but always ensured he kept a particular distance from their troubles, for fear he should suffer with them.

Patricia looked at Liz, who in turn looked at Bessie.

"Dan has to take the van back, and we have to unload our stuff," Liz explained.

"Well, can't you just put it into the front room?" Bessie replied.

"There's quite a lot of things, suitcases, boxes, and a few things from the kitchen."

"Well, you can put the kitchen things in there," Bessie said, pointing to the kitchen where John was making himself sick.

"No, we brought the washing machine and a few things like that."

"Oh," Bessie said.

"We have no way of knowing if I'll be able to get anything else, so couldn't afford to leave it."

"Well, don't mess around, put the big stuff in the back shed and the boxes in the front room," Bessie snapped. She was a kind and loving woman, but knew how to ensure control and order.

"Right," Liz said, as if they all suddenly stood to attention. Dan went first as the three went to work.

"You too, greedy," Bessie said, shouting to John. She could be loud when she needed to, and it was enough as he scurried past from the kitchen, mouth full of food while holding an unreasonably large piece of cheese.

They worked hard to get it done. As they emptied the last of it, Liz returned to the front room, back to her mother. Bessie was as always sitting beside the dying fire, looking tired.

"Mom, why don't you go on up?" Liz asked, pushing the hall door closed to keep the heat in.

"No, come on, let them do it," Bessie replied mischievously.

Liz looked back, thought about it and then agreed, pulling out a chair from the opposite side of the small square dining table Bessie was at. As she sat down, she breathed out wearily, not just from tiredness, but from all of the mental and physical fatigue she had felt for far too long.

Immediately Liz could feel those eyes on her. Her mother didn't need to say a word, but of course she always knew. She didn't have to say or ask much, but the bond between them was always so strong that words didn't matter.

"Are you all right?" Bessie asked, not because she didn't know the answer, but because she knew if she didn't ask, Liz would never say a word to her about it.

Liz nodded, resting her chin on her hands as she leaned heavily on the table. "So-so," she replied, feeling a well of emotion inside again. It was like a squirming beast inside her, always threatening to unleash itself on anyone nearby.

"That much, eh?"

Liz smiled. "I don't know what to do. Jack has just upped and gone. We thought something bad had happened, but the police said they looked, did all sorts of checks and now they won't talk to us."

Bessie frowned. "They can't do that. That's not right."

Liz shrugged. "Well, for the moment all I could focus on was getting somewhere to live, with the kids. Now I'm sorted I'll keep trying to get our own place, and once I have that, I will have to go and try to find out myself what's going on, why they won't help and who will."

Bessie pushed her frail hand across the table to her daughter, looking into her eyes, remembering the whole life they had shared, how some things never changed, and that look, whether tired, happy, sad, or angry, she was always Elizabeth. A real survivor.

Liz looked down at the table, feeling the tips of her fingers, more a reassurance that she was safe now, home for as long as she needed to be. For too long she had held her back against the wall, alone, struggling against others who simply didn't care. She had begun to wonder if there was no one left in the world that did care, about anything. Now, now she had her proof that wasn't right. She was thankful for the love and kindness, but it was always typical of home, in Yorkshire.

"Well, you have a home here now, all of you. Stay as long as you need."

Nothing more was said between them. Bessie knew her daughter would handle it, because she herself had been through so much loss, so much hurt and heartache. She knew that Liz would manage, because they were alike.

Patricia and John walked in to see mother and grandmother nattering away over two cups of tea, acting as if they had been there years.

"All done?" Liz asked.

"Yeah," Patricia replied.

"I think we had best get to bed," Liz suggested.

"Yeah, I guess so. Dan emptied the van and went," Patricia said, as if she were simply conveying what time it was, of no importance to them.

"Went where?" Liz asked.

"Well, he said to take the van back, but I think he just wanted to go home, to his flat."

"Really?" Liz said, looking perplexed. What she said and what she felt were two different things. She held on to the fact that she was angry and disappointed in him. She wondered if it were a thing now, how all men were going to be. It was easy to think so.

The look on Patricia's face didn't suggest surprise. Instead, it simply seemed as if she were tired. Anything more she knew wouldn't be said.

"Well, one less bed needed, I guess then. Let's go up," Liz suggested, at which they all made preparations to go.

"Mom, do you need any help?"

"No, love, you go on and I'll find my way up," Bessie insisted.

"I've been here managing long enough now, so I think one more night doing it won't matter."

Liz half smiled, before turning to go up. They knew where to go, having been so often to see her, as much as possible.

The house was like a relic from the past, with a large stone step up into the front door from outside, with no front garden and eave windows leaning out onto the street. In days gone by, all of the chimneys would be billowing smoke, and Bessie, along with others, could be seen on her knees scrubbing the steps, sweeping the street, and keeping a good house. Though the house had often been decorated, it still maintained an old-world charm, with small square light switches and power sockets sticking out from the wall, with a fragile switch for on and off. The fact that the house still had an open fire in the back room was enough to show its age, and that of the lady that called it her home.

The front room was a show room, decorated and maintained perfectly, but rarely ever lived in. It had a sofa, chairs, wooden cabinets, and fine pictures, all the trappings of an old-style luxury home. Even the carpet was thick and plush, not from being expensive, simply because it was never used to the flow of life.

The back room was cozy and functional, more like a cross between a dining room and a laundry room, with clothes across airers dotted around the place. Here on the walls were pictures of family, more emotive and intimate, a constant reminder of happiness, joy, and love. If Bessie had nothing else in her life, she had those memories, a long and deep reminder of the way she had lived her life, and instilled in all of those around her a sense of being right, fair, and good.

The kitchen appeared an extension out towards the back of the house, leading into an old, no-longer-used toiled, and a storage shed. The entire place was functional, holding all the utilities she would ever need, where her love of baking came alive. They were her offerings to anyone who would come in, through the back way, and those people numbered in the many, to see her, to hear her tales of experiences, not to mention that fine food.

Upstairs was a new bathroom and several bedrooms, all large and staid. The wallpaper reminded of the age when the rooms were freshened up, and the beds so solid they felt as if it would be like lying on a tree.

As Liz walked up the stairs, John and Patricia went ahead, aware of where they would be sleeping, having done so regularly since birth.

The Village of Carlin Howe wasn't a big place, on the edge of the old steel works and not far from the coast, but it was a busy place for all that. The people appeared not to have changed over time, as attitudes of respect and a quiet way were common. There were few things to do, but for a time it would be a nice place to visit, and there was always someone out doing something simple but fun.

John stopped at the doorway to his bedroom and looked back. Liz half expected him to ask for more food, but he appeared far more thoughtful.

"What's up, love?" Liz asked.

"How long are we going to be here?" John asked.

"Not long. If I don't get any response from the Council, I'll go back by myself, and sit in there and wait until they agree to help us."

"Quite a while, maybe?"

"No, a week or two, I won't allow any longer. Whatever it takes, I'm going to get us a home."

John smiled. "Cool," he said.

"Really? What's cool?" Patricia asked, wondering if she should even ask. She knew what he was like.

Again John smiled, pleased with himself. "I guess that means I get a two-week holiday," he said, beaming.

"Ha," Liz snapped wistfully. "You're back to school the moment we get a house," she insisted, at which John's face dropped like a brick.

"You dare to say such a terrible word," John mocked.

Patricia laughed. "Yep, back to school, back to all your favorite lessons."

John sneered at her. "Be gone, fools," he said, his voice deep as he puffed his chest out, before turning into his room and slamming the door gently.

Liz and Patricia both laughed. For Liz it was a good thing. He always seemed able to remain positive, so upbeat, and no matter what happened, he could always find humor and enjoyment in the smallest things, in the worst circumstances.

"Goodnight, Mom," Patricia said, entering her own room. Liz gave her a brief hug and bade goodnight before going into her room.

Hers was the smallest of the rooms, an oblong box room, used sometimes for storage, but it had a bed and some drawers. When she had visited her mother, Jack had never gone with them, appearing to prefer his own company than consider being on what was a fun holiday for them. She was used to being apart from him in this place, but never had the time to think of anything that might be wrong. She had spent far too long thinking of family, and what needed doing next. Next was all there was, to the point that it seemed in her own mind she no longer existed.

Liz sat on the bed, looking out of the tall but narrow window. She could recall living in the house with her sister, the enjoyment and fun that they had shared. Bessie had been good to them, providing as well as she could, but when her husband died, both girls were young, and of course so long ago it was a fight simply to survive.

She flicked off the light from the hang-down pull cord and simply watched outside. The air was cool, but it didn't matter. How she felt affected everything about her. For all her hurt and upset over Jack being missing, somehow she felt different. It was difficult to pinpoint what it was, but for all the nightmare engulfing them, at her center she felt a sense of hope, a spark of purpose that had been missing for longer than she could remember.

22

FINDING HOME

Bessie sat hunched over the cold fire, as she always was, soon after the first ashes of the night had passed. It was cold, but she was used to it, ignoring the pain in her fingers as she shuffled the brittle fire brush as dead coal and embers fell onto the collecting pan below. It was a routine she considered as much her life as anything. She would roll up sheets of the previous day's newspaper, and tie them into paper logs. Then she would walk slowly, holding a small brass coal scuttle, out into the back shed. Down it would go, onto the floor, and there she would take her well-worn long-handled spade, so small but good enough, and scoot some pieces of coal into it. It would be just enough for the day ahead, for the cold time, which to her seemed more and more often. Then she would bend over, slowly, carefully, picking up the scuttle, just about managing, and back to her seat, the place where she felt most at home.

It was the best part of it, putting the paper logs into the freshly swept fireplace, then one by one putting small pieces of chopped wood in place. That was one thing she couldn't manage. She couldn't get out to get the wood, so kind Mister Barker from up the road, he went for her, once a week, kindling in a bag, and opened it before putting it in place as a stack on her hearth. That had been a tradition so long, and before that was kind Mrs. Webley, and before her kind Mister Treat. So many good and kind people, but Bessie didn't realize it was she that brought the kindness out in them, the goodness, which reflected who she was.

With a few pieces of wood on top, then would go a dozen pieces of coal, and then a match, the smell of sulfur, the white smoke rising, dropped into the pile, and wait. It was as much a ritual as a chore, because it signified the beginning of her day, as its warmth spread throughout the room and eased her movement, so she could think and feel, and prepare for breakfast.

As the flames crackled, Bessie leaned her hands on her knees, mindful of the pain in her joints. She could see the swelling all around. There would be no getting better, only managing, but as long as she was alive, she would live it as best as she could. She leaned forward, pressed as best as she could, and began to lift herself, ready for the daily trip for breakfast.

"Hey Mom, hold on. What are you doing?" Liz asked, enough so that she could impress her concerns, but not loud enough to make her mother jump. That was the last thing she needed.

Bessie dropped back again onto the seat, looking up at her daughter. "Well, I was going to get something cooked."

"Mom, I can do it. I'll do something for us both," Liz said. As she looked at her mother, it seemed in some ways she never changed. She was always dressed as best as she could, in a smart dress, even if it was old, and soft slippers across her swollen feet. Her hair was done once a week by a lady that called for a wash and set, and white as her hair was, it looked big and curly and made her feel special again. She would look at people with a strong but sensitive gaze, but her features, her demeanor, and when she smiled, it reassured, that as disciplined with herself and others as she was, she cared very much.

"I don't mind," Bessie replied, and it was true. She would never complain, and viewed her entire routine as a good one, one that made her feel proud, because she would go on, no matter what tried to hinder her.

"I know, Mom, but I'm here for now, so maybe let me do stuff, and you have a bit of a break?" Liz said, her expression pained, as if she worried too much for her. She knew complaining about it would do no good—her mother was too independent for that—but it needed to be said, if only to show how she felt.

"That's fine," Bessie said, shocking Liz. It was usually something of an ordeal to convince her to sit a while. Still, even if she went to do something, it was obvious her mother would get up and go in to join in. Deep down she didn't mind, it was all the more special to still be able to do things together.

Liz looked behind the kitchen door, picking an apron from a hook. She placed it over her head and tied it off before retreating into the kitchen. The place was full, if a little haphazard. She knew her mother had everything she needed to cook, prepare, and clean after, anything that one could ever need.

"Would you like some egg and bacon?" Liz asked, at which Bessie smiled.

"You're up early," Bessie said before Liz could walk away.

"Yeah, I woke up and couldn't sleep. I didn't fancy lying there feeling sorry for myself, so I came down."

"So you thought you'd come down here and feel sorry for yourself?" Bessie asked, smiling at her. It was obviously a small joke, but with her it was never just that. Liz thought for a moment, but knew what she was getting at. It was a message not to dwell on things, because as she always said: worry sure keeps you busy, but it don't get you no place.

"I know, I know, chin up, keep going, get on with it," Liz said mockingly, trying to deflect attention.

"Make us a cup of tea, love," Bessie said, her voice softer. That always did it, not the stern words, not the lecture, or the hard stare, but the softening of her voice, the emotion in what she said. Liz felt she might crumble, but instead walked out, agreeing to do so.

At one time the window outside looked out into large fields and was a beautiful greeting to the outside world as the sun rose in the morning. Occasionally people would walk past, waving to Bessie, but often it would be the veg man, or the butcher or someone delivering. Her days were filled with people coming to and fro, never dull, and the sights she would see were a constant reminder of her past and her home. As with all things, change had taken over, as fields had given way to a growing housing estate. People that passed were often supermarket delivery, or parcel delivery, and the waves for good morning grew less. For all that, Bessie never changed; to her it was a window to the world, and she had the best seat available.

Liz brought two cups of tea, both in saucers. She preferred mugs of tea, but knew her mother still clung to old standards. Sugar was in a bowl on the table, with a small silver spoon always available. She placed them down, pulled out a chair, and sat down.

"So, how are you, Mom?" Liz asked, cupping the tea, as if it were the cup of life. Its heat spread throughout her hands, a welcoming moment to think and switch off.

"I was going to ask you the same thing," Bessie replied. She took the spoon, dropped a slither of sugar into the cup before stirring it, dropping the spoon and ignoring the cup.

Liz smiled. "So-so. Patricia and John are coping well enough, and I'm still managing. I was worried about Jack, but didn't say much, but since then all I could focus on was the house, where we were going to live."

"I didn't think things were bad between you?"

"No, well, neither did I. Turns out he left us with a lot of debt, and didn't pay the mortgage for months. I think he left us long before he actually did." Liz looked down at the table, feeling empty, wondering if she was at a dead end in life.

"So you think he might have just left, that's it?"

"I don't know. I'm scared he might have done something bad to himself, and might still do. I have no idea."

"The police haven't helped?"

"They did, but it just stopped, and they say they can't say why. I don't know where else to turn."

"There must be someone, some place you can go."

Liz shrugged, her mind reeling for answers. "Maybe after I have a cup of tea, I'll have a think, look through the yellow pages."

Bessie smiled slightly, picking up her tea and sipping. She felt concern for her daughter, but as much as she was worried for her future, it bothered her to think that she seemed so apathetic to it.

"What about a place to live? I love having you here, but school for John, and Patricia is growing up so fast, she needs—"

"I know, Mom," Liz interrupted.

Each wanted to say something more, but didn't for fear that whatever they said might be wrong. It felt like a powder keg waiting to go off, one wrong word and it would be a mess.

They sat in silence, each sipping on their tea. Bessie was simply glad of a moment's peace, but enjoyed being with her daughter.

Both jumped as the door slammed open. Brenda walked in, carrying bags of shopping, huffing and puffing. "Liz, oh, it's so good to see you."

Liz turned quickly to see, her heart sinking, but her face lighting up. "Hello, Brenda," she said, standing up and turning to hug. Brenda dropped the bags where she stood, leaning to hug her sister.

"Mom, why didn't you tell me they had gotten in? I'd have come earlier."

Bessie looked at her, and played quiet. It was obvious why she hadn't said anything, but it didn't need saying.

"Well, I'm here now, even if you have brought cold in with you."

"Oh, sorry, I'll shut the door, but it's getting icy out there now. At least there's a nice fire," Brenda replied, moving to kiss Bessie on the cheek. Straight away she moved to stand in front of the open fire.

"Hey, don't hog all the heat," Bessie snapped. There it was, that famous old mother's bark, move or else. They had heard it so long, they were used to it. Her bark, thankfully, was worse than her bite.

Brenda stepped back, mindful not to go too far. It didn't matter how old they were, she would always be their mother, and always in charge. She had worn a flowery silk scarf to protect her hair, always careful for how she looked. As she settled, she removed a faded green coat, but underneath looked immaculate with a fine-thread pink cardigan and billowing trousers to match. Her life had never been so simple, but she made the most of it, and showed a determination to live life on her own terms, which Liz to date had never been able to match.

"So, what do you have planned, sis? Shopping with me?" Brenda asked. Her cheerfulness grated, but all the same Liz envied her apparent innocence, as if she didn't need to have a care in the world.

"Yeah, maybe a bit of shopping, get some new clothes, some new shoes," Liz said brightly.

"Oh lovely, I like the sound of that," Brenda beamed. Though they were both similar ages, she always seemed to sound much younger. No matter how hard life got, she still maintained a happy outlook, and always a smile for her sister.

"Then maybe we can go buy some carpets, and some curtains, and maybe a new home for me and John and Patricia, us being homeless and all," Liz said abruptly. The moment she said it she regretted it, as Brenda's face dropped, her mouth open in shock, as much hurt as surprised.

"Oh, no, I'm sorry," Brenda said, much quieter. She looked away, unsure of what to do.

"Oh, I'm sorry. I shouldn't have said that," Liz said, feeling lower than she could ever imagine. Nothing seemed to be going right for her, and now she was her own worst enemy.

"Both of you stop feeling sorry for yourselves, and get on with it. Life does this to you, and sometimes people do as well. You pick yourself up, you don't complain about it, you get on with it. The day you stop living is the day you die, and anything that comes to hurt you, that's life. Deal with it," Bessie said. Any suggestion of emotion or tears were washed away. Any thoughts of regrets or dissent were ignored. Mom always knew best, and after the life she had lived, nobody could argue with her.

"Yes Mom," Brenda said.

"Yes Mom," Liz said.

It was like old times, all together, often so poor, but life was simple, and they were happy then. Both suddenly laughed at how it had turned out.

"You're right, Mom, as always," Liz said. Brenda nodded. "I'm going back," Liz said, looking between them both.

"What? You just got here," Brenda insisted.

"Yes, but I have to do something. I needed to come here, somewhere to keep what I have left, and for my children to have a roof over their heads. Now I need to deal with this. Instead of waiting for things to constantly happen to me, I need to go out and make things happen," Liz replied. Her comments were directed as much at her mother as her sister.

"Oh, OK," Brenda said, agreeing reluctantly. "No shopping then?" she said, laughing. Liz smiled, thankful she hadn't tried to talk her out of it.

"Good," was all Bessie said, making her feelings clear. Liz thought to make a joke of her comments, to say a mock thanks for it, but she wouldn't, no need to spoil what was a succinct comment.

"Liz was getting us some breakfast. Will you do us some egg and bacon please?" Bessie asked, looking at Brenda. It was as much an instruction as a request.

Brenda nodded, smiling at them both before leaving for the kitchen. The moment she walked out, Bessie turned to a small wooden unit behind herself. She opened a small door, took out a tin, and pushed the door again. She dropped the tin gently onto the table, lifting its lid. It was an old tea tin, finely patterned in black, but worn with time and use. Liz watched her, fascinated, wondering what she might be about to show her.

Bessie pulled a wad of bank notes out, mixed, folded over in a bundle. She held it out towards Liz. "Here, you need this. Take it," she said.

"Mom, I can't," Liz tried to say.

"Don't be daft, you know you need it, and I won't use it. Take it, please," Bessie insisted, continuing to hold it out.

"I can't, Mom, I just—" Liz continued.

"How will you get back to Elton?" Bessie asked. No matter how old she was, she never lost that sharp tack, that ability to see through the bull. There was no place to hide with her.

Liz laughed briefly before taking the money. She wouldn't insult her by counting it, but she could see it was enough to see her through what was needed. "Thank you, Mom, I'll pay you back eventually."

"Forget about it. When it's gone it's gone," Bessie replied.

Liz pushed the money into her dressing gown pocket. She thought of just going, there and then, getting dressed and out. She felt a need to do something, to change things. Nobody else would do it for her, she knew that much.

Before anything else could be said, Brenda brought through two plates of food. Liz had felt no urge to eat, until the smell of freshly made toast covered in butter wafted around. The deep, rich smell of bacon made it final, it was too good to resist, and mushrooms, egg and tomatoes too.

"Sis, you're the best," Liz said, her mouth watering. Together they all sat at the small dining table, tucking in. Nobody spoke, nothing more needed to be said.

The short moment of exclusion, the time when the three just sat eating, enjoying being together, was soon shattered as the hall door swung open. John ambled in, dressed scruffily in his baggy pajamas, hair a wild mess, rubbing his eyes. He was still half asleep, couldn't quite open his eyes, but he had an almost uncanny knack of avoiding furniture when walking. It was as if he had a sixth sense, but not just what was in front of him.

"What's for breakfast, Mom?" John asked, stretching his arms out while keeping his eyes closed.

Liz stopped eating, bursting out laughing. Neither her mother nor Brenda quite understood what for, but were pleased to see her happy in a way, properly for once.

"Yes, John," Liz eventually said, struggling not to laugh or choke with food in her mouth.

Brenda cottoned on to what the joke was, smiling. "I'll get you some, John," she said, standing to resume duties. John didn't acknowledge the kindness, but instead sat in his aunt's place at the table. He opened his eyes enough to see Bessie looking at him, smiling, as he picked up pieces of food from the plate in front of him, eating.

"You're a hog," Bessie said playfully.

"Yum," was all John said, wondering where the rest of his food was coming from.

"I'm going back, to sort things out," Liz said, elbows on the table, looking at him thoughtfully.

"Back where?" John asked, mopping up the last of the tomatoes with his fingers.

Again Liz chuckled to herself. "Back to Elton, and the northwest, because I need us to get a house, a home."

"So we're not staying here then?"

"No. You need to go to school."

"Mom, don't use foul language like that," John said, picking up his plate to lick it. Liz pinched the side of it, ensuring he did no such thing.

"I'll go, and then come back for you and Patricia and our stuff, once I work something out."

"We can live in a tent?" John asked. Liz didn't laugh.

"Well, if it hadn't been for mom, we might well have ended up in one, a cardboard box one." Before John could reply, Brenda picked up her now empty plate and dropped another one in its place, full of all sorts of cooked breakfast food. Then, finally, he was speechless.

"I'll go up and get dressed, and tell Patricia," Liz said, readying herself. Her mind was made up, she knew she would never rest until they had a roof of their own over their head.

As Liz got to the top of the stairs, Patricia came out of her room, looking as if she hadn't slept. "You look how I feel," Liz said.

"Yeah, well, not the greatest of beds, and it's hard to get used to being here, thinking of how long it might be," Patricia said.

"Well, I'm going to—" Liz began to say.

"Mom, I'm thinking of going back to stay with Dan," Patricia said, struggling to maintain eye contact.

Liz looked at her, shocked. "But, it's— Look, I know it's not easy, it's only for a couple of weeks. I'm going back now, today, to make sure we get somewhere to live, and get our lives back," Liz pleaded. Patricia remained silent but didn't look at her.

"Please, love?" Liz asked, struggling to hide her emotions. The thought of being so alone was too much to bear. "If you stay, I promise I will fix this."

"OK, Mom," Patricia agreed, nodding. The last thing she wanted was to compound her mother's misery. "I don't really want to live with him anyway. I'd only end up being his servant."

Liz quickly grabbed Patricia by the shoulders, pulling her into a hug. It was a difficult embrace, in an awkward situation for them both. Neither were happy with the direction of their lives, or the men in them.

"At least John's happy," Liz said, trying to be positive.

"Of course he's happy, he's getting fed lots," Patricia immediately responded. A moment passed as they looked at each other, before both burst out laughing. It was a moment of levity, one they could share and ignore problems, but it wouldn't last. It was obvious only one person could deal with it.

"Right, I'll get ready," Liz said.

"Do you need some money, Mom?" Patricia asked. "I don't have much, but—"

"Oh, love," Liz interrupted, hugging her again. "Your Gran gave me some, but thank you so much, for being you."

It was an important understanding, as her daughter took her first steps as an adult at a difficult time, but one that proved she had grown into a wonderful person.

"I'm very proud of you, Patricia," Liz said. She didn't wait for the response, just turning away before anything more could be said.

As she went into her own room, she began to think, not only of what she might do, but of the past, and how it had shaped where they were. Old illusions felt less important as she questioned the very basic elements of her life, and its value. As much as she wanted to continue, such thoughts would have to wait. Time was ticking, and obviously running out.

As Liz entered the back room again, John was busy licking his plate for any last taste.

"John, stop that. Mom, I'm going straight out. Brenda, Patricia needs breakfast," was all she said as she put her coat on. She kissed John on the head, who didn't even notice, then hugged Bessie before giving Brenda a quick wave.

As she walked out into the hall, Patricia was coming down the stairs. "I'll call, once I sort things," Liz said.

"OK, Mom. Where are you going to stay?"

Liz shrugged. "Wherever is cheap, and short, because I want a place to live."

Both smiled at each other, an uneasy understanding, fraught with worry. Liz left the house, walked off down the street and caught a bus to Middlesbrough, in order to catch a train South. Only as she walked did the reality of what she was thinking sink in, the cold air biting into her cheeks, the thought of how really alone she was. If she couldn't fix this, or find somewhere to stay, she might literally end up on the streets, sleeping rough. The idea haunted her, but so did the idea of being without her children. If she didn't find somewhere, and as importantly, get John back into school soon, matters would quickly be taken out of her hands.

As Liz walked down the road towards the railway station, she was reminded of times in the town as a child. It always seemed clean, but in times gone was much busier. She often wished she could remember more of her father, but for his loss her mother more than made up for it with her love and energy. The place had an old-world style to it, more Victorian buildings than modern architecture. Rows of tall red brick buildings preceded her, as the road led along tree-lined avenues. The semicircular yellow building at the end housed the station, leading to old but functional lines. Though they served a huge amount of people, and traveled in all directions the distance of the land, it was always a surprise to see so little done to change and modernize the place. Liz could never decide if it was a good thing or not, but all the same she felt good.

Whenever she brought the children up, they would always travel by coach, simply because it was so much cheaper. Now, though, all that mattered was she got back quickly, to Chester, and did something, anything.

The station had the old smells, oil and diesel, but as bad as it seemed, it was still welcoming. She had traveled through before, on nicer days when her mind wasn't focused on worry. Today was quieter, but there were still families around, young children running about, couples together, some alone, but all seemed to have a purpose.

"Morning," Liz said at the ticket window. "Can I get a train here, straight through to Chester?" she asked.

"Morning," the ticket man replied, ignoring the rest of her question. It wasn't a good start.

"Fifteen pounds and thirty-five pence, one way," the man said. He was dressed in a loosely fitting black uniform, his tie hardly held together around his neck. His face was stubbly, and his hair black and slicked to his head. As he spoke, Liz noticed a strong odor of cigarettes. He looked an unhappy person, just the kind of person she didn't need at the beginning of her day.

"Thank you, I'll take that," Liz said, producing a note to hand over. She still couldn't bring herself to look at the notes, to see how much it all came to, but it was obvious if she wanted to manage, she could have to figure it all out carefully. It seemed enough from what she had seen, it would be fine.

The man almost flicked the ticket at her thought the gap under the window before snapping the note away. A drawer popped out, from which he dragged out several coins for change, before dropping them heavily onto the counter. Liz watched him, aware of his attitude, but thought twice before saying anything. She had enough fights ahead without another from him. She picked up the coins, walking away, looking at her ticket for the platform. There was nothing mentioned. Her mind was abuzz, thinking of plans ahead, the platform, the man and his attitude, as she looked at the coins. It was short, he had given the wrong amount. *Should I go back?* she thought to herself. Again she was torn, what to do, whether it was worth arguing. She needed every penny, but the stress was already driving her mad, so she simply walked on.

"Excuse me, could you tell me the correct platform for," Liz began to ask a porter as he wheeled a trolley full of suitcases past. The man didn't stop, or even look at her, moving on, as if she were invisible. She wondered if that were the case, that she wasn't even really there, that she had died and nobody cared.

"Hey," a voice said, catching her attention.

Liz looked to see an elderly woman near her. She was wearing thick black shoes that appeared far too small for her, and a large flowery dress that looked older than time. She held oversize carrier bags, with bits of oddments sticking out. Liz wasn't sure whether to even look, let alone approach her.

"Hey," the woman said again, staring at her.

It was obvious there would be no ignoring her, not for the moment. "Hi, what's up?" Liz asked.

The woman approached, at which Liz immediately noticed a distinct smell of urine about her. "You asked him what platform for Chester," she said, without smiling.

"Yes, that's right," Liz replied, holding out her ticket.

"Up those steps, platform four," the woman replied, continuing to stare.

"Thanks, thanks so much," Liz replied, smiling, as much as the smell put her off.

As she turned to leave, the woman caught her arm. "Hey, I don't suppose you have any change, do you?" she asked.

Liz stopped. Her immediate thought was to ask what for, but it dawned on her that she simply wanted money, for anything. Her usual instincts were always to give, if it were only a little, it would do no harm. Now was different, now she wasn't far off being destitute herself.

"I'm sorry, I really can't spare anything," Liz said, looking at the woman. She thought to wait, to explain if need be, but the way the woman looked back at her soon changed that, as she sneered, an impression that she might react badly.

Liz turned quickly, walking away as the woman muttered something. It sounded like cursing, bad language, but there was nothing to be done about it. The day was already going badly, all she needed was another argument and she would break down completely. It was coming.

As she stood on the platform looking down the station, in the distance, all she could think of was going back to the place she ever wanted to be. It felt like an icy needle down her spine, as if the hands of fate were in control of her life, that she were a puppet and no matter what course of action she took, she would never be truly free to be happy.

Liz jumped as a loud PA barked instructions. *The train now stopping at platform seven for Chester, Ellesmere Port, Helsby...* The thought took a moment to sink in as she looked around to see the large sign proclaiming Platform Four, which she was standing on. She waited, frozen to the spot, as the PA repeated. Chester, Platform Nine. The woman had lied, or been mistaken. Without another thought she ran, feeling every bit of her age as she ran up the stone steps, over the bridge towards the right place. As she looked down, there was the train, beside an empty platform, guard standing half on the train, half off. Panic. As she ran, she lost a shoe, stopping to get it, before realizing she would miss the train. Off she went, clip, hop, clip hop, down the steps, towards the train, running across the platform, ignoring the bits her bare foot picked up.

"Hold on, don't go," Liz shouted, running towards the guard next to the open door. It was just going to be one of those days, she could tell, because it had been one of those months, or years, or lifetimes.

"Certainly, madam," the guard said, smiling at her. She smiled back, ready to hop in as he stepped over to block her access.

"Can I not get on?" Liz asked.

"Certainly, madam," the guard agreed. "Only this is the post wagon, parcels and letters only. Go further up and you'll find passenger carriages."

"Oh, thanks. I'm not too late then?" she asked breathlessly.

"No, we're not due out for nine minutes yet." Liz felt deflated, breathing out sheepishly.

"Thanks," she said, slowly walking away.

"Lost your shoes, did you?" the guard asked, looking at her bare foot. The thought occurred to her to be sarcastic, but he had been nicer than anyone else so far, so she decided against, simply nodding. She pointed back to where it had fallen off.

"Go get it then," the guard said, smiling again.

"I have time then?" Liz asked.

The guard pulled a watch from his pocket. "Yep, eight minutes yet."

"You won't go without me?"

"No, you have time, we won't go until time."

Liz hesitated a moment, but felt awkward for being rude, so walked slowly away. She needed her shoe, so off she went, but given how life had treated her she very much expected a whistle to blow and the train to speed off as fast as it could, with a guard hanging out of the window laughing manically at her.

The shoe was still where she had left it, all alone and waiting. She put it on, felt better for it, and hurried back to the waiting train. "Thanks," she said, before walking ahead to get on.

As she sat, she noticed a range of people nearby. All looked settled, happy to be where they were going. A family sat in a seat of four with a table between, food, drinks and games across the place. The two children, a boy and a girl, looked to their parents, seeming so happy and united. The man smiled at the children, the woman passing food. It all seemed so normal, because that was what normal was, when everyone was heading in the same direction, and wanted to be there. For a time she had wondered if anyone in life ever really was happy, but now, seeing this, she could see that was what most people had, and she had too, until now.

An old man sat in a seat of two beside her, with another lady of similar age. They seemed content, not unnecessarily happy or jumping around, simply at peace with one another and again, going in the same direction. The train journey she was embarking on appeared to her to be a metaphor for life, where the place they ended up resulted in something that mattered, that each had their own unified vision of what was right. There was no contention, no stress or fuss. It was an example, a way to be, the right way, and a course she determined to travel purposefully. Life had chosen her path, and now she accepted it. As the train lurched, pulling out to go, her mind calmed, focused on what had to be done. Reinvigorated, she decided nothing would stand in her way, not now, and never again.

23

THE LADY ROARS

If possible, it seemed colder in Chester than she remembered of Middlesbrough. The air seemed different, the place alien to her, as if she had been shorn of all her memories of it. She was there to do what was needed, but emotion hadn't followed her. Her mind was set, all she needed now was to get to the first place.

It was like a long walk to court for a trial where with the wrong outcome she would receive a life sentence. It was all or nothing, as she walked past secondhand shops, some boarded up, like an old mill town where most of its industries had closed down. When she had visited before, she felt weak, lost from being abandoned, but now all she felt was a grim fire in her stomach, borne of need. Life had never been truly great, just ambling along, days here and there of quiet supposed happiness, but it was enough, as long as her children were happy. She felt as if her life and anything of worth about her had circled a great drain and been swallowed up, but for all that, she would try not to revel in self-pity.

Where before the steps to the Council offices had been uncertain, dread filling her, now all she could think of were the wrongs and insults she had dealt with in recent weeks. She thought of almost begging for a home for her family, the sneers and dirty looks she had received. Then there was the bank manager, here to help, doing their thing, their slogan, only doing their thing was right, never hers. The debt letters, the telephone calls demanding something she didn't have, the calls at the door, demanding she leave her home because it belonged to someone else. It seemed to be relentless, attacks on her that she didn't deserve. Enough was enough.

Liz walked through the double doors into the Housing offices, to see three women behind the counter. Two were the same as before, and a third younger woman. The waiting area including all the seats were full, busy with people of all ages, most like her in serious need. She wondered how many of them were being told the same thing she had been.

There seemed to be a line on one side, but another group waiting in another corner. Some in seats were turned looking towards the counter, as if they were waiting either for a chance to speak or simply to be called. It seemed a mess, and one Liz expected one or two working there might enjoy or find funny. It was going to be a long day, and she had no time to waste.

"Excuse me," Liz said loudly, walking directly to the counter. Everyone in the office stopped what they were doing and looked at her.

"I'm sorry, but you'll have to wait your turn," one of the workers said. Liz looked at her, recognizing her. It was the same Margaret Fincher who she had seen before, that selfsame look on her face, a sour appearance, as if she lived for the misery she felt and inflicted upon others.

"I came in some time ago," Liz began to say.

"I'm sorry, but you need to wait in line," Fincher insisted, staring hard at Liz.

"What line? There is no line. It's a madhouse," an elderly man said, interrupting. Liz was grateful to him. He looked slumped over, beaten down by life, white hair and frail, but still took the time to don an old black suit. He was clearly a good man, but like her and so many there, in need. They were all fragile souls in their own unique way, each desiring of sympathy and understanding, but the response was nothing like it.

"I've been here three hours," another voice chimed in, a large woman in a deep velvet dress. Her hair was long and bedraggled, her cheeks heavy red as if everything she did was arduous.

"You'll all have to wait in line," Fincher repeated.

"We can't wait, we can't wait any longer. I have children, we have no home, we have nowhere to live. Do you want to see us out on the streets, is that what you are here for, to watch us all go on the streets, have our children taken into care? Don't you care?" Liz shouted, so loud and angry that all other dissent dissolved. She wasn't angry now, simply broken, beyond the end of her tether.

Before any of the office workers could respond, a door behind them opened. A short man stepped out, slightly balding, wearing a suit and tie but no jacket. He wore slim silver spectacles, and looked more like an accountant than a Council worker. He stood, holding the door open, looking around. Words were not important here, only his look, as the place fell silent.

"Can I have a word, please?" the man asked quietly, remaining otherwise still, looking now at Fincher. She made her way quickly to him as he leaned towards her, appearing to discuss something quietly. Within seconds he had stepped away, allowing the door to close. Fincher turned, refused to look at anyone else, returning to the counter. Without speaking she leaned underneath, picked at papers, all eyes on her, until eventually finding a folder which she lifted up.

Liz watched her, wondering just how much trouble she had caused, wondering if her application was about to go into the shredder, along with any last vestige of hope.

Something had changed, but all eyes remained on the woman, as she picked out a broad white envelope from inside the folder. As she took the note, it was clear her hands were mildly trembling, before she looked up directly at Liz.

Liz stepped forward, until she could rest her arms on the counter. She looked wide-eyed at the woman, feeling the intense stare and focus of the room upon her.

"We have a house available for you. It has been made available under the Emergency Homeless Housing Regulations. We attempted to contact you to advise you of this when it came available, and you can sign this tenancy agreement now, and collect the keys from your local housing office on the actual estate," Fincher said, attempting to speak deliberately but slowly, as if quiet enough so that the secret wouldn't get out.

Liz felt her heart soar. She didn't know whether to laugh or cry or simply hug someone. It was as if she were in a pit of despair, looking up at the sky with a plea for help from above, and someone had listened. In the moment of absolute desperation, she had found some kind of salvation. She didn't speak, unable to utter the words that would express just how she felt.

Fincher laid out a group of papers, all stapled together, pushing them towards Liz. "Please, just sign here, and here, and same again on the sheets below marked for signature."

It all felt too much, the heat in the room, the tension, all that had happened so quickly. Liz felt her head spin, her weakness so much that she trembled. She took the pen from the woman, not looking at her for fear she might break the magic spell that was happening. Her signature was usually firm and clear, but now it seemed like a doctor's scribble, as she sprayed across each section something like her name. It didn't matter, what had been set in motion couldn't be stopped, but still.

"Right, please take this top sheet to the office address given on the front. They will give you the keys and tell you where the house is. It's in Lache. You can get there by bus from the center," Fincher explained, before looking at Liz, her appearance different, as if she had just given to charity and felt somehow proud of herself.

"Ohhh, can't you do better than that?" a man asked, looking at Fincher with disdain.

"It's fine," Liz whispered, simply glad that she had something. She took the paper, refused to acknowledge the woman in front of her and turned to walk away. At the exit door she stopped, turned slowly towards the desk, looking at the women behind. Her face was stern, mirroring that of Fincher, that same sneering look, before turning to the others, those like her, waiting. Then she smiled at them, her face a broad picture of clear happiness.

"Go on, lass," someone seated shouted, as others laughed and smiled. She had been one of them, had been desperate, and stood her ground. She had won. It was only a small battle, the first of many, but it gave hope. Liz felt better than she could ever remember, and best of all she had done it by herself.

Laughter and mocking for the staff continued as she walked away, clutching the papers. They were like a treasure to her, not just a slip to keys for a house, but a link to hope, to a future where she could see something better. As she got to the bottom of the stairs and walked out, all she could feel was elation, freedom. She had left behind the office, now all she needed to do was get to the other office, get the keys and get in. Only then would she be certain that her fate was in her own hands.

24

A DAY OUT WITH AUNTIE

"You can come live with me," Brenda said, looking at John. He was in front of the television, watching a nature program and cursing himself for being too lazy to either turn it over or go and do something else. He thought of asking someone else to do it for him, or pass the television remote, but even that would need effort. Today wasn't a day for effort.

"I can't. I have college, and then there's Dan," Patricia replied. She had taken to peeling potatoes, because she knew her Gran would struggle, and besides, no one else would do it.

"All right, John can live with me. We make a great team," Brenda continued.

John turned to look at her. "Have you got a television?"

"Oh yes, a nice twenty-eight-inch one."

"Twenty-eight, that's tiny," John said, turning back in disappointment.

"Well, you can just sit closer, then it looks huge," Patricia said, looking at him mischievously. Brenda laughed as John pulled off one of his socks to throw at Patricia.

"Hey," Bessie snapped, in her own unique way. She wouldn't say anything else, she never needed to do. It wasn't about fear, or even respect, just behaving because they loved her, and were happy in her home, sharing it.

"You'll be going back to school shortly," Brenda suggested, looking again at John.

John shrugged. "If I have to. I don't mind, really. I miss it in some ways, miss my friends."

Patricia looked at him, surprised. She had never heard him sound so sensible. "You're not growing up, are you?" she asked.

"Nah, but I am hungry," he replied, pricking everyone's bubble.

"You're going to have to grow up soon, your mom will need you," Brenda said.

"It's fine, no rush, we'll be fine," Patricia interrupted before Brenda could take things further. "He has all the time in the world."

"Thanks, sis. Now go cook something," John said, laughing at her. Patricia smiled, throwing his sock back at him.

"Why don't you go out and do something?" Bessie said. It was a gentle suggestion, but not a question, more an instruction.

"Let's go to the beach, at Redcar," Brenda suggested, which was met with a mute response. The weather outside was dry but cold, and the skies had a vibrant white to them, suggesting it would be bitter out.

"Bit cold for that," John replied.

"No, it's lovely out. Come on, we can go in the arcade and then I'll buy you some fries."

"OK, we will," Patricia said, before John could object any more.

"Fries," was all John said, and he was convinced.

"Whose car are we going in?" John asked as he put his shoes on.

"Oh, let me see, erm," Brenda said, looking at him as if he were truly daft. "I don't have a car, we're going by bus." Patricia laughed, and even Bessie thought it funny.

"Oh," John moaned.

"Fries," Patricia said, at which he put on his coat and stood by the door. Everyone laughed.

Redcar, set in the northeast of England, in wintertime can be bitter and difficult for most, even those who have lived there all their lives. The beaches are soft sand and clear, and the sea foamy, but otherwise clean. Few ever ventured out in the worst of weathers, other than those hardy souls walking their dogs or picking for crabs or other edible shellfish.

The bus ride from Carlin Howe to Redcar was short but interesting, climbing such steep hills than even the newest of vehicles struggled. It was a bumpy, twisty, fun ride, through villages, towns, and hills, until it finally reached their destination. Redcar itself was a bustling place, destined to change, but full of shops in a long, high street intersected by a single road. Across the back was the beach, leading right along, and in the distance the steelworks, all chimneys, smoke and flames.

John stepped off the bus, wondering what he might choose to do first. Of course he knew; once the smell of food took hold of him, he knew what he wanted.

Patricia followed him, looking around, immediately feeling the cold as Brenda stepped off. She had her coat open, smiling as the brisk wind bit into the skin. She looked as if she were on a summer holiday, ready to hit the beach and top up her winter tan.

"Shall we go walk on the beach for a bit?" Brenda asked.

"Food," John said, only half joking.

Patricia pulled a face at him. "Food first, I guess, then a walk."

"Pasties or fries?" Brenda asked.

"Both," John said quickly, before Patricia could spoil it for him.

"Right," Brenda said, raising her eyebrows. "Patricia, you go get pasties over there, and me and John will go get fries."

"Large for me, please," John said.

"They don't do large enough for you," Patricia said, walking away before he could respond. He thought to say he would have another bag, but that was a given, no argument there or explanation needed.

As they finally all met up, full of fresh food, the three walked around back, onto the promenade. Concrete walls lined against the sand to protect against strong weather and to avoid erosion. Steel handrails lined alongside, and concrete seats were levied all along. It was bland and a poor reflection of the beauty beyond, but served a sensible purpose.

The three sat, dividing up the food, and began to eat. As cold as it was, with a strong easterly wind, the fries were freshly cooked and piping hot, covered in salt and vinegar, and the pasties equally fresh, making it bearable to be outside.

"I think I'm getting full up," John said, still chewing on a mouthful of food, his food wrapper almost gone.

"Wow, someone make an announcement," Patricia mocked, smiling at him.

"They're really nice, though," John said, at which the others nodded. No one wanted to speak, enjoying it too much to stop.

"I can't eat all mine, I'll put it back in the bag and save it for later," Brenda said.

"Me too," Patricia agreed.

"Yeah, good idea. I'll finish it for you," John said quickly, as he screwed up his empty wrappers and threw them into a nearby bin. Patricia thought to argue with him, but figured it would be an argument she would lose against her always hungry brother.

"Shall we walk?" Brenda asked finally. Both nodded, pulling their coats tighter.

"We must be mad," Patricia said as she stood up.

"Why? It's lovely out," Brenda said, looking around as if she had been sipping drinks by the pool outside.

Patricia and John looked at each other, frowning. "I guess there's nothing better to do besides sit indoors by a roaring open fire in front of the television, drinking hot chocolate," Patricia said. Both laughed, but Brenda ignored them, walking onto the soft, damp beach.

"Oh well, let's go," John said, before running off shouting *chaaaarge*. Patricia tried to follow in the same way, giggling, but the moment she got sand in her shoes she gave up, walking alongside their aunt.

"So, how are you both feeling then?" Brenda asked. Patricia thought of her question, aware that this walk and her talk were the likely point of it all, rather than simply a day out.

"I miss Mom," John said quietly.

"She's only just been gone since this morning," Brenda replied.

"I know, but it's cos we don't know when she'll be back, or what she's going to have to do."

"She will be fine, she knows what she's doing," Patricia explained, as much to reassure herself as she did for John.

"I know your mom, of course, she's my sister. She sometimes lets things happen, and goes along for the peace and quiet, but when she has to, when she really has to, she can do anything."

"Even find Dad?" John asked. It was an impossible question, he knew it, but he couldn't help but ask.

"Well, anything is possible, even that. If anyone can, she can. If he's around, she will find him."

"And if he's not around anymore?" Patricia asked.

"Then she will find out, in time. She's not the kind of person to let something so serious lie. She won't let him go easily."

The three continued to walk as the wind whipped up. The cold air blowing from across the North Sea filled their lungs with saltiness, making them feel as refreshed as they felt cold. Nobody else appeared quite so mad as they, to be walking in such conditions, but as harsh as it was, sunlight threatened to break through with deep blue skies piercing the white veil.

"What if we don't want him back?" John asked.

As shocked as Brenda felt at the question, Patricia appeared the opposite, almost allowing herself to nod in agreement. She smiled briefly at him before looking away.

"John, I'm surprised you should ask something like that. He's your dad," Brenda replied, looking straight at him. She stopped walking, pulling her coat closer.

John paused a moment, before turning to her. "He's not the best. Never does anything with us, never finishes anything. And he's always moody, angry about things. He's been like it for ages."

Brenda shook her head, wanting to say something, but before she could, Patricia interrupted her. "He's right. Dad would be there, but you could see he wasn't really interested. He wasn't a bad dad, just he seemed, I don't know—"

"Angry about everything," John interrupted.

"Angry, yeah, but as much with himself, and life I think."

"You think he might not just have disappeared somewhere, but have given up altogether?" Brenda asked, appearing even more shocked. She held a hand over her mouth, to cover her response.

"Could be," John said.

"I think so. I miss our old dad, from when we were much younger, but now he's gone, all that makes me sad is the thought that he probably gave up, and did something," Patricia continued. Each of her words brought more misery, but it was obvious they both felt the same. John looked down at the ground, clearly upset. Patricia looked at him before walking over and putting her arm around him. He was never one to show much emotion, but sometimes he couldn't help it.

"I'm sorry, love," Brenda said, placing a hand on his shoulder.

"The last time he got this upset, they had cancelled the new series of Blake's Seven on BBC One," Patricia said, smiling at her brother. John found it in himself to laugh, a moment of levity which broke the aura of sadness that had somehow washed over them.

"Let's go build a sandcastle," Patricia said, at which her brother looked up, tearful but wide-eyed.

"No, let's go have a swim," John cried. At which he ran off

towards the sea, Patricia in tow, shouting and laughing.

Brenda stood for a moment, bewildered by it all. "Hey, you can't go in the sea, it's too cold," she shouted. Neither took any notice, continuing to run towards the distant frothing sea. Brenda broke out into one of her runs, all legs and flailing arms, panicking at them both.

As she grew near, both turned to look at her, laughing uncontrollably. "Gotcha," they both shouted together, at which she stopped, breathlessly. The three laughed, enjoying the moment. It was a brief respite, away from the difficulties to come, from the misery, the struggle, the suffering. At least they had each other.

25

HOME AT LAST

The bus ride from the city hadn't taken long, the house being in a borough of Chester which she knew was called Lache. Even the name sounded ominous. As she traveled, she saw such a stark change, as the landscape and gardens went from being pristine gardens to weeds here and there, until in Lache litter and debris replaced even the weeds.

The bus stopped at a huge circular roundabout, with bus shelters on either side of the main road. Two other roads intersected off into smaller, narrow roads, with terraced housing either side. Surrounding all of the roundabout were shops, a fruit and veg seller, a post office, a butcher, even a newsagent. At least they wouldn't have far to go for basic things.

Liz stepped off the bus, feeling as if she had gone into an alien world. She had of course lived in Council areas before, only so long ago she had forgotten what they were sometimes like. It seemed quiet, and the sun had broken through, providing a short respite from the otherwise bitter day.

A few people mingled around, some waiting at the bus stop, others going in and out of the shops. As many people appeared to be using the betting shop as were using the other shops, something which surprised her. In some ways it appeared to reflect what she remembered of Carlin Howe, where she grew up, which to her mind, though far removed from where she wanted to be, was no bad thing.

Liz removed the papers she had received at the office, sifting through them to find a local office address, which stated an area of Lache, and helpfully provided a hopeless hand-drawn map. It was poorly photocopied, giving her little chance of finding the place she needed. She would have no choice but to ask.

Nearby was a tall, thin man, smoking from a roll-up cigarette. His face looked craggy and worn, as if time hadn't been kind to him. Beside him was a shorter, much larger woman, wearing a long light blue coat, which was far too big for her. The look on her face as she stared back at Liz made it clear she wanted to be left alone. As hard as she tried, she couldn't stop the sinking feeling in the pit of her stomach that all was not going to go well.

As she looked around, wondering who she might speak to, she noticed chimneys atop all of the houses, but most surprisingly smoke emanating from them. She couldn't remember the last time anyone she knew without gas central heating, or oil, or similar, even if all electric. The sinking feeling got worse.

As she stood looking more than a little lost, a man came out from the newsagent, carrying a metal sign. He dropped it heavily, looked at her with clear disinterest, and went back in. Whether it was a sign of how things would be, she had no idea, but the most important thing to her was getting a home, and all back together again.

The main road led on down to an open field and more houses. Of the two smaller roads off the roundabout, one led to a tight-knit bunch of houses, all the same darkened red brick, terraced, and worn roads. The final of the four routes likewise had houses, but at the end appeared different buildings. She herself was at a crux; she could stop someone and ask for help, or simply go walking to find out. There were few people around, and of those she didn't like to ask, so off she had gone, walking along.

Debris and litter were scattered all over the pavements, as if nobody cared about the place. She had seen much of the country over the years, traveling with family, and even in the northeast where she grew up as poor as it was, it was never so bad. She had to constantly remind herself that all she wanted was a home, what happened other than that didn't matter.

As Liz walked, she passed two houses; both appeared old but neatly kept, with fine gardens and clear of rubbish. Netting under the gates of each appeared to simply be in position to keep out litter, which suggested to her it was a constant problem from the shops.

To the right as she walked was an elementary school, with small children running round playing during break. She thought it unusual to see such young children wearing school uniforms, but in a way it seemed good that standards were so good that they enforced such discipline from a young age.

At the end of the short road was a small temporary cabin, beside a small building which simply said Lache Healthcare. It was another good sign, the local doctor's surgery, right within the local area, almost central. Wherever the house might be, it wouldn't be far from basic amenities. As she walked around, she noticed a sign on the side of the temporary cabin, written in black marker, saying Housing Office. There it was, the place she needed, also close. It was a mixed day, some good some bad, but better than she had experienced in recent times. To top it off, the sun had broken through properly and felt warm on her face, as if some kind of omen of good things to come. Whatever the reality, she would be glad of anything positive at such a point in her life.

Inside the office there were green filing cabinets off to the far end and one window with wire mesh covering it, clearly designed to keep people out. A door across the way led to another section with a plastic sign on it which simply said Private.

As she entered, a woman came from the opposite door, immediately looking at her. Straight away she smiled at Liz, quite the opposite of what she had been expecting, given her experiences.

"Morning, can I help you?" the woman asked, moving to stand behind her desk. She was white-haired, looking as if she were close to retirement. A pair of white plastic glasses hung from a bead necklace around her neck. Her hair was curly and well maintained, the same as her makeup, suggesting she cared about her appearance. Her kindly demeanor was a welcome change for Liz, leading her to hope things would be much better. The lady wore a two-piece dress, smart jacket and skirt, and dark, short-heeled shoes, looking as if she ensured she dressed according to her job, but also in a way that showed she cared about herself, and the impression she left on others.

"Hi, my name is Liz, er, Elizabeth Cornwell. I have this paperwork for a house, to get the keys," Liz said, fumbling for words.

"Oh, right," the lady said, taking the note. "I'm Mrs. Barker, I run this local housing office. We're only part time, and I was about to lock up, so it's a good job you got here when you did."

Liz thought about what she had said, realizing if the Central Housing office had delayed her as they wanted, she would have gone to find the house, only to find the local office closed. As hard as she tried not to be cynical, she wouldn't fool herself into assuming anything, but some things were just too obvious.

The lady looked at the note, before turning to one of the filing cabinets. She ruffled around before picking out a piece of card with keys attached. She looked at it before shaking her head silently.

"What's up?" Liz asked, feeling sick with the tension.

"Oh, nothing, really," Mrs. Barker said, continuing to ponder. She turned back to Liz, still holding the card, before looking up at her.

"Is everything all right?" Liz asked, feeling like she might explode any minute.

"Yes love, you have been offered a house. It's near to here. I'm not sure why they have offered you that house, but it's just along from here, number twenty-three, above the newsagents."

"It's fine. I'm not bothered by what or where it is, as long as it's a house, has a roof over it and I finally have somewhere for me and my children to live."

The lady smiled at her. "As bad as that, is it?" she asked.

"Yep," Liz replied, looking ruefully at her.

"All right, well sign here, and here," Mrs. Barker suggested, placing the card on the desk and crossing two spaces for her to write. Liz took a pen from the desk before scribbling her name.

"That first one is your tenancy agreement, and the other is your new tenant booklet. You can take both of those, I'll keep this other sheet, and there are your keys." Mrs. Barker handed the keys to her, smiling. She thought to say more, but it was obvious she needed to get on with it, into her new home. Liz took the paperwork and the keys, thanking her before leaving. As she walked away, the woman sighed to herself, feeling annoyed at what had been done, but for their own particular reasons they had given her such a place, and nothing could be done about it.

Liz walked along, looking at the house numbers, counting up. She could feel her heart beating stronger than ever, filled with a sense of hope that she hadn't had for far too long. As good as she felt about what was to come, she felt a sense of pride, of accomplishment, how she had done something for her family, and proved her independence.

As she counted the houses, she came back to the roundabout, with the houses stopping dead on twenty, and no more. She looked up and around, to see more people milling around. As the sun had come out, the place had become busier, with a large number at each bus stop on either side of the main road. She stood right in front of the newsagents, looking at the street name, the house number, it was all correct, but not there. Slowly she walked back, looking closer, until she saw a small black gate at the side of the shop. On the other side was a small garden, overgrown and littered with rubbish, dropped wrappers, bottles, and cans. An old armchair had been dumped upside down on the back wall, with cushions strewn all over. As she stopped to look, she looked at the high stone steps leading up to the front door. The door was light blue, with tattered brass lettering, showing the number twenty-three.

Then it hit her, the thought of why the woman in the office had shaken her head, she knew what the place was, what it was like. That sense of elation faded, but the inner strength she felt, that which had been building in her, demanded of her to move on, get on with it, deal with it.

Liz pushed open the rickety old gate as it skidded off the concrete. She walked in, slowly ascending the steps to the door. It had three small oval windows at the top, each frosted so nothing could be seen inside. To the right was a large window, suggesting it was a front room. As she leaned back a little looking up, it seemed that the house was across the side and top of the shop. As much as she tried to be positive, everything she saw and felt was a constant barrage, a reminder of how far she had come. It was difficult to decide whether her life had risen or fallen, but she couldn't escape from feeling deeply low.

There were two keys on the tied white string, one clearly for the front, another for a back door. As she looked around, she could see a small driveway which was part of the house, leading through a high brick archway. At least there was a back entrance, and perhaps a back garden. She wondered if the back was as bad as the front, but couldn't bring herself to go look.

As she lifted her hand to push in the key, she noticed it was shaking, not just with nerves, but perhaps with fear of what she might find. She turned the lock, then pushed open the door. Inside was different to how she had imagined, to the left stairs leading up, and to the right a hallway leading to a door on the right. The entire place appeared clear of anything, its walls cream-colored but clean enough. The floor was a solid black, coated concrete, but the stairs, all wood, were bare. A single cord hung down, carrying a light bulb. Otherwise, the place was empty, as if it hadn't been lived in for a generation.

Walking in, she shut the front door, then walked slowly down to the end of the hall. As she peered in, it was dark, light cut off from boards across the large front window. She could see through gaps that the window had small square panes, but each were broken out. The window was an old Victorian style, which might have appeared picturesque in any other setting, but given the circumstances simply made her feel worse. Ahead was another door, hanging open, with a steep step down to what appeared to be the kitchen area. Before she could head over to it she spotted the fire, a great open fire with a mantelpiece above it. It had a dusty old grate in the center, covered in ash and rotten pieces of gray coal. That would be fun, lighting that every day in winter, not to mention having to buy coal.

She knew there was no point in dwelling on it, she would have to check the rest of the place, then confirm she would keep it. It wasn't as if she had much choice in the matter.

It was difficult to describe the kitchen as such, more an oblong storage room. The large square enamel sink had been bolted to the wall, with a sheet of metal clipped to its side to act as a draining board. Liz laughed when she saw, unable to resist the temptation to touch it. It immediately fell to the ground with a clang. It would certainly hold up pots easily.

The kitchen window sat at the back of the sink, and was uncovered. It, too, was Victorian style, small square, but to her relief not broken. The windows were too grimy to see out, but she could see enough to notice it was overgrown with weeds throughout the broken concrete. There was one cupboard on the wall nearby, which looked as if it might be of the same strength as the draining board. She would be sure to only put plastic pots on there, unless she fancied some smashing times.

Through and up the stairs she went, only then realizing how large the place was. It had four bedrooms, and a bathroom, each looking empty but clean enough. All of the walls shared the same basic cream color, wooden floorboards, and large windows. Again each room had open fires, no radiators, no gas, just paper, wood, and coal if they wanted to be warm. It felt to her like her childhood, back home in

Yorkshire, lighting the fire every day, freezing until then, and then waiting for the warmth to come through, feeling good again. Mornings were the worst, but nights were good, especially bath time with loads of hot water. She couldn't decide whether it was a good thing, but it wasn't so bad, she hoped.

A tinkling noise came through, catching her attention. It sounded like a shop bell, hardly surprising to her, given the house was at the side of a shop, and above it. As she looked to see where it came from, she was shocked to see gaps in the floorboards, and through them light and movement from below. As she leaned over to look, she could see people moving around, the colors of the displays, and the flooring below. So it was, no covering from the ceiling of the shop, no filling, nothing other than thin plaster tiles with holes in and wooden flooring she was standing on. It was the oddest thing she could ever remember, as if the divide between her new home and a shop selling newspapers were so thin, she could almost cross it by a single step. She could cover it with flooring, and it would no longer be a problem, but then there was the problem of buying such things.

Liz turned and stood, looking out of the expansive window. It was oblong in shape, but unlike the others had much larger panes, so she could clearly see out. She felt like sitting down, but there was nothing to sit on. The weather had changed yet again, as dark clouds came over, matching her mood. The house was poor, so basic, but it was something, and meant she could bring her family back. Liz felt as low as she ever had, no money, in such a place as she had never lived, expecting the worst. If it were a play it would be a tragedy, where all was lost, no love, no family, alone and without anything to her name. If she were in her twenties, she could get on, begin again, forget the past and forge a new future. She wasn't in her twenties anymore, no longer what she would consider young, but worst of all it felt as if everything she had ever worked for had gone, been destroyed in the blink of an eye. Then, finally, she was angry, with him, the man she couldn't name. He had let her down, taken everything from her. Whether he was alive or not, she couldn't stop her from being angry with him. Whatever it was that took him away, even then she could forgive him, he could come back, they would fix it, make it right, and be right back where they were. Even if they were poor, it didn't matter, because they would be together again. That moment she accepted she still loved Jack; for all his faults and failings, they had still shared half a lifetime together, and she would still take him back for all the wrongs he had done.

Rain began to patter down, finally making the scene outside complete, not so much a beautiful winter's day, but a harsh and bitter time, which appeared to her the way it would always be. She was in Limbo, stuck in a place where time stood still, and that time was all bland, gray, and sullen. Her mood reflected it.

A clanking noise interrupted her shallow thoughts. As she broke her concentration to see where it was from, she noticed the keys on the floor. Something inside her sparked, that same sense of strength and independence, borne of her need for her children, to provide for them, and protect them. Maternal instincts alive from her mother, from what she knew of family, reasserted themselves, and once again she was ready to act.

"Right, Liz, you have the house, you have the keys, go accept it, and start making telephone calls," she said to herself. On that day she turned a leaf, being open and honest with herself, accepting things for how they were, and prepared to change things where she could, for how she needed them to be.

26

THE PRICE OF MONEY

"Hello, is that the benefits agency?" Liz asked, hanging on to the telephone as if it were her connection with life.

"Yes, can I help you?" a man replied, his voice light and polite.

"I need to make a claim for benefits. I have been made involuntarily homeless, and don't know what to do. I have two children." The line went dead, as if he had hung up. The meter on the payphone continued to count.

"Hello," a voice suddenly appealed, the line crackling with its loudness.

"Yes, hello," Liz replied hopefully.

"Can you give me your name, and some way to contact you, and I can make an appointment for you."

"Thank you, yes," Liz replied, proceeding to give out what she could. It occurred to her to wonder what they might do if she was literally living on the streets, and had no means of being contacted, but she still maintained some small semblance of hope that if that were to become a reality, they could cope.

"OK, madam, if you call at this office for two o' clock, then we can take your claim and process it. Are you actually on the streets homeless now, or do you have somewhere to live?" the man asked belatedly. Liz smiled to herself, thinking that perhaps the social safety net wasn't that bad after all.

"Yes, I have just taken the keys for a house in Lache, and will be moving in today, though I have no money, and nothing to put in the house."

"Right, well, you will get help with paying the rent, and for local taxes, and you can apply for an emergency grant or loan to assist with basic needs. We can discuss that with you when you come for the appointment."

"All right, thank you," Liz said, struggling with mixed feelings. In her life she had always worked, until Jack earned enough so that she didn't need to, and had never claimed money or appealed for help. It felt odd, wrong somehow, as if she should be ashamed of her failure. Again the small voice in her head reminded her, *think of the children, do what is right for them*, and she settled.

"Please don't be late. Bye," the man said before hanging up. Liz stood, telephone in hand, feeling as if she had been cut off, hanging by nothing more than a cord. *Move on*, the voice inside her head insisted.

Liz pressed the button and inserted more coins. More money, more cost, less for what they would need, but needs must. She dialed again and waited.

"Hello," a familiar voice came on. It was as much a relief that he was in than anything. He loved the pub for a drink, and needed little excuse to go, but it was still early, even for him.

"Hello, Dan," Liz said. She didn't even need to see him or hear his response to know how he would be reacting right then, after his decision to leave to go back to his comfy little flat. It didn't matter, it couldn't because she knew she needed him, and for that reason she remained polite.

"Oh, er, hello Liz, nice to hear from you," Dan replied, his words stuttering. It was good, she thought, because then she could try at least to be in control.

"Whatever you're doing, I need you to get that van again, and come and pick me up, then we're going on another journey." It wasn't a question, simply a statement.

"Erm, I'm not sure if work will let me borrow it again," Dan said, sounding reluctant. She knew him well enough that he would say such a thing simply to get out of doing anything, even if he had no reason to.

"Tough, I need it, we need it, and we need you. If need be, steal the damn thing, just get it," Liz said. Her tone shocked him; he had never heard her be so assertive.

"Right," was all he said, still sounding unsure.

Liz felt assertive. She had accepted the cards that life had dealt her, and figured if she had no choice but to fight for what her family needed, then she would damn well fight for everything she could get.

"Do you know Chester?" Liz asked.

"I think so, yeah."

"Good, I'm at the shops, at the roundabout, at Lache, near where we're going to be living. Get that van, don't waste time, don't dawdle, I'll be waiting here for you, come and pick me up," Liz ordered. She waited, listening for any hint of dissent. Any word out of order and she intended to scream down the phone at him if necessary.

As if Dan could feel the tension down the telephone line, he hesitated, then spoke quietly. "All right, Liz, I'll get it and be there as soon as I can," he said, realizing if it were a battle then he had surely lost the war.

"Fill up the tank while you're at it. We're going to be busy," Liz said, before hanging up. Time and money were precious. She would need to work fast, and certainly intended to do so.

As the line went dead, Dan slowly replaced his own telephone handset. He sat a moment, pondering just what had happened. A fleeting thought occurred to him to ask himself if Patricia really was worth it, all the hassle. The thought didn't last long. For all of his faults, he still cared about her, and them. He would simply get on with it.

Time stood still for Liz as she thought a moment. She looked up, wondering what her next move would be. She could go back into the house, check it out some more, see if anything were needed. If not then look around.

A tapping noise against the side of the telephone booth she was in interrupted her decision. She looked out to see a young man staring at her. "Are you going to be long?" he asked, sounding more polite than she had expected. Liz pushed open the door and leaned slightly out, looking at him. He was slightly shorter than her, wearing a scruffy, worn T-shirt, its shoulder having been ripped off, or fallen off. His hair was cropped short and he was covered in tattoos. She thought he had the look about him of someone not worth offending, so she stepped away from the box, letting the door go.

"Sorry, love, if you still need it, that's fine," the man said quietly. He had a Scottish accent, and piercing blue eyes. His appearance offered what she would have imagined a threat, but his tone, his voice, the way he talked to her, seemed the opposite.

"Oh, no, it's fine, I was leaving now, thanks," she said, feeling a sense of confusion over what she saw and how he really was. She accepted it was the classic looks being deceptive, which was good, a nice start to life in Lache.

The man smiled at her, taking hold of the door, and stepped past as she moved. As he moved around, Liz noticed another young woman behind him. She also had a shaved head, and was covered in tattoos and body piercings. She wore a skintight dress and long, black, high boots. She didn't smile, or speak, simply choosing to lean against the telephone box, to wait. Liz smiled at her a moment, then looked away before walking off. It was surely going to take time to grow accustomed to the people of the area, and for her to change some unwanted preconceptions.

Things were moving along, if only in a bare minimum of how it all needed to be. The truth to her was that it was the best she could expect, for now, and perhaps for a long time to come. A thought hovering in the back of her mind which she refused to give life to was that her children were growing up. In time it would mean they would be off and living their own lives, at which point she would be truly alone. It was something she couldn't bear to consider, something far off and best avoided, otherwise that pit of depression might swallow her right up.

She considered going back into the house, but with nothing in there to even sit on, it wasn't the best option. Instead, she decided to look around, to see what the place and the other shops were like. If Dan arrived and she wasn't there it was tough, he would have to wait.

Across from the newsagents was a post office, and beside it a small food store. She walked close by, looking through the windows of the first. Several people milled around looking at the few shelves in there, but the largest group of people were queuing for counter services. At the top were banners offering Road Tax, Parcel Delivery and Benefit Cashing. It occurred to her, the image of all these people, waiting to collect benefit money: that would be her, that was her future. A few weeks ago she had been living in a decent home that they owned, had money in the bank, security of employment for the man she had spent most of her life living with, and now she was stuck in a rundown Council house with no money, no job, no security, and possibly no future. Something she never quite admitted, even to herself before, was her own attitude to others who had nothing. Now that belief screamed at her, that she had the cheek to judge others, for being too lazy or ignorant to go and do better for themselves. Now that the tables were turned, she could finally see how easy it was to slip into a trap of deprivation, struggle and loss. She wondered how many of them had ended up in similar situations simply because of someone else, or which of them lived such a life because they had no understanding of how to change it.

It was a reminder that for her, she must find her way, for her own sake as much as her children. This life could not become all of her, that whatever it took she would overcome, and move on. It was a stepping stone to better, for all of them. It was something she used to reassure herself of intent; whether that would become the truth, she chose to ignore.

The small food store looked useful, if expensive. As always, prices in the place were much higher than larger supermarkets, because it was a captive audience. Still, it would prove useful at a pinch, which was the point of it being there really.

Each of the shops in the circle had houses as part of them from the side and above. Most had nets across the windows for privacy, some smoke coming from chimneys. As quaint as it was for her mother to light a fire every morning, she had no desire to follow the same routine.

Across the way was a shop selling flowers, and beside it another selling fruit and vegetables. She thought of walking across to see some prices, but as she walked to the curb, a white van passed, blocking the view. She looked down the long road, to see on the far right a large grassy field with children playing on it. It was the one thing she most loved about the young, was no matter how cold it got, they would still go out, often in shorts and T-shirt, and play endlessly. She figured there was something to learn from it.

As she stood daydreaming, her focus was broken by a honking sound. She quickly turned to see the van nearby was being driven by Dan. It was different to the one they had used before, same size but older, much older.

"Will that thing even get us to Yorkshire?" Liz asked, walking over to him.

"Yeah, should do, I think. It was the only one they would let me use. So I brought it anyway, just in case," Dan said, leaning through the side widow.

"Needs must," Liz replied, walking around to climb in. "I have an appointment at the benefits agency, and then we can get off to Yorkshire. I won't waste time phoning again, we'll just go."

"Right, sounds good to me. I'll wait in the van when you go, because the locks aren't very good. Don't want anyone pinching it."

Liz nodded at him. "You know where it is?"

"No," Dan replied, shaking his head as they set off for Chester City Center.

"I have an idea. You can drop me and then find a place to park. Drive back for me after about an hour and I'll wait where you drop me off."

Dan nodded, sitting a moment in the van as Liz departed. He too had noticed how the journey to Lache started out as so pretty, with seasonal flowers still in bloom on all the verges, rows of houses all fine and beautiful. It seemed as if the wealth of the city ran out the further away they got, until the unwanted got what was left.

Liz dropped out at traffic lights before walking down a steep incline. She knew she was going to be early, but didn't want to miss her appointment. To the outside, the place seemed as fine as anything else in the city, its Roman walls looking old but well maintained, and some of the surrounding visuals quite splendid. As she walked through the old brick archway, things changed, with plastic signs attached to the walls and neglected waste bins spilling out rubbish onto the floor. Bushes and greenery surrounded the entrance to the dark building, more to do with not being cared for than any deliberate intent. It was like walking up a hill to be sentenced, rather than an entrance for somewhere that cared for others. Liz couldn't help but pity the people who worked in such a place as much as those like her who needed it.

Inside wasn't much different, except if possible appearing darker. A few people stood in multiple lines, each with a sign overhead demanding people wait according to the first letter of their surnames. At the far end was a sign which offered New Claims. Liz walked over to it, trying not to stare at others. As difficult as she found it, she couldn't help but wonder if they thought the same of her, that they could see her desperation.

The line for new claims was much longer than others, but dealt with quickly. It felt like a prison sentence to her, as if she were marching to receive gruel for the day and her orders of which cell she might be in for the night.

"Hello, good afternoon, how can I help you?" the woman behind the desk asked cheerfully. She looked young, and far too happy for such a place, but she smiled nonetheless. Her hair was long and blonde, bright and bubbly to match her demeanor. She wore a delicate silk-type cream blouse, and her fingernails were polished bright red. She looked as if she had just stepped off a flight from New York as an attendant, breezing into the wrong place, but made the most of it anyway.

"I have a new claim, my name is Liz Cornwell." The words sounded stilted, as if her mouth was made of clay. They were things she didn't want to utter, an admission of her complete failure. She had no choice, it was what it was, her life, and the direction it had taken.

"That's fine. Please take this form, fill it out and then stand in line over there, according to the first letter of your surname, then someone will go through the form and get you seen to," the polite woman explained, before offering another trademark smile and a pause which meant *next*.

Liz took the form, picked up a pen from the stack on the desk, and walked across to a row of dedicated shelves nearby. Others were already leaning on it, some smoking, others looking out into thin air, daydreaming. It was a kind of no man's land, where those who entered were swallowed up by the system, its tentacles wrapped around you, if the right answers weren't given you were spat back out, ready to live on the streets.

The form was large in size and thick. As she opened it, leafing through, she could see it asked everything imaginable, from employment history to reasons for not working. Much of it would be blank for her, because she had spent so long simply living off Jack's wages. At the time, the last she worked it had seemed a good idea. She could change things, do so much more, learn more, and raise the children. In reality all she had become was a maid, as well as a full-time mother, her life subsumed into serving others. For so long that she had forgotten what it was like to simply be herself, who she really was. She was in for a rude awakening, that much was obvious.

The form was intensive, asking everything about her. The questions felt invasive, as if no stranger should ever be allowed to ask so much, but she knew she was there begging for money, for help with paying her rent, and local taxes. She was in no place to argue with them, so filled out the form as best as she could.

The last part of the form suggested it was optional, her sexuality and ethnicity. She thought or writing something sarcastic, such as being a monk due to no longer wanting to ever know any man ever again, but they wouldn't see the humor in it, so decided against. Besides, all that mattered was the money. At least she would have some to use for essentials.

Finally she flipped over the cover and walked to stand in line. She had no clue how long she had waited, but mentally it seemed like days. Her neck and arms ached with the tension, but in a way she could see the light at the end of the tunnel.

The line slipped by easily enough, each taking their turn, going to sit and answer questions until it was her time. The man she was to see sat behind a Perspex screen, surrounded by wooden enclosures for supposed privacy. Such a word was a mockery, because amid all that concern for her rights, the form still took everything from her.

"Hello," the man said, not quite as polite as the previous lady, without bothering to look at her. Liz replied, sliding the form across the worn wooden desk, under the thin gap under the screen.

The man appeared young, like the girl. His hair was short and dark, contrasting his bright white shirt and short tie. He looked clean cut, but acted like a robot, scanning through the pages, ticking off sections with his pen before flipping to the next part.

"You say you haven't worked in a long time?" the man asked, as if he had simply asked her for the time of day.

"No, my husband worked and I didn't have to."

"Oh," the man replied quietly, his *oh* sounding like a drawn-out drizzle of words, leery and suggestive of her failure.

"I'm homeless, or was until today, and I have children," Liz said, undecided whether to become angry at him or cry.

"Yes, I know you have children, you wrote that on the form."

That was it, forget anything else, now she could be angry. "Well," she said loudly.

"You didn't mention you being homeless now, though, on the form. I'm sure we can expedite things for you," the man said, closing the form and finally making the effort to look at her.

Liz looked at him in sheer surprise. She had just been about to sound off on him and he had somehow knocked her sideways with an absolute change in outlook. Such a surprise and a moment of happiness wouldn't last.

"There are a couple of forms for you to sign, already filled out. Then you'll get your money order."

"Money order?" Liz asked, looking as if she had just been poked with an ice stick.

"Yes, everyone gets one."

"I, I don't have a bank account."

"That's fine, it can be cashed immediately at the Post Office in Lache."

Liz breathed out heavily, a sigh of relief. "Oh, thank goodness. I had worries I wouldn't be able to buy any food tonight," she said, finally allowing herself to smile at him. From the woman at the local Housing Office to the man at the phone booth, and now the two in this place, it seemed some people were on her side after all.

"Right, well it gets sent to your house, and will be there in about two days," the man continued, pleased by her reaction, and his ability to help her.

Once again Liz looked up at him in shock. "Two days?" she asked, unable to mask the emotion in her voice.

"Yes, because we don't do them. It's processed from a different place. There's nothing I can do about it, sorry," the man said, looking at her as if she were a lost puppy in need of a hug.

It was like being swallowed up by a whirlpool. Each time she thought she had a moment of positivity, something else would come along to shatter her illusions. She could argue, but so far she had learned that disagreeing with anyone never changed anything.

"OK," she said, looking down, trying to suppress her emotions.

"Sorry," the man said again, his tone as much suggesting *next* as it did an apology.

Liz stood up, ignoring him from that point on. The next person in line sat down, ready for their own disappointment. Nobody looked at her, as if they feared she might be contagious. No one wanted that kind of bad luck, the possibility that they too might be declined money they so urgently needed.

Leaving the building was the only positive feeling from it, as much as she knew in time she would be better for having something to buy food with. Her need was so great she hadn't stopped to ask anyone how much she might get paid, but it didn't matter, it couldn't because as small as it might be it was still more than she had there and then.

As she walked back up the uneven pathway from the offices, she spotted Dan waiting in his dilapidated van on the corner of the road. It was an intersection of traffic lights with cars passing each way and people all around. Dan had a look about him as if he were worried that at any moment someone or something might crash into him. As Liz walked close, his expression changed, not from worry to relief, but to even worse concern as a police officer walked past right up to him.

"Right, you'll have to move this vehicle. It's in the way," the officer insisted, staring at him hard.

"Right, yes, I'm just," Dan began to say, struggling through stuttering speech.

"Now," the officer again ordered. There would be no third time.

As Liz opened the door to step in, Dan began to drive off. "Hold on," she shouted, holding on to the open door.

"Sorry," Dan said, glancing at Liz.

"Move," the officer shouted again. Dan glanced sideways at him, then back to his girlfriend's mother hanging on for dear life, trotting along as he moved away. His mind couldn't cope, stuck between a rock and a hard place.

"Dan," Liz screeched, at which he hammered his foot to the brake, causing the van to lurch. Liz stood, glaring at him, as if he had lost his mind. She thought he might at any moment suddenly squeal away again, so jumped in, slamming the door behind herself.

"Don't fall apart on me now, Dan, we need you," she said curtly. Before he could respond, a tapping noise on his door interrupted him. He turned to see the police officer glaring at him in a similar fashion to Liz. He began to mouth something in response, but unable to control himself, Dan simply hit the accelerator and once again the van lurched off, while he was still speaking to thin air. Off they went, traveling along, police behind, heading away from the angst of it all.

As they rounded the high corner heading towards a roundabout with fountains in the middle, Liz said something to him. He didn't hear, his mind so focused on worrying about everything, he couldn't cope.

"I said," Liz repeated.

"Pardon?" Dan asked, not listening at all.

"I said, will you please," Liz continued.

The van roared as he pressed the accelerator even harder, even as he approached the stop.

"Will you please," Liz called out, turning to look directly at him. Dan knew she was angry, so much he felt like crying. It was all too much for him, nothing like the quiet life he wanted.

Once again Dan hit the brakes, so far from the stop that a huge gap was left between them and the roundabout. Cars behind honked horns, cars in the other lane slowed, drivers looking at him as if he had gone mad. Dan simply sat, hands clenched tightly to the wheel.

"Dan," Liz said again, only much quieter.

Without looking at her he spoke, mirroring her tone. "If you keep on at me, I'm going to get out and walk off," he said.

Liz laughed, feeling such a burst of humor as she hadn't felt in too long. "Really Dan," she mocked, smiling at him like he was a child. "It seems that's what all the men want to do lately, just get out of their cars and walk off." It was a succinct point, one he acknowledged, but one he objected to regardless.

"No," was all he said in response, hands still fixed on the wheel, staring ahead. Other cars had begun to move around them, some beeping horns, others winding down windows to shout at them. It didn't matter, neither had any attention for them at the moment.

"No, what?" Liz asked.

"No, I'm not like that. I'm not the smartest of people, I'm not the bravest or the best, but I don't quit, not in life, not for Patricia, and not now. I just can't do with you shouting at me. Not now," Dan said. He showed little emotion, but it mattered what he was saying.

"All right Dan, we can go. I won't shout anymore," Liz said, her voice quiet to match his mood.

Without saying another word or looking at her he moved on, the van slowly dragging ahead. They passed the roundabout, moving over into the left lane, and off down the road.

Leaving the city was a series of winding roads and roundabouts, with traffic coming from all directions. Neither spoke, simply prepared to go where they had to.

"Stop," Liz shouted, making Dan jump so much he almost lost control.

"Don't do that," he shouted, looking immediately for a way to stop without blocking traffic.

"Pull over, in there, that road," Liz insisted, pointing out a small side road. Dan did as he was told, edging along until the road ended in front of several small buildings. On the one side of the row was a fish and chip shop, between the two a boarded-up building and at the side was an all-glass fronted building, its entry to the side.

Dan turned to Liz, looked her square in the eye and spoke. "Seriously, you made me stop so urgently, almost causing a crash, because you're a bit hungry and fancied going into the food place for some food?" he asked, clearly annoyed.

Again Liz laughed at him. She loved his immediate naivety. "No you fool, I saw that other place, and no, not the one boarded up. I just need to go in there, and see what they say."

"All right, no problem," Dan said quickly, feeling more than a little sheepish.

Liz stepped out, slowly closing the door, as if she were wary about what she was doing. She walked equally slowly, cautious in her approach, before going around the glass-fronted building.

As she looked at the front, two large glass doors stood before her. Inside, it was all light, simply furnished, a desk in a corner with an unmanned leather chair behind it. A filing cabinet stood in one corner, and the walls were covered in posters, offering all kinds of help, support, and assistance. One showed an African child, leaning its head to one side, with bold white letters above pleading for help.

As she opened the door, warmth swept out, a barrier between the bitter chill eating away at her outside and the welcoming warmth inside. The lights were all on, making it clear just how dark the skies outside had become, signifying the possibility of a storm coming.

Her heels clicked on the white tiles, echoing around the room. Before she could say anything or call for assistance, a woman stepped out. Liz immediately drew the conclusion that she must be from Africa, as she was black, before berating herself for being so stereotypical.

"Hello, how are you?" the woman asked, smiling at Liz as if she had known her all her life. The badge on her lapel said it all, and was the reason why Liz had been so in need to stop. In bright red letters were the words Red Cross. It was just a whim, no real reason for why she should need to go in and speak, but she had put Jack so much out of her mind, spent so much time fire-fighting, that she hadn't had time to dwell on her missing husband, or think to do more to find him.

"Hello," Liz said, suddenly finding herself lost for words. She had ignored the emotion welling within herself for so long, it was as if a tsunami of tears might flood over her, making her so weak again she couldn't do what needed to be done.

"Oh, love, are you all right?" the woman asked, holding out a hand to her. If she had remained uptight, stood off a little like so many did, then she could have coped, stiff upper lip, absolute resolve, and managed. The fact that she seemed so kind, so supportive destroyed any hope of pretense she might maintain. Tears rolled down her cheeks, as she lifted her hand to her face, trying to hide the shame.

"Come on, come sit down, talk to me," the woman said. She walked over, taking a chair from beside a wall, pushing it closer for Liz to sit down. Liz did as she was offered, struggling not to let go altogether. There was work to be done, even if it meant she would be doing it while crying. It was one of those moments where nobody could help, nothing could be done to take away the pain of loss or being abandoned. No arm around the shoulder could change anything, no amount of love or friendship. It was just one of those things that had to be borne, and because of her children, and because of the love of her mother and sister, she would cope.

The woman pulled out a chair of her own, sat across from Liz, one hand on her arm, looking at her with sympathy. She was smartly dressed in a thin black skirt and a soft flowered blouse. Under the name of the Red Cross badge was her own name, Tabatha Simpson. She was young, but clearly not ignorant of how things could be. It didn't seem simply to be her training which made her so good to be around, simply because she cared, and it showed.

"You can tell me if you want to, but you don't have to," Tabatha said quietly. She turned quickly to her desk, pulling over a colorful square box, before pulling several tissues from it. She handed them to Liz, waiting patiently.

Liz wiped dry her nose and the tears away from her face. The constant nagging at the back of her mind, that she must get on, ate away at her desire to express. It felt good to release to someone different, knowing she might not burden others in the same way that she might burden a loved one, who might already be struggling with their problems.

"Well, I won't bore you with it all, but my husband, Jack, he has gone missing. It's been quite a while now, and he left us with a lot of debt, and homeless. I have been fighting, I got a house, and signed on for money, and have our two children with me to move in. But as I'm all set for that, it just hit me to think of him. In a way I worry that he has done something terrible to himself, or been hurt somehow and can't find his way back to us. I've fought so much for all of this that I never had time to stop and think about doing more to find him," Liz said, the words rolling off her tongue as if they had been like her emotions, built up and waiting to be released.

"I see," Tabatha said softly. It was obvious she had been affected by her obvious hurt and pain, but she was too good at her job, too strong to allow herself to show it. "Have you been to the police?"

Liz nodded. "Yes, they were helpful to an extent, they did search for him, asked people, but then it all stopped all of a sudden, and they just said they couldn't really do anything more with it. I mean, it just stopped, and that was it, they were gone. It made no sense," Liz said, tears being replaced by frustration.

"Oh dear, I can see that is making you so upset," Tabatha said. Her response didn't gel with Liz, making her wonder if she were simply sounding off to someone who could never share what it meant.

"I guess I'll just have to get on with it," Liz said, her voice a mixture of hurt and anger.

"Well, the fact is, what we find from time to time is that the police won't say what they know, because they can't. Sometimes they do find a person, and when they do, that person might say they no longer want to ever go home, and that has to be respected. Now it might not be the same with your husband, but it's possible."

"You're seriously saying to me that if Jack left on purpose and they found him, and he told them to leave him alone and that they weren't allowed to say anything about him, then the police would simply walk away and not tell even his children a thing?"

Tabatha nodded. It was a delicate moment, one she knew from experience could lead to sudden outbursts. She was ready for it.

"No. He wouldn't do that to us. I know he loves his children too much to do that. My instincts are telling me that he is either hurt, and doesn't know who he is, or that he isn't alive anymore, and that's it." Liz struggled again with tears, but whatever the outcome, she knew things would never be the same again. Now it was all on her.

"Well, I hope that you find out one day, because I know there is nothing worse than someone going missing and never knowing what happened to them."

It was a small comfort that she had such empathy for her, but she appreciated the gesture, and the opportunity to vent. She knew all too well that her husband of twenty-seven years would never simply walk away and abandon them. If he did, she knew he would never walk away from his children in such a way.

"Thank you, for talking to me," Liz said, feeling stronger for it all. She felt refreshed, having unburdened herself a little.

Tabatha smiled at her as they both stood, before opening her arms and hugging her. It felt odd, but most welcome at the same time. As if a stranger were showing her the kind of love for another stranger that offered more help and support than she'd had since her family fell apart.

"You're very welcome. Please come and talk any time you need to, and if you find out what happened, please do tell me. We are here for you," Tabatha said, still offering that same unconditional smile.

Liz left, walking back to the van. By the time she got in, she showed no more signs of emotion, simply nodding for Dan to drive on.

"Where next?" Dan asked.

"Yorkshire. We're going to get the family, and back here to move into our new house." She knew they had no carpets, no curtains or furniture to speak of, but it didn't matter. They would be together again, and take one more step on rebuilding their home, and their lives.

27

ONE LAST TIME TOGETHER

"So you think he's dead then?"

"I didn't say that. Anything could have happened."

"Kidnapped by aliens?"

"Now you're being daft."

"Just eat your burgers and let's get back," Brenda insisted. She had heard enough of John and Patricia arguing between themselves. It had been a worthwhile time out, taking their minds off the problems.

"How come you never had children, Brenda?" John asked suddenly. Brenda stopped mid-munch to stare at him. It wasn't simply the nature of the question that surprised her, but the fact that it had appeared so out of the blue.

"John, really," Patricia said, unable to look at her aunt.

"Sorry, just making conversation," he said before biting down, shoving the rest of his burger whole into his mouth.

Brenda had been about to reply, right up until the moment he stuffed so much food in, she felt shocked again. Patricia looked at her, shrugging. She was used to it.

"Well, perhaps I didn't want to have a greedy hog like you who shoves whole meals into their mouths and asks daft questions," Brenda replied, deliberately nibbling at her own meal. She too wanted to take a large bite out of the cheese, bacon, and pork burger, to satisfy her hunger, but she wouldn't be a hypocrite, so tiny morsels would have to do.

"Oh, right, so you chose not to have children, because children stuff their faces and ask silly questions?" John asked.

"You said it, you always ask silly questions," Patricia interrupted.

"Yeah, but I'm not always daft. Like I know I have to go to a different school soon, that I might never see any of my old friends again. We may never go into a house we own again, rarely ever have any money, and life will probably never be the same, even if Dad does come back," John said, before eating some of his fries. He didn't make eye contact, knowing full well that after what he had said, the impact would be just what he intended.

Neither Brenda or Patricia spoke, but neither ate anything more. Today was a day of shocks and surprises, and none more than the young man beside them. Brenda thought to herself that he was growing up, saddened by the thought of how he had to, and why. It was the last age of his true youth, and any remnants of innocence would probably be stolen by his missing father.

"Do you want my fries?" Patricia asked, without saying anything more.

"No, thank you," John replied, still staring at the last of his meal.

"Really? That's not like you. Not hungry anymore?" Patricia asked.

"Yeah, famished, just don't want yours after you've had your grubby hands all over them."

"Ah, there it is, that same old John, the one we know, love, and can't stand. Welcome back," Patricia said, throwing a fry at him.

"Come on, wrap it up, let's get back," Brenda said, gathering the wrappings and empty drink cartons for the bin.

"Why, are we going home for tea?" John asked, at which both Brenda and Patricia laughed. Neither were sure if he meant it, but it was funny nonetheless.

It had been a successful day, with each being bought nice things by their aunt. Brenda was just one of those people, always upbeat, always cheerful, a glass-half-full kind of person. Her innate happiness was infectious, and a stark change from how life had too often been with their parents.

As the three sat on the back seat, riding the bus back, John turned to Brenda, giving her a look which made it clear he was going to say one of his *things*. She looked back, waiting with bated breath.

"Thank you for today, and what you bought me. It's been great," he said, before looking back outside.

Brenda looked away too, only because she almost burst into tears. There were times when she regretted not having children, because of the love they could and did show. It was so nice to have someone to share things with, others to have such a different outlook on life, being so young. She held back her emotion, because it wouldn't be fair to burden others with how she felt, given what they were going through. It was tough, because she loved family.

"Sometimes, John," Patricia began, before biting her lip. Her first instincts were to be sarcastic, but she could see from the look on his face, the relaxed, almost mature appearance he offered that he was in a difference place now, and she should reflect it. "Sometimes, I really love you," she finished.

John's eyes widened, as if in shock horror. He had expected something funny or sarcastic; the last thing he wanted was her to be *nice.* For the first time in his life, he was lost for words. Quickly he turned away to avoid her seeing he was blushing. Still, it was good to have people care about him, and though he would never admit it, he cared about them just as much.

The bus ride as usual was winding and bendy, up and down steep hills until it reached Carlin Howe. The views were often beautiful, smooth and clear beaches, wildlands of grass and dunes, heather laid in sporadic patches. It was an empty and lonely place in cold times, but brought to life by all the myriad of people milling about their lives. Neither Patricia or John could imagine ever staying in such a place, but for all that they could still appreciate how wonderful it could be.

The bus finally stopped outside the old steelworks in Carlin Howe, at which the three dropped off and began the long walk up the hill. On either side of the narrow road were endless terraced houses, built after the war and each gaining their own unique character over time. People did that, it was their affect, demonstrating the nature of themselves and their imprint on a small place in Yorkshire.

John went first, up the steep concrete steps, turning the handle, knowing it was hardly ever locked and in through the long dark hallways. The others followed, each carrying new bags of things bought for them. As John opened the hall door to go into the back dining room, his face lit up to see his mother there, in the old chair beside Bessie, and Dan by the window, looking out of place as always. He seemed to have that look when around Patricia, but more so when he had done something for himself and not others.

"Mom," John said, louder than he had intended. He dropped his bags to the floor right where he was before engulfing her in a loving hug. He had even fooled himself just how much he had missed her, and for such a short time. He was never one for showing emotion, but it was such a time, and he felt no choice. Liz hugged him back, arms wrapped tightly around him, her eyes closed, feeling as if all were right again.

Patricia walked in behind him, quickly looking at the two hugging, and smiled. Immediately she glanced at Dan, her smile dropping quickly as he looked back at her. She was annoyed at him, and would be sure to let him know how much soon enough.

Brenda struggled in, dropping arms full of bags to the floor, smiling at them all. "Hello, Liz, back again," she said happily, wary of prying too much.

"Not for long now they have a house," Bessie said, stealing the thunder. It was a double-edged sword, because on the one hand she was pleased to see her daughter having a place to live for them all, but on the other hand she would worry, what kind of place it was, how she would manage, and how much she would miss having them there once she was alone again. She would never say as much, but still, it all mattered.

"It's fantastic, Mom, well done. What's it like?" Patricia asked. It was a question that to Liz had no reasonable answer. She couldn't be too negative about it, because she wouldn't want her children feeling as she did, but she also couldn't be too kind about it, because she knew once they got there they would see it for how it really was. Some subtlety was needed.

"It's big, it's got four bedrooms," Liz said, intending to continue, but decided to simply lead with that and see the reaction.

"It's in Lache," Dan said, until Liz glared at him, at which he simply shut up.

"Wow, sounds pretty good then," John said, sounding unusually interested.

"Yeah, I think you'll like it. Needs a bit of work, but we can sort it out, I'm sure."

Bessie looked at her. She knew her daughter too well, able to read between the lines. She was putting on a brave front, but nothing would be said for now. As much as her instincts were for her to suggest they stay, and settle there, closer to where they had family support, she knew her daughter was independent and wouldn't want to. Besides, there would still be the problem of a place to live, a home of their own.

Liz glanced at her mother, knowing full well she was aware of things, but neither spoke. It was what it was, as always.

"So, what now, are we packing to go today?" Patricia asked.

"No, you can't go now, it's late. It's dark out and cold. Wait till morning," Brenda suggested, sharing Bessie's concerns for being suddenly left, especially after such a good day.

"Don't be daft, Patricia, of course we can't go now," John said. All eyes were on him, waiting for his own unexpected nugget of wisdom. "We've not even had tea yet," he continued, his expression quite serious, as if it were even more important than having a home.

"Food again?" Liz asked, hands on her hips, as if she were about to scold him for being so foolish. John looked at her without saying a word, afraid if he said anything more if might be a problem.

"All right then, Dan," Liz said suddenly. He didn't quite jump to attention as much as turn white as a sheet. "You and Patricia can go to the place up top, and get five rounds of fresh fish and fries," she continued. All eyes lit up at the thought, the lovely freshly caught Yorkshire fish, covered in batter, lathered with salt and vinegar. It didn't matter that they had eaten so much already, at the back of Liz's mind she wondered what their meals would be like once home, and money dried up. They would make the most of it, for now.

"Bread with mine, please, three rounds—no, make that four," John chimed in, acting like a small puppy excited at the prospect of a bone which it could never hope to finish.

"Sure, John, you can get into the kitchen, get all the plates out, knives and forks, and prepare your own bread," Liz mocked.

"Me?" John simpered, remaining steadfastly where he was.

"Yeah, you," Patricia said, pouting at him as if they were both young children again.

"I have to go help carry the fries," John insisted, jumping up to put on his shoes and coat. Liz smiled at him, knowing full well he wouldn't do much to help unless she insisted. She wouldn't, not now, because she wanted him to be happy. Times ahead wouldn't be as good, that was a fact.

As Dan and Patricia put on their coats, ready to go out, Liz stopped them, touching Dan by the arm. Both turned to look at her.

"Oh, and by the way, thank you for helping so much," she said. Dan blushed a little, unsure whether to smile and thank her, or whether she was being sarcastic.

"You're welcome," he said quietly, hoping that was it, all said and done. It wasn't.

"Oh, and by the way, you're paying for the food, Dan," Liz said quickly, without a hint of a smile. Dan tried to speak, but words failed him. He just nodded instead, figuring it was easier to just go and do it. Patricia gave him a wry smile, thinking he had gotten off lightly for simply leaving them when he did.

"I'll come and give you a hand in the kitchen," Bessie said, at which she struggled to stand up. Her legs ached, but no more than the rest of her. Her limbs had grown swollen over time, making any kind of movement difficult, but with pain, like life, it was something she accepted and just got on with it.

"No, Mom, you stay there, I'll do it," Liz insisted.

Bessie ignored her, forcing herself to stand up. She took a wooden walking stick and pressed on it, leaning enough that the rest of her body could get her moving.

"Seriously, Mom," Liz said again, quite aware that she was wasting her time complaining.

"I've been doing this since before you were born," Bessie said, walking past her without looking in her direction.

Both stood, side by side in the kitchen. Bessie buttered bread and prepared drinks as Liz moved around gathering plates and cutlery. Liz never spoke, but she felt emotional over it. Her mother was the one true bedrock in her life, someone for all of her life she had been able to depend on. The moment would be a short one, so close together, and in a way so safe, but it mattered, and gave her strength to do the same, to be the same for her own children in the days ahead.

"Food time," John shouted, bursting through the living room door from the hallway.

"Hey," Bessie snapped, with her typically loud voice. Loud when she wanted it to be. John ignored her, dropping the bags of hot food on the small table by the window.

"Bring it in here, John," Liz said. She was used to his behavior, and knew he had an immature streak, but it was fine to her, because she knew he was changing. For her it was sad in a way, because how he grew up and changed wouldn't be natural, it would be forced, and there was nothing she could do to change it.

John picked up the large carrier bags of food, carrying them into the kitchen. Immediately he spotted a large plate covered in freshly buttered slices of white bread, piled high. Deftly he grabbed a slice, folded it over, then over again, before shoving the entire thing into his mouth. He expected a chastening for it, but nobody said a word. It was food, there to be eaten.

Only Bessie and Liz sat at the table. The others sat on chairs, plate in hand, drinks beside them, fully focused on the wonderful fresh fish and fat-cut fries, smothered in salt. John picked up bread, filled it with his food and scoffed it quickly, but nobody had time for chatter. It was a communal moment, shared by the enjoyment of the local food.

Patricia finished first, wiping her mouth with a cloth, then looked up as others were finished. "Thanks for that, Dan," she said succinctly.

Dan looked at her, quite surprised. It never occurred to him that he would be thanked for anything.

"Yes," Liz said, finishing the last of her meal. "Thank you for that, and for the van, and for helping us. I don't know what we would have done without you."

It was a shock to hear them being so pleasant, but especially Liz, who rarely ever said much to him. "You're welcome," Dan said, looking down at his food. It was a nice gesture, something that helped to reassure him, he mattered too.

"Thanks," John said.

"What for?" Patricia asked.

"Thanks, to me, for thinking of this," John replied, continuing to eat but regretting that his plate was almost empty, but his stomach didn't feel full.

"Er, no, Mom thought of it," Patricia said.

"Nope, me, food," John said, standing up quickly. He dropped his plate onto the table, looking at Bessie. Her plate was still half full as she picked bits of fish here and there.

"No, John, leave Gran alone," Patricia said, ready to pounce if he tried anything.

"It's all right, he can have it. I'm finished," Bessie said, handing her plate to John. He took the plate, nodding thanks, as if it were a peace offering and it was his duty to consume it.

Together they ate the food, and enjoyed the warmth of the

crackling open fire. The entire room was warm, just right, and being all of the family, it felt good.

"You like this fire, nice and warm, John?" Liz asked.

"Yes," John said, struggling to eat and speak at the same time.

"Good, because the house we're going to has open fires too."

Patricia looked up at Liz, clearly surprised. "I didn't think they still had houses with open fires like this. I thought Gran's was the last of them."

"No, well," Liz began, not wanting to say much more. She needed everyone home, no doubts, no regrets, and then they would deal with who thought what when it occurred.

"Mom," John said, picking up the last of his fries, finally feeling he was satisfactorily full.

"Yes, love?" Liz replied. It was a quiet moment, one on which they all reflected something different.

"Do you think Dad is dead?" John asked. If Liz had been still eating, she might well have choked, but it was enough of a question, probably the hardest thing she had ever been asked. It was enough that she felt lost for words.

"John," Patricia said, aware of the rising emotion welling from his words, for them all.

"No, I don't," Liz said firmly. Deep down, she had no idea, but suspected the worst. She had tried to be positive, her mind running through various scenarios, but how she felt about each changed with her own moods. At times she would be hopeful, at others disinterested, sometimes so hurt by it all she would lay at night weeping. There were no easy answers, not for her, or anyone else.

John didn't answer, or look at her. All remained silent, as if waiting for some kind of wisdom to make it all easier for them.

"I don't know, John. I don't know where he is. I know he's your dad, and still my husband, and until I find out one day what happened, I will be asking that same question," Liz finally said.

"How come you haven't done more to find him, then?" John asked. It was obvious they were things he had been thinking about, until finally he simply had to open up.

Liz almost laughed to herself, realizing it might not look right if she did. She maintained a firm expression before him, aware that they were all looking at her.

"I called the police, they did what they could. I spoke to the Red

Cross."

"You never mentioned that," Patricia said.

"No, well, I never had time. They said much of what the police did, that sometimes people didn't want to be found."

"Surely if he was dead they would keep looking?" John asked.

"I don't know. Obviously they keep it open, but if there are no leads, I think eventually they kind of drop it, and move on to the next."

"Unless it's a child, in which case they keep it a priority," Brenda said, interrupting. "Then they will carry on for ages. Susan Marple in Darlington had one of her daughters go missing. They kept on at it for weeks, until they found her living with her dad. He had taken her and kept her without telling anyone."

"Well, that's good to know, but it doesn't help us," Liz said, far from impressed.

"Sorry," Brenda said, unsure what the fuss was.

"For now, all we can do is get on with our lives, and hope things change, that we find him or he finds us, and then we will see what happens," Liz said, trying to sound optimistic.

"Still doesn't sound like we're doing anything. I mean, can't we try to find him?" John asked. Liz understood his need to know, wanting more, but she was already at her wits' end, without ideas. She found herself wondering more and more whether she even cared. She would never admit to it.

"When we go back, and we're settled in the new house, I will go back to the old house in Elton. I will ask around, knock on doors, put up postcards and maybe some posters, and try to find out what I can for us. All right?" Liz said, feeling she might simply tell him to shut up if he carried on. She could empathize with his concern, but she was only human, subject to the same stress and suffering. Especially when she had no answers of her own.

"Sounds good. I could go with you," John suggested.

"Oh no," Liz said, her voice lighter, as if she were ready for him.

"Why not?" John asked, falling for it.

"Because, my dear boy, you will be in school, your new one, in your shiny new uniform."

John's face sank, as if he were Superman faced with a chunk of kryptonite. "Dark days ahead," he said, at which everyone laughed. Liz chuckled at him, finding it ironic he had something worse to worry about than being homeless or missing a parent.

"I think we all need to get to bed. Going to be up early, load the van and get to our new house," Liz said.

"Yes, well, I'll have to get home. Call me when you can, so I can come and visit you at your lovely new home," Brenda said, standing up to put on her coat.

Patricia stood up to hug her. John simply sat, not wanting a hug in the least, but Brenda leaned over quickly, kissing him on the cheek. He almost melted, shying away from the pleasantry, but it was nice all the same. Finally Brenda hugged Bessie, telling her she would be back soon.

"I'll see you out," Liz said, standing beside her sister. Brenda smiled at her, nodding.

As Liz walked through into the hall, Brenda turned to look at them all, smiling. "See you soon," she said cheerfully.

Liz opened the front door, stepping out onto the top step.

Brenda followed, out into the night air, pulling her collar close round. "It's going to be cold tonight," she said wistfully.

"I think it's going to be a cold winter," Liz replied.

"Keep the fires burning," Brenda said, offering her sister a kindly smile. The two hugged, feeling the need to be tearful, but neither did. There had been enough of that, and no doubt in time much more, but not for now.

"Take care, and if you need anything, call me. I will come down when you're settled, help you any way I can," Brenda said, holding Liz's arm. It was a kind moment, well meant, and helped. Liz wondered how life might have been if she never had children, were an only child herself, no mother or father around, no one to care. She knew the only reason she could go on and fight was because of the love behind her.

"I look forward to seeing you soon," Liz said, pulling Brenda close again for a hug. Brenda smiled once more before leaving, walking off down the street. For all their young lives it had been the only house they had known for their mother. Coming back, and seeing such things, reminded her of their time as children, walking off to school together, and to work, away all the time, but always coming back. It was good to have family, and memories.

Finally she turned to go in, closing the door. The next few days would be the biggest trial of her life, worse than anything she had experienced, but at least she knew she had people around her who cared.

28

THE SEEDS OF HOPE

"I know how to get there, I've been there already."

"Yes, but don't forget."

"I won't. What? Forget what?"

"That fundamentally, deep down, you're useless." Everyone laughed. Everyone except Dan.

"Yes, well, I got all this stuff into this van, I drove us here, and," Dan began to say.

"And then you got lost," Patricia said, following up on her theme, laughing as she did.

"No," Dan insisted.

"We're nearly here," Liz said, interrupting them both.

"Cool," John called, eager to see, but unable to as he was stuck in the back of the van, surrounded by boxes, and as he saw it, junk.

As they turned the road from Saltney to the road into Lache, all eyes were on the place itself. At the top end were perfectly laid gardens among large houses. Even the roads were flat and clean, nothing out of sight. As they moved on towards Lache, the houses changed. Most were older terraced, built in the nineteen forties and fifties. Some had chimneys, none showing signs of life, still welcoming with well-maintained gardens. Patricia watched closely, as Dan drove them slowly down the long road towards the center. The difference was obvious, looking dark, the walls of houses seeming muddy with time, smoke, and age. She had only ever known one place in their lives, one house, one type of place. It was a culture shock to see how things would be. For the first time she felt poor, but not for the first time she wondered if she could go to live with

Dan, if she, like him, could get away with it.

Dan drove the van slowly to the large roundabout surrounded by shops, turning towards the house, as Liz directed him to pull up in the small driveway near the brick archway that led to the back.

"Do we have anything to sit on, Mom?" John asked quickly.

"What about beds, where will we sleep?" Patricia asked. It immediately occurred to her to wonder if then would be a good time to mention her living with Dan, but for the moment held off.

"I will sort it. Just let us get in, and give me time. I will sort things as I can," Liz said, pleading for patience.

As the van stopped, Dan opened his door to step out, at which the others followed suit. John remained, trapped inside but eager to see.

"Hold on, John," Liz shouted, pulling the house keys from her pocket. He did no such thing, clambering to get over boxes, pushing things away until he managed to find his way to the van's back doors. As Liz walked around the pathway to the front gate, he banged heavily on the back windows. She turned to look, to see him wide-eyed, almost manic, like a crazed dog trying to escape.

"I think he needs a bowl of water," Patricia said as she followed Dan. She hadn't bothered to look at the house, simply accepting what it was going to be, refusing to be drawn on her own feelings of how things had turned out.

Liz opened up the doors, at which John breathed out a huge sigh of relief. He jumped out quickly, brushing himself off before stopping to look up and around. To him it was very different, starkly so. Everything seemed so much darker, the walls of the houses, the sagging, green-tinged roof tops, the smoking chimneys. Even the road seemed dull, as if the life had been run out of it, uneven and discolored. Finally he turned to the house, seeing it abridging a newsagents shop, as if the house had somehow grown around it. Liz watched him, almost breathless, waiting for his reaction. She hadn't thought about it until then, how he was affected by it might affect them all. He often seemed bulletproof; no matter what happened he just got on with it. If he showed any signs of a loss of spirit, then surely none of them would cope.

The tension was clear and obvious, as all of them stood, as if time stood still for a moment. John looked on at the house, not blinking, his emotions and thoughts unclear, hidden, perhaps from him too.

Liz looked at Patricia, but she had nothing. Nobody knew what to say. It was obvious Patricia would cope, she would manage, because she had an out, she could walk away and was young enough to rebuild her life. Without John, Liz wasn't sure if she could do the same, not in the short term.

John turned to look at her. "Well, open up then, I want to get in and see my room," he said, still without giving anything away emotionally. Liz almost burst out laughing, or crying, she couldn't decide which. Picking the keys from her pocket, she headed through the gate and up the steps. She couldn't help but feel some embarrassment at the state of the garden, but it would keep John busy by kindly allowing him to clear it for them. As she opened the door and stepped in, it became clear that the place was musty. She thought to open up the windows, but most downstairs were boarded up, to cover the broken glass anyway.

The four walked in, along down the hallway and into the living room. It was dark, but enough light filtered through to see the place and what it represented. It was only at that point that Liz felt anything from being inside the house. Before she felt nothing, simply a need to get a home, get settled, and rebuild their lives. Now, as it was all becoming clear to her, that this was where they would remain for nobody knew how long, just what it was truly like.

"Nice color on the walls," Patricia said, looking at the bright orange around the room. Black damp had set in around the corners, and white paint flaked from the wood on the sills and skirting. The floor was bare wood, with a stone hearth around the open fireplace.

"Oh cool, an open fire. Just like at Gran's," John said suddenly.

"Er, yeah, should be lovely," Liz said, unsure of just what to say, for fear that he might somehow object or change his view.

Patricia walked through and down the step into the kitchen area, or what was supposed to represent a facsimile of one. She also gave nothing away, but Liz knew she was like her, that she would just get on with it, even if she didn't like it.

"Might be a bit draughty when it snows," Dan said, with his hands in his pockets. His remark was meant to be humorous, but as often it fell flat. Liz glared at him again in her way, at which he looked away, quickly trying to think of something positive to say. He couldn't manage it, as his mind kept telling him to say how nice it was he had his own flat.

As they all stood watching, a huge cracking sound made them all jump. Liz looked around quickly as John stepped away from the fireplace he had been inspecting. The cracking sound grew louder as a chiseled breaking sound mixed with it.

"Are they knocking down our house?" John asked, looking at his mother in the way he used to, the frightened look on his face which only she could comfort him over. Even if for a short while, he was still her little boy, in a way.

Liz thought to quickly react, to rush outside and berate whoever was doing wrong to them. Before she could move, one of the large wooden sheets fell away from the living room window, bringing with it bright, cold sunshine from outside. Each shielded their eyes, having grown accustomed to the darkness, as if it were an entwined part of existence in the new place, that it were natural and no other possibility existed.

Finally, eventually it became clear, as they adjusted, to see a man standing outside. He pulled the boards away, dropping them slowly onto the garden beyond, then turned to look in, like some savior, brought to provide a reprieve from the madness of the hovel they had inherited. He stopped, looking at them, almost as surprised at seeing them as they were to see him. It was an odd experience for all, where the answer was obvious, but needed saying anyway.

"Are you supposed to be here?" the man asked. He was a burly man, wearing a light green high-visibility jacket, even though the sun outside was bright. He wore thick leather well-worn gloves, looking as if he were well used to being outside in all weathers.

Liz looked at him, feeling confused for the moment. "Well, the bigger question is, are you supposed to be here?" she asked, feeling indignant.

"Yes, I am," the man replied in the same tone. "I have a work order here to repair and replace all the broken windows."

The comment immediately brightened her outlook, as she realized he was there for their needs. "Oh, right," Liz said, laughing. "Yes, I'm just moving in today. I have keys."

"Ah, right, well I guess I'm here for you, then. Won't take long. All the rubbish has been cleared, and the chimneys are open, so I'll do this now and it will be much warmer for you," he said, at which the mood all round lightened considerably.

"All right, have a quick look at the house, and then let's unload the van," Liz said to the others, rubbing her hands together. Though it was sunny outside, the air had a considerable chill to it, and a clear night ahead would mean it would be bitterly cold at night.

"We haven't got any beds," John said, offering an unusually balanced insight into the truth they faced, one which until then nobody had mentioned properly.

"We haven't even got anything to sit on," Patricia kindly explained.

"Let's not worry about that, we don't have time for sitting or sleeping. We have work to do. We will worry about that sort of thing when we're done," Liz responded, in a manner which left no room for dissent. The three looked at one another, shrugging, accepting her wisdom.

"Dan, go to the newsagents, and get me a local newspaper. Patricia, John, get into the van and begin unloading boxes, leave heavy stuff for us all to handle," Liz continued. Without further ado, each took to their tasks, leaving her to stand, watching outside, thinking ahead.

The green-jacket man appeared again outside the window. He held a small oblong cardboard box, inside which lay equally sized panes of glass. The frames, although fine, were all metal, single pane and in need of paint.

"I shall clip out all the old and put fresh new glass in throughout," he said, at which Liz smiled. As he smiled back, she suddenly felt a chill, for allowing herself to be overly friendly with another man, all while her own man was still missing. She wondered again of what to do, if she were to blame, that he was gone because of her. She asked herself was she a bad wife, a bad person? She caught herself, feeling sorry for herself, and dawdling while she had the cheek to insist others work.

"So you're moving in here today?" the man asked, stopping her just as she was about to walk away.

Liz looked at him, wondering whether she should say anything or just nod and carry on out. It was something which stood out for her now, how she was the main person in the house, the one in charge, and most responsible. In the past if there was trouble, a problem or simply something needing doing, she would call Jack, leave it to him, let him deal with the hassle. It was a reminder of her own faults, for all of his. Now she had no choice.

"Yes, yes we are, I guess," she said hesitantly. As much as she knew it was true, she still struggled to deal with the fact of it, or to express just what it meant in words.

As he worked, unpacking the box and ladling putty into the metal frame, he looked at her. "You know there are other houses empty around here," he said, deciding not to make direct eye contact with her. He could see she was struggling in all sorts of ways, but the kind of person he was, he couldn't help but chat.

"Really? Like where?"

"Up the road. Proper houses, not like this, and in better condition."

"Right," Liz said. She didn't want to admit how she felt about the house, but felt equally annoyed at what he was suggesting.

"Just how they are, but it's not nice that they put you here. They could have given you better," he said, leaving it at that. He pressed a pane of glass in and cut off excess putty, before walking away.

For the moment Liz felt anger, but as bad as she felt, it was still a home, and she was in no position to argue. It was what it was, and she would have to make the best of it. Besides, the last thing she wanted was to upset her children over it. They were there with her, and for now accepted it. Without another word she walked out, left for the van and grabbed a sweeping brush.

"Oh, you're helping out after all then," John said as she passed. The look she returned proved it was an unwise thing to say. He remained quiet, pulling out a box which looked small enough for his skinny frame to handle. Dan could take the rest, he figured.

Liz went back into the house and began sweeping the hall. It was already well cleaned by the Council, but it didn't matter, because she would work out her emotions by doing something useful.

"Where shall I put the boxes?" Patricia asked, struggling through the front door.

"They're all marked, for each room," Liz replied.

"Erm, no, they're not."

Liz frowned. "We did that, didn't we?"

"Nope," Patricia said, deciding against sarcasm. Things were stressful enough without that.

"Great. Another thing to worry about. Just put them in the living room, and we will have to open them and go through them one at a time to see where they belong. Put the suitcases in whichever bedrooms you want. That's if you're going to stay with us." The moment she said it she regretted it, but it was one of those things she couldn't help think, nagging at the back of her mind. It was a stupid thing to give life to, she knew it.

"Thanks, Mom, but I'm not going anywhere. OK?" Patricia replied quickly, not bothering to wait for a response.

"Love," Liz tried to say, but she just pushed past her, into the living room. John was already there. He was in his own world again. If he had heard, or been interested in what was said, he didn't show it. He never did. There was nothing more to be said, better to leave it. Liz carried on sweeping as Patricia dragged her brother back to the van.

As Liz swept, Dan returned, carrying several newspapers, sweets, drinks, and even comics. Liz looked at him, feeling impressed. "Oh well done, you thought of us," she said, lifting the newspaper from his arm.

"Yeah," Dan replied hesitantly.

"What did you get us to eat?"

"Erm," he replied, with no idea of what to say. As Liz looked at him, it dawned on her that what he had bought was enough for one person, and that was him.

"You have a look at the newspaper, I forgot something," Dan finally said. He turned to leave, without waiting for her response. She figured it was a good idea.

"Drinks too, Dan," she said, leaning the brush against a doorframe. She looked through the newspapers, a national paper, a sports paper, all as useless as he could be at times. Finally the last was a local paper, which she opened to the classified section.

"I'm hungry," John suddenly said, making her jump.

"Don't do that," she said, louder than she had intended.

"Watch it, Mom's on the warpath," Patricia said, sliding past them both. Liz wanted to say something, but before she could, it was too late.

"Right, who wants what?" Dan said, as if he had deliberately timed it to save the day. Tension was fraught, but as always something came up to help.

"Ooh, food," John said quickly, picking through the things Dan had brought back.

"Don't worry about me, I'll just unload the van alone," Patricia said, walking past again. Ignoring her, John picked out a few packs of sweets, a pasty, and a sandwich, before walking out also.

"Thank you, Dan," Liz said, picking a pack of mints from his collection. "What drinks did you get?" she asked. Dan looked at her like a lost puppy, only then realizing what he had forgotten.

"Doesn't matter. I have a little bit of money, I'll go back and get some," she said, folding up the newspaper and dropping it onto the nearby stairs.

"Sorry," Dan said, but it didn't matter much. He had done something anyway.

As Liz walked out, John was returning from the van with what might have been the smallest box he could find. "Where you going, Mom?" he asked.

"To get us some drinks. Might help to cool us all down a bit."

"Nice. I'll have a pint," he replied, looking more cheerful than she had expected.

"Go up and see which room you want," she said, catching him at just the right time. It was a good way to see what he wanted, but also avoid helping with the van.

"It's fine, I'll do it all," Patricia said, carrying a suitcase and carrier bags. Liz thought to say something abruptly, finally giving in to her own sense of frustration and anger, but before she could say anything, a man walked up to her, as if he were in two minds over how to approach.

Liz looked at him. "Yes, can I help you?" she asked.

"Yes, I have some mail for you," the man said, at which she realized he was simply a postman. She had been so involved in what was going on that she hadn't even noticed his uniform.

"If it's a bill, it's not for me, we're only just moving in," she said, wanting to sound cheerful but simply betraying her own emotions though it.

He had no idea what it was, nor cared, so simply handed her the few letters, smiled, and walked away. There were three letters. The first was white, marked for a Mrs. Bell, with the correct address. Liz decided to simply cross out the name, write on it "not at this address" and post it back, or she would if she could find a pen. The second was a brown envelope with a clear window. She turned it over to lift the flap. She thumbed along it, tearing it open. Inside was a green oblong piece of paper with black print across it. She had never seen anything like it, feeling a little lost, but it had her name printed on it.

"Oh, nice, you have a money order," Dan said as he walked past, carrying a box.

Liz looked at him, feeling confused. "What do you mean?" she asked, looking through the envelope. There was nothing else in it.

"It's a money order. You can take it to the post office over the road and cash it," Dan said, as if she had won the lottery.

"Really?" Liz asked, suddenly feeling much better. Patricia had intended to say something curt again, but upon seeing all eyes were on the letter, she stopped, feeling curious about what was going on.

"Yep, it says in that small box, one hundred and sixty-eight pounds and fifty-eight pence. It's from the Benefits Agency," Dan explained, before walking off with his box. He was finally pleased he could do something that didn't make her angry.

"Oh wow," Liz said suddenly, feeling as if she had just won the lottery. "We have money, we can get food, get stuff," she said, holding the paper tightly, as if it might somehow blow away in the wind and she would be broke again.

"Cool, can I have a pair of football boots?" John asked, having stepped from the house once again silently.

"No, don't be daft. We can go out and get some stuff in a bit, and I have an idea," Liz said, looking at them both. Patricia was smiling again, so finally it was all coming good again.

"Does it involve food?" John asked hopefully.

"No, well, yes, but not right now. Come inside with me, I will show you."

Liz walked off as the others followed, back into the living room, which was slowly darkening as new glass panes were added.

"Right," Liz said, picking up the local newspaper. She leafed through it, until she found what she was looking for, then leaned across to Patricia and Dan. "This classified section has listings for items for sale. Look through, and you will see a few cheap items, including sofa and chairs, and beds. I need you to go to the telephone box, and call a few of these, the cheap ones, and then arrange to go look at, and buy things that we need."

Patricia looked at Liz, raising her eyebrows. It wasn't the best suggestion she had been offered recently. Dan looked at her, wishing he were somewhere else.

"It's fine, just get cheap, get the price and address, and arrange to go pick it up, and I will carry on here sorting things." Again neither answered, but knew it would be pointless arguing.

"What about the money? I mean, Dan and I don't have much, if any," Patricia said. She knew Dan might well have more, but would be loath to spend again. He had already bought fuel and had no desire to do more, that much was obvious.

"I will go cash this money order, and give you the money out of that. It's either that or we sit on the floor in here, and sleep on the floor in the bedrooms."

"OK, we'll go do that then," Dan said, taking the newspaper. Patricia glared at him, annoyed that she didn't have time to consider a good reason not to do it. The last thing she wanted to do was traipse around looking for furniture in the houses of strangers. Dan chose to ignore her, simply deciding to get on with it. He took the newspaper, closed it, and walked out, feeling very much in charge. If he had to choose between who to anger, Liz or his girlfriend, he figured it might as well be Patricia, because she was nowhere near as bad as Liz for barking orders and being angry.

"John, you grab a brush from the back of the van, and get upstairs and begin sweeping," Liz ordered, looking around for things to do.

"OK, I'll get right to it," he replied, not intending to do anything except go choose a bedroom.

Things had begun, windows being fixed, floors being cleaned, boxes unpacked, and new things arriving. It was far from perfect, but to Liz felt natural, the way it should be. One way or another she would have her home back, only this time on her own terms.

29

THE LADY ALONE

Mavis muttered to herself as she walked. She was the old lady of Lache, the woman everyone knew, but no one spoke to. She was large even though she never stopped. Few knew anything about her, like so many who seem different than the normal, she was almost invisible.

She wore flat-soled shoes, but never worried about her feet, full of calluses, bruised from the constant procession from one place to the next. She wore a simple dress, full of faded flowers, a slight rain jacket hanging loosely from her shoulders. Her hair was white and curly, showing signs that at one time if may have been cared for, but not anymore.

The expression on Mavis's face appeared blank, but she stared at the ground, whispering things that only she knew about. She called a name that nobody would know, talking to no one but herself.

It was a long, lonely walk, through the streets or Lache, in and around, but always there, up and down Cliveden Road, around Sycamore Drive and into the streets near the health center, the school, the shops, and back. Every day would be the same, wandering as if she were a free spirit destined to roam around looking for a kind of peace which she would never find.

People knew her, or of her, vaguely of her first name, the few that took any notice of her movement around their homes. Nobody cared to ask what her story was, just that she was the crazy lady who walked out in all weathers, who people crossed the road to avoid. She had troubles which were beyond help, with answers and no future. People didn't talk to her, in case she followed them, in case she wouldn't let go, in case what she had was infectious.

Mavis had a secret, one which she couldn't express, a dirty one. Hers was a tale of loss, which everyone could feel, but nobody wanted to. She was a haunted woman, surrounded by the surreal, nightmares so bad she could never wave hard enough or wake screaming loud enough to make them cease. Hers was a dark life, always in the shadows, never able to feel the joy of a smile, unaffected by human company, as if it were all a mirage to her.

The path ahead was a hard one, but she never complained, never cared for how it felt underfoot, only that she had to walk, and never stop. If it rained, or snowed, she would find a way, never truly looking ahead.

"Morning, Mavis," a voice called. It might have been Ben, the local butcher, but she didn't know. He always said hello, was always so kind, so generous, but that was it with him, a nice hello and gone again. He never stayed long enough to see how she was, just enough for a smile and then he was gone. Mavis never replied.

The large double-decker bus waited as people climbed on, each finding their way, full of purpose, ignoring the strange lady as she walked. Mavis crossed the road, carrying on like she did. The driver pulled away, then stopped for the large lady blocking his way. He thought to beep the horn, but didn't, because he had seen her before, and knew she would be gone in a moment, and besides, he wasn't sure she was all there.

The lady went, and so did the bus, and on it went, strangers ignoring each other, as Mavis walked some more. She called out, whispered, muttered, and from time to time, called so loud it sounded like a cat crying.

When it rained it was the worst, because the tears rolling down her cheek weren't from the heavens, but from her own grief. It seemed as if she used the storms when they came as a means to hide her own sorrow, that only then she could express her feelings when alone in the rain. If that was how it seemed, it wasn't the truth. The truth was a secret belonging to her, one that she could never properly share with others.

Mavis walked alone, surrounded by people, but known to nobody. No one cared, no one stopped to talk, hers was a life of loneliness and emptiness.

Sorrow stalked her, blinded her to others, except when they shared her loss. Today was a sunny day, bright and cold. Today was different to her, but how and why she had no idea. Not yet.

30

ONE STEP AT A TIME

As hard as Liz swept the floor, it didn't help her perception of the place much. The orange walls and tacky brown and white woodwork didn't look any better. The fireplace looked grim, full of cobwebs and dead rocks which might once have been called coal. Dust had settled everywhere across the hearth, but she had no cloths to wipe anything. There was no alternative but to go to the shops, finally, and cash her money order. As she went to walk out of the living room, she spotted the workman at the window, still looking at her with that cheeky smile. It was as if nothing could affect him. She imagined throwing a brick at him and he would still smile back. He was lucky, one of those people who just loved their jobs, no matter how simple it was. The man spoke, but made no sound. She felt confused at first, until it occurred to her why, and what he was saying, that he had finished. The windows were fine again, dirty, but sorted. No more rain and wind right in the middle of their home.

A knock at the door interrupted her enjoyment of the small but important change to her new home. As she opened the door, there he was again, that man, at the bottom of the steps, smiling like a Cheshire cat.

"Hey, I'm all done here," he said, with his hands in his pockets.

"Oh, marvelous. I did see it was done. Thanks," Liz replied expectantly.

"So that's it, then," the man said politely.

"Nothing else to do?" Liz asked.

"Nope," he said, shaking his head. It was only a split second, a tiny hesitation, as the two looked at each other, each waiting for the other to say something. Neither did. Liz felt something, but was in no mood for anything other than getting on with what was needed. In her mind, he seemed like a nice person, someone good to talk to, but in the cold light of day, it was simply too soon. She thought to herself how she hoped she would see him again, get another chance, but common sense told her such things never happened.

"Thank you for that," Liz said, a little quieter, reflecting her changed tone and emotions. It was a subtle response, but one that he was old and experienced enough to read.

"You're welcome. Anything else, just go down the road to the office and tell them, and I'll be sure to come back and get it done," he replied without looking at her, no point in pushing the matter too far, but he retained his cheerful smile. Liz nodded back at him, even though he couldn't see. It was an unspoken agreement each respected.

That one small moment was a kindness she would not forget. She had been left behind, ignored, unwanted by men, but for a short time with someone she didn't know and would likely never see again, she was able to feel normal. It was a good thing, which presented her a small amount of hope about herself.

The workman took his tools and left with a short wave goodbye. Liz closed the gate, huddling to herself for a moment, taking the time to look at the freshly repaired window. It wasn't much, but it made it like she had some control over her home. It was the first of many things that would go to make life just a little more bearable.

Time was getting on. She could see Dan and Patricia across the road, in the telephone box, one of them talking. She had her things to do. She walked indoors and looked upstairs. "John," she called, waiting for a response. Nothing. "John," she called again. Silence continued. Worrying, she quickly walked up the stairs. The front bedroom was empty, large but clear. The back bedroom, also empty, but clear. As she opened the door to the first of the two small rooms, the air inside was stuffy. It was small, obviously rarely used, its window half covered in ivy. Again there was no sign of John. Panic began to set in, the horrible thought that he too might have gone, walked out and left her, or taken, something terrible happened.

Liz quickly rushed out to the forth of the bedrooms, the last, small room, opening the door. She almost burst into tears as she saw him sitting on the floor, back against the windowed wall, clearly enjoying a moment's sleep. She held her breath, forcing herself to withhold tears. The shock left her shaking, her hands trembling as thoughts raged through her mind over what if.

"John," Liz shouted, immediately regretting doing so.

John jumped, looking at her awkwardly. "What?" he struggled to say.

"I thought, well," Liz began to say, realizing whatever she said would sound foolish, instead choosing to leave it alone.

"Is the food here yet?" John asked, closing his eyes again. Quietly Liz slipped away, back downstairs and out.

As she crossed the road, money order tightly in hand, she almost bumped into a woman ambling slowly past. Clouds had slowly gathered as rain threatened to fall. A tight wind wound around the circle of shops, suggesting a storm might be approaching. As she walked, she thought anything the weather could throw at her wouldn't matter, because it would be nothing compared to what life had sent her way.

Patricia opened the telephone box door, leaning out. "Mom, the first one didn't answer, but the second one has. They have a sofa and a chair, usable they say, bit worn, for ten pounds. We thought of skipping that and going for the next one, which is fifty-five pounds."

"Oh, no, we have to buy food and transport, curtains, all sorts with this little bit of money. I don't know when I get more money, so it had to be as cheap as possible. Go and get that ten pounds one," Liz insisted. It was obvious what they would get might be poor, but they were in no position to argue.

"Right, Mom, we need the money now," Patricia said as she nodded for Dan to agree to go look at the suite.

Liz agreed, quickly leaving for the post office. As she entered, she was immediately met by three large lines, each full of people holding similar money orders to hers. She knew things were tough, unemployment was high, jobs locally were hard to come by, but they had been sheltered from it because of Jack. Since he was no longer there, they had become like a lot of the masses, insecure and dependent on a welfare state which was struggling to cope.

Few bothered to speak as the lines crept forward. People at the counters processed and stamped money orders, sifting through cash, ignoring the faces of those who were so desperate. Nobody wanted to know what it was like, the divide, between those who had and those who needed. Nobody wanted to share, to be equal, only to just be different.

Eventually, after what felt like so long she wondered if it would be too late, her line took her to the front. Liz handed over the money order, feeling a mixture of shame and sadness at what she had to do. She had fallen so low as to be in need of help, with everything. To her mind, it didn't matter that she was entitled to it, or that it was the nature of the system in the country that those who struggled would be supported and cared for. All that mattered was she was effectively begging, and had no other choice, but for her children. It wasn't the life she wanted, but for now it would be what it was. One day at a time, she reminded herself. Take one simple step at a time, and take whatever came as it did. Don't prejudge, no expectations, but don't give up hope. One day it would be better. It had to be.

The woman looked at Liz briefly, before opening the drawer to count the money. "You know you can cash this in any post office," she said, without smiling.

"Oh, I didn't know that. How can you tell?" Liz asked.

"If it has the name of the post office where it has to be cashed, then you can only go there with it. If not and it is blank, you can cash it anywhere. So I can do this for you now, but if they're open then you can get your money any place."

Liz smiled. It was only a small thing, minor in the grand scheme of things, but still, it helped. "Thank you," she said, taking the money. It wasn't much for a family to live on, but to her it was a king's ransom.

As she walked out of the shop, Patricia and Dan were outside, waiting.

"Did you get the address?" Liz asked.

"Yep, we can go now, but need to finish emptying the van," Patricia replied.

"Unless John has done it all for us," Dan said, looking over at the house.

"Nope, he's asleep, or he was last time I saw. We'll all have to muck in quickly and get it done, then you two can get out," Liz said.

"OK," Dan said as he and Patricia walked to the van to finish up. Liz knew very well what her son would be up to, or thought she did.

As she walked back into the house and up the stairs, she knew full well what she was going to do. She would burst into the small room, shout again, only laugh this time at his response.

As she quickly pushed open the door, she got a shock of her own, as he was standing at the window, looking outside. He turned to look at her, as if he had been waiting for her.

"My bed will go there, drawers there, need a television there, and some shelves, and all my posters can go on that wall, and I'll paint it all red, and woodwork white, and," John said, so quickly he could barely get the words out.

"Wow," Liz said, pleasantly surprised. "So all you need now are a bed, drawers, shelves, posters, and paint. Cool. I'll get right on it." John nodded at her, looking at her with all seriousness.

"First though, we unload the van, and then Dan and Pat can go get what we need."

"Right, off you go then," John said, struggling not to smile at his little joke.

Liz felt pleased again that he remained upbeat. He seemed immune to the suffering she felt, and for as long as she could, she would keep it like that.

"Well, if you help and do a good job, we might be able to get a few bags of fries from the local," Liz said, walking away.

John chased after her. "Come on, let's get it done then," he shouted, rushing past her on the stairs. She held on to the banister rail, laughing at his excitement.

Together they emptied out the van, dropping boxes, kitchen items, and suitcases into the new house. The place was a little dark, the air inside stuffy, and everything so old it seemed as if they had stepped back in time, but still, it was a place to be safe, and united.

"I'll go get that sofa," Patricia said, looking at Liz, then Dan. Dan nodded, at which they both left.

"Now," John said, slapping his hands together. "About those fries."

Liz laughed again, looking at all the mess of boxes all over. It would wait, there were better things to do for the moment.

John walked down the steps as Liz locked the door. As the two walked out of the gate, John stopped a moment as a woman passed. He watched her go before turning to Liz, smiling. "Did you hear that?" he asked.

"No," Liz replied, frowning.

"She was having a right go about something, chattering away."

"Well, she might be angry, or upset about something. You

shouldn't judge people, you never know," Liz said. To her it wasn't just a matter of good manners or being kind, she could see how something awful could happen, in a way that could break people, leading to them ending up in a similar way. In her darkest moments she too wondered if she could cope, if it hadn't been for her children. She couldn't bring herself to imagine what it might be like to be in such a position, if truly alone in life.

As John agreed, walking off to find the fish and fry shop, Liz stood a moment, watching the woman go. She was an unusual lady, wearing what must have once been a lovely dress. The way she walked, how she looked caught Liz's eye, wondering if that might be her in time, if she didn't keep it together. She internally berated herself, for being so negative about someone she knew nothing of. They were busy now, so much to do, to keep track of, but she determined that if they met again she would do better.

As the two sat eating fries, light began to fail. It only then occurred to her that the place had no light bulbs. Leaving her half-finished fries on the windowsill, she stood up to look around. The living room had two hang-down strings with connectors, no lights. The kitchen had a bulb, but it didn't work. The hall had nothing. As she searched all over, it was clear nothing worked, and in a few hours they would be sitting in darkness.

"Can I have your fries?" John asked. Liz ignored him, more concerned with getting things done.

Just as she was beginning to panic, the front door swung open as Patricia backed in, struggling to hold on to the sofa.

"John, they're here," Liz called, to no avail. He was lost in his food again. She quickly ran to Patricia's side, trying to take a hold of the sofa as Dan pushed from the other end. Looking it over as they all struggled, she could see it was black, fake leather, quite worn with patches of the topping material missing. It all seemed solid enough, but most importantly it was clean.

"Oh, well done," Liz said as they finally struggled it in. It wasn't the reaction they had expected, having first seen it and wondered if instead they should be taking it to the local refuse tip.

Far from being lazy and filling his face, John had taken to moving boxes and creating space. As they walked in, the place for the sofa was just right.

"Well done, John, well done you two," Liz said as they placed the sofa down. It didn't matter to him how it looked, all that mattered was he had a place to sit while he ate the last of his mother's fries.

"There are two chairs with it, not one. He was going to only give us the one, because he used it, but when I said we were moving into an empty house he just gave us it," Patricia explained, heading out to the van for the rest.

"Things are looking up," Liz said, looking at Dan as he was about to follow.

"They are, although we didn't see any beds for sale," he replied, turning to walk away.

"Oh no, we wouldn't want used beds. If need be we will either sleep on this suite tonight, or go find some cut-price new ones," Liz insisted.

"Well, that man did mention a superstore not far from here, in the middle of an industrial estate. Said it had beds and stuff in there, not sure what they're like."

"Dan, are you coming to help or just talking all night," Patricia called as she struggled once again with a large armchair.

"Right," he said, quickly moving to help.

"John, get ready, we're all going to the shops. Dan, Patricia, hurry up and get that in here, we're off out," Liz snapped, ordering this way and that.

As if time were on a cliff edge and any hesitation would lead to disaster, the four hurried and harried, moving the rest into place, then set off for the store.

"Where did you say it was?" Liz asked, climbing into the side seat after Patricia.

"Well, I'm not sure of the name, but I know the road to get to it. He gave us directions," Dan replied, pointing to a man across the way. Liz looked over, to see he was shifting bags of food around outside the shop.

"Hold on a second," Liz said, ignoring the odd looks from the others as she walked over to him.

"Now where's she going?" John asked.

"No idea, let's just get into the van," Patricia replied, at which they all climbed in. Dan revved the engine, as if to let Liz know they were ready, but she seemed in her own world.

"Hi," Liz said to the man, at which he stood up straight, looking at her with bright eyes, smiling.

"Hello," the man said as a bag of fresh potatoes spilled across the ground outside.

"My children said you knew of a supermarket that sold beds. I didn't know that any did that?" Liz asked, looking at him without smiling.

As the man looked at her, another much older woman came out from the shop he was tending. Outside were foldable wooden racks, full of fruits and vegetables. The woman looked at Liz with a faint smile, betraying her own difficulty with life, borne of age more than anything.

"Hi," Liz said, looking at her. The woman nodded back, smiled a little more before going back into the shop.

"Yes, yes," the man said, watching the woman go back in. "I'm Simon," he said, holding out his hand for hers.

"Oh," Liz replied, laughing a little, feeling awkward. It seemed odd to shake his hand, given he was simply a shopkeeper and she a stranger to him, but in time she would come to find the place had enough truly decent people around that Lache was more of a community than most ever realized. "I'm Liz," she said, gently shaking his hand before stepping back a little.

"Yes," Simon replied, which confused her even more. "I mean, there is a place, it's like a supermarket, but it's a warehouse, and they sell all sorts, everything. I explained to your son about it, and how to get there."

She looked at him, tall and thin, slightly thinning hair, but kind eyes and a cheerful disposition. She felt better for knowing the place, as poor as it seemed, had such decency.

"Do you need directions again?" Simon asked.

"No, no, I'll be fine getting there. I'm married," Liz said abruptly. As soon as she said it she could feel herself blushing, as if she had stepped outside her body and someone else was controlling her, that all she could do was regret the actions of the stranger inside her.

"Right, that's good," Simon said, picking up the spilled potatoes. "I work here with Mom. It's her shop," he said, not losing his positivity for a second.

"Thank, thanks," Liz struggled to say. She wanted to say more, but the urge to walk away was too much to bear. "Thanks," she said again, smiling quickly, then walking off. Simon watched her go, thinking she was a nice lady, hoping to see her again, before carrying on with his work.

Liz climbed into the passenger seat of the van without looking at anyone. "Right, let's go, we need three beds," she said, looking straight ahead. Dan fired up the engine, reversing quickly out. As he did, he quickly slammed on the brakes, making them all jump.

"What did you do that for?" Patricia demanded.

"Because someone walked behind me, some silly woman not looking where she was going," Dan replied, resuming moving again. As they moved away, Liz looked out of her window, catching a glimpse of what Dan had meant. There she was, the same woman, head down, talking to herself, looking down at the ground as she walked. It seemed as if she walked hand in hand with sadness, expressing something much worse than words could ever convey. As much as she felt curious to find out more, they had enough of their own problems, so it would have to wait. As if their own problems might ever cease.

31

WHERE NOBODY KNOWS YOUR NAME

"Hello, how are you doing today?" Simon asked. He was busy sweeping up after the spill, always cheerful.

"Simon, there's a delivery out back," his mother called. Together they made a great team, always doing well, but she was such a hard worker, even at her advanced age. He felt as if he knew the business, how to make it work, everything about it, just still, every day she still felt the need to remind him of what to do and when.

Mavis stopped a moment, which she rarely ever did. To her he was just a minor nuisance, a hindrance to her search, for something no one understood.

"Not stopping to say hello?" Simon asked, deliberately ignoring his mother. He stood watching the woman, smiling at her as always, wondering if that would be the day she would speak to him. For a moment she seemed to hesitate, slowing briefly, before once again resuming her walk.

Simon watched her pace ahead, thinking of how long it had been since he first saw her doing so. Every day she would walk around the shops, never going into them, off around the back streets of Lache, to the outskirts and back in again. He was aware she never left the neighborhood, always in the near location, but for some reason he didn't understand, she would never set foot beyond.

Wrappers and debris dropped by shoppers blew around, creating a mini maelstrom. As colorful plastic and bits clattered around, Mavis slowed her walk, as if something had caught her eye. She looked sideways at the spill, while still walking a path she knew so well, it might have been on tracks.

"Your favorite," she whispered, almost daring a smile. Simon almost laughed, so surprised at the sudden response from her. He had watched her go for years, and never once had she properly stopped to speak. What most stuck him was no matter how bad the weather, she would be out there. Often when it rained she would wear a thin but light coat, as bright and colorful as the rest of the things she wore. Her shoes were always flat, never boots or running shoes, always the same thin-soled flat slip-ons.

"Have a nice day, Mavis," Simon said, ready to turn to go inside.

"Nice day," Mavis mirrored, almost turning to look, but instead walking away. Simon felt both shocked and surprised, pleased that she was still aware of others nearby. She may well walk with her head down, but she never bumped into anyone, never fell over, always avoided traffic. She was like a bat, using the sounds of the streets to guide her. Her instincts appeared everything, where sight showed nothing, and how she felt dictated her day ahead and where she went.

"I opened the door for them, they're dropping food in now. Didn't have time to wait for you," Simon's mother said, interrupting his thoughts.

"Sorry, Mom, coming," he replied, turning to walk in.

The shop was much darker than inside, and at first glance quite sparse. Rows of wooden racks held fresh vegetables and fruits, all brought in throughout the day as needed. In one corner sat an old-fashioned non-electric till, something which his mother always insisted on having. She simply never trusted technology, even attempting to stop the installation of a telephone, until Simon insisted.

"The sacks of potatoes are out back, they need bringing in and separating," his mother insisted, standing in the middle of the shop, hands on hips, as if she were barking orders at a team of staff, rather than just her son. She would never admit it, but she knew all too well she couldn't manage without him, and that her life ultimately revolved around him. For all her angst, the need to berate him from time to time, he was always good-natured with her, and together they got on well.

"I'll get to that right away, Mother," Simon said, looking at her cheekily. He was a man in his forties, and yet still retained an air of youth when around her. Life had been difficult for him, suffering the death of his wife so close after being married to his childhood sweetheart. He had struggled with it, but never married again. To him life was good now, quiet and settled, and free of pain. One thing it had taught him was to value people, and his reputation in the neighborhood was one of true respect. Money was never the issue, if someone had very little, he would always be there to help, and the community thanked him for it.

As he walked past his mother he smiled at her, as she looked at him with a curious smile. He stopped a moment, before intending to carry on, thinking he was mistaken in what he had expected from her. He wasn't.

"I used to be friends with her, you know."

Simon looked at her, at first curious, then confused as to what she meant.

"Mavis," his mother continued, leaving it at that.

"Oh, right," Simon replied, struggling for something to say.

"You'd be surprised how different she was then."

Simon looked at his mother, at least intrigued, but unsure whether he wanted to know more. He liked the person Mavis was, but felt awkward at knowing more about her. On the one hand he liked her apparent innocence, and how she lived simply, but perhaps happily. On the other hand he felt a natural instinctive need to know, who or what was her life about. It suggested a Pandora's box of secrets and unknowns, which few bothered to question.

"She seems happy enough. Seems like a simple woman, maybe lonely I guess," Simon said, aware that he was verging on prompting his mother for more, as uneasy as he felt.

"She doesn't say much, does she?"

"No, not much." It was a simple response from him, but it was clear his mother had things to say, and other than telling her to leave it, she would go on anyway. Too late now.

"Back when I was first here in this shop, with your dad, she was younger, and married, and had a little girl."

"She had a little girl? And she was married?" Simon asked, offering a look of shock. "All this time I have seen her wandering around here, all those years, I couldn't imagine that. I thought she was simply a little slow, learning difficulties."

"No, they had a house up on Sycamore Drive. Seemed pretty happy the three of them, and she used to come in here for her fruits and vegs. I'm surprised you don't remember her better."

"Well, I was away for a long while, wasn't I, studying."

"I know, and working, and then married."

The word "married" hit a sore spot in his subconscious, an unspoken word about something he chose not to remember, simply because he couldn't cope with anything else.

"During the time you lived away, things happened. I don't know too much, but I do know that like a lot around here they struggled for money, and I think her fella turned to selling drugs to make money."

"Really?" Simon asked, looking stunned.

"Yep," his mother said, nodding earnestly. "Did it for quite a while, and from what I was told he ended up using it too."

"Wow, that's a shock. Well, not that much, I mean, you do see it, but I'm amazed at how she was to how she is now."

"That's what the difference in her is all about. All I knew was that he went off the rails, and then one night the place was full of police, and he ended up getting arrested. Something was said about he had beaten Mavis up, apparently not an uncommon thing."

"That's terrible. I'm shocked. Poor Mavis, who wouldn't hurt a fly," Simon said, wondering if he might need to sit down. It felt right that he had been wary to ask about it, and part of him regretted allowing her to continue.

"That's not all," his mother said, the tone of her voice now sounding as if she were simply spoiling to gossip, welcoming his interest.

"I'm not sure," Simon began to say, too late. She had to say it now, as if to unburden herself.

"The worst of it was they found blood all over the place, but no sign of the daughter. They reckoned he had murdered her, in a drug-fueled rage, an beaten her up, and then run off. They caught him in the end, and he was tried and convicted for it, but they never found the little girl."

"My God, horrible. I don't think I want to hear any more, Mom."

"No, well, if you wonder why she's like she is, that's it. She ended up back here, rehoused in a different home. Since then it seems she always been wandering round, looking for something. I bet she's looking for her child."

It was enough. He didn't want to know more, choosing to walk away into the back room. There was nothing more to be said, but at least he understood her a bit more now. It would be nice to be able to talk to her, but at least he could appreciate why it might never happen.

"Simon," his mother called. He peered back through the doorway, listening reluctantly.

"Yes," he replied.

"Why don't you ask that woman, the new one over the road, ask her out?" It was a mischievous question, one that he chose to ignore. He had work to do.

32

ROUGHING IT

"Hey, Mom, what about this one?" John asked, jumping as high as he could before landing hard on a deep-set king-size bed.

Liz looked at him with a mixture of disdain and disbelief. "John, get off there," Liz snapped. "You're getting a single if it's cheap enough, in fact we all are, and only if they're cheap enough," she insisted. Regardless, John would wait a moment, because he was as comfy as he had been at any time.

"These are the cheapest single beds I can find. They're forty-nine pounds each," Patricia said, looking at one of the beds as if it were a cardboard box with a white pattern on it.

Liz shook her head, feeling on the verge of panic.

"What about these?" Dan said suddenly, sounding pleased with himself. He was stood well away from them, in another section of the huge superstore.

Liz looked across, seeing sleeping bags and camping gear. She thought to shake her head, before being reminded of the cost of a basic single bed.

Patricia walked over to him, looking at what he was pointing at, before turning to her mother. "Sorry, Mom, but I think that's what it's gonna be. They're only nineteen ninety-nine each, so sixty pounds for three cot beds. Dan can sleep on the floor," she said, without bothering to look at him.

"Stick three in the trolley," Liz replied, refusing to give it another thought. She picked up three rolled-up quilts and some basic bedding. It was far from ideal, but she knew they were in no position to do anything about it. Dan had money she figured, but he had done enough, with diesel and other things. He had his own to contend with, so no more.

"What about curtains?" Patricia asked.

"What about carpet?" Dan asked.

"What about food?" John asked.

Liz felt like exploding as she cupped her hands to her face. She wanted to burst into tears, but wouldn't, because it was how she felt all the time, and crying wouldn't help, so she kept it in, remained strong, refused to give in.

"Curtains will come soon enough, when we can find some very cheap, and have more money. Carpets, well, they can come one day, but for now let's worry about food for the weeks ahead. Might be a couple of weeks before we get paid again," Liz said, walking ahead with a sense of purpose which drove all other thoughts from her mind.

"We could paint the floor," John said, his remark offhand and sudden. Liz almost stopped, bursting out laughing. It had been unexpected, but still welcome. She could still appreciate a moment of silliness.

"You can paint the walls," Patricia said, holding up a large tin of bright red emulsion.

"Oh yeah," John said, reacting to his favorite color. Liz looked at the tin, the color, then the price, almost ten pounds. She shook her head, deflating all hopes he had of making an impact in his room.

As they walked into the food court, each pointed to different things, the colors and smells of foods which made them all hungry, but Liz remained firm, only putting in what she knew they needed and had to have. Luxuries would have to wait, in her mind for a very long time.

Finally with a full trolley they paid up, as Liz looked at the little money they had, stressing about how quickly it was going down. She had shopped cautiously, buying bulk items of potatoes and vegetables. Loafs of bread were good, eggs and basic cereals, things that would go a long way and still fill them up.

"Can we have some food when we get in, some tea?" John asked. He was like a metronome, set off on his routine quest for food by the smallest reminder of his need. It was tiresome dealing with it, but at least she understood why he was like it, for his age, and how quickly he was growing.

"You're going to be bigger than your dad," Liz said suddenly, without thinking. She regretted it the moment she said it, as an air of silence descended upon them. Nobody spoke of it, each choosing to ignore the remark, but it was done.

After quickly loading the van with the bags, bedding, and food, the group edged their way back home. Light had begun to fail as orange streetlights lit up one by one. It blanketed the appearance of the place, as the estate hid in the darkness from its sullen look.

"Er, Mom, we forgot light bulbs," John said, his face a picture of worry.

"Well, it's a good thing one of us is awake, because I saw a pack for a pound and picked them up. We have enough for now," Liz said, feeling proud of her chance to gloat. There had been little to feel good about in recent times, but she could allow herself a little pride over how things were going.

"Well done, Mom," John said as they pulled into the concrete path at the front of the house.

Liz stepped out of the van and walked over to open the door, before looking back. "Right, John and Dan, get the pack of bulbs out of the bags and fit them where needed, then get the beds and the bedding upstairs, into the right rooms. Patricia, when they're in, you go make up the beds and things for the night."

"Yes sir," John barked back as he jumped from the van. He held his hand so tightly to his head in salute, it sprang like a band, vibrating. Dan laughed at him, until he saw the look on Liz's face and jumped to work.

"What are you doing, Mom, sitting on the new luxury chair beside the roaring fire?" Patricia asked. Liz ignored her, realizing it was late and they were all tired. All she could think to do was get in and get everything sorted.

As she walked into the living room, with what little light was left, she could see the place looked like a bombsite, with boxes and bags all over. One chair was still on its side near the empty fireplace. It looked as if there had been a war and the residents had suddenly fled, leaving anything that wasn't important. All that she had, that they had to show for their lives, seemed like junk. It had come to this, boxes of trash, a few suitcases of clothes, and camping cots to sleep on. With less than a hundred pounds in cash to last them two weeks, she doubted she could ever feel lower in her life, but at least they were in, and it could only get better. She hoped.

"Push, will you," a voice shouted. Liz looked back into the hall to see John fixing a light bulb in while Dan and Patricia dragged in two beds at once.

"I thought I asked John and Dan to take the beds up?" Liz asked.

"Yes, but neither of us could reach high enough to do the bulbs, so here we are," Patricia replied. It was only then that Liz noticed how much John seemed to be growing. It seemed in only the blink of an eye that he was her little boy, short and sweet, and there he was pushing a light into the socket without having to stand on anything.

"Whatever," Liz replied, simply because she couldn't think of anything else to say. She walked past them to the van, grabbed several carrier bags of food, and returned to the house.

"John, we need a light in here," Liz shouted.

"Yeah, I know," John said, standing right behind her. She jumped, almost dropping the bags.

"John, don't sneak around," she insisted, looking for somewhere to place the bags. The kitchen was sparse, too sparse, with only the cooker, washer, and refrigerator suggesting it actually was a kitchen. It looked depressing, as if someone had tacked on a shed outside the back of the house and said make do with that. They would have to.

Suddenly light poured over everything as John flicked the switch on the wall. "There you go, all perfect," John said. Liz chose not to respond, unable to think of anything good to say.

"I shall go bring light to the darkened walls of this house," John finally said, clutching at the pack of bulbs. Liz smiled, thankful that he was positive anyway, if only at the thought of more food.

"I will get the pots out and do us some tea," Liz offered, at which John suddenly stopped.

"Can we not go to and get fish and fries again?" he asked excitedly.

"Sorry, love, but you've had your treat for the day. It'll have to be potatoes and a couple of eggs."

John looked at her like a lost puppy unable to find its toy. "Funny, but what are we really having?" he asked.

"No, really, you've had fries earlier, and that's all we have for now. It has to last us till we get paid again."

The expression on her son's face changed decidedly. "What about carpets?" he said, sounding sullen.

"Sorry, no, we can't eat carpet either."

"You're funny again. I mean, when are we getting carpets down?"

"I said, I don't know, we don't have any money," Liz insisted, her voice breaking. She had maintained an even temper, controlled her emotions, but deep down she was ready to break down.

"I don't want to live like this, I want to go home," John replied. His voice began firm, as if he were to shout, but as he spoke his voice broke, like hers, betraying his real feelings.

Liz looked at him, tears in her eyes, struggling to find the words. "I'm sorry," she said, as if she held all the blame in the world on her shoulders. The two stood together, barely looking at one another. She could manage, just about keep it together, but she knew her son was young, at an impossible age amid the maelstrom around them, the disintegration of their lives. She could always just about do it, manage to make it work, but she couldn't make him happy if he couldn't do it for himself.

"I want Dad back," John said finally. It was the kind of sentence she had expected him to say all along, but never had. Jack had never been the best of dads, rarely ever around, lacking the ability to show much empathy or even affectionate, but that was all her family had ever known.

"I know, love, I think in a way we all do, but I don't know where he is, or even if he's still alive. No one seems to know, and it seems other than us, no one seems to care," Liz replied, moving slowly towards him. She was wary of a backlash, that he might blame her, perhaps even become physical. She couldn't imagine her own son behaving in such a way, but they were all on edge now, ready to jump into an emotional abyss.

"Why can't we go back to Gran's? Why can't we live there?" John asked, struggling himself not to break out crying.

Liz looked at him, differently now. "No, no, that's not going to happen. This is our home now, and we will make it nice, and we will live here and find our own way. Right," she said, harder than she had intended. She waited, tense, holding herself for the reaction. It never came, as he looked down at the ground, tears rolling down his cheeks. Instead he just nodded, sort of shrugging, before clutching once again at the pack of light bulbs.

"I'll do us some food, and you can have a few slices of bread with it, that will cheer you up," Liz said quietly. It wasn't much, but she had nothing else to give. John sniffed heavily, nodded again, and headed back into the living room. He struggled around boxes, placing bulbs into sockets, before going on to the next room. As he walked out, he flicked the wall switch without looking. The room lit up, reflecting garish orange around the place from the walls. It was almost comically bad, but it would change, get better, for all of them.

"You make up the beds, unpack them and get them ready, and I will go get the bedding and pillows and set them up, OK?" Patricia suggested, only it wasn't a suggestion to Dan, it was an order. She was learning quickly how to deal with adversity, courtesy of mother's instructions.

The bedrooms were stuffy, in need of airing, but it was too cold out to open up. With no curtains, they wouldn't do much for the night, but she was thankful they had somewhere to sleep.

As Dan continued setting up the small beds, she walked off down the stairs, passing John as she did. "Looking busy there, John," she said, unsure of whether to be abrupt or pleasant. It was her brother, after all, so either approach would do.

As he walked up, her brother ignored her, simply looking ahead.

"Are you all right?" Patricia asked, stopping to look.

John stopped, turning slowly. "Yeah, I'm just hungry, that's all," he replied, looking at her blankly.

Patricia smiled, laughing briefly at him. "Yeah, that sounds like you," she said, before continuing to the van. It was enough, just the right thing for the right moment, helping him shift away his sense of anger, so he could focus on being better.

As the three finished up what they were doing, locking the van's front door, a sense of reality set in. They were no longer setting up or preparing to go into a rough and ready house, they were there, doors closed, lights on, everything in the house, at least all that they owned. They were in their new home now, for better or worse, and there was nowhere else to go.

Patricia, Dan, and John all stood in the living room, looking at the boxes stacked up, the dilapidated sofa and chairs threatening to fall apart before them, each seeing the white mist of their breath as cold set in. The place looked like a warehouse, there for storage, nothing so absurd as a place to live in.

"We need a fire," Dan said, aware that they were all thinking the same thing.

"I agree, shall we burn that chair?" John asked, looking at the armchair on its side. There was a pause, a hesitation as each thought about what he had just said, before Patricia burst out laughing.

"Yeah, then we can go on to the sofa, and maybe some boxes," Patricia struggled to say through fits of giggles. It was silly, but a good release from the tension.

Liz walked through, carrying a plate of food. It had potatoes and eggs on it with several slices of bread at the side. Steam rose from its top, showing disparity between the food and cold of the room.

"There you go, John, sit somewhere and eat that," Liz said, handing the plate to him with cutlery. She left and quickly returned with two more plates of the same.

"It's getting cold in here. What about a fire?" Patricia asked, doing her best not to laugh while eating.

Liz didn't see the joke, wondering what to do about it. "I think we'd best finish our food and then go to bed. Not much else to do. Besides, we have no coal."

Dan looked around, trying not to appear like an idiot. "Er, where will I be sleeping? Shall I go home?" he asked hopefully.

"No," Patricia said quickly, imagining if he did go he might not come back until all the work was done.

"I never thought of that," Liz replied, thinking of the two of them in a single camping cot.

"He can sleep on the sofa," John said, annoyed that he had to stop eating in order to offer help.

"Oh, good idea," Liz said, smiling at Dan. To him it was the worst idea possible, sleeping on a rough old sofa, in such a cold and empty place.

"I don't have any covers," Dan said, his mind racing to think of any way out of it.

"It's fine, you can use our coats to cover yourself," Patricia said, smiling at him, not at all innocently. Dan gave her a look of mock despair, realizing he couldn't win. Sometimes he just had to take it on the chin, because to him, she was worth it. Sometimes.

John scraped the last from his plate, at which Liz took it from him. "Right, let's all go and get into bed, and get a good night's sleep. Big day tomorrow," she said, rubbing her hands together as if she meant action.

"Why, what's happening?" John asked.

"Cleaning this place, properly, and sorting boxes and unpacking. And let's not forget, later this week we're getting you back into school, locally," Liz continued, sounding full of purpose but feeling the opposite.

Dan circled a few times, gathering coats, trying to delay it as much as possible. There was no television, nothing to do, on a mess of a sofa, covered in coats, for a long, cold night.

Liz went first, followed by John and Patricia, as she bade Dan goodnight, still trying not to laugh.

"Mom, I put you in the front room. John, you know where yours is, and I'm in the back double room, for what it's worth," Patricia explained. The three stood on the landing, each silent, wondering what to say, but the house was so cold, so bare and empty, it seemed as if they were all standing at a dead end, none of them having any idea what to do.

"It's cold down here," Dan said loudly, at which the three laughed again.

"It's going to be cold up here too," Patricia replied, before shouting goodnight.

Liz quickly hugged John, then Patricia, before going into her room. In the center of the ceiling was a single-cord hang-down bulb. It was like a prison cell, only with wooden plank floors and faded purple walls. There was nothing to cover the windows, as orange sodium lighting outside argued with the white bulb inside. Privacy was an obscure concept in such a state.

She felt hungry, not having eaten with the others. She couldn't escape the nagging thought of running out of money, as well as food.

The bed looked small, low down, but the covers seemed good and would no doubt be enough. She turned off the light, allowing street lights to flood in, shadowing her with an odd color as she undressed. There were no chairs, no wardrobes or dressers for clothes, simply the bed on the floor. She felt like a stranger having walked into an empty house off the street, in a place where she had no right to be. Her home was just an outline, a blueprint of what one might be built on, but deep down she wasn't entirely sure she had the strength to build such a thing. She would find out, because there was no other choice.

33

CLOSE TO BEING ALONE

It was a long night, full of aches, bitter cold, and emotional recriminations. Liz fought a tiger inside herself, of self-doubt and self-loathing, where the love and belief in her family collided with the nagging voice in her head which blamed her for it all. She felt suffocated by it, that she was enveloped in the mess of her life, the lack of a future, the futility of it all.

As long as she had her children, she would carry on. She lived for them now, anything else would be a bonus.

Liz sat up on the bed. It didn't matter how old she was, such a poor place to sleep and the awful cold would affect anyone. She leaned over to the bottom of the bed, picking up the small jacket she had worn the night before. Inside the pocket was a small bundle of notes and coins, the last of the cash she had. She spilled it onto the bed, sifting through it, separating note from coins, and then each into their respective denominations.

"Mom," a voice called. It was Patricia, outside the door.

"Yes, come in," Liz replied.

Patricia opened the door, walking slowly in, holding her arms, trying not to shiver. "It's frosty out," she said, doing her best not to let her teeth chatter.

"Oh, right," Liz replied, continuing to count the money. "I guess we're going to have to go and buy a small bag of coal," she said.

Patricia looked at the small pile, watching her mother count. "You know, Dan has to go to work, and I'm going to have to go to college," she said.

"I know, love," Liz replied, muttering to herself.

"I don't have any money for bus fare. Dan can drop me at work, but getting back, and other days. He won't have the van, only his motorbike, and it's too far."

"Yeah, I know, love," Liz replied, staring at the small pile of change. "We have about thirty-four pounds left to last us for who knows how long, and," Liz said, intending to say more, but again choosing not to for fear of burdening her family.

"All right," Patricia said, standing up. "I'll get dressed, and we can get to work sorting the place out." Liz smiled at her, thankful for some small understanding.

"Shall I wake sleepy bones, John?" Patricia asked before leaving.

"No, leave him. We'll do what we can, and he can sleep some more."

Liz got up quickly, thinking constantly about what to do. She knew they wouldn't last, no chance. She could telephone her mother, or sister, and ask. She knew they would help, but it wouldn't change anything. Ultimately she was going to have to get a job, if such a thing were possible. She was middle-aged, in a nation of age discrimination, at a time of mass unemployment. She knew choices were few and the way out difficult. It was like a chess match where no matter what she chose she would end up losing out.

As she walked down the stairs and into the living room, she had expected to see Dan, either sitting or lying, shivering and feeling sorry for himself. To her surprise he was still asleep, covered in coats, and towels from a newly opened box, and was snoring heavily. It seemed he had not only slept well, but didn't have a care in the world. She envied him, and her own son, for the ease with which they took life and its problems in their stride.

Hunger ate at her, reminding her she hadn't eaten, but for all that she simply didn't want to. She felt sick from not eating, but felt equally sick from the thought of food. It would have to wait.

It had been a restless night, not only for the cold but because of trying to adjust to being in a strange place. Worries over money strangled any other thoughts in her mind, like a trickling river of fear running down her spine, as each day passed and little by little it would diminish to nothing. Then what?

Just at the moment of her worst, when she feared she might lose it all, lose control, lose her family, a spark of inspiration hit her. Her mind had been a frenzy, trying to think where she might get money from, what she might sell to get it, what she might do to make money. Anything was possible. Then, like a mirage before her, an idea, something of value. Without saying, or allowing the thought to transform into doubt and hopelessness, she leapt towards the pile of boxes.

In their haste to get away, they had filled marked boxes, each one with something different: pots and pans, towels, kitchen stuff, tools, odds and ends, but then she found the one she had been looking for.

"What's up, Mom?" Patricia asked, just as Liz appeared to be at her most frantic. As she bundled towards the boxes, she half stood on the floor and half on the sofa, treading on Dan as she did.

"Ow, hold on," Dan shouted, withdrawing so as to not make it worse.

"I'm looking for something," Liz replied, tugging at one of the boxes on top.

"I can see that," Patricia continued. "What?"

Liz didn't answer, instead lifting the box away as best as she could. Lack of food and sleep made her weak, as she dropped the box sideways from her arm. Down it went, banging off the top of the sofa, before landing hard on Dan. He lay there, not saying anything as the box split, sending papers all over.

"Mom," Patricia said, walking around to help.

"It's fine," Liz said, scrambling through the papers. It had seemed she was sorting them, but as she looked through them, the mess simply got worse.

"What are you looking for?" Patricia asked, increasingly concerned.

"Don't mind me," Dan said, which he knew was the case anyway.

"Got it," Liz said all of a sudden, as she pulled out a faded brown folder. She stood back up, leafing through it, eager eyed, ignoring anything else.

Patricia looked at Dan as he simply lay there, feeling like he was the least important thing in the room.

"Are you going to tell us what you have?" Patricia asked one final time.

"Yes, yes, love," Liz said, picking out two sheets of paper, stapled together. "It's this," she said, showing it to Patricia.

"What is it?"

"It's our small pension, from when I worked at Nabiscos. It isn't worth much, but I can cash it in, and we can get some stuff for the house, and pay some bills when they come in."

Patricia stood, looking wide eyed at her mother. It felt like a relief, but more that her mother wasn't losing control of herself.

Liz flipped over the pages, quickly reading the back. "It's supposed to pay out in around fifteen years, but doesn't matter. We need it now."

"That's great, how do you sort it out?" Patricia asked.

"Says I have to fill this page in on the back, but there isn't a form. I'll go get cleaned up and go ring them. You can get John up, and once I'm done, we can get working on this place."

"Well, I have to go to work, while I still have a job, and I have to take the van back to work," Dan insisted, wishing he could just get back to some sense of normality. It failed to occur to him that all of them felt like it, but only he had any kind of choice.

"Yes, yes. I know all that, just get on with it then, do what you have to, and I'll deal with this," Liz replied, her mind lost in other matters.

"Mom," Patricia said, looking at her mother. No response.

"Mom," Patricia said again, trying to be patient but doing a poor job of it.

"Liz," Dan finally snapped as he tried to sit up from the sofa as it sagged in the middle.

"What?" Liz finally answered, looked at them both, but still clearly elsewhere.

"Patricia is going to need bus fare to get home, and for the rest of the week. I need to get up and get out, and you need to listen to us a moment," Dan said quickly. It was the sharpest he had ever spoken to her, always so meek and quiet, yet it showed he had a side which suggested there was more to him.

Liz looked at him a moment, as if she were still lost in thought, but it wasn't what it appeared. "Wow, Dan, I didn't know you had it in you," she said. Her words were far from mocking, instead appreciative of what she saw. He too thought about things, how she spoke to him. She had always been so polite, but apparently not so much anymore.

"No, well, I guess that makes two of us now, doesn't it? You've changed too," he replied. Liz chuckled briefly to herself, thinking it had been an experience that was going to change them all. As tough as it was, she appreciated their lives had the chance to be better for it.

"Sorry, love," Liz said, looking at Patricia. "I have enough. You get dressed and ready, both of you, and I will sort out what you need for fares and lunch. I'll go get this paperwork when you're out and about."

Patricia smiled at her. There was nothing else to be said as each went about their business. Dan finally got up and dressed, into his work uniform, as Patricia did the same.

"What about breakfast, do you want something?" Liz asked, looking at them both, as they stood in the hall, waiting to leave.

"No thanks, Mom, I will get something light from the canteen. I'm sure someone will help out," Patricia suggested, beginning to walk to the front door before her mother could object.

"Dan, surely you?"

"No, Liz, I get free and I can go to my flat and get something, 'cause it's close enough for me. Thanks."

Liz handed coins and a note to Patricia, before both headed out, closing the front door before any objections could be made. Though neither would say it, it would come as a short relief from the oppressive atmosphere in the house. Liz appeared ready to quickly adapt to her new circumstances, even it appearances were false, but to both of them, it seemed as if all they wanted was an escape.

Liz watched the door close, her stomach rolling over as her upbeat feelings sank lower. She heard the rusty gate move and close, then the van fire up and pull out. All the while, she stood, just staring at the door, as if it might magically open and they would rush in and hug her. Life wasn't like that, it wasn't so simple. It never would be again.

It occurred to her to perhaps go and wake her son up, but she would never do that, because she couldn't bring herself to drag him into her sadness. She would smile, continue to do what was needed, and get on with it. It would either work out, or it would all fall apart, but whatever happened, it wouldn't end up like it simply because she gave up.

Ideas trickled into her mind, what to do, where to begin. It filled her with a fragile hope, that she could do it. There were all the boxes to empty, things to put away, the fire to clean, lots of cleaning, and perhaps make the place a bit more manageable. She knew she couldn't ignore the pension papers, that they could help them a lot. It was a sacrifice, but perhaps a necessary short term one.

Without thinking anything more, she determined to freshen up and get to it. As she quickly walked up the stairs she looked ahead, seeing shafts of sunshine flooding through the narrow side window in the house. She knew it was daft to think such things, but she figured why not? She allowed her mind to wander, because it gave her hope, so she saw the sun as a roadmap in her life, small things that guided her on when her choices were good ones. There was no harm in believing in something good around her.

Just as she got to the top of the stairs she stopped abruptly, as a yawning lurch exited the room nearby, almost oblivious to her presence. John had woken, and he stretched, stumbling around, staggering who knew where.

"Oh, the monster awakes," Liz said, making him jump. She was pleased for company, even if it meant dealing with his never-ending needs.

"Yeah," the monster replied, finally ceasing yawning long enough to look at her. "What time is it?" he asked, looking bleary eyed.

"I believe it's about nine thirty. Good you're up, you can help me sort out," Liz said, smiling at him.

"Nah," John said, before quickly turning around and dropping back onto his bed. He just lay there, half-pulled his quilt over himself, and went back to sleep. Liz laughed again, noticing how his feet were sticking out of the end of the bed. It was another sign of just how quickly and how much he was growing. With all that, he would need more food. It was going to be difficult.

Liz redoubled her efforts to get on with it, quickly getting cleaned up and changing her clothes. She counted out some coins, feeling a sense of panic at how quickly it was going down, before going outside to the telephone box. She looked at the front garden, seeing sweet wrappers, empty tin cans, and papers all over, mixed in with the tall grass and dead plants. It would be a big effort to sort it, and given their location, so close to shops, she knew it would continue to gather rubbish. Another thing to put up with among so much.

The air was cold out, but the sun continued to shine. A few people milled around as buses and cars passed by. For all it was a small area on the outskirts of Chester, it seemed busy anyway. People around had a similar look, tightly wrapped up for the cold, but no one dressed particularly smartly, clothes seeming old and worn, much like the place. A fine tint of ash stung the air, from the myriad of chimneys on each rooftop. It was an anachronism, a place permanently at odds with the rest of the city. It was something she would never get used to.

As she walked up to the telephone box, a young man stepped out, holding the door for her. It seemed to be the most popular place in town, apart from the shops. Any time someone went to use the phone, someone else left, and when they left there was always someone to go in after them.

The phone itself was worn and old, but as long as it worked that was all that mattered. It was a lifeline to so many, a doorway to opportunity or an answer to their needs. Liz dropped in several coins, lifted the paperwork to find the number and rang.

The other end of the line was poor, a slight buzzing and a faint voice, but eventually someone answered. "Hello, Ashurst's Insurance, can I help you?"

"Yes, good morning, I have an insurance policy, for a pension agreement with you. I would like to know if I can cash it in please?" Liz asked, her heart pounding, more out of fear that they might decline and hang up. She felt as if she were hanging on by a thread, that all other options were dead to her. This was it, the last. If this didn't work she might slump down to the floor, there and then, crying.

"Hold on please, I'll put you through," the feeble voice offered, before the line clicked.

"Hello," Liz shouted, thinking the line had gone dead. As she was about to call out again, music began to play, suggesting she was on endless, interminable hold.

"Hello," a voice suddenly asked, as Liz pushed more coins into the slot.

"Hello, yes," Liz replied, almost praying for help.

"I understand you want to cash in your insurance policy?"

"Yes, I need to. We have no money," Liz said, feeling awkward for saying it, but it was a sign of her desperation that she would say anything.

"Right, do you have your policy number?"

Liz nodded, before realizing he couldn't see her. She agreed, reading out the numbers from the top.

"Right. I will need some information from you, to prove who you are, and then I'll action that for you immediately."

"Oh, thank you," Liz said, slumping a little as she finally felt able to believe it might work.

"The name of the policy is joint, however the primary name on the account is Elizabeth Cornwell, so I can action that with your confirmation. Is that all right?" the man asked, sounding as polite as any she had met in a long time.

"Yes, yes. That's great," Liz said, trying not to sound too cheerful or desperate as she spoke.

"OK, I'll sort that out for you, and get a check out for you. It should be out today and you should have it tomorrow."

"That's brilliant, thank you so much. Did you say check? Because I don't have a bank account to clear it through."

"Right, well, it will have to be through an account, otherwise we can't pay out. We have no alternative payment methods."

It was like hitting against a brick wall, two steps forward, three steps back. All Liz could feel was anger and frustration. Her mind rolled over, thinking of options.

"Do you have a family member, that we could pay it to?" the man asked, as if he could sense her need and was prepared to do anything to help. She felt uplifted that for all the bumps in the road of her life, there were people all over that could and wanted to help.

"Yes," Liz replied quickly, trying not to allow herself to well up with tears again. "Er, the name is Dan Forster. He is my son-in-law, and has an account. If you make it out to him, I can pay it in there."

"Right, I shall do that, it will be in the post to you shortly. Ordinarily we require a signature for this, but I'll fill out the form, and expedite it, so that will come with the check tomorrow. If you can please be sure to sign that and return it, I will be sure to get it all squared away."

"Thank you so much, you don't know how much this helps," Liz said, wanting to shout and cheer, but just about managing to hold it down.

"No problem. Is there anything else I can do for you today?"

The first thing that came to mind for her was the need of a hug, but knew that was a step too far. "No, you've been so kind. Thank you," Liz said, losing her voice.

"Thank you, bye for now," the man said as the line went dead.

Tears rolled down her cheeks as she opened the door, only to see a young woman outside, glaring at her.

"Sorry," Liz said, smiling and crying at the same time.

"Took you long enough," the woman said, grabbing the door

from her before shuffling past.

Liz thought to say something, but decided she was in a good mood, and didn't want to spoil it. She walked back across the road, feeling as good as she had for a long time. Things were definitely going to be on the up. As she walked through the door, she looked up the stairs and thought to shout, get up, but stopped herself. It was fine, he could enjoy the last of his vacation, before going back to school.

The place was in need of a good clean, and lots to do. She would spend the day doing what was needed, and when everyone came home, she would share the good news. It was going to be all right.

34

A TERRIBLE THOUGHT

"No Dan, it's not going to be all right. Right," Patricia said abruptly.

The comment almost made him swerve off the road. "I thought you were fine about things?" he asked, forcing the wheel back straight again.

"I was, I am I mean. I'm not sure. Mom isn't saying much, but I know she had almost no money left, and we're living in a house which is barely fit to live in."

Dan glanced around at her to gauge how she really was. The look on her face suggested anger, but the puffiness in her eyes suggested she too was struggling to cope.

"I don't know, I don't know what to do. I guess go to work, and me to college, and do what we can to help when we can." It was a sensible suggestion, the best that they could do, but Patricia was in no frame of mind to be sensible.

"I'm still training, I am on very little income through my college, and a lot of that will be swallowed up by bus fares and lunch costs."

"Well, I can pick you up some nights, on my bike, and I'll buy you some apples for lunch," Dan replied. The sensible moment he had had was lost in an instant, the moment he tried to plan anything for her.

"Just drive," Patricia said, ignoring anything he said afterwards.

As they pulled up outside the college, Dan stopped and turned to her. "I'm doing my best, struggling to cope with things as much as you and your family," he said. There it was again, the kind of thing which made her care for him in the first place. He had such a tendency to say the worst things, but it seemed when he spoke honestly, and didn't let his ego interfere, to her he could be the best.

Patricia finally looked directly at him, softening her approach.

"But I have my own problems too, bills to pay, motorbike

payments, and I have to go out with lads too, I need money for that," Dan continued, unaware of just what he was saying. He was like a runaway train, where at times it seemed normal, and others like no one was in control of his thoughts or his mouth. Any hint of agreement was lost in that moment.

"Thanks for the lift, Dan. Don't worry about us, we can manage, I'll sell something if I have to," Patricia said, jumping out and slamming the door behind herself. Dan continued to speak, trying to paper over the cracks in his own lack of sensitivity, but before he had finished she was gone, walking away and up the steps into the building. Even then he still thought to carry on explaining himself, even though he was alone by then. It summed him up as a person, so much in his own world at times, the center of his own life, that he only truly needed to justify it to himself, and he could live with anything.

Dan fired up the van and drove off, smiling. Job done, off to work while he still had a job.

Patricia walked into the college building, along to her class. It wasn't much of a career choice, but better than being unemployed or signing on for benefits.

As she entered into the room, the class had started. From her dad's insistence she had been training to become a seamstress, something which she thought would be useful and interesting, turned out to be monotonous and dull. The teacher noticed her enter, before continuing with explaining sewing techniques. She knew it wouldn't be Mrs. Barker, in a different class, but hoped for the best. Patricia took her place at a bench towards the back, dropped her bag and prepared for the routine struggle to stay awake.

"Right, so if you cross-stitch here, and use clamps to hold the edging in place, then you can see how the line remains straight," the teacher explained, loudly so that all could hear, all twenty highly bored students.

Patricia looked around for her friend Hannah, someone she found helped to break up the boredom of the classes. For one reason or another she would often miss classes, which made it all the worse. The skies outside were gray and dull, looking as if any moment it would rain heavily. She knew once the day finished she would have to find her way home, likely on multiple buses, and then the following day it would all begin again. If only she could lie down her head and sleep it off. Perhaps if she did that, when she woke up it would all be right again. Life, it seemed, was far from perfect.

"Did you do the homework?" the teacher asked, an inane question, barely worthy of anyone's attention, let alone Patricia's.

Silence descended, as all eyes focused on her. She was lost, thinking of a better life, in which money was never a worry, and she could do all the things she ever wanted to.

"Miss Cornwell," a loud voice boomed, interrupting her thoughts. The teacher was right in front of her, glaring down like an eagle looking for food. Until that moment just who or what he was had never occurred to her. He was an unusually tall man, completely bald, and excessively thin. He wore a simple plaid shirt and narrow bland-color trousers. He peered at her over black round spectacles, declining to bother blinking as he eyed her, awaiting her response. Now that she finally looked at him, in all his glory, he looked just the kind of person who would teach upholstery and the intricacies of becoming a seamstress. That, and no doubt a love for train spotting. He was the epitome of boring, what it would be to live a shallow life full of little things and nothing more.

Patricia looked at him, wide eyed, wondering if she could be as condescending towards him in the same way as she thought about it. She could think of nothing good to say, so remained silent.

"How are you, Patricia?" the man asked, almost whispering. Then, at that moment it struck her, how wrong she was about him. He looked at her, not with eagle eyes, but with kind eyes, sensitive and sincere. His had no look of anger, simply one of caring and thoughtfulness. She stared back at him, struggling with the thought that she didn't even know his name.

It was a delicate moment, one where she felt various things, such as the need to run out, or shout, or say something personal, to admit all she was going through. Whatever it was that held her back from being honest, she had no idea, but it was the kind of thing that ruined relationships. It seemed nobody was perfect, not even her.

"I think I was a bit hard on my boyfriend, this morning," Patricia replied, no longer looking at him, or even in the room, but into her own life and how she dealt with it all.

"Maybe you're just a little too hard on yourself?" the teacher asked. He didn't move, not an inch closer, remained calm and not the least bothered by what anyone else thought in the class.

Patricia didn't respond, instead she bit her lip, trying not to break down. She had a well of tears waiting to spill out, but crying would do no one any good, so she sucked it up, held it in, and showed strength as if it mattered.

Before she could say anything, or hear anything that might have helped, Hannah burst in, carrying bags and a rucksack, as if she had taken a detour to the shops before class began. Whatever moment it might have been building up to was gone in that haphazard moment, a rush of excitement, cool air, and noise. Hannah plonked down beside her friend and smiled widely.

The teacher looked at her, still in that moment, but aware that any hope to help would have to wait.

"What's going on? What have I missed?" Hannah asked brashly.

Patricia looked at her, for the first time, wondering how good a friend she really was. She was good for leaning on, to lighten the boredom, but anything more and it seemed she perhaps lacked the maturity to deal with it. Given the circumstances, it seemed a good idea to find out for sure.

"My dad went missing a while back, and it's left us homeless. We have no money, and no idea where he's gone, and we're all having a breakdown over it. I don't cry about it 'cause it won't do any good, and we don't have anyone to turn to," Patricia explained, refusing to give in to tears. For now.

"Oh wow, that's awful," Hanna replied. She dropped her bags and looked at her friend for a moment, aware of the close presence of the teacher. The class had remained silent, all looking at them, but being so young, no one had any idea how to respond.

"You know, you can talk to me, or one of the faculty any time. We're here to help any way we can," the teacher said, remaining kindly quiet with his words.

"Awful, like the weather today. I just don't know what I'm going to do with my hair," Hannah said, pulling a compact mirror from one of her bags and looking into it.

"How awful," Patricia said, feeling more lost than ever.

"I know, I'll have to have a hairdo," Hannah said again, giggling over herself.

Patricia looked up at the teacher, her eyes finally betraying her emotions as they filled with tears. "You see, even if people wanted to help, and I get some don't, there's nothing anyone can do for us."

She stood, up, picking up her own bag, realizing she had made a mistake.

"Come on," the teacher said, standing up and walking around the back of the bench. He held his arm out, ignoring the others, his attention purely on Patricia.

It was an act of kindness, perhaps futile, but still it helped, even if only to reassure her that some people cared.

Patricia took her bag and walked towards the door, ignoring her shallow friend. Hannah continued to say something, but whatever it was, it wouldn't help. She would never be the type of person who would help anyone but herself.

Patricia followed the teacher out into the hall as he closed the door after himself, determined to ensure no one followed or listened.

"Where are you living?" he asked, showing that at least he had listened.

"We got a house in Chester, local Council. It's not much, very run-down, but better than nothing," Patricia replied.

"Well that's one good thing. You should go home now, and stay home until you manage to sort out what really matters. This doesn't matter, it can wait."

Patricia nodded, looking down at the floor. He was being so kind, she feared if she looked at him she might simply break down.

"Do you need a lift home?" he asked, continuing to look at her. She knew then he was a good person, and a good teacher. She felt bad for how she had looked down at his classes, and her time at the college, realizing that they weren't just there to teach, but because they cared.

"No, thank you. I'll go get the bus, it's fine," Patricia said, unable to imagine anyone going to their new house, to see what it was like. She would feel ashamed, more embarrassed than she already did, if it were possible.

"I'll let Student Services know that you will be taking an extended time off, and if traveling is too much, Chester has several colleges, and I'm sure you could transfer to there to carry on your studies," the teacher explained, in such a kindly manner it simply made her feel worse that she had never given him the time he clearly deserved in class.

"Thank you," Patricia said quietly, wanting only to get out and head home. It wasn't much of a home, but her mother was there, and that was enough.

"OK," the teacher, said, smiling at her.

Patricia began to walk off for the door, not at all bothered about missing her friends, if such a term could be used to describe them. Instead she would miss him, the man who turned out to be much better than any of them. She had found it out too late, but was intrigued by the idea of studying elsewhere.

As the two walked away, Patricia stopped and turned back, before he could go into the class. "Before you go," she began, at which he stopped and turned to looked at her, still smiling. "I never even knew what your name was?" she asked.

"Funny. My name is Paul, Paul Burke," he said, before wishing her good luck. Patricia nodded and headed out of the doors. As she walked down the steps, she plotted her next move, likely to the bus stop and then to the station before getting yet another bus.

"You're out soon," a voice said, sounding familiar. Patricia looked up to see Dan, on his motorbike, sitting sideways, looking at her.

She couldn't believe it, the last thing she had expected, after what he had said, and how she reacted. Even if she had seemed angry and bitter, it didn't matter. To Dan it was like water off a duck's back. Nothing affected him.

She thought to say something, to ask him all sorts of questions, but it didn't matter anyway. She would take him at face value, and now, because she knew he was worth it, she began to cry as she walked over and hugged him.

Neither spoke as Dan held her tightly. It was a brief moment, but a beautiful one, and one that left her feeling that her future was with him, as long as he had it in him to do what he had that day.

Both climbed onto the bike and set off for home, ready together to do whatever it took to make it all work, for all of them.

*

"No, love, when I said put that over there, I didn't mean lie down on the sofa and put your feet on the arm," Liz said, smiling at John. He laughed at her cheekily, feeling at last different, now that they had begun to arrange things. It might not be a home as such, but it was better than the first moment they walked in.

"I'm going to try lighting this fire. We don't have any coal at the moment, so I guess we'll just have to burn the scrap papers and catalogues we have to try and warm the place up," Liz explained. It was cold and getting colder as the day progressed, but she felt warm from all her exertions. She had continued relentlessly, emptying boxes, putting what little they had in each room, and sorting the kitchen so it was at least functional.

"It's not too bad," John said, struggling to keep his eyes open.

"Oh, well, I'm glad you're feeling like that. It's good you're positive about it," Liz said, beginning to feel better about things. For too long she had felt as if her stomach were full of snakes, writhing around, trapping her nerves, to the point where she wondered if she would ever feel happy again. It was far from perfect, but it was a base to begin again from. As long as her children were happy, she could be too.

"Now that you're settled, we can go to the local school tomorrow and get you registered," Liz said, smiling at John.

John suddenly sat up, all ideas of sleep swept away. "What?" he asked abruptly.

"Yep, you need your education."

"Noooooo."

"Yes, bright and early tomorrow."

John didn't speak again, simply looking down, as if he were deflated again and unhappy. Liz knew it was an act, that he would adapt, because he was like her, strong.

Just as she thought to offer him some food as a peace offering, a thudding noise hit the front door. It occurred again before she could get into the hallway to see what was going on.

"Burglars, Mom," John said, which was hardly funny given how little they had, and for sure nothing worth stealing.

Liz walked down the hall, trying to peer out of the small frosted glass panes at the top of the front door. Obviously someone was outside, moving around, but there was no spy hole and no way to be sure who it was. She would just have to open the door and find out.

The moment the door opened, a rush of air kicked in, cold and bitter. Standing before her were Patricia and Dan, the last two people she had expected to see.

"Oh my, what are you doing here?" Liz asked instinctively.

"Sorry, Mom, we just couldn't stay away," Patricia said. Dan simply stood smiling at her, as if he had lost something in his mind.

"I thought you were at college, and Dan you had to be back at work?" Liz asked.

"Yeah, well, we thought we missed you, so wanted to come back," Dan replied.

"I wanted to come back and help sort out," Patricia said.

"Oh, sure," Liz replied, not buying it for one moment.

"Well, I wasn't in the right frame of mind to be in college, and surprisingly they understood, so I came back."

"I didn't want to leave on bad terms from Pat, so I waited for her. I knew she couldn't do without me, and expected her to come rushing out to meet me, which she of course did," Dan said, a cheeky grin on his face. Patricia thought for a moment to decry his comment, but it was sweet and fun, so left it.

"Right, well, come in," Liz said, standing aside, feeling awkward for making them stand outside to explain themselves.

The three went in as the moderate heat from the place contrasted well with the increasingly bitter cold outside.

"Wow, this is much better," Dan said as he walked into the living room. The fire wasn't much, quickly burning low without attention, but it had affected the place, and gave a color to the room which had been missing. It had gone from an orangey gray to a flickering reddish warmth, as if life had been breathed into the broken home. It was a small thing, but made a big difference to how they felt.

"Seems to be coming along nicely," Patricia said, looking at her mother wistfully.

"Yeah, well, early days, but we'll get there," Liz replied, feeling as good as she had for a long time. At first she struggled to put her finger on what had changed, but an idea presented itself to her, that she was finally in control of her life, of her destiny. She now had choices that she could make, rather than being strung along by life. Whether it would be felt odd at that moment, but she still sensed a change for the better.

"I think things are gonna be all right," John said, looking at them all, still lying across the sofa as if it were his and no one else could go near. Nobody spoke. It was the kind of thing no one expected him to ever say, sounding mature well beyond his years.

"Don't grow up too soon," Patricia said, smiling at him. He ignored her, instead wondering if now was a good time to mention he was hungry.

"Well, when that check comes tomorrow, we can fast cash it and…" Liz began to say, trailing off, as if her thoughts had run dry.

"What's up, Mom?" Patricia asked, wondering if her mother were about to have the kind of nervous breakdown that seemed overdue.

Liz stood there, mouth open, lost for words. Before anyone could say anything else, she began searching, looking all over, on the mantelpiece, in empty boxes, searching through the living room then the kitchen.

"What have you lost?" Dan asked, wanting to help, but as so often feeling left out and useless. He was the kind of person who frequently wanted to help, but rarely ever knew how. He was the master of the odd question, but a peasant for a proper answer.

"Mom, what are you looking for?" Patricia asked, her voice insistent and concerned.

"Paperwork, the thing I had," Liz replied, explaining nothing.

Patricia was about to ask again, thinking to put her arm around her mother, to try and reassure her, but before she could, Liz stopped, looking deeply concerned, daring to look at them.

"I think," Liz said, suddenly bending over to the couch. She shoved John's leg out of the way, lifting the cushion up, grabbing out the paperwork.

"What is it?" John asked, sounding louder than he had intended.

Liz stared at the papers, flipping it over, reading quickly.

The three waited, watching Liz with bated breath, all aware that there was a problem. It couldn't be dealt with, or even accepted until she actually said what it was.

Liz stopped, before looking up at them. "I think I made a terrible mistake," she said, lowering the papers to her side.

"What?" Patricia asked, increasingly annoyed that her mother was being so obtuse.

Liz held the papers up again, showing them to Dan and Patricia.

"What? What's wrong with it? Are we not getting the money?" Patricia asked.

"Oh yes, we will. Except I forgot something. I forgot to change the address, to tell them what our new address was. The check will go to our old home," Liz explained, looking as unhappy as she ever had.

"That's not too bad. Either go there tomorrow, by train from Chester station, or maybe the day after, and pick it up. I'm sure someone will be there. If not, pop into the building society and ask to get access," Dan said, unsure whether he was making any sense or not.

"No, the house will be empty, and even if there is someone in there, they won't just give us the letters. They won't know who I am or if they're my letters," Liz said, feeling sick with herself.

"Go there early, and wait. Get there before the postman drops the letters through. If it's the one we know, he'll probably give you the letters anyway," John said. The moment he said it he figured it would be an idea destined to be shot down in flames. It was how it was, how they always were with him.

Liz turned to look at him. "Yeah, I could do that," she replied, surprising him.

"Can't you just telephone the insurance place, and ask them to send out a new check?" Patricia asked.

"No, I don' think so. They won't want to send two checks out, and if they do, they might charge us to cancel the old one, which we can't afford," Liz said, her mind reeling with ideas.

"I can give you a lift on my motorbike," Dan said, trying to be helpful again.

Liz laughed. "No thanks, love, I don't want to go on that thing," she said, at which Dan looked at her as if he had been stung.

"I'll get a very early train tomorrow, and get there and see if I can be there before he delivers. If it's not there, I'll just have to go again the day after," Liz said, resigned to how it would have to be.

"Great," Dan said, clapping his hands together.

"Great," John said, clapping his hands together. "Now, what's to eat?" he asked, not entirely hungry, but wanting to eat for something to do.

"Potatoes," Patricia said sarcastically.

"Fine by me," John replied, aware of her intent but throwing it back at her.

"I have some bad news for you, John," Liz said, at which once again everyone held their breath.

"Oh, right, what's that?" John asked.

"I'll be out tomorrow, so no time to go to the school. It will have to be the day after," Liz explained, a look of mock annoyance on her face.

"Oh, terrible," John said loudly. They all laughed, aware that however much they tried to plan things, life had a way of doing the opposite.

35

MADNESS

Liz woke up without an alarm clock. The usual one they used reminded her too much of waking up with Jack. It was the last thing she needed. It didn't matter, because for so long she had been waking up fitfully, just as first light edged over the horizon. It beckoned some kind of warmth, and for them into the old house which threatened frost and bitter cold inside as much as out.

Her arms and legs ached from the cold, reminding her of the need to find money soon, for coal as well as food. In all of her years she had never quite struggled as she had in recent weeks. She knew all too well from stories on the television and in the newspapers how much people were struggling, but until then they had avoided it. Now they were poor, dirt poor, and life was perennially on a cliff edge of uncertainty.

She had slept in a night dress, and kept her dressing gown and slippers on. The quilt was half decent, but still not enough. It seemed an absurd idea to have to light open fires in the bedroom. Most houses had gas heating, oil heating, even closed-door Parkray coal fires, so to actually be in a house with open fires in such modern times seemed an insult. She felt as if she were behaving in an unreasonably privileged manner, at the same time as living in complete poverty. Her conscience was an unwanted distraction from the reality they all lived.

With no carpet down, the floor creaked as she dressed. She had no intention of waking anyone, wanting them to sleep. She would be the protector their father had failed to be. She would live up to her responsibilities that their father had abandoned. It was how she had been raised, to be a good person, caring of others and treating everyone fairly. It seemed that life didn't make that so easy.

As she gently closed the door, her stomach rumbled. She wouldn't waste food on herself, maybe a snack later, when she got in. If there were buses into the city so early, it wouldn't matter to her, because she wouldn't pay the bus fare, even if she had it. The night before she had sat on her low bed and counted what money they had left. One five-pound note and a bag full of coins. It wasn't much to last for another week, but some of it had to be spent to allow her to chase off for their life-changing check.

The walk offered a kind of peace that had been absent from her life for too long. The air was beyond cold, but she had wrapped up well, in a decent coat Jack had bought her years before, and a thick scarf around her neck. She kept he hands in her pocket, because she couldn't find her gloves.

The walk wasn't too long, but wound its way around houses, increasingly large and decorous. Beyond were a few woods, across the river and a stone bridge into a city which seemed disconnected from poverty and by a winding river.

The city itself was large, and anyone in it would feel enamored by it, such large buildings, the ancient Roman walls. One could feel rich simply by walking through it, that they belonged with the good and the great. The truth was never in sync with it, that you could rub shoulders with millionaires and homeless alike.

Few cars passed by at such an early hour, but slowly the place was coming to life. Liz walked past all the shops, signs lighting up and staff milling around, ready for the hordes of shoppers to come. Down the old cobble streets she walked, as if on a mission to collect some great treasure that only she knew about. If she could get the check, she too could feel well-off, and a welcome part of the place, at least until a short time later when the money was gone.

The railway station was obvious from the smell of diesel far off, winding down a long street to the bottom, where the old yellow facade greeted passengers for generations. Deep down Liz felt apprehensive, in part because she knew life being so fickle, that the check may well not be there, or that the postman might suddenly decide she couldn't have her post, because she was poor, recently homeless and unwanted. What most ate away at her was the thought of having to go back to a place where it had all begun, and ended in a way, so badly.

It helped that the ticket master was so kind. The day hadn't worn him out yet, so he had a smile and a kind comment for all. She bought her return ticket, winced at the cost, and refused to give in to the fear that she was on a fool's errand. She had one direction, one place to go, and anything else would be to give in to hopelessness.

The train was late, all too often, which made the butterflies in her stomach all the worse. Anything that didn't go to plan, that didn't go smoothly, would make it worse, because it was a sign, an ominous sign that something was going to go wrong. She wouldn't think about it, but still it was a nagging voice in the back of her head that refused to go away. Once she had the check, she could get on her way back, and if only symbolically she could put it all behind her, look forward forever.

As positive as she tried to remain, the train as it clicked along reminded her of what she was doing. On through Frodsham, past Helsby, stopping each time, closer and closer until they arrived at the station at Elton. She had been so often, always coming back from the shops, carrying bags, dressed smartly. She always looked forward to being home, but in her mind all she could think of was being in her home with her children. It often seemed like an admission that she loved her husband, a mental process involving thought, rather than anything she naturally felt. She had always accepted it was a natural part of being married for so long, ignoring that others married for far longer seemed still so much in love. She would never think to ask herself if she loved him, just that she did, and that was the end of it.

The walk up from the station seemed longer and more of a struggle than ever before. The sun had remained low in the sky, faded by a white mist of bitter frost around. Her heart beat stronger, as much for the way she felt as for the endless walking. She felt thankful it was still early, so that she might avoid bumping into anyone she knew. There would be the awkward questions, the looks of sadness and mock sorrow. There would be offers to help which never came to anything, and then those who stood back and made noises but simply wanted to keep their distance.

As she walked along the main street through Elton, School Lane, heading to the road which branched off, towards that old house, she looked ahead, trying to keep her chin up, not to allow her emotions to control her.

It was still early enough that she knew the postman wouldn't have been. He never came before nine in the morning, and it was only just past eight. She would have to walk around a bit and keep an eye out for the postman. The last thing she needed was to miss him.

The walk down towards the house was the worst of it, a reminder of a life that had long disintegrated. It seemed like a ghost house, far away at the very end of the road. Either side were rows of prim and proper houses, gardens lined with flowers and hedges, all trimmed and neat. Nothing was out of place, in their gardens, their houses, or their lives, except like everyone their lives were often a mess, only well-hidden from reality.

Liz slowed her walk, as if she were walking in treacle. She could face the house, it was only a house after all, even with all the memories. It was the thought of bumping into local neighbors she dreaded most.

Sun flicked over the top of the houses, brightening the day immensely, shining a warmth to her face which eased any tension she had. The house came clearer into view as she slowed her walk to almost a snail's pace. It seemed so unusually normal, as if she were simply going home, ready to walk in and get things ready for tea. She could feel it so much, it seemed so real. All she needed were the front-door keys and she could just go in, but she had none, and the place was no longer hers.

As she rounded the corner, looking to see the all-glass front door, the large windows, and the wide panes of open glass, she felt shocked. It was no longer that of her memories, but so different. The large metal garage door was bright green, no longer the red of old. The front door had been changed, now a dark brown oak, with small panes of glass at the top and brass fittings around, all shiny and new. The grass had been cut fresh, and a border dug. It all seemed too much, that the building society had taken it over and done so much simply to sell it quickly.

Liz walked around, standing at the edge of the short driveway, unable to take her eyes off it. It seemed as if she had been in a time warp, life had moved on too quickly, where hers had almost stopped. She felt envious of it, that they never experienced it so.

A thought occurred to her, as absurd as it seemed, that as she looked on, the door might open and Jack would step out, asking her where she had been. She dreaded the thought, as much as she wanted it. She would take it too, simply to end the nightmare of need that they would have to endure.

Unable to stop herself, Liz walked up the driveway, to the door, then around the front, looking through the glass. It all seemed so fresh and new, as if it were no longer the same house. Of course it didn't matter how it seemed, because some things could never change.

An abrupt whisking noise made her jump, as she looked to see the front door suddenly open.

"Hello, can I help you?" a voice asked. Liz looked to see a woman leaning out from the doorway. She seemed as if she had just woken, dressed in a flowery dressing gown, her hair tied in a net, no makeup, looking shocked to see someone staring inside.

"I'm sorry," Liz said quickly, struggling for words.

"Do you need something?" the woman asked. She sounded reasonable, but the look she returned suggested she was anything but.

"I'm sorry," Liz said, trying to regain some composure. She was already nervous having to come back, but the reaction and what she had seen of the changes left her feeling lost. "I used to live here."

"Oh, right, well, we live here now," the woman explained curtly. She thought to say something more abrupt, but could see how badly Liz was handling it, so paused a moment.

"Right," Liz said, walking slowly to the woman. "I'm sorry. I didn't want to be rude. I was here to see if we had any letters left. I'm just shocked they have sold the house already."

The response Liz gave lowered the tension, sounding more human than the woman had expected. "Oh, I see, no problem. We've not been here long, only a few days. It came up cheap, and we had the money, we made an offer, and they were in a hurry to sell, so here we are."

Liz felt a mixture of feelings, sadness that her life had been discarded so quickly, but also upset that she mattered so little in it all.

"That sounds like them, the bank I mean," Liz said. The woman nodded, smiling slightly.

"There haven't been any letters before today," the woman explained, looking out at Liz, her demeanor completely changed.

"Oh," Liz said, her hopes dashed. If the day could have been worse, she couldn't have imagined how.

"Though he did drop one through just now," the woman said, lifting a single white envelope from a shelf inside the doorway. "What name did you say it was?"

Liz almost exploded, daring to believe that finally just one thing could go her way. "It should be in the name of Cornwell, Liz

Cornwell."

The woman looked at the envelope, then back to Liz. "It does say Cornwell, but not Liz, or even L as the first letter."

"Oh," Liz said, patting her forehead, admonishing herself. "No, it might be a J, for Jack, they might have issued it with that name," Liz explained. She thought to say what it was for, and how their life had ended up where it was, but it was so much, so long and complicated, it seemed an impossible task.

"Yes, that's it," the woman said, smiling as she handed the letter to Liz. Liz pried open the seal on the back and peered inside, to see a check. It was a large amount, everything she had hoped for. She felt like bursting into tears, but held off, because the day was going to be fine after all.

"I can see you've been through a lot," the woman said, her voice so quiet it was almost a whisper. Liz looked at her, nodding, but unable to speak. She no longer had the words for it.

Nothing more was said as Liz forced a smile at her and walked away. The woman watched her go, wondering of her story, whether anyone would ever hear what had happened.

Liz walked back along the street, almost crawling. She held the envelope tightly, as if all their lives depended on it. Inside was a golden chalice, a doorway to freedom. She knew it was only the start, that she would have to get a job, and John would have to go to school. The house needed work, and they had to find a new direction for their lives, but this was the start of it, a step up, help in some ways.

Finally, for one last time, Liz stopped, turning back to the house. It was time to say goodbye to it, knowing she would never return. Never again would they mention it, or think about it. She looked on, staring at the place, and thinking of all the years they had lived there, all the memories, so many good, and thankfully very few bad ones. She felt better about herself, as if she had come full circle, and was a better person, a better mother for it.

Liz's thought were interrupted by a clanging noise beside her. Her mind still a flux of ideas, she turned to see a metal bin, its lid held up in the air as a white rubbish bag was dropped into it. Her eyes wandered to see a man going about his chores, doing what he did. For a moment it seemed surreal, as she focused, grew aware that she was looking at Jack, standing there in baggy boxer shorts and knee-high socks. He wore a stained white T-shirt, covered in a worn dressing gown. His hair was unkempt, face full of stubble, round blackness under his eyes, looking tired and drawn.

It seemed like a dream, that she might blink and any moment would wake up from the absurdity of it. The man, Jack, hadn't seen her. He was ambling along, sorting out the rubbish, ready to replace the lid and go back in through the open door. It was one of the rows of pretty houses, perfectly tended lawns, oh so lovely and perfect.

As Liz stood, watching, struggling with a wild panic in her emotions, a woman stepped from the house. She wore a white nightgown, her hair a mess, looking at him as if he were taking too long. Neither initially noticed Liz, instead going about their business, as she stood watching them.

Tears threatened Liz, a torrent of emotion, but she held firm. She felt confused, that perhaps he had lost his mind and forgotten who he was, but that was too absurd to bear. She wanted to rush over and wrap her arms around him, but she was too honest with herself for that. She knew the truth, but didn't have the strength to give it life.

At first the woman looked up, finally realizing they were being watched. She gave a brief easy smile, like she would to someone kind passing by, then stared, wondering why Liz was staring at her, and Jack so hard, her eyes boring into them.

It was a frozen moment as each looked on, and nobody spoke, until finally Jack replaced the bin lid, clanging again slightly as he did so, almost without any interest in what he was doing.

Slowly Jack looked at the woman, then up to see what she was looking for. His eyes focused as if he had been melted to the spot, that what he was seeing was beyond comprehension. It wasn't so much as being caught with another woman, it was simply being found to still exist. For so long he had held out, pretended to himself that life had only just begun when he walked away from what had gone before. That life never existed, it was never real, it didn't matter. All that had gone on to matter to him was the moment he lived in, and the only emotion that mattered were the ones he enjoyed.

"Jack," Liz finally muttered, more annoyed that she had failed to say it louder. The intent was to shame, but all she felt was betrayed. No amount of excuses could explain away the sense of what she felt then.

Jack looked at her, mouth open, trying to say something. It

seemed he wanted to somehow say sorry, but the word wasn't big enough. No matter what he did or said or felt, he could never quite do justice to what she needed, or deserved.

In Liz's mind she tore down the path, arms and fists flailing, showering him with rage. She taught him just the kind of lesson he deserved, for simply choosing to walk away. It wasn't her way, not the way she was brought up, or how she lived her life. Besides, he simply wasn't worth it.

Liz breathed in deeply, arms stretched, and opened her mouth. "Bastard," she shouted as loud as she had ever done. "Bastard, bastard, bastard," she repeated as she lost the battle not to cry.

Jack's mouth quivered as he tried to look at her, finding he couldn't and looked away, only to look again because he had to. What little sense of shame he had forced him to look at her. As poor a man as he was, he still knew that much, that he had to show enough decency to look at her and take what was coming.

"Why, Jack? Why didn't you just tell us? Why didn't you just do it like a man? Why leave us with nothing, no money, no home? Why, Jack?" Liz pleaded, not at all interested in his answers. They weren't questions, they were blades, to cut him with their accusations.

Liz sobbed, angry with herself as much as with him, for showing him it mattered. She wanted to walk away, but gave him one last sneering look. He looked broken, unable to defend himself. She could tell he wanted to talk, to say something, perhaps to defend his honor, but he had none, so remained silent.

"Look what he did to us. He'll do that to you too, one day," Liz said, looking at the woman. Before either could say anything, she walked away, struggling to get a grip of her emotions. She had the envelope, gripping it tightly. She had what she needed, and now she knew the truth. It was a bitter truth, but would be enough to close the book on that chapter of her life forever. Liz walked on, not bothering to look back, accepting in her mind that with each step, that man and the woman he was with faded, no longer existed, to her or the world. They were dead, and so was her life with him. The tears dried up, the memories faded, and she walked off back to the station, satisfied that her life would be better.

36

A NEW WOMAN

The journey back had been a cathartic one, allowing Liz's emotions to settle. She had gone into the bathroom and washed her face, then taken in several deep breaths, before getting onto the train. The ride and the walk from the city was a welcome one, allowing her to come to terms in her mind with what was to come. In her mind were only three images as she walked, those of her son John, her daughter Patricia, and her son-in-law-to-be, Dan. They were the light and the life for her, and her reason to live.

Lache wasn't the best, but it had her family and her home there. It was her home, it belonged to her, and as a family held her and their destiny. She walked down the street, enjoying a brief moment of warmth from the sun as it flowed right down the long street. She felt as if she had been reborn, come again from the time of fear and worry, of not knowing, to being aware of everything, about herself and what she was capable of. Most importantly, she felt a right to be happy with herself, and who she was. That mattered as much as anything.

As Liz walked around the corner from the first shop, she almost bumped into someone. She had still been lost a little, her mind wandering, almost knocking over the woman coming in the opposite direction. As she looked up, it occurred to her how alike they were, each on a wandering mission, lost in their own thoughts, ignoring anything else that went on.

It was Mavis, doing her thing, seemingly happy with her lot, but still so sad, that air of grief that appeared to hang over her.

"Hey," Liz said, stopping to look at her. She figured Mavis wouldn't hear her, and carry on anyway, but instead she stopped, slowly turning to look back.

Liz smiled brightly. "How are you today?" she asked.

Mavis stood, her attention fleeting between Liz and what mattered in her own thoughts.

"Penny for your thoughts," Liz said, standing watching, and

hopeful.

The look on Mavis's face changed, no longer so focused on what she was doing, but stern, as if something bothered her. "Penny for your thoughts. That's what she used to say," Mavis said, looking down at the ground.

"Who used to say that?" Liz asked, shocked that she had spoken, let alone stopped her wandering for so long.

"Penny for your thoughts," Mavis repeated. She went to turn and walk away, ending the slight moment between them, but before she did she stopped again, daring to look at Liz, eye to eye. There was a sense of sharpness there, that she still had something, still thought about something. "Sally-Anne. She said it, she always did," she said, almost a whisper, before turning to walk away again.

Liz stood watching her go, as Mavis repeated the name over and over.

The day had been beyond surreal, and if it was a mark of things to come, then at the very least it would be an interesting time ahead. Liz laughed a little, feeling curious. One day, she figured, she would find out more about it.

Still, life had to go on, and things were there to be done. Liz unlocked the door and walked in. As she walked into the living room, John, Patricia, and Dan were sitting on the scruffy old sofa. The three looked up at her expectantly. Liz stood at the doorway, wondering what to say, if anything at all.

"Well?" Patricia asked, mirroring all of their feelings, the need to know.

Liz pulled out the white envelope from her pocket, holding it up to them, breaking out into the broadest of smiles.

"Come on then, you need to go get this check cashed," she said, at which they all cheered.

Life was tough, as it was for everyone. The key to dealing with the problems in life, as Liz and her family discovered, was to never give up, to never lose hope. They would cope, and succeed, and most importantly, they would do it together, as a family.

END

Liz Cornwell will return in:

Missing

The Disappearance of Sally-Anne

ABOUT THE AUTHOR

DJ Cowdall is the author of the hugely popular 'The Dog Under The Bed Series'. He is a British Author, having spent many years writing and publishing short stories, now writing novels of all types

Released January 2018, his novel, '"The Dog Under The Bed", is a charming and funny tale about a stray dog in need of a home, which has received a huge response from readers

He has also authored a book about his time living in Africa and his experiences with his two amazing dogs, titled 'Two Dogs In Africa'

Following the success and acclaim of 'The Dog Under The Bed', David has released a follow up titled 'The Dog Under The Bed 2: Arthur On The Streets', which is available now on Amazon worldwide in Kindle and paperback

Also available from DJ Cowdall are a varied selection of books, such as 'I Was A Teenage Necromancer' series, 'The Kids of Pirate Island' and 'The Magic Christmas Tree'

Due summer 2019 is the conclusion to the 'Dog Under The Bed' series, subtitled: 'What Happened Next'

He is the father of one Daughter, Maya, and she is his biggest fan!

Check out his website at:

http://www.davidcowdall.com

Sign up on there for his newsletter and for details on forthcoming novels and events.

Feel free to contact him any time at:

d.cowdall@gmx.co.uk
https://twitter.com/djcowdall
https://www.facebook.com/DJCowdall
https://www.goodreads.com/author/show/15502553.D_J_Cowdall

Made in the USA
Columbia, SC
26 October 2020